TOTAL COMMITMENT

Elizabeth Waite

severn House

This first world edition published 2008
in Great Britain and in 2009 in the USA by
SEVERN HOUSE PUBLISHERS LTD of
9–15 High Street, Sutton, Surrey, England, SM1 1DF.
Trade paperback edition published
in Great Britain and the USA 2009 by
SEVERN HOUSE PUBLISHERS LTD

British Library Cataloguing in Publication Data

Waite, Elizabeth
  Total commitment
  1. Adult child abuse victims - Fiction 2. Nannies - Fiction
  3. Widowers - Fiction
  I. Title
  823.9'14[F]

ISBN-13: 978-0-7278-6684-4   (cased)
ISBN-13: 978-1-84751-094-5   (trade paper)

All Severn House titles are printed on acid-free p

Typeset by Palimpsest Book Production Lt
Grangemouth, Stirlingshire, Scotland.
Printed and bound in Great Britain by
MPG Books Ltd., Bodmin, Cornwall.

One

'If you've got that bloody door locked there's gonna be trouble, I'm telling yer.' Mike O'Brien's bawling could be heard halfway up Milner Road. He was a towering hulk of a man who could put the fear of God into you with just a look.

His daughter, nineteen-year-old Paula, got quickly to her feet and folded the sheet she had taken from the local newspaper into a square before pushing it into her handbag. Heaving a sigh of relief, she thanked God that she had finished writing her letter and that too was safely tucked away in her bag.

Her father had reached the top of the stairs and he hurled himself with such force against her bedroom door that it swung inwards, banging against the chest of drawers that stood behind it.

'You're the only one, Dad, who ever locks my door,' Paula told him, and there was no missing the hidden meaning in these few suggestive words.

'Watch yer mouth, my gal. Yer mother tells me you're after applying for a new job, one yer found in today's paper.'

'Yes, that's right, Dad; a change of scenery for me is long overdue.'

'You can't do that, Paula, not without my say-so – you're still on licence. Besides, you've got a damn good job, so you 'ave, with Boots the Chemist, an' you'll stay there until I tell you different.'

'Dad, you've played that tune so many times over the last five years that you've come to believe it yourself. Whenever possible you walk me to work and nine times out of ten you're there to meet me when I finish work. You don't allow me to lead my own life.'

'How many more times do I 'ave t'remind you? You're still on licence. You can't go about chopping an' changing jobs.'

'You made that story up to frighten me when I first came home. I am not "on licence", as you call it. You've said it so many times that you've come to believe it. Well, it's a load of rot.'

Michael O'Brien's face was by now so red one would think his cheeks were going to burst, but Paula was quite used to his rages. He was always so full of his own importance. She hated his arrogant, overbearing manner that he used to get her to do things that she had no wish to do. She was older now and knew that so much about her life in this house had been wrong. She was still very fearful of her father but she no longer allowed him to intimidate her as much as he had done when she was a child.

'I could always 'ave you put away again, and ye didn't like being in prison, did yer?' he blustered.

The colour drained from Paula's cheeks and she clenched her hands into such tight balls that her fingernails were digging into the palms of her hands. 'I was never in prison and you know darn well I wasn't. I would probably have had a much easier time of it if I had been. No, between you and your kindly priest you saw to it that I spent over a year in an asylum, a bloody loony bin, where I was made to work like a dog and was fed worse than any animal. I was thirteen years old, Dad. And you have a lot more knowledge than I do as to how and why I was sent there in the first place.' Paula felt she had never been so brave. Never before had she ever stood up to her father with such vehemence. Well, she hadn't quite finished yet.

'Time and time again I have pleaded with you for an explanation but you will never listen. You've done your best to convince me that I was a bad lot. That I caused trouble and that what happened on my thirteenth birthday was entirely my fault. To this day I don't know who was the cause of me being shut away for over a year. But you do! And the day will come when you will be forced to tell the truth, and make no mistake, Dad, I shall live to see it and you can take that as a promise. Now will you get out of my way because I am going downstairs to see Mum and then I am going out for the day.'

'May the Saints preserve us,' he mumbled, as he made the sign of the cross. 'He's the devil himself that has got into you this morning.' But he made no attempt to stop Paula as she left her bedroom, and she felt happy and a little light-headed as she tripped down the stairs.

Heads turned as Paula O'Brien walked down Milner Road, which was in a quiet middle-class area of South Wimbledon, south-west of London. Paula was tall, slim and graceful; her face could be described as nothing less than incredibly beautiful, her cheeks were a peachy tone, dark lashes lay above her lovely dark green eyes, yet it was always her long, shiny auburn hair that attracted the most praise. The fact that she had such poise as she walked and that she spoke so well was down to her early education. From a young age she had been a pupil at a private school, the Sacred Heart of Jesus, which was situated in the centre of Tooting, roughly two miles from the house in which she lived with her parents. This house had been bought outright by her mother's father and given as a gift to her parents when they had first married. Her attendance at such a school had been largely down to her mother, not that her father had ever objected to the school itself – he thought of it as a magnificent academy for young ladies – he just hated the fact that he had the fees to pay. Her mother's biggest regret was the fact that her daughter's education had been so wickedly cut short on her thirteenth birthday. Frances O'Brien also had to live with the fact that she had never been able to make amends for what had happened to her daughter on that disastrous day six years ago.

As Paula walked towards Blackshaw Road where Fred and Laura Wilson and their two boys, Jack, aged five and a half, and Ronnie, just four, shared a rented house with Laura's mother, Molly Owen, she felt she was on a mission. Laura was her best friend and had been like a second mother to her over the years, at least whenever she had been given the chance. This small but scrupulously clean council house had always been a refuge to Paula. In time of anxiety, when her father's behaviour became too spooky, she had always been sure of a welcome and a cheerful hug from Molly Owen and she knew that today would be no different. In fact when she told Laura and her mum what she was thinking of doing she was sure that they would give her the encouragement she would never get from her own parents.

With that thought in mind she quickened her pace.

Jeffrey Lawson was seated at his leather-topped desk in his oak-panelled study, carefully scanning the *Tooting and Merton Borough News*. Having found the page of small adverts, he ran his forefinger down the column until he found the one he had paid for: the advert looking for a nursemaid. Leaning back in the comfort of his chair he breathed a heavy sigh, whether it was from relief or sheer desperation it would have been hard to tell. He was amazed that he had finally put into action an idea that might turn out to be either a lifesaver for him or the dullest thing he'd ever done. Oh well, just have to wait now and see what replies were forthcoming, if any.

Thirty years old, well built, his shoulders broad, Jeffrey Lawson was six foot tall, with dark wavy hair and dark brown eyes. He wasn't just good-looking; he oozed charm although he himself never seemed to be aware of that fact. He and Sheila had met at Raynes Park Tennis Club, married when she was twenty-six and he was twenty-seven. Sheila had not been a virgin and he himself had had his fair share of lady friends. Their meeting had truly been a matter of love at first sight and within three months they had agreed that whatever had happened before they met wasn't relevant to their future life together.

Their future life – so many ideas, so many plans – and what did the future hold for him now? Three wonderful years together, that is all they'd had, and now Jeffrey looked across the study of this large house that his grandma had left to him when she died. Yes, in that respect he had been extremely fortunate. He had been just twenty-five years old when Grandma Lawson's will had been read out and he had come to realize that he was the owner of her valuable home.

He folded the newspaper, laid it tidily on his desk and walked across the hall to the lounge. Quietly he turned the door handle, entered the room and walked across the carpet to where in the bay of the window stood two cots, each holding a sleeping baby boy. His twin sons were seven months old and he was at his wits' end. Sheila had died giving birth to these two babies and it wasn't fair. He had tried everything, he really had, but he was now ready to admit that even with all the help he had received from the social workers, and two so-called professional nannies, both of whom had turned out to be an utter disaster, he just couldn't cope any longer.

He stood a while, silently looking down at his baby sons. Neither Sheila nor he had had any ides that they were expecting twins. Not until after the first baby had arrived. He spread his fingers and gently stroked the soft, silky down-like hair of his son Peter, who was the oldest boy by ten minutes. Sheila had always maintained she was carrying a boy and had even chosen the name of Peter before he was born. His own mother, Mary, had named the other baby David. Good plain names. They hadn't given either of them a middle name – one Christian name is more than enough for any man, was his thought on the matter.

He had called the midwife as soon as Sheila had started having pains. It had been about ten o'clock in the morning, and she had arrived at eleven o'clock. Straight off the midwife had sensed trouble and had called Dr Wainwright, their family physician, who on arrival had immediately called an ambulance, despite the fact that Sheila had always been adamant that she wanted to give birth at home. The four-hour wait at the hospital seemed endless, only to be told he had two sons but had lost his beloved wife.

His own mother had been a godsend. She had organized everything, from rushing around the shops to buy enough clothes, an extra cot and bedding for the second baby that hadn't been expected, to rearranging the furniture in the nursery that Sheila had so lovingly prepared. Jeffrey had been so grateful when she had come rushing up from North Devon where she now lived with her second husband. Sheila had no close relations; she had been an only child and both her parents had died in India some years ago.

He felt guilty, having allowed his mother to stay so long. His mother had been on her own for six years, after his father had died so suddenly from a heart attack, making her a widow at the early age of fifty-one. His parents had been such a loving couple, doing everything and going everywhere together whenever it had been possible. Those past six years his mum had been so lonely, never seeming to get over his father's death, and then out of the blue she had met Arthur Blackmore. He was a true Devonian, a widower aged fifty-nine, two years older than his mother, up here in London on business, when the two of them had met and found happiness in each other's company. Within six months they had married quietly at Wandsworth Register Office and Arthur had whisked his mother away to live in Coombe Martin, North Devon, where Arthur owned a very successful garden centre.

Jeffrey had been torn in half when urging his mother to return to her husband. Much as he wanted her to stay he knew he was being very selfish. 'Arthur is a good man, and you two should be making the most of your lives together,' he had told her more than once. Finally she had agreed, on condition that he brought in more paid help. 'I will manage fine, Mother,' he'd said for the umpteenth time as he handed her into a first-class railway carriage.

'All right then, Jeffrey. I will telephone you tonight and you must phone me whenever you need advice, be it day or night.'

'I will.' He had repeated his promise as he stood on the station platform until the express train was out of sight.

But deciding he could manage and doing so are two different things.

That had been four months ago and since then he had been a lost soul, lurching from one catastrophe to another. He felt he couldn't go on. Yet what was the alternative?

His mother's returning to Arthur had made him aware of just how much he had come to rely on her during those first three months of the babies' lives. Almost every day he had been on the telephone telling her about the bossy nannies who not only argued with him over the slightest detail of the twins' well-being but the pair of them argued with each other, counteracting each and every decision that the other one made. Supposed to be professionals, they were stiff and starchy and they were utterly opposed to any suggestion that he, a mere male, might make. *What did men know about babies?* they constantly asked.

It was two weeks ago, during a lengthy conversation with his mother, that he had come to the conclusion that he should have taken her advice in the first place. She had recommended that he search for a homely woman who would deal with the large amount of dirty washing that came with babies and also to be on the lookout for a younger person to be a nursery maid, a young lady who must love children and would also have the energy to cope with the lifting and carrying, not to mention walks in the fresh air: pushing a double perambulator was no task for a weakling.

Later, when he had related the gist of this conversation to Joyce Pledger, his housekeeper, she had been dismayed. 'Oh, Mr Lawson, who do you think has been doing the washing and the ironing since your mother went back to North Devon? Certainly not those two uppity dragons that call themselves nannies; they don't know the meaning of the word. Do you ever see them showing love towards Peter or David? I might not have any children of my own but I come from a big family and I know that to be loved and cherished means a lot.'

That long speech coming from Joyce Pledger had made him stop and think. When he had first brought the babies home, Social Services had sent three different employees to visit at regular intervals. He could have cheerfully killed one of them, who had brightly asked if he had considered having both babies adopted! Two no longer were involved, but the third one, Esmé Wright, was a blessing. A big woman in her early forties, she was of Irish descent, but had grown up in the east end of London. With two children of her own she was a typical working mum – kindly, jolly and caring – and she had certainly proved her worth.

Later, when Jeffrey had disclosed not only his mother's feelings to Esmé Wright but also those of Joyce Pledger, she had gone off the deep end. 'It needed somebody t'tell you you were wasting good money on those two stuck-up, so-called nannies,' she had yelled at him.

After that he had invited Esmé and Joyce to join him in the lounge, have a drink and to feel free to air their views. The outcome was that Joyce would now regard being involved with the twins as part of her workload while Esmé, instead of drawing her wages from Social Services, would come to Ridgeway at least four days a week, and her own choice of a title was that she would be more than happy to be known as a general dogsbody. Both women also urged him to take up his mother's suggestion and advertise in the local paper for a nursery maid. 'What we want is someone friendly, easy-going, who loves kids, and if she don't know something she should be willing to ask an' take a bit of advice now an' again, with no backchat.'

Later that evening, Jeffrey found himself going over what had been said at that meeting and he was chuckling away like mad. Both women were loyal, kind and helpful but he had never in his wildest dreams thought that he would be in such a predicament that he would be forced to seek their advice. If and when he was able to get back to work in his office he would be very tempted to show his colleagues a copy of Esmé's job description for a nursery maid . . .

Now Jeffrey Lawson was in the newspaper offices still wondering if he was doing the right thing. *Right or wrong*, he told himself, *it is done and now I have to wait and see if anybody will apply*. He hadn't put any telephone number or private address, but instead had taken the advice of the young lady clerk who had inserted at the foot of his advertisement a box number. 'All replies will be forwarded to you in a large plain envelope, Mr Lawson. You have paid for the advert to appear in Wednesday's and Friday's editions for three consecutive weeks. If, however, you find a suitable applicant before the final date please let us know and we will cancel for the following copies.'

Jeffrey thanked her and, wrapping his scarf more tightly around his neck and pulling on his gloves, he made to leave. As he pulled the glass door open, a young woman pushing a perambulator made to enter. He stepped back, holding the door open, and she smiled her thanks at him. As she passed Jeffrey could not resist glancing into that pram. He couldn't see much of the baby as it was snuggled down with pretty pink blankets protecting it from this wintry weather. Somehow he felt disappointed but reminded himself it was still only the tenth of January. Why was he so sure? Because it would have been Sheila's birthday today.

He practically ran to the nearest coffee shop. The service was swift, the coffee excellent – as was the Danish pastry he had ordered to go with it. He loosened his clothing and did his best to relax but it was no good; his mind was full of memories and each and every one focused on Sheila. He thought of her lovely face, her blue eyes that laughed. She had been quite short, only five foot five, but extremely fit. He remembered the first game of tennis they had played together – he had won but it had been a well-fought game. He remembered the first time he had taken her out to dinner and how afterwards they had strolled along Cheyne Walk and then along the Embankment. Even then he had wanted her with such intensity that it had shocked him, but he had never so much as breathed a wrong word. And then he remembered their wedding night, at the Savoy Hotel in the Strand. She had lain in his arms, talking had not been necessary; they both knew they had found a love that was strong, that would endure for ever.

Next day they had boarded the Orient Express from London to Venice and from there to France. She had given him two sons but they would never know their mother, never feel all that motherly love she would unstintingly have given them. Jeffrey began to shake. He put his hands together tightly, wishing that he might feel the comfort of her on this, her special day. From now on life was never going to be easy, he realized and sighed. Some days it was almost impossible to bear, but of course he had Peter and David and they must now be his first concern.

Two

Laura's expression was gleeful as she opened the front door to find Paula standing on the doorstep. 'Christ, you look ravishing,' she told her friend as they hugged each other closely. 'How the 'ell 'ave yer managed to get out so early on a Saturday?'

'Well, I only get one weekend in four off and I was determined to make the most of it. Besides, Laura, I have so much I need to talk to you about – I don't know that I want your advice, more like your opinion if you don't mind.'

'Since when 'ave we minded what we say to each other? Anyway let's get out of this draughty passageway; it's cold enough this morning to freeze the brass balls which hang up over the pawn shop.' Laura pushed open the kitchen door and the heat hit them both; the fire was roaring halfway up the chimney.

'Where is everybody? I've never known this house to be so quiet,' Paula said as she unwrapped her long scarf from around her neck and unbuttoned her coat.

'Fred's taken Mum to the market – the weekend load is too much for her to carry on her own – and the boys pleaded to go with them. Crafty little sods, the pair of 'em, they know damn well if their father doesn't buy them something their gran most certainly will. Here, give me yer coat and things, I'll put 'em in the front room.'

'I'll make myself useful,' Paula called out as she went through to the scullery and was immediately struck by how chilly it was out there. Lifting the tin kettle from the black-iron gas stove Paula brought it to the deep stone sink and held it under the solitary brass tap. While it was filling with cold water she glanced around. One whole wall of this scullery was just bare bricks – no wonder it was so cold out here. Before she had time to light the gas under the kettle Laura was back. 'No, don't do that,' she said, 'we don't used the gas stove unless we 'ave too. When Mum is doing a big bake she moans all the time that she is forever feeding money into the gas meter. The big kettle on the range in the kitchen is on the boil, just bring the teapot to it and there's a bread pudding in the oven on the side, we may as well cut ourselves a chunk before they all get back from the market or else we won't get a look in.'

The two young women sat facing each other, their cups of tea and pieces of the pudding, which was packed with currants and sultanas, both steaming in front of them. Paula leant forward, resting her elbows on the kitchen table. It never ceased to amaze her just how much she always felt at home as soon as she stepped into this house.

'Good, ain't it?' Laura grinned before taking another bite at the spicy pudding.

'It sure is,' Paula replied, all the while appreciating what a good friend she had in Laura. Six years older than herself, Paula could still vividly recall the day when Laura had first come to her rescue. She had been waiting just inside the gates of her school at Tooting Broadway for one of her parents to meet her. A gang of rowdy lads had thought she was fair game, wearing her posh school uniform; it had been fun for them to remove her hat and pretend to play a game of catch with it. Laura had been waiting for a tram, only yards away, and had come charging to her rescue. Paula had been six years old and Laura had been twelve; from that day to this Laura had taken Paula under her wing.

Laura Owen was like her mother, Molly. Cockneys born and bred, with a wonderful sense of humour that brightened Paula's spirits whenever she managed to spend some time with them.

Even though Fred Wilson had married Laura when she was seventeen and he was twenty-four, it had been two years before Jack had been born, and during those two years Laura hadn't forsaken Paula. Fred and Laura had taken her out and about with them and often saw to it that she was given little treats, all of which had to be kept secret from Paula's father. Paula's mother had taken to Laura, despite the fact she deplored the way Laura spoke and was often heard to declare that Molly Owen would be a very nice person if she didn't gossip so much. For all that, Frances O'Brien had encouraged these secretive meetings even though at times she would maintain that it wasn't a sensible thing to do.

'I've answered an advertisement that was in yesterday's local paper,' Paula suddenly blurted out.

Curiosity was instantly eating away at Laura, leaving her longing to jump straight in with numerous questions, but for once she bided her time, telling herself Paula would tell her everything when she was good and ready and if she didn't, well, then that would be the time to jump in with both feet.

'It's a gentleman advertising for a nursery maid for his seven-month-old twin boys. He states that qualifications are not necessary but a love of children is essential. I have written and applied for the job but the letter is still in my handbag,' Paula carefully explained.

'Would you really want to be responsible for two young babies?' Laura asked, astonished that Paula would even contemplate such an idea.

'Well, I haven't posted the letter yet; it was as I read the advert that the thought just came to me. It opened up such an opportunity – the advert states "own room and all amenities", and that would be my number-one priority. Just think, Laura, how many times have we discussed me leaving home? And always we've come back to the inevitable question: where would I go? Of course, I know nothing about what the job would entail, but I can't see any harm in me applying. I'm nineteen years old, going on thirty it seems at times, and I still can't break away from my father. If I remain living under his roof nothing is ever going to change. I will be under his thumb, living by his rules, repeatedly being reminded of how wicked I've been in the past. Must I endure all of this for the rest of my life?' Paula's speech ended on what sounded like a sob.

Laura looked at her friend. Her head was bent low, her face covered by her gorgeous auburn tresses, and Laura's heart ached for this dear girl who she had always looked upon as a young sister. She sighed heavily; there were times when Paula acted as if she were afraid of her own shadow and there was no doubt the cause of her inability to take charge of her own life was down to that brute of a father of hers. Mike O'Brien was a pig of a man and many's the time she'd been tempted to tell him exactly what folk did think of him. But what good would that do? No good whatsoever; that man had a skin as tough as old boots. What a pity Paula didn't have any grandparents she could turn to. It was well known that her mother came from well-to-do parents, had grown up in Hampstead, had been given a good education with the family owning a business and a country cottage in the Lake District. Her father had suffered a stroke when he heard his only daughter had eloped with Mike O'Brien. Her parents had bought and paid for the house which the O'Briens still lived in, but neither one of them had spoken to their daughter from that day to this.

About one fact, Laura was really sure: a few weeks after Paula had turned thirteen years of age, that girl had been spirited away and neither sight nor sound had been heard of her for a whole year. She had never been able to work it out for herself. Mrs O'Brien had invited her to a small tea party on the actual day of Paula's thirteenth birthday, and at the time she would have said it had been a quiet but happy occasion. At least that had been what she had thought. When the disappearance of Paula became known, every kind of rumour imaginable had been flying around, but those who knew what had happened were not saying a word. There must have been a very good reason that had persuaded those involved to have remained silent all these years.

'Paula, you'll make the right decision,' Laura assured her, reaching over and patting her shoulder. 'You've got too much sense not to.'

Liking the sound of that, Paula watched as Laura picked up the teapot and asked, 'Want a refill?'

Without waiting for an answer she took the pot to the big kettle and added more boiling water to the tea before refilling their cups. Paula was thinking how well her friend looked. The weak winter sunshine was streaming through the closed windows and it was turning Laura's long, bushy head of blonde hair into a silvery mane and shrouding her in the kind of look that made her seem holier than thou – which Paula knew was far from the truth. In her teens, boys had referred to Laura as Blondie and because of her own auburn hair she'd always been known as Red. Laura was smiling now in that affectionate, teasing way that Paula knew so well. Although life had dealt with each girl so differently they had always remained as close as their conflicting lives would allow. Surprisingly, there had never been any jealousy shown between them. Both had been attractive lasses with fabulous figures and an abundance of beautiful, long thick hair.

They sat silent for a while as they sipped their fresh cups of tea, and then it was Laura who spoke first. 'Like you said, Paula, it can't hurt to post your letter now that you've taken the trouble to write it. Your decision, but if you don't go ahead with what you've started you'll never know the outcome, will yer?' Then a moment later she added, 'I would miss seeing yer, if you go away to live in.' She stared directly into Paula's green eyes. 'I do agree that if this job were to come into being it would probably be the best thing that could possibly 'appen to you. It would be the chance you've bin waiting for. Cut the ropes that tie you so tightly to that father of yours. Just lately you've been looking really done in and any change 'as got t'be a change for the better.'

'Thanks, Laura.'

'What for? I 'aven't done anything.'

'You've listened and you have given me your opinion, which is what I asked you to do and I am grateful,' Paula said, sounding close to tears.

'Oh, for God's sake, don't go all bloody weepy on me. The kids will be 'ome soon and they'll wanna know what I've done to upset their Auntie Paula.'

Paula delved into her handbag, retrieved the letter she had so carefully written, and handed it to Laura to read.

'Oh, very formal. 'Aven't let yer hair down much, 'ave yer?' Laura, having slowly read the letter, word for word, felt entitled to pass judgement.

'I haven't told him my life story if that's what you're getting at. If he replies and offers me an interview there will be plenty of time to decide what to tell and what to leave unsaid.' Paula sighed deeply before saying, 'Believe me, Laura, there's nothing I'd like better than to be able to make a clean break. Life in my parents' house is sheer hell; it does not get any better – in fact, if it's possible it gets worse by the day.'

'Paula, I am now going to tread on ground that both me and my family 'ave always avoided because you've always told us, quite plainly, that's how you've wanted it . . .'

Paula let out a soft moan. 'Don't suppose I can stop you.'

'No, you can't. Today I'm gonna say my piece. Whatever it was that happened to you six years ago is still a mystery to most folk – me included – and of course everyone has formed their own opinions. Well, we are all entitled to our own beliefs but I firmly believe you went to hell and back and you have never, and I mean

TOTAL COMMITMENT

never, fully recovered. I've watched you and it has almost broken my heart when on some days I know that you are walking about all normal like but living a ruddy nightmare.

'I've made myself a promise over and over again that if I ever learnt the truth and was able to do something about it, I would. Even if the effort proved too much, at least I would have tried. But not knowing! Helpless! Yes, that is exactly how I 'ave felt for the past six years since you came 'ome and I got my first look at you and I needed no telling you 'ad been to 'ell an' back and I wanted you to get well and strong again but more so I wanted some bugger to be made to pay for what had happened to you.'

The two friends fell into each other's arms, both of them sobbing. Each knew that it would still be a very long time before the truth was brought to light, but enough had been said for today.

In silence they went into the scullery and washed their hands, slapping the cold water over their faces and into their eyes.

On the spur of the moment Paula said, 'Laura, I want to make you a promise: I will post my letter and *if* I do get this job and *if* after three months I am still there I will tell you what happened on my thirteenth birthday and the horror of the months that followed.

'Perhaps I should say here and now that I can only give you details of certain events that took place on that day, because most of it is a complete blank. I won't ask that you believe me. As of yet I haven't found one person who does. All these years, Laura, you, Fred and your mother have taken me on trust while I have pushed that part of my life behind me – or at least I have tried to. So will you bear with me?'

'Of course I will, yer silly cow. We, all of us – me, me mum, Fred and our two boys – regard you as a big part of our family, no matter what,' Laura said warmly, 'and don't you ever forget it. And should the time come when you're ready to talk, you know darn well we'll listen with an open mind. From the little I 'ave found out over the years and the image I still 'ave in my mind of the way you looked when you first came back to us, I know your story will be gut-wrenching.'

Paula knew that when she left to post her letter Laura would go to her room and weep buckets. Laura was like that. Hard on the outside and given to sudden outbursts, yet soft and gentle on

the inside, and Paula thanked God that she had been given such a
dear, true friend.

Normally Jeffrey Lawson loved this house and felt himself fortunate to have inherited it. It was a rare house, very beautiful, but
it was his grandparents who had made it a home. Its very name,
Ridgeway Manor, told of its beauty. Every room in the house was
spacious and just to enter the high-ceilinged entrance hall was to
feel the peace and joy that the old house offered. Sheila too had
fallen in love with it. Soon after they were living here together
they had come out of the house at the dead of night and walked
across the great smooth lawn and had lain down on the soft earth
beneath the huge oak tree and he had made love to his wife.
Whether it was the time of year when the brickwork was washed
with warm sunlight, or when the bracing winds of winter beat
against the windows and the smoke from the fires came back down
the tall chimneys, turning the flames of the log fires to bright
blue, warning that a severe frost was to follow – whatever, he
loved this house. But after Sheila's death would he ever be able to
look upon this house as a home again?

This evening he was slumped back in an armchair, staring out
at the frost-covered garden. There was a glass of whisky in front
of him, the only thing that gave him any comfort these days. Try
as he might he couldn't set his mind to anything since Sheila's
death. Day after day the pain of her loss did not get any better;
the fact that she was gone for ever tore at his mind. His strong
hands gripped the arms of the chair. How on earth was he supposed
to cope for the rest of his life without her? The loneliness was
unbearable and he just wouldn't be able to be both a mother and
a father to his two sons. Over and over again he told himself that
there must be many more men and women who had found themselves in the same predicament. But that was no consolation to
him.

Esmé Wright had expected to see an empty bottle at Jeffrey's
side when she looked in on him before going home late in the
evening, but was delighted to see that there wasn't.

He put his book down and fluttered his hands. 'Checking up
on me? Look, bottle still two-thirds full. Honestly, Esmé, I have
really cut down since you saw fit to lay down the law. I'm grateful

to you; your lecture was exactly what I needed and since then I haven't had anywhere near my usual quota.'

'Glad to hear it.' She grinned. 'So what did you regard as your usual quota?'

'Oh, two or three glasses of an evening.'

'And now?'

He nodded his head towards the glass that was placed on a table in front of him. 'That is my first drink tonight. Esmé, I do understand your concern and I have taken your warning to heart. Truly I have. Now that I have given the nursing agency notice that I shall no longer require the services of two nannies after this week, I feel I shall be imposing on you and Joyce more than ever.'

Quick as lightning Esmé shot back, 'Now, don't you go worrying yerself sick over that. Joyce and I make a good team. Besides, by then you should have some answers from the advertisement you put in the local paper.' Then, letting out a great belly laugh, she said, 'Be fun to see what answers turn up. You never know, we might get a real old dragon who will think it's 'er job to keep you in order as well as the two babies.'

'God forbid,' Jeffrey muttered nervously to himself, as Esmé called, 'Goodnight, see you in the morning.'

The week was finished, and on Friday the two nannies had left in a huff. Somehow they had managed to get through the weekend. If on that Friday evening you had told Jeffrey that he was going to enjoy the coming weekend he would have disputed the statement to the utmost.

The babies had been good, maybe because Joyce and Esmé had them out of their cots for long periods. Set down on soft blankets which Joyce had spread on the floor, surrounded by toys, often picked up and given cuddles, they seemed a whole lot more contented. Esmé's explanation was that 'babies can't 'ave too much love and affection'. For a while their father had been left in sole charge of the nursery while the two women prepared the Sunday roast and he surprised himself with how much enjoyment he got out of being alone with David and Peter.

No standing on ceremony was allowed. Jeffrey carved the leg of lamb and the three adults ate together grouped around the kitchen table. The big perambulator was wheeled in from the garage and the two baby boys sat one at each end enjoying the attention, and Jeffrey had been smiling as he had remarked that this was the first time that either of his sons had seen inside the kitchen of this house that was supposed to be their home.

'Yeah, an' I bet it's the first time they've been given a crust of bread dipped in gravy to suck on,' Esmé said aside to Joyce, and they both grinned knowingly.

It was eight o'clock on the Sunday evening. Esmé Wright had long gone home to her own family when Joyce came into the kitchen to say she was going to her room but would leave the door wide open so that she would hear the slightest murmur from the twins.

'Mr Lawson, why are you still sitting in the kitchen?' she ventured to ask. 'Both the lounge and your study are really warm, wouldn't you be more comfortable there?'

The sad look he gave her was enough to break her heart. She knew only too well what it was like to suffer the loss of a loved one. Her fiancé had been killed in France. 'Come on,' she urged him, 'but before you go upstairs, why don't you take a peep at David and Peter?' She had almost added, 'And start to count your blessings,' but her common sense had told her she had said enough.

Three

Jeffrey Lawson had received three replies from his newspaper advertisement. Over the telephone he had read all three letters to his mother and had asked if she and Arthur would give them their consideration and advise him as to whether, in their opinion, it would be to his benefit to interview any of the applicants. A couple of days later his mother rang back and he thought it remarkable that their preference had been for the letter that was signed Paula O'Brien. They said it was well written, short, yet had given the most essential details. It was the same application that had appealed the most to both Joyce Pledger and Esmé Wright, and incidentally to himself.

Nevertheless he was still feeling dubious as he picked up his pen to write to Paula O'Brien, inviting her to come to the house for an interview.

Paula had been on the lookout for the postman each morning as she made her way to work. Purposely leaving home earlier than usual, she had waited at the corner of the road hoping to waylay any mail that might have been addressed to her. Should it have been delivered to the house there was no doubt her father would have opened it, read the letter and then there would be all hell to pay. On the third morning her vigilance had paid off. Thanking the postman she slipped the letter into her bag, telling herself that she would wait until her mid-morning break before opening and reading it. *Then*, she argued with herself, *you'll be irritable all the morning if you don't find out what the letter has to say, you'll take it out on the customers and for what? Stop being so cowardly and open the flipping letter.* Paula was grinning as she once again held the letter, addressed to Miss Paula O'Brien, in her hand.

Her eyes quickly scanned the handwritten letter, immediately giving her the gist of the communication. Quickly she walked in to the doorway of a shop that had not yet opened for business, and took in great gulps of air, holding them, then letting them go in little steadying gasps. Then, hugging herself, she spoke out loud. 'I've got an interview, I really have. I can hardly believe it but he must have thought my application wasn't too bad.' Then the thought came to her that she still had no idea who *he* was and no idea as to where she had to go to keep the appointment. Come to that, she hadn't even taken in the date or the time when she had to present herself.

The notepaper was thick and expensive, Paula thought, as she looked at the signature at the foot of the page. Jeffrey Lawson: nice name, she noted, allowing herself a small smile. Her eyes then went to the top of the headed notepaper: Ridgeway Manor, Copse Hill, Raynes Park, Surrey. She was still smiling even if her pleasure was tinged with apprehension. Raynes Park wasn't too far away; it was easy to get there – in fact there were several means of public transport that she could use. She wasn't over familiar with the area but enough to know that either side of the borough boundary with the Royal Borough of Kingston-upon-Thames there were the more expensive areas of Copse Hill and Coombe, with their large detached houses, golf course and gated lands. She knew about the golf course because Mr Thorpe, the manager of the branch of Boots the Chemist in Wimbledon where she worked, was a member of the club there and played on the course as often as he was able to.

'Time's getting on,' Paula said, scolding herself as she glanced at her watch. She mustn't be late, because this evening she would want to leave work dead on five o'clock – come what may she was going to call in to see Laura on her way home; she couldn't wait to tell her and Molly that she'd received a reply from her letter and that she'd been offered an interview. But what if this was one of the evenings that her father chose to come and meet her? Oh, to hell with him! For once she'd make sure he had a long wait, for she'd be going out the back entrance and through the loading bay. She'd worry about him being bad-tempered later on. Too many years she'd allowed him to boss her around, making her life a thorough misery.

Even with her new determined attitude, when she arrived at her place of work she still ended up feeling shaky and anxious, still not sure that she should even be contemplating not only changing her job but upping sticks and leaving home for what would seem to be an entirely different way of life.

Whoa, hold on, Paula said, chastising herself. *You're jumping the gun a bit here! To have been granted an audience with this Mr Lawson is a long way from being offered employment in his household. Just get yourself through the day, then have a good old chinwag with Laura before going home and you'll feel a whole lot better, but don't forget to keep the whole thing to yourself once you get home to Milner Road – don't want Father getting wind of your intentions.* He'd been so secretive and domineering about everything to do with her past that for him to upset the apple cart now that she'd been brave enough to start the ball rolling would be outrageous.

No, she'd much rather struggle along, keeping her intentions under wraps for as long as she could.

Paula was grateful that she had been kept busy behind the counter for most of the day, yet all the same the hours had seemed endless until at last at five o'clock she was on her way to Laura's. *What a winter we're having*, she was thinking. During November the whole of London and Surrey had been blanketed with freezing grey fog when at times you couldn't see a hand in front of yourself. Over Christmas it had been bitterly cold, with ice forming around the windowpanes, and now January was here and the wireless was forecasting snow. *Surely it's too cold for snow*, she was thinking, banging her hands against her thighs as she walked.

As Paula turned in to Blackshaw Road, Fred Wilson and his two small sons were approaching her from the opposite end of the road. Catching sight of their auntie, the two lads let go of their father's hands and came running. It was already almost dark, the street lights were on and as they came nearer the two little boys made a pretty sight. Jack was wrapped up warm in a navy-blue coat, a huge white scarf wrapped round his neck and a peaked cap was pulled well down on his head. By his side was Ronnie. He too wore a warm overcoat, and his long woolly scarf was bright red as was the bobble hat he wore on his head and the gloves he had on his hands. Paula knew at once that Molly, their grandmother, had knitted all of these items for the little lad. The boys went either side of Paula, each grabbing hold of her hand, and dragged her along until they reached number 47 where Laura was waiting in the passageway with the front door wide open.

'Mum, Mum, we've found Auntie Paula,' Ronnie called out as he neared the small iron gate which enclosed the little front garden and shut the house off from the pavement.

'Bet yer didn't know you were lost, did yer, gal?' Laura chuckled as she hugged her best friend. 'But it's lovely t'see you unexpected like,' she told her as she ushered them all down the passageway into the warmth of the kitchen.

'You poor thing, you look frozen t'death. What's brought you round 'ere on a Saturday night when you've bin at work all day? Come on, take yer coat off an' get nearer the fire.' All this rambling from Molly hadn't stopped her from kissing Paula's cold cheeks. 'Kettle's boiling. I'll make a brew straight away,' she said, bustling over to the dresser to take down the cups and saucers.

'About time too,' Fred told his mother-in-law, at the same time giving Paula a sly wink. 'Suppose you and Laura 'ave 'ad yer feet up in front of the fire best part of the afternoon.'

'Nobody forced you t'go out. You could 'ave stayed in and given us an 'and t'do all the vegetables for tomorrow's dinner,' Molly jeered at him.

'No, Gran, don't 'ave a go at me dad. He'd promised t'take me and Ronnie to the Vale this afternoon. There wasn't any football on when we got there cos the ground is frozen but we 'ad a good time at the park.'

'Jack, I was only joking with yer dad. I'm glad he took the pair of you out, got some fresh air into yer lungs, as long as you ain't got too cold.'

'No, we're all right,' he said, grinning as he put his arms around his gran's neck and planted a kiss on her rosy cheek.

With all outdoor clothing removed, the adults turned to look at Paula. It was very unusual for her to call in on a Saturday evening but it went without saying that it was Molly that shot the first question at her. 'So come on then, lass, I know I'm a nosy mare but by the way you're smiling it's got t'be good news you're gonna share with us.'

'Mum!' Laura cried in exasperation. 'Why do you always 'ave t'jump in where angels would fear to tread?'

'It's all right, really it is, Laura, I was only waiting for everyone to settle down before I broke my news. I've had a reply to the application I sent off for that job as a nursery maid and the gentleman has asked me to go to his house for an interview on Wednesday afternoon.'

'Good on yer, gal! Just don't go acting all spineless-like, when it comes t'telling yer father. This might just be the break yer've been waiting for.' Molly's voice sounded loud and harsh in the small confined area of their kitchen.

Laura's voice was much calmer. 'I am so pleased for you, Paula – at least it's the first step in the right direction, and at this stage I don't see any reason why you should say anything to your parents.'

'Funny you should say that, Laura, Mr Lawson has asked me to go to his house in Raynes Park on Wednesday afternoon and he suggests at two o'clock, but he does say for me to telephone him if those arrangements are not suitable. For me he couldn't have set it up better. As you know Wednesday is my half-day, since all the shops close at one o'clock, and I'll be able to go straight from work without saying a word, even to my mum, and I won't have to sneak out of the house praying to God that my dad doesn't come home unexpectedly.'

Not a soul questioned Paula further; it was enough that she had called in to see them all and the welcome she'd got was as usual enough to raise her spirits sky-high.

After Molly had made sure that everyone had been given a steaming cup of tea, she came to sit beside Paula. 'I'm that pleased for you, Paula, love. I'll be thinking of yer on Wednesday and even saying a little prayer. Try not to show that you're excited over the next few days, love; play yer cards close t'yer chest. If you don't like the gentleman, or the sound of the job he's offering, you can just walk away and you won't ever 'ave t'say anything to anyone. But I'm proud of yer, I want yer to know that. Done this off yer own back. Yeah, you go an' see what the bloke 'as to say, suss everything well out, ask loads of questions, make sure you know exactly what you'd be letting yerself in for before yer make a decision and then if yer decide that the job ain't for you, well, you won't 'ave lost anything and yer parents won't be any the wiser.'

Molly was such a good-hearted, motherly kind of woman and Paula felt the sting of tears at the back of her eyes as she answered. 'One thing I have learned over the years, Molly: nothing is ever how we would like it to be. I have found the best way to cope is to take one day at a time. All the same, thanks for being so understanding.'

Molly shrugged. 'We all do the best we can. You just keep at it, gal; you ain't done bad so far. You've just got to keep trying, day by day, and the day *will* come, please God, when everything will get sorted out.'

Silently Paula was wishing that Molly's prediction would come true.

Four

Joyce Pledger sighed for the umpteenth time. She'd be jolly glad when this day was over. All morning it had been debatable as to whether or not Mr Lawson was going to conduct the interview he was supposed to be handling this afternoon. Repeatedly he had asked her if she would preside over the interview with the young lady who was applying for the job as a nursery maid.

'No, sorry, Mr Lawson,' she stated firmly. 'After all, I am only an employee in this house. It is you, yourself, who must decide if the applicant is suitable. She will want to know what her duties would entail, what wage you are offering – in fact she will, more than likely, have numerous questions to which only you, yourself, are in a position to answer.' He was still doing his best to convince her that it would be far more beneficial if two females sorted the matter out. At that point she hadn't been able to stop herself from laughing.

'You've a funny sense of reasoning,' she told him, shaking her head. 'You're a solicitor, you work in the City, and most of your friends that came here often when poor Mrs Lawson was with us are well up in the legal profession, others that I've made meals for have been stockbrokers and Mrs Lawson once told me that your great friend, Mr Montgomery, is a trader on the Stock Exchange. You're surrounded by such brainy colleagues yet you're baulking at sounding out whether or not an applicant will be suitable to take care of your two baby sons.' Shaking her head, she couldn't resist adding, 'You are unbelievable!'

'Put like that, I do sound a bit gutless, don't I?'

They both laughed and Joyce said, 'You'll be fine, and I will be on hand; just call when you want the tea brought in or if you just need a bit of a nudge.'

'Thanks, I do appreciate you bearing with me.'

Joyce just nodded. *As if I've got any choice*, she thought, though at same time she longed for this house and the people in it to get back on an even keel. But that wasn't going to happen until

Mr Lawson got back to going to the City every weekday. Men were like fish out of water when their routine was upset and as if the death of his dear wife hadn't been bad enough for him to bear he had been left with those two dear little babies to care for. Naturally, at all times he had done his best, but he had found it hard to cope. It was also a certainty that his life had become tedious, humdrum. He needed to return to his work so that his brain could be stimulated and then perhaps he would feel more able to face the future.

Jeffrey had made himself presentable in dark grey flannel trousers and a freshly laundered white shirt, top button left undone. He wore no tie but an immaculately tailored navy blue jacket, his dark hair, well brushed, for once did not appear to be quite so unruly. He was walking the floor of the front lounge, the windows of which looked out over the front of the house. He glanced backwards through the open doorway into the hall to where the tall grandfather clock stood majestically against the far wall – the clock was only one of the many treasures he had inherited along with his grandmother's house. He and Sheila had had everything that they could possible have asked for. They were set up for life, and then to have her so cruelly taken from him . . . Utter despair was creeping over him again. Why, oh why, had he put that daft advertisement in the paper? And even worse, why had he agreed to today's meeting? The clock struck the hour, two loud chimes boomed out. it was two o'clock – maybe she wasn't coming.

He held the letter from Miss O'Brien in one hand as he pulled the floor-length curtain back with the other. The snow was falling heavily, great white flakes that were settling on the shrubs and trees, already giving the grounds a white fairy-tale look. The first sign of movement attracted his attention; a young woman was approaching the house, leaving her footprints in the snow as she walked along the main pathway. Her head and shoulders were tilting forward in an attempt to avoid the wet snow touching her face. First impression was that she was much younger than he had imagined the applicant to be, and why he had thought she might be dressed in black, he couldn't for the life of him have said. She certainly wasn't.

Esmé Wright glanced across the lounge to where Jeffrey stood. He appeared to be mesmerized and she had to come forward and nudge him to get him to move as the doorbell rang. He seemed incapable of moving off the spot and it was left to her to hurriedly move to open the front door.

'Hallo there, you must be Miss O'Brien. Come in, come in. Not the best of days to be travelling, is it?' Esmé, who was on the short side and inclined to be plump, leant her head back to look up at this tall young lady. 'I'm Mrs Wright, a friendly home-help and a general dogsbody.'

Paula, who up until a few minutes ago had been feeling terrified, found herself smiling at this warm, friendly greeting. 'Yes, I'm Paula O'Brien,' she said, stamping the snow from her boots on the huge doormat and at the same time removing and shaking the tight-fitting felt hat that she had worn to keep her head covered. Now standing in her stockinged feet she was about to remove her coat when she saw a gentleman standing behind Mrs Wright and at the same moment Esmé too caught sight of him.

'Oh, there you are, Mr Lawson. This is Miss O'Brien – shall I leave you two to get acquainted?' Without waiting to hear his reply Esmé took herself off to the kitchen, in a great hurry to tell Joyce Pledger of the beauty that had landed on their doorstep. She was enough to make any red-blooded man's eyeballs stick out on stalks!

Left alone, Jeffrey had his first clear view of Paula O'Brien and he drew his breath in sharply. He had not only imagined that she would be dressed in black but that she would look much older. She was quite tall: without shoes as she was now she must have been five foot six or seven. She had a glorious head of auburn hair piled high on her head, which he hadn't noticed as she had walked up the drive. Her heavy brown coat had a deep fur collar which framed the beauty of her face. She wore only a faint trace of make-up and the bloom on her checks had probably been caused by the bitterly cold weather. At that moment he could think only of what a picture of loveliness she made.

Lack of confidence had Paula glued to the spot. She had no idea how to communicate with this well-dressed, good-looking stranger. Suddenly it was as if someone had pressed a button within Jeffrey Lawson, and he sprang to life. 'What am I thinking of? Please let me take your coat.' He was all fingers and thumbs as he helped her off with the coat and when he had it slung over his arm, he said, 'I'll settle you in front of the fire in the lounge; that is where

Mrs Pledger has laid tea out for us, so much more informal than having it in the dining room, and then I'll take your coat to the kitchen where Mrs Wright will hang it up to dry – or would you like to wash your hands before we have tea?' Jeffrey knew that he was speaking too quickly. He was used to reading contracts with great speed, but this was different. He must slow down. He should be able to deal with this young lady's application with ease.

'Yes, please, I would like to freshen up. If that's all right?' The sound of Paula's voice brought him up with a start.

'Of course, there is a downstairs cloakroom, this way.' They walked side by side and as they passed an open door he pointed. 'That is the lounge. We'll have tea in there when you're ready. You'll be able to find your way back because the cloakroom is only across here and then down rather a long corridor which will be on your left.'

Paula lingered in the lavatory, hoping that her heart would stop thumping and that she could escape attention for as long as it took her to calm down. *I'm supposed to be here for an interview for a job, but it's all going wrong. This handsome stranger comes out of the blue and treats me as if I was some do-gooder from the church that he has invited to take tea with him. I'm all at sixes and sevens – or as Laura would say I don't know whether I'm on my 'ead or me 'eels.*

Jeffrey Lawson seemed equally bewildered. Miss O'Brien seemed to be a very nice, well-spoken young lady, but she looked and acted as if she was out of her depth. She had a well-formed figure and a face that was so beautiful it had taken his breath away. One minute she seemed confident, even self-assured, and the next minute she appeared to be trembling, but why was she frightened? The fact that she was scared made him feel very awkward.

Jeffrey had already seated himself in an armchair by the fire, but with his back to the door. As Paula timidly came into the lounge he didn't hear her come in. She cleared her throat and at that moment Joyce Pledger entered the room bearing a heavily stacked tea tray. Everything seemed to happen at once, Jeffrey jumped up so quickly he knocked against the table which was standing between two armchairs and on which Joyce had already set out the necessary cups, saucers and plates. The bone china rattled, Jeffrey was trying to apologize and Esmé was calling out that she was leaving now.

Joyce took charge. First she put her tray down then indicated that Paula should take the armchair that was opposite the one in which Mr Lawson had been seated. Having introduced herself as the housekeeper she stated her name and said she was pleased to meet Paula, all the while taking plates of food from the tray and setting them out on the table which was now in front of Paula. 'All I have to do now is bring you in the pot of tea and a jug of boiling water,' Joyce said, as her eyes roamed over the plates she had set out. 'Oh, I forgot to ask, do you prefer milk in your tea or a slice of lemon?'

'Milk, please,' Paula answered, still thinking what a lot of fuss everyone was making. Never for a moment had she envisaged that her interview would turn out like this. She turned her head and looked around at this beautifully furnished room, only to find that she was alone. Now she was worried. The huge fireplace had an open grate and logs were piled high, burning brightly, crackling, sending out an occasional shower of sparks. Oh, if the circumstances weren't so odd she would think she had landed on her feet. Although the room was large, the ceiling high, lit by three table lamps with shades made from soft cream silk from which hung long ornamental golden tassels, it still gave off an atmosphere of cosiness and she was tempted to snuggle down in the soft velvet upholstery of her chair and close her eyes. But if she were to do that there was the possibility that she would fall asleep and when she woke up she might find that all of the happenings of the afternoon had been a dream. So instead she stared into the fire, loving the smell of the burning logs, and nuzzled her stockinged feet into the deep pile of the carpet.

Meanwhile Jeffrey had grabbed his chance. As Joyce was setting out the food he had bolted from the room, calling to Esmé to wait a minute.

'Where do you think you're going?' he asked even before he had caught up with her.

Tugging her hat well down over her ears and winding a long scarf twice around her neck she told him, 'I'll be back about six to help Joyce feed the twins and see them settled down for the night.'

'Won't you come back into the lounge, please – stay for tea?' Jeffrey pleaded, not wanting to conduct this interview on his own.

'No, you'll be fine; just carry on as normal and make your own decisions,' she told him firmly, buttoning up her long coat and pulling on her gloves before picking up her shopping bag. 'If I'm lucky I might still catch a few of the market stalls but if the weather has sent them packing there's a good greengrocer's near Wimbledon Station where I can pick up enough vegetables to make a grand stew for my lot. I'll see you later.'

'Yes, all right then,' he said, resigned to his fate. Realizing he was being idiotic he quickly added, 'Thanks, Esmé, it can't have been easy for you, all the hours you've put in here over the past few months. I owe you and Joyce a big debt.' He seemed to be considering his words although Esmé was impatient to be on her way. 'Even if things do work out well with this young lady I hope you will still continue to regard this as your full-time job; I wouldn't want you considering whether or not you'd be better off if you were to return to Social Services.'

From the sound of his voice she could tell that he was genuinely concerned. Esmé laughed, really laughed, and her eyes glinted with wickedness. 'Mr Lawson, you are a pushover. 'Aven't you got enough t'worry about without this? Put yer mind at rest, those two babies of yours 'ave tugged at my heart strings and I aim to stick around to see them grow into strong 'ealthy lads. I was never lucky enough to 'ave regular work with the Social, they only called on me when they were desperate. Besides, you let me change my hours when I 'ave to take me own kids to the clinic or whatever, and to top all that you pay me more than I ever got working for the council. Now, you get in there and work yer charm on that young lady. She's just what we could do with around 'ere; she'd bring a bit of life into this big house. Anyway, like it or not, I'm off. See yer later.'

Jeffrey watched as she closed the door behind her, telling himself that Esmé Wright was a character and a half and at this moment he was especially grateful that she was around.

Jeffrey seated himself in the chair facing Paula and the atmosphere was suddenly strained. Paula took it upon herself to play mother, and pulling both cups and saucers near to her she asked, 'Do you have milk in your tea?'

'Yes, please, just a little,' he replied.

Paula poured tea into both cups and then sat back and eyed the food. There were plates of savoury titbits and an assortment of cheeses adorned with fresh salad, as well as fruit scones with a dish of strawberry jam and another dish of thick clotted cream. Paula kept her hands folded in her lap until Jeffrey urged, 'Now, do please help yourself.' The moment of awkwardness passed as he held out the plates to Paula and soon they were both smiling as they began to eat their tea. It was all very pleasant, Paula was thinking. *This gentleman is making himself very likeable.* With no apparent effort he was making small talk, telling how well his two baby sons were doing and how very much he had come to rely on his housekeeper and Mrs Wright. More so since he had dispensed with the services of the two nannies and that brought him to describe in detail the goings on in this house last weekend. He gave a blow-by-blow account of himself, Mrs Wright, and Mrs Pledger eating a roast dinner sitting around the kitchen table while the babies lay one at each end of their perambulator and were fed titbits from the table that he wasn't supposed to have seen. If it had been his aim to try and make Paula relax, he had certainly succeeded, because he almost had Paula wishing she had been there. She couldn't believe how the time was flying by. Mr Lawson had such an endearing way, there was no side to him and he most certainly was not arrogant, but all the same he hadn't yet touched on the reason for her being here.

Jeffrey was aware that he should bring this conversation round to a business level yet he was loath to do so. He needed to know how he should address this beautiful young woman and he badly wanted to ask why she was seeking a position as a nursery maid to twin baby boys who were only seven months old. Had the advertisement made his requirements quite clear? An essential condition was that the successful applicant would be expected to live in and that he was a man on his own. Though he would empha- size that Joyce Pledger also lived in and that there were many nights when he, himself, had to stay in town.

He had just about managed to express these doubts and had tackled the hardest part, telling of how his wife had died giving birth to the twins. Now he sat upright in his chair, trying hard not to be captivated by her big green eyes, and said, 'Miss O'Brien, if you have any questions that you would like to put to me, please, fire away.'

Before Paula had a chance to have her say, the quietness of the house was broken as the crying of both babies could be heard coming from the nursery.

Jeffrey was on his feet in an instant. 'I was afraid of this,' he said mournfully. Joyce Pledger appeared in the doorway. 'I have their bottles already prepared, Mr Lawson, but if I might make a suggestion . . .'

'Please, whatever it is, just tell me.'

'Why don't we take Miss O'Brien up to the nursery with us? She has to meet David and Peter some time and right now seems as good as a time as any, don't you think?'

Jeffrey turned his gaze to Paula and raised his eyebrows in question, saying, 'Would that be imposing too early? We've hardly had time to talk.'

'I think it would be very appropriate, sir, after all the babies are the main reason that I'm here today.'

Jeffrey liked the sound of that but not the fact that she was referring to him as 'sir'. Time enough later to go into that and all the nitty-gritty. He found he was actually looking forward to seeing how she would react when she came into contact with two wailing babies whose nappies would certainly be in need of changing.

'Fine. As you say we might as well throw you in at the deep end, at least that way you will know what you are letting yourself in for and you will be better able to decide whether you consider this is the occupation you are looking for.'

Already Paula was telling herself that she liked Joyce Pledger; there was nothing hoity-toity about her. It was she who had reached the two cots first and, lifting the first baby out, she had handed him to Paula and then, leading the way with the second one in her arms, had shown her how to lay them down on the changing table, remove their soiled napkins, wash their bottoms and finally gently powder each baby until he smelt sweet. Now they were sitting side by side on low nursing chairs, each baby boy contentedly sucking away at his bottle. It was a scene that gave Jeffrey Lawson hope, not only for his own future but for that of his two sons.

Paula was thinking what a sweet little soul David was, so at ease in her arms now, so trusting that she, a complete stranger, would not harm him. She eased him more tightly into the crook of her arm, bent her head forward and kissed the top of his downy head.

All at once there were too many memories – alarming, threatening memories that she didn't want to recall. She had nursed so many babies when she had been thirteen years old and shut away in the institution. Yet not one of them had been hers. Oh yes, she had given birth – but to a son or daughter? She had never been told which. Nor had she set eyes on that baby. It had been whisked away the minute it had come into the world without her even knowing whether it had been born dead or alive. Had some caring parents adopted it? She'd had no way of ever finding out. It hadn't even been given a name.

'You're handling David well; do you come from a big family yourself? Are you comfortable with him or shall I take over from you?' Jeffrey was smiling gently as he spoke to Paula.

'I'm fine, thank you. We won't disturb him; let him finish his bottle.' Paula had kept her head down as she answered, but now she raised her head and looked at him. 'I am an only child, but when I left school I had a job working with other children and there were quite a few babies there from time to time.'

'Well it would seem that you have never lost the knack, though in your letter you said you have worked for Boots the Chemist for the last five years.'

'Yes, that is correct,' she answered, still avoiding meeting his eyes. 'My first job didn't last long and I've been at Boots ever since. Caring for young babies just comes naturally, I suppose, and he is a beautiful little boy – they both are.'

She hadn't told any lies. It had been her first job, a very hard one without pay and no days off, when she had been shut away from the eyes of the world, but he didn't need to know about that sad episode of her life.

'We'll talk some more later, but meanwhile perhaps you'd like to consider a trial period. I propose that you come to Ridgeway for a month, see if you consider it a worthwhile occupation, or if the babies would be too much for you to cope with. Mrs Pledger, who by the way prefers to be called Joyce – "Mrs" is only a courtesy title for women in service who have never been married – lives in and has agreed to help with the twins. Also Mrs Wright, who has two children of her own, will be here at least four days a week and she will take on all the heavy work such as the washing. Before you make a decision I'll get Joyce to show you the room you would be occupying should you decide to accept my proposal. If at the end of four weeks you decide that taking care of two babies is not for you, then we will part on friendly terms with no animosity on either side.'

Paula's head was buzzing. Mr Lawson appeared to be a straight-forward sort of gentleman and his offer was fair and the wage generous. The room she would have to herself with the full use of a bathroom right opposite was superb – more than twice the size of her own bedroom at home – but there were so many what-ifs! What if her father tried to prevent her from leaving? What if after four weeks she found she couldn't cope with the duties required; would she be allowed to return home?

Jeffrey was using the telephone in the hall as she and Joyce came back down the stairs. Joyce shook hands with her, said she hoped to see her again soon and took herself off to her kitchen.

'Well, Miss O'Brien, have you made a decision?'

'Yes, sir, I have. I would like to take you up on the offer of a month's trial, but when would you want me to start?'

Jeffrey looked puzzled. 'Is the date going to be a problem?' he asked.

'I do have to give my employers one week's full notice,' she explained.

Jeffrey's face broke into a grin. 'No problem. I should have anticipated as much, and seven days is fair. You will have other matters to attend to besides. Where are we? It's Wednesday today, so shall we say a week on Monday?'

'That would suit me well, thank you, sir.'

'Good, let's hope our arrangement will suit us both equally well. I'll fetch your coat. I have already telephoned for a taxi to take you home.'

Paula started to object. 'Sir, the bus . . .' She got no further.

He raised his hand. 'It is treacherous weather out there. I wouldn't dream of allowing you to walk down the hill to catch a bus – and by the way, I use this taxi firm frequently and have an account with them, so at a later date when you let me know approximately what time you will be leaving home to come here, I will send a cab for you. Can't have you struggling with your suitcases on the bus, can we? You have the telephone number for here; it is on top of the page of the letter I wrote to you.'

'Thank you. You have been more than kind,' Paula told him.

He walked her to the door, came down the steps with her, and handed her into the back seat of the taxi. 'I hope we shall meet again soon,' he called as the taxi moved off.

'So do I,' she murmured. 'So do I.'

Normally she would have laid her head back and rested, wallowing in the sheer comfort of a taxi ride. She couldn't begin to relax. She had committed herself. She was going to leave her job, leave home – though how she was going to get away without her father going absolutely berserk she hadn't yet worked out – and as for a taxi coming to their house in Milner Road to carry her off to this new life, the very least he would do would be to throw a frenzied fit, and that would be after he had slapped her a few times and told the taxi driver in no uncertain terms where he could go. Oh, well, she sighed, but it wasn't much of a sigh because suddenly she was laughing. *You were going to make a break*, she chastised herself. *Well, I have to say this: you haven't made a bad start.*

'Sufficient unto the day,' Paula decided as she asked the driver to stop at the top end of her road. She'd get out here, since it wouldn't do for either of her parents to see her arriving home in a taxi. That would throw a spanner in the works before she'd even started. She had eleven days in which to work out a strategy of just how she was going to break free from her old life and begin this entirely new-found one.

How on earth was she going to go about it?

Five

Molly Owen had an answer for everything.

'In the cupboard under the stairs we've got a couple of suit-cases, a bit battered I'll grant you, but they'll serve your purpose, Paula.' Molly glanced at her own daughter and the lovely Paula who were both sitting on the hearthrug in front of the fire. 'What I suggest is that each morning from now on, you put on an extra jumper, cardigan, or whatever pieces of clothing you decide you want to take with you. Then call in 'ere on yer way t'work, strip the bits off, and leave them 'ere an' I'll do yer packing for you.'

Paula and Laura gazed at each other and burst out laughing. 'You really are a proper card, Mum,' Laura said when she got her breath back.

'Well, somebody's got to think sensibly about what Paula's doing. If this change is t'her liking then I say good luck t'her and I think she's real brave t'set about changing jobs and leaving 'ome. Not that I don't think it's long overdue. What are yer now, Paula? Nineteen coming on to twenty, an' that daft bugger of a father of yours still wants to lead you by the hand. Will only let you do anything or go anywhere that he approves of. Half the bloody time he 'as yer housebound. It's a wonder he ain't tried chaining yer to the scullery sink.'

'Mrs Owen, I don't know what I'd do without you. I have risked telling my mother about this job; she just didn't want to know. She covered her ears with her hands to prevent herself hearing what I was trying to tell her. I can appreciate her point. She insists that if my father even gets wind of what I am planning to do he'll take it out on her and what she doesn't know she can't tell him.'

'Doesn't it make you mad that she won't stick up for you?' Molly asked, disbelief obvious in her tone of voice.

'It's always been the same, Mrs Owen; you don't know the half of it. The weird things my father would make me do and some that he would do to me. My mum has known for years what has been going on, right from when I was a very small child, but she never once made any attempt to stop him. She said he looked upon it as his right to be with me, to discipline me. I was his daughter and he wanted only what was best for me.'

'May the Good Lord 'elp her!' Molly cried. 'Sounds t'me like that woman is more than half doolally 'erself.'

'I've often thought that.' Paula sighed. 'When my parents have a row I've always tried to shut myself away in my room and when I did come down I always assumed that the smashed crockery was down to my dad.'

'But you doubt it now?'

'Let's just say I'm trying to keep an open mind, but only this morning before I left for work Mum threw a cup at me. I was going to even the score and throw something at her but then I looked at her face and I got a fleeting sense of what an ordeal her life, since she married my father, must have been like. I tried to put my arms around her but she wasn't accepting any sympathy or comfort, at least, not from me. "Too late," was all she kept muttering. Then just before I left the house she did kiss me, very gently, and told me I was doing the right thing just so long as it doesn't all blow up in my face. So, what am I supposed to make of that?'

'Only you can answer that,' Molly said, but there was a smile in her voice as she added, 'We're going to miss you.'

'No, we're not, we'll see just as much of her, perhaps even more,' Laura protested. 'She'll get days or at least half-days off.'

'I've just 'ad a thought,' Molly butted in. 'If you want any new undies, couple of pairs of knickers or whatever, I can get them for you when I go to Kingston Market and pack them straight into yer case – and I'm gonna buy you a present,' she said, sounding pleased as punch. 'I'll get you a new washbag complete with soap, flannel, toothbrush, paste, comb and brush an' that way you won't 'ave t'sneak them all out of your bathroom at home and give the game away. Good idea of mine, don't you think?'

'Oh, Mum, you really do take the biscuit. You sound just like the kids do when their dad gives them a penny to spend,' Laura managed to say once she had stopped laughing.

'See, we're all of us going to help yer on your way to this new life in this big house you've been telling us about,' Laura said, getting to her feet.

'Where you going?' her mother asked.

'To put the kettle on.'

'I'll do it. You stay with Paula. She's been on her feet all morning at work; she must be dying for a cuppa.'

Paula laughed. 'I could murder a cup of tea and then I should really get going, though I did have the sense to tell my mum I had to work this Wednesday afternoon, stocktaking. She can tell that to my dad and it has given me a chance to pop in here for a while.'

'In that case if you've got all afternoon you're not going anywhere; you'll 'ave yer tea with us.'

Left alone the two girls held hands as they stared into the flames of the fire. It was Laura who spoke first. 'So, come on, love, let's both cheer up. You've taken the first step and that alone shows you've still got some guts left in you. What you've got to do now is just keep telling yourself that you have the right to your own life. Even if you make mistakes, so what, they will be of your own making,' Laura insisted.

'That's just it. Do I have the right to clear out and leave my mother to it?' Paula asked, still sounding very emotional.

'Paula, we both know how difficult it has been for us to remain friends over the years, but we have managed it. We are not just fair-weather friends so I want you to know that no matter what I will always be 'ere for you. Since Fred and I got married and we continued to live 'ere with my mum our life has been really good. Look around you. We ain't got much in the way of worldly goods but we all get on well, we care for each other and we respect each other. Let me assure you we can always make room for one more. It was my mum's idea to tell you this, just in case at the end of the month's trial you decided that job wasn't for you. We want you to know you do 'ave a place to come back to. Our two kids would think it marvellous if their Aunt Paula moved in.'

Molly came in from the scullery with a plate of rock cakes she had baked that morning and as she set the plate down in the middle of the table she turned her head toward Paula. 'I want yer t'know that I go along all the way with what my Laura 'as just told yer. We don't need the front room, only use it Christmas an' high days and holidays, can't afford to light the fire in there other times, besides it's much warmer out here in the kitchen and a darn sight more cosy. So I'm telling yer, if this job does turn out to be different from what you're imagining and you don't want to carry on with it yer needn't be afraid that your dad won't let you go back home. You can, and you will come here with us. Have you got that?'

'Yes.' Paula struggled to hold back her tears as she smiled at this kind, big-hearted woman.

'That's settled then – oh, hang on, my Laura was talking about your time off. Where else would you go but 'ere? Second home from now on, agreed?'

Paula was so moved she almost choked on her response. 'Why are you all so good to me? I will do my best to show you how grateful I am.'

'Stop that. No thanks are needed. I know about the gap in your life and there must be some dark, awful reason for it. I don't care what it is. I really don't give a damn. You, Paula O'Brien, are a good-living, kind, caring young woman, and from what I've listened to about this Mr Lawson I reckon he came to that same conclusion. What he wants is someone who will show a bit of love to his babies, someone who will become a stand-in for their real mother, and if I were to meet up with him now I would tell him he's made a bloody good choice. One I'm sure he'll not regret.'

Paula wiped her eyes and managed a smile before saying, 'Do you know, me saying that I would like to accept this job on a month's trial is the first decision I have ever made for myself.'

Fred Wilson had just stepped in through the back door and had heard Paula's last remark, 'Crikey, we ought to go somewhere and celebrate.'

'Hello, Fred.' Paula grinned, always pleased to see this easy-going, hard-working man. 'No, we're all rushing things. There's quite a lot of planning for me to do before I can safely walk out on my mum and dad and it is not going to be easy.

'Dad won't let me slip way without causing a rumpus. He relies on me for so many things. I wish he was different, but he's not going to change now. He's set in his old-fashioned ways. "Duty" and "honour thy parents" are his belief, but at the same time he firmly believes that he has the right to rule me with a rod of iron. I'm quite sure he has been expecting me to live with him and my mum until the day that I die. He believes it is my duty. He's told me, on more than one occasion, that he is the only man I need in my life.'

Seconds ticked by and nobody spoke because they were all so moved. It was impossible to know what to say.

Finally, Paula broke the stillness that had settled in the room. 'As much as I want to I am still not sure that I will be able to make the break,' she muttered, sounding really desperate.

Fred was frowning deeply as he said, 'I've known your dad for years and t'be honest I've always thought him to be sick in the 'ead. Not so long ago he had a showdown with you out in the street for all the neighbours t'hear. It was all about the clothes you were wearing; I thought you looked dead smart and so did everyone else, but not him. Raving like a lunatic he was. You went indoors and changed an' when you came out the clothes you 'ad on looked as if they had come out of the Ark. Why do you always go along with what he says? I reckon he'd never let you out of the house if he 'ad his bloody way.'

Paula didn't know how to answer. She knew Fred to be a good man, cheerful and warm-hearted. She had always been taken by his tousled head of fair hair and his friendly, outgoing nature. Do anything for his family and even his neighbours, would Fred. He was particularly fond of Laura's mother. His father had been killed whilst working on the railway and his mother had been unable to cope. Six months after his death she had committed suicide leaving three girls all under the age of six and Fred, aged seven. The girls had been farmed out to relatives and Fred had been all set to go into the workhouse. Then Molly Owen, out of sheer pity, had taken him to her house, to muck in with her own kids. There had been Florrie, Laura's sister, and two brothers, Tom and Len, so the house had been pretty crowded. None of the children had been very old when Mr Owen had died from tuberculosis. Molly had somehow managed until Laura's siblings had all married, moved into their own homes, and produced offspring. Fred and Laura had married but had stayed put, having sworn they would take care of Molly for the rest of her life. Sunday afternoons seldom passed without some of Molly's children turning up with grand-children in tow.

All this history served to prove to Paula what a real mum Molly Owen had always been and still was. A real old-fashioned mother, with her greying hair pulled back into a bun. She wore dark-coloured dresses always covered by a flowery wraparound overall. It was she who made this humble house a real home. Many's the time when Paula had felt the warmth of this house in Blackshaw Road and she wished that her own home could have resembled it.

'If only,' she would murmur as she walked home, knowing full well there was no comparison.

Love was everywhere in Molly Owen's house. Fear reigned where she lived.

Laura felt panicked by what Paula had been telling them, though not all of it was news to her. She and Fred and her own mother had often spoken of the distressing way poor Paula was made to live her life. Now, Paula had made the situation sound absolutely hopeless. If she weren't careful she *would* end up staying with her parents and sacrificing the whole of her life to fit in with her father's needs.

'You are going to think seriously about taking this job, aren't you?' Laura forcefully asked. 'You've told us that you'd agreed with Mr Lawson to give it a month's trial. You're not gonna let him down, are you?'

'I don't know,' Paula answered honestly. 'While I was in that lovely house it seemed as if I was being granted a new start in life. I told myself that there was so much in my past that I would dearly love to wipe out and that here was the place and the time being offered to me. A solution that would enable me at least to make a start. Those babies were adorable. I found myself yearning to take responsibility for both of them; it would to me be such a privilege. If at that moment, when I was nursing David and giving him his bottle, Mr Lawson had asked me to stay, start living there, become their nursery maid, I would have cried out, "Yes please." But now, back in my familiar situation, it seems an impossible dream.'

Paula suddenly looked so sad, every bit as sad as Laura felt for her.

'We'll think of something. I can't promise what, but we'll come up with a plan, never fear.' In spite of her own brave words Laura felt worried and unsure.

'If only my dad would disappear, get offered a job far away, just for a week. Just to give me time to safely get out of that house. But that isn't going to happen, is it?'

Laura didn't like the sound of 'safely get out'. She took a deep breath before saying, 'Paula, you're grown up, you're no longer a child that he can control when the mood takes him. From what I've gathered, when you were little if he said jump you did and you've told me many a time that he believed it was his God-given right to discipline you. So are you just going to carry on, week after week, letting him rule your life until you become a dried-up old maid?'

Paula hung her head but she made no attempt to answer.

Laura closed her eyes and gritted her teeth. *I've just said that Mike O'Brien believed he had the right to discipline his only child. But what I'd like to know is to what lengths his discipline went?* Paula, as a child, wouldn't have lived in terror of him if all he had been doing was reprimanding her and yet she herself had never seen any visible signs of ill-treatment, no bruises or black eyes. There was of course a great many ways of terrifying a young child without using physical violence. Fred had once remarked that his drinking mates often referred to Mike O'Brien as an obstreperous old git. Too fond of making smutty, bawdy remarks about young women and not backward in mauling them, given half a chance.

She sighed, looked down on Paula's beautiful thick head of hair, and said gently, 'Just for once, love, why don't yer just face up to yer father? Look him straight in the eye and tell him you've 'ad enough. Tell 'im you've got a new job an' you're leaving 'ome. What would be the worst thing that he could do?'

Paula realized that if she started to answer that question she would be in over her head. She did her best to calm down but still her voice trembled as she said, 'He would make it his business to find out who was offering me employment and then he would take great delight in telling Mr Lawson exactly where and why I was put away for a little more than a year.'

Laura felt unexpectedly sorry for her. Her voice softer now, full of compassion, she said, 'I know you always like to stick to the truth but for Christ's sake what did you tell this Mr Lawson? He must 'ave wanted to know where you've worked before.'

'I didn't tell him any lies, if that's what you're thinking. It was while I was nursing David that he remarked about how well I handled the baby. I told him that I'd had a great deal to do with babies in my first job and that it had only lasted a year and for the rest of my teens I had worked in the chemist.'

'You were really referring to the time you spent in that home?'

'Yes, but I didn't elaborate. He didn't ask about my earnings and I didn't volunteer any details.'

'There you are then, you got yerself out of that quite nicely. Ooh, you make me so angry! You're bloody capable enough with everyone except that sodding father of yours.'

Despite herself, Paula smiled at her. But Laura didn't smile back; instead she rolled her eyes in exasperation. 'All that awful time you went through, there must 'ave been someone to blame, yet you never utter a wrong word. Keeping things to yourself is one thing but some day the truth will have to come out. And the sooner you realize that, the better off you'll be.'

It took a while for Paula to form an answer.

'I made you and your mum a promise and I have thought long and hard about it. If the time should come for me to keep my word it will mean that I shall have been living in Ridgeway Manor for three months and must have proved to Mr Lawson that I am well able to take care of his two sons. That can only mean one thing: that I have stood on my own two feet and gone some way towards putting the past behind me.' Shaking her head, she rubbed at her eyes, feeling the tears beneath her fingertips. The memory of what she had promised to disclose had her feeling sick. 'Presumably I shall be feeling a lot stronger by then and, Laura, I will tell you the whole sordid story – or at least as much as I know myself.'

Laura stood up. 'I shall keep you to that. Meanwhile I think we've talked enough for one day. Come on, we'll wrap ourselves up warm and go for a walk to meet Ronnie and Jack when they come out of school – the boys will think its great to see their Auntie Paula.'

Calling out goodbye to Molly who was in the scullery, they opened the front door and went out to brave the weather. As she closed the front gate Laura thought perhaps she should make it her business to tell this Mr Lawson how good her friend was with her own two boys. Then came an afterthought. He'd find out quick enough that he had a gem on his hands with Paula. To know her was to love her.

Six

The day that Paula was to start her new life had dawned and she was beginning to think that the angels were on her side. Her father and his brother, her Uncle Patrick, had got themselves a building contract, working on the other side of Clapham Common, which meant they left for work at six thirty in order to see that all their labourers clocked on the site by seven thirty. She would be able to leave the house this morning without becoming involved in an ugly scene with her father.

It had been a remarkable week. Her mother had apparently had a complete change of heart. She had washed and ironed practically every item of clothing that Paula possessed, laying the items on the foot of the bed and each day she had included at least one newly bought article furtively slid between her own clothes. She would accept no thanks, neither would she enter into any discussion about Paula's plans for the future. She still insisted that what she didn't know she couldn't tell. Fully aware that her mother was as frightened of her husband as she was of her father, Paula made herself accept that. Even though he was not in the house, her mother was frightened and with Paula gone she was going to be so lonely. *What can I do?* Paula asked herself over and over again. If she didn't cut the ties and break free now she might never get another chance. Her heart ached for her mother but there was another side to this story. For years, whenever the mood took him, her father had ordered her to go upstairs to her bedroom where he would quickly join her and once inside he would lock the door. Her mother must have known that what took place on these occasions had not been right. Yet not once had Paula ever heard her make a protest. Then weeks after her thirteenth birthday, when she had started to be ill, her mother had been quick to join in with her father in his condemnation of her. Could her mother have stopped that kindly priest from taking her away? She had never been allowed to ask that question.

Her mother broke into Paula's thoughts to tell her that the cab she had ordered had just turned into the road. Paula closed her eyes, a feeling of euphoria surging through her. She really was going to go through with it. Then suddenly her mother was crying like a baby. Paula blinked and sighed. How many times had she tried to analyse their relationship? Mother would always side with her father, at times even lashing out at her, being especially harsh when it came to verbal abuse, only to be conscience-stricken and loving as soon as her father left the house.

The doorbell rang. Paula walked down the hall, opened the door and said good morning to the taxi driver.

'Any luggage, miss?' he asked, smiling broadly.

'Only those two holdalls,' she said, nodding her head to where they stood at the foot of the stairs. 'But we do have a couple of suitcases to pick up from number forty-seven Blackshaw Road, if you wouldn't mind.'

'No problem, miss, it's not going out of our way,' he assured her as he stepped into the hallway and picked up both cases.

Cautiously Paula turned towards her mother. Wonders would never cease, she almost cried out. Frances O'Brien's face had been wiped of all trace of tears and now she was showing one of her most winning smiles. Paula breathed a prayer of thanks and felt herself relax for the first time this morning.

'It is time for you to go,' her mother said quietly, but as Paula made to put her arms around her she took a step backwards. 'I shall pray for you. Paula,' she said, and with that Paula had to be content because as she walked down the path towards the taxi she stopped halfway and turned to look back at the house. The front door was already firmly closed.

What a different send-off Paula received from Laura and her family. Jack was sitting on the doorstep with his young brother Ronnie watching for his aunt to arrive. 'The taxi is coming,' he yelled through the open doorway before taking hold of Ronnie's hand and dragging him down to the gate. The wheels of the cab had hardly stopped turning before the two lads were on the pavement ready to hug Paula as she got out of the taxi. Seconds later Molly and Laura appeared with Fred bringing up the rear carrying two very old suitcases.

'You got away all right then?' Molly wanted to know, but Paula wasn't listening. She and Laura had their arms round each other and for once it was Paula that was urging Laura to calm down.

'I won't be far away, you big ninny, I shall probably have more freedom than I have ever had in my life up to now. Besides, there is a telephone at Ridgeway and I shall ask Mr Lawson if he would allow me to receive a call from you, say once a week.' All the same, both girls were now snivelling.

Fred made eye contact with the cab driver and they both raised their eyebrows. 'You in an 'urry, mate, or would yer like to come in an' 'ave a cuppa? Me boys 'ave got t'ave their kisses an' cuddles yet, never mind Molly standing there waiting 'er turn to pass on a load of advice. Anyone would think our Paula was going to the other end of the world. She's only going to bloody Raynes Park.'

At the mention of tea the whole tribe went into the house.

'Are you sure you're all right?' Molly asked as soon as she could get a word in edgeways.

'Yes, Molly, a bit apprehensive because everything had moved so quickly, I just cannot believe it,' Paula confessed. 'It's as though this job is too good to be true. If it does turn out well it could be the answer to all of my prayers. On the other hand, what if I can't cope? Honestly, Molly, there's such a big difference between Mr Lawson's way of life and mine. I just hope it doesn't turn out that we are like chalk and cheese.'

Concern was obvious in Molly's eyes as she said, 'Look, love, you've got t'stop putting yerself down. From what you've told me I think I've worked out exactly what this Mr Lawson is after. He wants a full-time mother for his twins, not just a couple of posh nannies. I expect it was a bit of a shock to him when you turned up. My bet is he thought you were too young, and he couldn't see a lovely young lady like you wanting to care for two babies. Then he had a chat with you and saw how you handled one of his boys. Then he knew straight off there was a bloody sight more to you than a pretty face. So he offered to take a chance on you. And if you ask me he's bin dead lucky to 'ave found you. Now don't you think it's time you drank up your tea and got going?'

'Oh, Molly! You're like a ray of sunshine. Whatever would I do without you?' Paula said before she moved to place her arms around this woman who meant so much to her and gently kissed her weather-beaten cheeks.

'Dunno about a ray of sunshine, more like a dose of Epsom salts,' Laura remarked cheekily, but she made sure she was out of her mother's reach when she said it.

Jack and Ronnie were good-naturedly ragging their aunt about going to live in a big posh house, when out of the blue Jack became serious. 'You always talk more posh than we do, Auntie Paula, will yer get worse now that Nan says you're going up in the world?'

'I promise not to, just as long as you don't stop loving me, Jack,' Paula answered him, as she pulled him close to her and gave him a hug.

'I'll always love you too, Auntie Paula.' Ronnie wasn't going to be left out, yet there was a sob in his voice and it almost had Paula in tears again as she gave this dear little boy his reassuring hug.

'I've put yer cases in the back, miss, an' I think it's time we were on our way.'

'Yes, I am sorry we have delayed you so long,' Paula said, still with one arm around Ronnie's shoulders.

'Not at all, my love,' he answered with a huge grin on his face. To himself he was thinking, *What a difference. At her own house the atmosphere had been so different. That woman must be a right frigid cow, never even came out to wave her off.* No doubt about this lot being different, he thought. From the kids right up to their parents and their gran, they had feelings for this lass and they weren't ashamed to show them.

He had only been driving for about ten minutes when he slid open the glass partition that separated him from his passenger, turned his head and said, 'You all right, love?'

Paula nodded and smiled. 'Never better,' she said.

'Good. Mr Lawson 'as an account with this cab firm. I know him well, you'll find out for yerself, but I can tell yer now, he's a good bloke.'

Although she'd visited the house before, as the cab neared their destination Paula found herself looking at so much flourishing greenery and was taken aback. They were not that far from London but the views of the surrounding countryside were beautiful. It was the end of January and the snow had disappeared as quickly as it had arrived. The sun was shining, though it was weak, and the sky was colourless and low, still the air was clear enough for her to see for miles, the fields and hedges all looked so good and hardly a sound coming from anywhere. It was all having a calming effect on her – so much so that already the knots that had clustered inside her chest were beginning to unwind.

'Oh, my,' she murmured as the cab drove up the long shingled driveway and Ridgeway Manor came into view. It was just as solid and awe-inspiring as she remembered. Before she was even out of the cab the huge front door was opened and both Mrs Wright and Joyce Pledger were standing at the top of the stone steps.

Everything seemed to happen at once. The cabby opened up the back of the taxi and removed her two battered suitcases and her two holdalls. 'I'll take them up and put them inside the hall for you, miss,' he said. Then grinning broadly, he turned to Esmé Wright, who had quickly come down to stand beside Paula. ''Ow yer doing, me old love?' he asked her. 'Worked yourself a cushy number here by all accounts.'

'I'll 'ave less of the "old" from you, Tom Brown. Yer not exactly a spring chicken yerself.' Esmé was smiling like a Cheshire cat as she reprimanded him.

By now Joyce Pledger was on the other side of Paula and was doing her best to explain that Mr Lawson had gone up to town for the day. 'Business he just had to attend to, apparently, but he said for us to make you feel welcome and if it did turn out that he was unable to return home this evening he would telephone and he would see you tomorrow.'

'Oh,' was all that Paula could think of to say.

'We have your room all ready for you, the babies are fine; come along in and we'll get you settled.'

As easy as that, Paula was thinking, looking up at this splendid house that was, at least for the time being, going to be her home.

In the hall Paula thanked the cab driver, opened her handbag and was about to offer him a tip.

'Put yer money away, lass. I told you, Mr Lawson has an account and he always adds a tidy sum to be shared amongst the drivers.'

'Well, if you're sure, thank you very much.'

'Hope you settle in well. Mrs Pledger has been here a long time and I can vouch for her – she'll see you all right – but I don't know so much about that one.' He nudged Esmé with his elbow at the same time he was winking slyly at Paula.

'Don't push yer luck too far, Tom,' Esmé warned, 'or we'll not be offering you any tea.'

'Now there's a funny how-do, cos I'll not be needing any refreshments today. Earlier on Miss O'Brien called at some friends of hers and we got a great welcome and a good cup of tea, so, ladies, I shall love you and leave you and look forward to seeing you in the near future.'

They all three, still chuckling, gathered at the front door to see the taxi driver away, and then it was Esmé who took charge. 'Joyce, you and Paula take a holdall, I'll bring both the cases, then we'll leave her to see what she thinks about her room before she goes to see the twins.'

By one o'clock Paula was telling herself it was all too good to be true. Her room was delightful; someone had put a vase of sweet-smelling cut flowers on her dressing table and a small box of chocolates with a note beside it, which said, *Hope you will be happy here in your new job.* The note was signed *Pledger*.

She and Joyce had fed the two baby boys, played with them for a while and now they were happily settled in a playpen in the kitchen. Nearby was a table set for three and Esmé was urging them to sit down as she was just about to serve up lunch.

So had begun Paula O'Brien's first day as a nursemaid. As she ate Esmé's tasty shepherd's pie, Paula was almost praying that she wouldn't wake up and find it was all a dream.

Seven

With trembling fingers, Paula took the telephone receiver from Joyce. Everything had turned out so well she could hardly believe her good fortune. She listened to the deep voice of Mr Lawson asking if she had settled in all right and apologizing for him not being there when she had arrived. 'Everything is fine, thank you, sir. Mrs Wright went home about an hour ago and Mrs Pledger and myself were just about to take David and Peter upstairs and settle them down for the night.'

'As long as you are sure that you have everything you need.' His concern came down the line and Paula was pleased that he had asked to speak to her when Joyce had answered the phone. After she had again reassured him that she had been made welcome, he said he would be home the following evening between six and seven o'clock. She said, 'Goodnight, sir,' and handed the receiver back to Joyce.

She desperately needed to believe that she had made a good move. During the last week there had been many times when she'd felt misgivings. As the shock of what she had done began to subside at last, she felt incredibly weary. Sinking into an armchair by the fireside she leaned her head into her hands and closed her eyes, trying to shut out the enormity of her actions. All she had to do now was to get herself into a strict routine, and she knew it wouldn't be hard to love those two precious little boys who had already captivated her heart.

Seated opposite to Paula, Joyce Pledger already felt that it would be no hardship to form a friendship with this young lady. The atmosphere between them on this, their first evening alone together, was nicely companionable and the day had gone quite well. Perhaps it had been for the best that Mr Lawson had had to go to his office and even better that he would not be returning until tomorrow. It had given her and Esmé Wright the chance to take their time, show Paula the ropes, tell her of the routine they had drawn up between them for the good of the twins. Paula appeared to have many good points, and what she didn't know she readily admitted and proved herself most willing to learn.

Joyce Pledger was a small, dark-haired lady in her mid-thirties, always with a ready smile on her face. She was a capable lady who didn't stick to the rules, employed originally as a housekeeper when Sheila Lawson was still alive. Both she and Mr Lawson used to leave early every morning to work in the City. At that time the Lawsons had employed a cook but, for reasons unknown, Mrs Stevens had failed to turn up one morning and to this day nothing, as far as Joyce Pledger knew, had been heard of the woman.

Without any formalities Joyce had taken it upon herself to slip into a routine. After all, at that time the Lawsons employed a cleaner three times a week and although this was certainly a very large house, herself and Mr and Mrs Lawson were the only inhabitants. The Lawsons saw to their own breakfast and had left the house each morning by seven forty-five. Joyce had taken the first step, and had gone to a lot of trouble. She had shopped, bought food and the necessary ingredients, prepared and cooked a dinner and laid the table in the dining room for a few evenings. Such was the appreciation shown to her by the Lawsons she had been more than pleased to accept their proposal to carry on being cook-cum-housekeeper. She had also appreciated the rise in salary that they insisted she be given.

The household had come through a bad patch, as Mr Lawson had faced devastation at the loss of his wife, and sheer bewilderment that he was left with two newborn sons. Now at long last she could look back and thank God that Mr Lawson had survived all his trials and tribulations.

It also suited Joyce to make herself indispensable. She felt well established in this household, which had become a sanctuary. She had had a childhood sweetheart, and they had grown into adults together and made plans, become engaged when she was nineteen and he had been twenty-two. Then in August of 1914 Germany had declared war on France and had also invaded Belgium. It was inevitable that Britain would then declare war on Germany. Frank Johnson, who if he had lived would have been her husband, had survived in the British Army until 1918 when he was taken prisoner by the Germans at the Battle of Amiens. He was not held in captivity for long. He had died as a result of his wounds.

She herself had been an only child and at the death of her parents she had seen service in a private household as a way of not only earning a living but also putting a roof over her head. With the death of so very many young men in that terrible war the young women left behind had not stood much chance of finding a husband, and so Joyce often felt grateful to Mr Lawson for having provided her with some security.

Her biggest regret was that her Frank's body was buried in a foreign country and so she didn't even have the consolation of being able to put flowers on his grave.

Paula had been laid back in her chair with her eyes closed and deep in thought when the sound of Joyce adding another log to the fire brought her upright with a start.

'Would you like a drink – sherry maybe? Or tea, cocoa or Horlicks?' Joyce asked as she got up from her knees.

'I don't think I want anything more to eat or drink tonight, thank you, Joyce, but I would like to take a glass of water up to bed with me.'

'No need,' Joyce answered promptly. 'I have filled the bottle beside your bed and topped it with a clean glass.'

'Oh, please, Joyce, you mustn't start waiting on me.'

'Don't worry, I have no intention of doing that, but until you get yourself familiar with the house and its layout, I will do all I can to help. We have already gone through the night's procedure so let's hope the twins don't decide to prove me wrong.'

The big lounge was very warm and cosy. Joyce had told her that besides the open fire there was a back-up system behind the fireplace that never went out. Three big lamps that she had admired so much on her first visit were lit, shedding soft, golden pools of light, and the heavy floor-length velvet curtains were drawn tightly shut.

'Let's hope the babies don't wake you up too much on your first night.'

'I shan't mind if they do; I'm not likely to sleep too heavily tonight – different bed, strange bedroom and all that. I do admire how everything has been planned right down to the last detail.'

'Yes, Mr Lawson put a lot of thought into those two rooms. Two friends of his, who have children of their own, came round and gave advice.'

Paula had been very anxious about getting up in the night to see to the twins but now she had made herself familiar with the set-up she felt she would be able to cope. Three rooms on the first floor had been entirely made over for the well-being of Mr Lawson's sons, and the nursery seemed to be equipped with every apparatus known to man.

Connected by a sliding door was what Paula would call a wash-room. It contained a massive, heavy-looking washing machine – the first one Paula had ever seen – as well as a deep sink and two long trestle tables, one laid out with every item that was needed when changing a baby and the second table held a miniature bath. Shelves along one wall held neatly stacked white towels in three sizes and so many items – Johnson's Baby Powder, lotions, creams, antiseptic ointment – that it resembled a display from Boots the Chemist. One corner of the room had been set out as a small kitchen, with a gas hob which had four burners and on which stood a shiny copper kettle. There was also a deep white sink with just one tap for cold water, and fixed to the wall above was a slim gas water heater. A shelf fixed to an adjoining wall held tins of Pablum baby food – another new invention, and very convenient – and glass jars filled with Farley's Rusks and a large sugar basin.

These two rooms contained every item that was needed to look after the health and well-being of both babies. The third adjoining room had been made into a bed-sitting room for Paula.

'Do you mind if I go up and check on David and Peter? Then I'll finish my unpacking,' Paula asked hesitantly, not wanting to put a foot wrong on her first night here in this beautiful old house.

'Paula, there are no restrictions on you. I know it must be a bit scary – new job, unfamiliar surroundings and the fact that you've made yourself responsible for two wee mites – but you'll come to love them. In fact when you were feeding Peter earlier on I thought how quickly you were bonding with them.'

'Thank you, Joyce. It certainly won't be a hard task to love those little boys, and I hope within a few days I shall have mastered the best way to look after them.'

'I'm sure you will have. Now, if you're sure you don't need anything I'll say goodnight. Remember my room is only at the other end of the same corridor as yours. I can hear if they cry, and if they do then I will come with you for the first few days until you feel you can stand on your own two feet.'

'Thank you, Joyce. I do appreciate all the help you're giving me. Goodnight.'

It only took a short while for Paula to unpack her belongings. She hung her navy-blue dress in the wardrobe along with her dark brown coat, remembering how her father had never allowed her to wear bright colours. She put her underwear in the top drawer of the chest of drawers, laughing as she handled the warm white panties and vests that Molly Owen had bought her from Kingston Market. Two jumpers and two skirts she laid flat in the second drawer and then, shaking the creases out of two blouses, she stopped and held them to her face. One was a pretty soft pink with long sleeves, and the other one was baby blue with a sailor's collar. Both blouses were brand new and had been bought by her mother. She had to swallow hard to rid herself of the lump that was threatening to choke her. She was close to tears as she put the blouses on hangers and hung them in the wardrobe.

In her nightdress and dressing gown, with blue fluffy slippers on her feet – a present from Laura – and with her thick long hair brushed and hanging down over her shoulders, she looked closer to fourteen than nearly twenty as she walked the short distance to the nursery.

As she stood between the two cots and looked down on first Peter and then David, she felt a peace that she had never felt whilst living at home. The baby down that had been on their heads when first born had vanished and already showing was darker, shiny real hair; it was plain to see they were going to be the image of their father. Gently, using her forefinger, she stroked each forehead and then in turn she touched each plump little hand. Already she felt it would be no hardship to give her devotion to these two babies and hopefully she would be privileged to see them grow into sturdy little boys.

It was hardly possible to contemplate that this could happen some day.

Eight

Paula had survived the month's trial at Ridgeway Manor and Mr Lawson had been so generous in his praise that she felt she must already have become an accomplished nursemaid. In fact he had told her that she had far exceeded his expectations.

'I hope you aren't thinking of leaving us now,' he said, grinning and showing his brilliant white teeth.

Nothing had been further from her thoughts.

Living in Milner Road, the daily routine had become dreary. Here the twins woke her early and once she had given them their first bottle of the day she had time to look out at the garden and the rolling fields beyond and excitement would rise inside her at the prospect of the day ahead.

She thought less and less of her father now. The horror of the year she had spent in what had been a military hospital at one time began to fade. The twins had become her life. They were a good reason for living. It was she who tucked them into their cots at night, sang them songs, recited nursery rhymes and tickled them until they chuckled loudly. She had spoon-fed them their first solid meals, endlessly changed their napkins, took them for outings, pushing that heavy double perambulator, and already she was utterly devoted to the pair of them.

The two women she now shared her life with had made an enormous difference to her way of thinking. Joyce Pledger had been her friend from the off. She was a kindly soul, though Paula suspected that before she came here to live, Joyce had been a very lonely lady.

Esmé Wright was an entirely different story. Paula really liked Esmé, who was overweight, well into her forties, her blonde hair frizzy from being permed too tightly and she was what her own mother would call 'common'. But she was kindly and always jolly. It was Esmé who had taken Paula under her wing and told her she didn't believe in bringing babies up according to any book. Lots of loving and a bit of spoiling never harmed any child, at least in Esmé's opinion. In fact, when watching her as she nursed one of the babies, Paula was often reminded of Molly Owen, that lovely lady whom she regarded as her second mum.

Yes, she firmly told herself, one way and another, with a lot of help and kindness, she had made a good move, and she felt she had just about started to put the past behind her.

There was still one thing that niggled away in her mind, the fact that she hadn't been able to make contact with her mother. She had written one letter each week for the past four weeks, begging her mother to meet her on her free half-day, and suggesting that either Kennards at South Wimbledon or Joey Lyons at Tooting Broadway might be a good place to have tea together. Perhaps her father had got hold of the letters and had forbidden her mother to make any contact. If that were the case she knew her mother would be too afraid to go against his orders.

There wasn't much else she could do, she thought ruefully.

Then one night, for no reason she could fathom, she had a nightmare. Nothing like it had happened in the weeks since she had left home. She had wakened sweating, yet shivering; the ferocity of the dream was such that she couldn't control her limbs. Realizing that in her dream she had been flung back into that hellhole to which she had been banished for so long, she crossed her arms across her chest, hugging herself tight, then closed her eyes and rocked her body from side to side.

Now wide awake she sat up in bed and told herself she was safe, she was in the pretty bedroom that had been hers since she had come to take care of Mr Lawson's two sons. It was no good: even though she repeatedly told herself that she had left home, started a new life, all the confidence she had built up had now vanished. The problems between herself and her father still existed – they would never go away until she confronted him.

Oh dear, Paula sighed heavily, she'd thought she had succeeded in putting the past behind her, but now she mournfully told herself, *It is never going to go away. It is always going to be there.*

A sudden thought occurred to her. She hadn't taken any time off in the five weeks that she had been here – not from any righteous feeling or trying to curry favour with Mr Lawson, it was just the fact that she needed to get herself and the babies into a set routine. She wanted the babies to get to know her, to rely on her;

she felt even at that young age they needed assurance and in many ways she knew she had succeeded. They recognized her voice, held out their arms to her and laughed when she talked to them. Each day she discovered something new about these babies, and found them a constant delight. Their dark hair was now long enough for her to brush into a curly cockscomb. What amazed her was that their features were identical and yet they had already developed different habits. Peter was a contortionist: with ease he could bend his chubby leg from the knee and put his big toe into his mouth and lay in his playpen on his back contentedly sucking away. David was absorbed by his plump fingers; holding them up in front of his eyes he would stare as if mesmerized by the fact that they belonged to him.

In so many ways it was good to be here at Ridgeway. To be amongst people who accepted her for what she was, who didn't know of her past and therefore had no reason to judge her. Right from the start she had steeled herself against thinking beyond the next day, treasuring each moment of her new life.

Only last night Esmé had pressed her to let her know when she wanted to start having her half-days, and then she had offered to come in at one o'clock and stay until nine on those days, rather than her normal day of nine till five.

'Joyce and I can manage easily enough now. We'll see that nothing untoward comes to your little darlings an' we promise not to over-feed them. So get yerself off. Go see that mate yer always talking about, and tell us how good life is when yer living with the nobs.'

Paula had laughed at Esmé's suggestion at the time, but now she felt a few hours with the Owens would bring her back down to earth. A good old chat with Laura was just what she needed. Perhaps Laura would have met her mother in the street and she would be able to tell her if she was looking well. *Yes*, she decided. *I'll get the twins all set for the day and then when Esmé comes in I'll ask her if she was serious in her offer. If so I'll tell her I would like to have tomorrow afternoon off.*

Sighing again, she looked at the one and only photograph of her mother that she had, it was a very old one and her mother looked so young and happy as she relaxed in a deckchair in the garden. If only her mother would agree for them to meet up. A good talk would clear the air and she would be able to convince her mother that the change she had made was working out well. It was understandable if her mother was cross with her – after all she had left her on her own with her father. *But fair's fair and she must have been partly to blame for sending me away when I was still a child.* Her heart ached. Recalling that awful year, she stared hard at the picture of her mother and watched it become blurred by her tears.

'Please write to me,' she murmured. 'Don't try and pretend that I don't exist, please, Mum. At least I shall be able to leave a message with Laura in the hope that she might be able to make contact with you and pass it on.'

And with that thought she had to be content for the moment because with two babies to look after there wasn't much free time for daydreaming.

Nine

Paula didn't get time off in the end. Both babies started to develop sniffles and whereas Paula was ready to call in the doctor, Esmé advised her to wait.

'I'll lay my last shilling that they're cutting their first teeth,' she had loudly declared – and of course she was right. During the night both Joyce and herself had walked the floor, soothing them, patting their backs, all the while crooning until it was safe to lay them back down in their cots. From the moment the tooth had pierced the gum they seemed to advance in leaps and bounds, and the fact that they were starting to crawl had their father in raptures. It also had Jeffrey thinking that it was about time he had them christened.

No sooner the thought than the deed!

The day of the christening was a day that Paula knew she would remember for the rest of her life. Jeffrey's closest friends, Andy and Hilda Burrows, were godparents to both Peter and David. 'Keep it as simple as possible,' is what Jeffrey had said. After the ceremony at St Andrew's Church the guests had made their way to the Belmont Hotel. Mr Lawson had booked a private room in the hotel and there were about fifty guests present to celebrate the occasion. All adults, mostly men – Jeffrey's colleagues. They all brought great gifts but not suitable ones. Jeffrey's mother Mary and her husband Arthur had travelled up from North Devon.

'I have to compliment you, Paula; you are doing such a grand job. Peter and David are a credit to you.' Mary smiled as she made the comment. 'Of course it will be better when the boys start school; they'll meet other kiddies and you and my son will meet up with their parents.'

Paula looked up, startled. 'You and my son will meet up with their parents.' Why was she coupling the two of them together as if they were the boys' parents? She was so happy here in this job, she felt so safe, and she certainly didn't want any complications.

Aloud, Paula said, 'It will be three years at least before their father thinks of them going even to nursery school.'

Mary laughed. 'Only thinking of the day, are you, Paula?'

'Well, yes, I suppose I am,' Paula answered timidly. 'Never in a million years did I think I could have landed a position as good as this one.'

'Well, in my opinion nobody could have done a better job than you have, right motherly type you've turned out to be even though you are only a youngster yourself. I will be eternally grateful to you, because before Jeffrey found you he was at his wits' end. Now in the few days that I have been staying in the house I have become well aware of how you have everything under control.'

'I have had a great deal of help both from Mrs Pledger and Mrs Wright,' Paula was quick to add. 'I couldn't have got by without their help.'

Mrs Blackmore just smiled again as she moved off to mingle with the wives of Jeffrey's associates.

Joyce came to stand beside Paula. 'Thanks for putting in a good word for me, but then if I say so myself I haven't done too badly since I stepped into the breach and you most certainly have done remarkably well. Come on, let's go and get ourselves something to eat.'

Paula first checked that the twins were being well cared for then grinned as she helped herself to sandwiches and a variety of salad whilst watching Joyce hold out their glasses for a refill. There had been many a day as she'd cuddled David and Peter, made up their bottles, prepared their baby food and washed and ironed their clothes, when she'd wondered what she would do if this job were to come to an end. She mustn't – she couldn't – let her thoughts dwell on such an awful possibility. She had to tell herself to live for the day.

'So, don't tell me you aren't looking forward to your day out with Mr Lawson tomorrow,' Joyce said, grinning broadly.

'I'm only going because it is part of my job. My time will be taken up with watching out for the twins.'

'That doesn't mean you can't have a little fun, too,' Joyce said quietly, thinking that Mr Lawson was thirty-one and Paula was only nineteen or twenty at the most. The age shouldn't matter. She had a gut feeling Jeffrey Lawson was becoming inter-ested in Paula, although there was no serious evidence of it yet, despite his seemingly casual efforts to be friends. She had noticed Jeffrey watching Paula quietly as they ate their evening dinner together, although Paula seemed oblivious to it. In fact she shied away, Joyce was sure of that. It was work alone that filled Paula's mind. On all subjects unrelated to the twins and their well-being she had a reserved, cautious air about her. Almost as if she had something to hide. She certainly never wanted to discuss her own family. *Don't be silly*, she chided herself, *you're letting your imagination run away with you*, and a few minutes later she went with Paula to retrieve David and Peter from so many drooling women.

Paula had been very wary about the invitation to accompany Mr Lawson on this river trip. Over and over again she told herself there could be no harm in it: He could hardly take the twins on the river on his own.

Monday dawned bright and sunny, and the rush to pack everything they would need into the boot of Mr Lawson's car seemed an awesome task.

Paula was ready and waiting when she heard Mr Lawson's car being driven out of the garage and Mr Blackmore's car turn in to the drive. Arthur had been to fill his car with petrol. Jeffrey was now helping his mother into the front seat of Arthur's car. Late last night Jeffrey had invited Joyce Pledger to join everyone on today's outing, a fact that pleased Paula immensely because she could only carry one of the twins at any one time. Their father was now leaning against the body of his car as he watched them manoeuvre their charges down the front steps.

Paula glanced at Jeffrey and quickly looked away. He looked different again today because he was dressed casually in grey flannel trousers, a white open-necked shirt and a navy-blue blazer. She hoped that she had dressed suitably. She had on a lightweight short-sleeved navy-blue dress and a matching long loose coat. Both coat and dress were edged in white. It was an outfit that suited her slim figure very well. She had packed sunglasses and a hat to wear later, but at the moment she had pulled her long auburn hair well back and fastened it with a huge tortoiseshell comb.

Joyce had chosen to wear a fawn-coloured linen suit with a very pretty dark brown blouse. Both women, on advice from the men, were wearing low-heeled shoes. There was a real holiday feeling in the air when they finally reached Hampton Court. Paula felt a thrill run through her whole body. What a treat. She thought she'd never been so happy.

As Jeffrey parked his car in the private car park behind the yacht club the sun was sparkling on the river and heat shimmered on the towpath. It was a perfect summer's day. Only Bushy Park on the opposite side of the road offered shady, cool places to sit. Paula and Joyce, with Mary following, picked their way slowly down the steps to the private yacht club. The girls were carrying the twins and Mary was carrying folded deckchairs, the idea being that they would set up their resting place on the hard standing above the slipway rather than struggle for space on the riverbank, which today was thronged with people.

Andy and Hilda Burrows came running to meet them with the information that their own two children were with their grandad and were already on the river in their boat. Arthur helped Jeffrey set up the chairs while Mary and Paula kept a tight hold on the twins as they stood watching swans back-paddling to catch the bread some small children were throwing to them. The river was very busy, as it always was on May bank holiday . Joyce was keeping a tight hold on the two wicker hampers she had packed.

Even before the christening, Jeffrey had told Paula that Hilda Burrows was a nice person, a great sport, and he was sure that they would hit it off. Jeffrey had been right: on the few occasions that they had met both Paula and Hilda felt that they would become good friends.

The men set out blankets, towels and more folding chairs while Joyce and Paula set about taking the boys' clothes off, dressing them in just a sleeveless vest, a pair of shorts and a wide-brimmed sun hat.

Paula was busy getting Peter dressed when he started to wriggle. He shrieked, pointing with his chubby forefinger. A saloon steamer was coming into sight. Passengers were sitting on the decks and they waved to the children.

Hilda told the boys to look across the river to the opposite towpath. A lumbering great carthorse was slowly towing a barge. The barge was brightly painted and was towing another boat which was heavily loaded with timber. Three scruffy, sunburnt lads all aged about ten were sitting astride the timber. They spotted the twins and they cupped their hands around their mouths calling loudly and cheerily, 'Hi, little uns!'

To everyone else the twins were identical, but not to Paula. It hadn't taken her long to work out that David's eyebrows were a slightly different shape and much thinner than Peter's. Each had dark curly hair the same as their father, and both were strong, sturdy little boys. Now as she watched their open, smiling faces she felt so grateful that somehow she had landed this job – only it was so much more than a job; it was a whole different way of life and she had never been happier. She had never known it was possible to feel so contented and safe day after day.

Andy flicked a strand of his fair hair from his face as he took the pair of sunglasses Hilda was offering him. 'Jeff, are you thinking of taking your cruiser out?' he asked, grinning and nodding towards the river.

'Well, yes, I was, but I didn't realize the river would be so busy. Although I should have known it would be, more so when the weather is as good as it is today,' he admitted sheepishly. 'And with it being a Bank Holiday too.'

'How about if I call my boys in and before we start eating we take them all over to Bushy Park? Peter and David can paddle in the stream there.'

At that moment Andy became aware of a gentle splashing and looked to see his father and his uncle, with his own two lads seated behind them, rowing a dinghy peacefully upstream. He watched the water rippling away from the dripping oars, marvelling at how effortlessly the boat moved.

'We're going to leave all the gear here and go over to Bushey Park for a while. There's more shade and the twins can paddle in the shallow stream.' Andy's voice carried easily across the water and it was Freddie, his eight-year-old son, who shouted, 'Did Mum bring loads to drink, cos we're all gasping?' It was his mother, Hilda, who answered him.

'Yes, we have bottles of water, orange squash and lemonade as well as tea and coffee for the adults.' Still smiling, she turned to her husband Andy and said, 'I'm right pleased to see that your father has made sure our boys are wearing life-jackets.'

'No fear on that score,' he said, frowning. 'The club officials wouldn't let anyone go afloat from this slipway without one.'

Jeffrey was leaning on the wall regarding the two boys, who had grown up calling him Uncle Jeff, and as he waved his hand to them a sad smile was on his lips. It moved Hilda to ask, 'Why so sad on such a lovely day, Jeff?'

Sighing, he told her, 'I was just thinking how Sheila would have loved being here today. She will miss all the joy of seeing our boys grow up.'

Hilda did her best to smile but wasn't very successful. If only there was something that could be done to bring Jeffrey and one of his female colleagues together. She had suggested this to Andy but he had said there wasn't any way he could think of, and even if there was, it would just be interfering. Looking now at Andy running along the bank, laughing with their two boys, she told herself to remember to warn Andy not to flaunt his own happiness. It wasn't fair on Jeff.

The transfer to Bushy Park was achieved without any disasters. Andy carried Peter and David was carried by his father. Arthur, Mary, Hilda, Joyce and Paula carried all of their drinks and food over to the park.

It was nice and cool in the park and even more so under the trees.

By the time the twins were settled on a rug, their bottles filled with milk, and every adult had a drink of their choice and were delving into the glorious food, Mr Burrows senior, his two grandsons and their uncle had arrived, and they lost no time in securing a drink and some of the goodies that were on offer.

Looking around at this group of people, Paula was acutely aware of the kindly, pleasant sociability that existed amongst them as a group.

This day had been an eye-opener for her. Another day that she would never forget.

She was learning quickly how the other half lived!

Ten

Mary and Arthur had been deep in conversation with Jeffrey for the past twenty minutes when his mother said, 'Well, if that's all right by you, Jeffrey, I shall go straight upstairs and tell Paula what we have all decided.'

'Thanks,' Jeffrey said, though he still sounded doubtful. 'You will have to speak firmly, Mother; she won't easily agree.'

'She will when I point out that it is for her own good.' Having said that Mary strode out of the room with a definite purpose in mind.

Mary stood unseen in the doorway of the nursery, and what she was looking at made her more determined than ever to get Paula to agree to their decision. Paula O'Brien, she felt, must have been sent to them by God Himself. When these two babies had been six months old, Mary had left her son and gone back to North Devon to be with her new husband, but it had been a reluctant decision because she had feared that her son would not be able to cope. The loss of his wife had been so devastating he had almost lost the will to live. However, Sheila had left him two beautiful healthy baby boys. What man would have known how to cope with such a situation? Especially with the upbringing that Jeffrey had been given, as an only child whom both parents had loved wholeheartedly and with grandparents who doted on him. He had never wanted for anything. Had never really learnt how to look after himself, never mind care for two newborn babies. God knows he had tried! He had suffered humiliation from two dragons who had declared they were professional nannies and it was she, herself, who had suggested that he advertise for a young but sensible girl.

And along had come Paula.

She had watched every move the girl had made and could find no fault. In her opinion Paula did not just do her duty where Peter and David were concerned, she actually loved them. It was apparent in her every look and every action.

'Hello, Mrs Blackmore,' Paula cheerily called as she spotted her standing there. 'Peter is all clean and fed if you want to pick him up. He's over there in his playpen. I won't be long tidying David up. He thought his Farley's Rusks would look better on top of his head this morning than in his mouth.'

They both laughed and Mary said, 'It is you, Paula, I want to speak to. I'll go and sit with Peter until you're finished with his nibs and then we'll have a good chinwag.'

Twenty minutes later a dapper-looking David was in the playpen contentedly trying to pile up a set of wooden bricks only to have his brother throw them around.

Paula, having made two cups of coffee, handed one to Mrs Blackmore and then sat herself down beside her. She was a trifle anxious as to what had brought Jeffrey's mother to the nursery in order to talk to her, but on the other hand she told herself it couldn't be that she was doing something wrong because yesterday, when they were all at Hampton Court, she had been loud in her praise.

'Paula my dear, my son is more than pleased with the way you have settled into his household and he is sure you don't have any idea of what a burden you have lifted from his shoulders. However, he is a little worried that you have not taken any free time for yourself – not one day since you first came here.'

Mary paused and Paula felt she was waiting for an explanation.

'Thank you for your kind words, Mrs Blackmore. It is just that I haven't felt the need. To me this job has opened up a whole new way of life. I had no experience of being a nursemaid and your son took a chance on me. As I saw it I had to get myself and the twins into a daily routine and in the early days I didn't want to cause any disruption.'

Mary took a sip of her coffee, replaced her cup on a side table, then leaned across and patted Paula's hand. 'That is very admirable, and I am sure you are aware just how much my son has appreciated all of your efforts, but the time has come for you to be able to relax a little.'

Paula's head jerked up and her eyes showed the apprehension she was feeling.

'We want you to take a long weekend, go somewhere nice, enjoy yourself.' Seeing that Paula was looking flustered, Mary hurried on. 'Arthur and I are going to stay on here for another ten days at least. With Mrs Pledger to guide us I am sure that between us we shall be able to keep strictly to your daily routine with the twins. So, my dear, it is now just a question of whether or not you trust my husband and me with Peter and David.' She stopped briefly but was smiling as she added, 'Remember they are my grandsons and I give you my word we shall take good care of them. So what is your answer to be?'

'Well, it is very nice of you to think of me but what would I do with myself? A long weekend would seem endless! Even if I booked into a hotel I would still be on my own. A half-day now and again would be nice if that is all right with Mr Lawson.'

'From now on you will regularly have a half-day each week, but please take this opportunity while my husband and I are still here and have a good break. I have been given to understand that you did not have an entirely happy home life and that your parents do not keep in touch with you, but what about your friend that you receive regular letters from? Wouldn't she be pleased to see you?'

Paula's eyes shone at the thought! To spend a whole weekend with Laura and her family was something that she hadn't dare dream of, but now the suggestion had been made, she was thrilled.

'Oh, Mrs Blackmore, if only it were possible! Of course I know the boys would come to no harm, but I am not sure if Laura would have room for me. She has a husband and two little boys and they all live in her mother's house.'

'My dear, there is only one way to find out: you have to ask them. Are they on the telephone?'

Paula half smiled to herself. In her mind's eye she could just see Molly's face if anyone suggested that they have a telephone put into the house! 'No, unfortunately they don't have a telephone, but I could send a postcard asking if it would be convenient for me to stay a couple of nights. When exactly would I be going?'

'How about this coming Friday, returning on Monday? Then Arthur can make arrangements for us to travel on the Tuesday. He will be glad to get back to Devon as he always thinks no one can run his business like he can. Not that he doesn't enjoy coming here,' Mary hastened to add.

The postcard was in the post by midday and by return the next day a postcard arrived for Paula. It was Mr Lawson who picked the mail up from the mat and he was chuckling as he gave the card to Paula. 'Sorry, Paula, couldn't help but read it!'

For a moment she almost felt irritated that he should have read her card but a quick glance and she was laughing with him. Printed in huge capital letters were a few words: COURSE YOU CAN. CAN'T WAIT. LOVE MOLLY.

Thursday came and Paula was going over the written instructions that she was leaving for Mrs Blackmore. She was like a young child excited to be going to see her friend – and indeed the whole family. To Paula it would be like going home. She had been ironing for hours, making sure that the twins' clothes were left in good order. She put her own newly pressed skirt on a hanger and followed it with one of the blouses that her mother had bought for her. How glad she had been for these; since leaving home she had not once been to the shops to buy anything, indeed she would have a nice tidy sum of money to put in the bank when she was ready. She hadn't spent any of her wages because every single item was provided for her here at Ridgeway. Now striding over to Peter and David, who were playing on the floor with a toy bus and a wooden cart that Arthur had bought for them, she hung her skirt and blouse on the clothes dryer to air. She smiled at the twins, who were coming up to their first birthdays and were simply gorgeous. Undemanding, easy-going, there were still times when she was frightened she might wake up and find that her new life in this beautiful house with such a lovely garden was all a dream.

Recently she had experienced an awful nightmare which had served to remind her that the past could not be wiped out. The horror of that whole year, when she had not set eyes on her mother or her father and had been shut away and made to feel that she was wicked and had much to atone for – even though she had only been thirteen years old. There wasn't a day when she didn't beg that all this security and happiness wouldn't be snatched away.

She also asked the good Lord to let it continue, because in the back of her mind there was always that unhappy house where she had been brought up. Memories of the weird things her father would do to her still loomed up to haunt her from time to time. How often she'd pleaded with her mother to stop him from taking her upstairs to her small bedroom and locking the door. Without fail her mother would turn away, and then shun her for the rest of the day. There had been one time when she had dodged in front of her mother, blocked her way, and demanded to know why her father was allowed to carry on in this way.

'He is your father,' was her mother's reply. 'He has every right; he doesn't hurt you, does he?'

'Did your father treat you in the same way then?' Paula had found the courage to retort. Even that tactic hadn't worked. Her mother had steered clear of her for days after that.

She had been so intimidated by her parents, her father in particular, and there still were many times when she asked herself how on earth she had ever found the courage to answer that job advertisement in their local paper.

Sheer desperation was the only answer she had come up with.

There was the odd time her relationship with her mother had been on an even keel – never close, certainly not intimate, yet always there quietly in the background. Was her mother ever happy? Not really. More resigned to the way her life had turned out and accepting of the fact that there was nothing she could do to change it. How she wished her parents had had other children! Her biggest regret was that she had turned out to be such a bad person, a daughter of whom both her father and her mother were ashamed. Oh, they would never admit as much; they did their duty by her down to the last letter, but that smouldering feeling of resentment was never far from the surface. If the truth was ever to come to light that would be a different matter. She had always been under the impression that both her parents had been reluctant to have her home – after all it must have been a joint decision to put her away for a whole year. To have her father treat her as if he owned her was bad enough, but a mother at loggerheads with her daughter, unable or unwilling to speak the truth, that was an age-old conflict, Paula thought, smothering a sigh. For a moment she covered her face with her hands, wanting to weep but knowing the time to shed tears was long past.

Paula had been all set to order a taxi, but Arthur Blackmore wouldn't take no for an answer.

'Now, listen here, my dear, I'd not be much of a man if I let you go on your own. No, I will take you to your friend's address and I shall be there on Monday to pick you up and bring you back home,' he had insisted and Paula loved the fact that he had said he would be bringing her back *home*.

By eleven o'clock on Friday morning Paula was sitting on the sofa in the front room of Molly Owen's house. There were just the three of them: Paula, Laura and Molly. Ronnie and Jack were at school and Fred Wilson was at work.

'We'll 'ave a cup of tea t'be going on with and then when you've got settled in we'll 'ave nice bit of lunch and you can bring us up to date with all your news.'

Laura couldn't take her eyes off Paula. Breaking away from living that sad miserable life she'd been forced to live in Milner Road had certainly been for the best. 'Paula, you look an entirely different person,' she finally said, meaning every word. Again she looked at her friend, taking her in from the top of her stunning mane of red hair to her face that had filled out, her rouged lips, the suit Laura had seen before but the blouse was new and Paula's figure, though still very slim, had filled out in all the right places. Only her flat-heeled shoes spoiled the picture but then her father had never allowed her to wear high heels.

Laura made a decision: she was going to let her friend settle in and breathe a little before she told her that her father had been round demanding to know where his daughter was living. Mr O'Brien had always been unpredictable, Laura knew, and he hadn't changed, not one scrap. He had always made it difficult for the two of them to be friends, and if he'd had his way he would have stopped them seeing each other years ago.

Laura had tried to be a good friend because she had come to love Paula, but she had never tried to pry, even after Paula had returned home from a long convalescence all those years ago, but there had been times when she had wished that Paula would break down and let all of her fears and worries come tumbling out. Was it ever going to happen? She had promised that if she lasted in this job for three months then she was going to tell her the real reason she had been spirited away for such a long time. Well, Paula had kept her job for a whole lot longer than three months, and judging by her letters and the fact that she was now here for a long weekend, she must have made a great success of her new life.

Molly's neighbours in Blackshaw Road couldn't help but hear

the laughter in her house as the six of them later sat around the kitchen table for their evening meal. Molly had made two huge steak and kidney pies with a massive rice pudding to follow. Jack and Ronnie wanted to hear every detail about the twins.

'And do yer 'ave to do everything for them, just like as if you were their mum?' young Ronnie demanded, while Jack was more interested in the size of the house that their Auntie Paula lived in now. 'Mum said you don't bath in front of the fire like we do cos you got a real bathroom and the bath is stuck to the floor and it 'as its own taps, an' she said the governor of yer house has a motor car. Is all that true?'

'Yes, Ronnie, I do take care of Peter and David most of the time because their own mummy sadly died, but they are too young to know that and they seem to like me well enough. While I am staying here with you their grandmother is helping to look after them.' Young Ronnie seemed to be satisfied with her answer until he suddenly burst out, 'I wouldn't mind you looking after me and Jack some of the time, Auntie Paula, but I'm ever so glad our mum didn't die.'

Paula did her best to hide a smile before she turned to answer Jack. 'Everything your mum has told you about the big house is really true. Some day soon I will try to draw pictures of the house and gardens and send them to you.'

'Oh, that would be great. I'll take them to school and show them to everybody – but yer still 'aven't said nuffin about the car, 'ave yer?'

'Well, it is true my boss does own a motor car but I don't know much about them. He doesn't use it on weekdays because he works in London and he travels up from Raynes Park by train. I'll tell you what, Jack, I shall also do my best to send you a picture of Mr Lawson's car, will that do?'

'Cor, yes please, Auntie; that will be smashing.'

The adults had nearly as many questions for Paula but they decided to wait until the boys had gone to bed. Fred explained that as it was Friday night he had no option but to take himself off to the Railway Arms. He explained that he ran a money club which members paid into each week and the savings were to be shared out in the first week of December so that the women would have money to do their Christmas shopping.

'Oh, and don't forget to tell Paula that you also play darts and down a few pints of ale while you are collecting in the cash,' Laura bawled out, but she did have a wide grin on her face.

'My gal, I'm not sure that I should leave you the present I got. But as I bought it mainly to let Paula know how pleased we are to see her again after such a long absence I suppose I better had.' Having stated his case, Fred disappeared out into the passageway and came back bearing a brown paper carrier bag from which he took a half bottle of Bell's Old Scotch Whisky and a bottle of Stone's ginger wine. Placing both bottles in the centre of the table, he said, 'Enjoy yerselves. I'll see yer all later.'

'I say, what about us, don't we get anything?' Jack yelled, outraged.

'Yeah, 'ave we got to go to bed right now so they can 'ave a drink?' Ronnie was equally put out by the unfairness of life.

'Wait for it,' their father said, producing two packets of Smith's crisps and two bottles of cream of soda.

'Thanks, Dad,' the two lads said in agreement.

By eight o'clock the two boys were tucked up in bed. When Laura came downstairs, Paula went up to say goodnight and to give each lad a storybook with lots of coloured pictures in them. She had asked Esmé to fetch them for her from W.H. Smith's in Wimbledon. Esmé had young boys of her own so she was more able to judge the type of book the boys would enjoy.

'Thank you, Auntie Paula, this book has got pictures at the back that can be coloured in,' Ronnie told her seriously as he placed his arms around her neck, kissing her goodnight.

'Yes, I know, Ronnie, and I have bought you a whole pack of colouring pencils which I will give you in the morning if you are a good boy and go to sleep quite soon.'

Ronnie thought about if for a moment. 'Can't I 'ave them now? I could sit up in bed and do one of the pictures.'

'You, young Ronnie, heard what I said. Book now; crayon pencils in the morning.'

'All right.' Ronnie sighed heavily, which made Paula smile.

Apparently Jack was quite pleased with his book and was snuggled down beneath the bedclothes with the book propped up against the pillow. Paula bent over to kiss his forehead and to say goodnight.

'Goodnight, Auntie Paula, this is a smashing story.' A contented Jack suddenly remembered his manners. 'Oh, thanks for buying us each a book.'

'You are more than welcome, boys. I shall see you tomorrow,' she whispered as she made for the door, but Ronnie hadn't finished with her. 'And the next day and the one after that cos Mummy said your boss had let you stay with us all those days.'

Paula was really laughing as she walked back down the stairs. Molly had made three generous glasses of whisky and ginger wine and when the three of them were seated comfortably she nodded at her daughter before saying, 'Suppose you'd better get it off your chest. She'll 'ave t'know sooner or later and best while little piggies with big ears are not around.'

Oh dear! Paula's heart sank down into her boots. From Molly's tone of voice she knew that what Laura was about to tell her was not good news.

Laura was steadily gazing at Paula. She looked so happy. Or she had until Molly had spoken up. Immediately the look on Paula's face had altered, she had clenched her hands until the knuckles showed white and her whole body had started to tremble.

'Hang on, Paula, luv. Don't go jumping to daft conclusions that something terrible 'as 'appened to yer mum, cos it hasn't. It's just that yer father came round here shouting his mouth off, demanding that we tell him where you were living.'

'Twice,' Molly muttered to herself.

Paula had to take a deep breath before she was able to say to Molly, 'Did you say that he has been here more than once?'

'Yes, love, but the second time there was only me in the house and I reckon that I gave your father as good as he tried to give me.'

'Oh, I am so sorry! He didn't attempt to strike you, did he?'

Molly and her daughter could not believe the change that had come over Paula in just a few minutes and with the mere mention of Mike O'Brien. There was no mistaking the fear in her eyes and her cheeks were drained of colour.

'Take a sip of yer drink, Paula, and try yer best t'calm down,' Molly advised. 'It appears he got hold of one of the letters that you've been writing to yer mum but you 'adn't put an address on the letter and that was like a red rag to a bull. So what does he do? He comes charging round here in a raging temper, knowing full well that you would also 'ave been writing to our Laura. I wouldn't mind but he was swearing and cussing and telling me what he would like t'do to me and me family. I was grateful that the boys were at school and Fred was at work else there might 'ave been hell to pay.'

Molly could see tears were stinging at the back of Paula's eyes, but she was doing her best not to cry. It broke her heart to see this lovely young girl so upset. 'I never should 'ave told you. I'm an idiot at the best of times. I am sorry, love.'

'No, no,' Paula protested. 'I'm glad you have told me but I just can't forget it. But, on the other hand, what can I do about him?'

'Let me ask you some questions,' Laura said earnestly, trying her best to sound confident.

Paula nodded her head and wiped her handkerchief across her eyes.

'How have you been since you left 'ome? Do you still fear yer dad? You 'ave often in the past told us that there was so many questions that you had never been able to get anyone to give you the answers to. Has all that nagging worry gone away?'

Paula didn't answer but concentrated on her Whisky Mac. Having taken several sips she finally said, 'Molly, do you mind if I go upstairs and put my night clothes on? When I come back down again I have just one piece of paper that I would like to show to both of you. I think now is the time for me to tell you what really happened to me when I was thirteen years old.'

Mother and daughter looked at each other in disbelief when Paula had left the room. 'That girl is so strong-minded and far too proud to ask for help, more's the pity!' Molly exclaimed.

'You certainly know what makes Paula tick, and you love her as if she were yer own, don't you, Mum?'

Molly smiled. 'Yes, I do, and I know they broke the mould when they made her. Got a heart of gold, 'as that girl.'

Eleven

Paula had had half an hour to think about what she was going to do and she remained determined to talk about the period of her life that still gave her nightmares — that was until she came downstairs. Dressed now in her cosy dressing gown it didn't seem right to burden her good friends with all the sordid details that still rattled around in her head.

Sinking down low in the armchair she knew she had the full attention of both Laura and Molly. If she did manage to drag it all out into the open, how in God's name could she expect them to believe her? What had happened to her all those years ago was so awful, so incredible, it had taken a long time to fathom it out for herself and to this day she was no nearer to getting the whole truth. Her parents had deceived her, blamed her, punished her in a way so cruel and evil she hadn't been able to let the horrible memories come back into her mind. She hadn't known what to do at the time, had not had a soul to turn to, and now it was all too late.

'I'm sorry, Molly, I just don't know where to begin . . . it's far too late,' she said, sounding thoroughly bitter.

Laura only wanted to help. In no way was she just pretending to care or being inquisitive, so she took the bull by the horns and jumped in. 'Paula, when you were shut away for all those months on end . . . did you give birth? Did you 'ave a baby?'

After a long hesitation, with eyes cast down, Paula muttered, 'Yes, but how did you know?'

Laura leaned over and laid a hand on her shoulder but it was Molly who answered the question. 'The way your mum an' dad acted, most folk around 'ere guessed. But, Paula love, I never did get t'hear the true reason why you were spirited away. The good Lord knows I tried 'ard enough. When Laura became so upset because we didn't know where you were or what had happened to you, I went with her, round t'your house, and pleaded for you to be allowed to come back with us and 'ave a bit of tea. Even though I wasn't allowed to put a foot over the doorstep I knew you weren't in that house, and I came away with the awful feeling that your mum was terrified to open her mouth. I honestly thought she was scared out of her wits. She kept looking backwards, over her shoulder, and she spoke in little more than a whisper. Local gossip was, and always has been, that you'd got yourself pregnant and that yer dad had sent yer somewhere t'ave an abortion. That never washed with me. Say what yer like about the O'Briens but they are Catholics to the core, and abortion would never 'ave been on the cards. Never in a million years! When, over a year later, you came home again, and from the few bits you did tell me or told Laura, we did come to the conclusion that you must 'ave given birth to a baby. But why in heaven's name was you kept locked away for such a long time? '

Paula looked horrified. 'That's the thing though, Molly. To this day I don't know how I ended up there or why my father chose to send me away for so long. Please, both of you, believe me I never knew a thing about it!'

'Oh, come off it,' Laura said, a touch scornfully. 'Even you couldn't have been that naive. How the 'ell do you think it got inside of you? You must 'ave known what was 'appening at the time *and* who the man was!'

Paula was taken aback by Laura's sudden criticism.

'That's just it. I swear to you, Laura, even to this day I have no idea who it was or how he did it.'

Staring at Paula's face, which by now was stark white, and seeing the hurt in those big green eyes, Laura wanted so much to believe her, although her story sounded so unlikely.

Paula had expected Laura's disbelief but it still rankled. All she longed for was to forget all the misery that birthday party had brought into her life – yet how could she wipe it completely from her mind when she still couldn't remember exactly what had happened?

'Laura, I never expected you to believe me. In all these years nobody has, so why should you be the exception?' she said quietly. Leaning back in her chair she closed her eyes, and after a while she said, 'You don't think . . . I mean, could I . . .? Would I be able to blot something out of my mind so completely that I have no recollection of it at all?'

'I suppose people 'ave been known to,' Laura answered, but without much conviction.

Paula nodded. 'I assume it happens when it's something too terrible for the conscious mind to deal with.'

It wasn't a question so neither Laura nor her mother bothered to reply.

'Do you want me to carry on?'

It was Molly who answered. 'Yes, love, as long as you don't get too upset you keep going and I promise you that if not tonight then one day in the future we will get to the truth, cos I'm gonna make it me life's work from now on – an' pet, that is no idle promise. No matter what, I've got a bit of savings and I'll spend every last penny of it digging away until we do find out the name of the bastard who was responsible for this, cos t'me it is an open an' shut case of bloody rape and should 'ave been reported to the police at the time.'

Paula was terrified by Molly's outburst but at the same time she felt such love for this homely woman who obviously cared so much for her. It served to ease some of her pain and embarrassment.

'I can tell you what happened when I woke up on the morning following my birthday party. I was hurting all over, my whole body was battered and bruised, and my head ached so badly I thought I had been hit over the head with a brick. There were deep scratches at the top of my legs and between my thighs the flesh was red raw and there was blood all over the bed sheets. At first my mother hadn't been angry, more like desperately sad. At the time the only thing that seemed to matter to her was that she had to get me bathed and the bloodstained bedclothes removed. All she did say was, "What's done is done, get yourself out of that bed and help me to clean this room up." There was no sign of my father; he wasn't in the house.

'When we had the room all clean and tidy my mother dragged the tin bath in from the garden and when she had it half filled with warm water she helped me to wash my whole body – she even washed and rinsed my hair. As I got out of the bath she wrapped me in a large towel and told me to pray.

'From that day I don't think I have ever really been free from horrifying nightmares.'

'So what happened after that?' Molly asked.

After Laura's initial disbelief it seemed that her conscience was pricking her and she'd decided to leave the questioning to her mother.

'I wasn't allowed to go to school because I was so badly bruised. Even my face was a mess and I remember one eye had practically closed it was so swollen.'

'For Pete's sake!' Molly clenched her fists. 'Why in heaven's name didn't yer mother call the police – or at least tell someone? You, pet, must 'ave put up one 'ell of a fight, unless the bastard had drugged yer and then got his fun by using you as a bloody punch bag.'

'At home, Mother and I were getting back to normal, until about four weeks later when I started to be sick every morning and that's when my mother went berserk. I would be leaning over the kitchen sink vomiting my heart up while she seethed with anger. She screamed horrible things at me like, "You're a wicked girl, you knew exactly what you were doing and it will serve you right if they lock you up and never let you come home again." I just couldn't believe my mother could change so completely. Sometimes her eyes were terrible, flashing with fury. She would get so angry all the time. I truly did not know what had happened to me or even that I had done anything wrong. There was one day when my mother and father had a terrific row. It was the first time I'd ever heard my father actually being violent towards my mum and that was the day they both turned on me. It was as if they had come to an agreement and in one fell swoop all the blame was on me. I was a tart, I flaunted myself. I was asking for it.'

Paula got out of her chair and stood up straight.

'Molly, I am telling you the truth. In all these years this is the first time this matter has been discussed. I hadn't, and I still do not, have any recollection of how I became pregnant!' She took a few deep breaths before adding, 'If you paid me a king's ransom I would not be able to name the father of my child.' Sitting down again she was smarting at her own stupidity and felt at an utter loss as to how to deal with it.

Laura stared at Paula's pale face. The fear and sadness were still showing in her eyes and she felt she had never loved her dear friend more than she did at this moment. Now she did believe her every word, though she could scarcely begin to imagine what an ordeal the past years must have been for her. But what could she do for her friend? For the moment she would just gather her up in her arms and hold her tight. If only taking her into her arms would wipe away all those hateful, hurtful memories! She was well aware that it would not make the slightest difference. There and then, like her mother, Laura vowed to do everything within her power to get to the truth of what exactly had happened to Paula when she was still a thirteen-year-old child.

'Your parents, they must have given you some explanation,' Laura gently probed.

'No, they never did. They talked in whispers and whenever I came into the room they clammed up.'

'Paula, I'm going to ask you some questions, if that's all right with you, but please, I don't want you to be upset.' Molly's voice sounded so gentle and Paula tried her hardest to smile as she nodded her head.

'You don't remember one man in particular that was at your party, a man who made a fuss of you, or even an older boy? Who took you upstairs to your bedroom and encouraged you to take all your clothes off and a little while later perhaps he got into bed with you?'

'No, Molly. I am truly sorry, but I have no recollection of anything like that ever taking place.'

'Okay, love. Let's try another tack. A few friends were there, some adults, and you had a birthday tea, right so far?'

'Yes, I remember all that and my mother brought in an iced cake with thirteen candles on it, everybody sang "Happy Birthday" to me and I blew the candles out.'

'And what happened after that?'

'We played pass the parcel and postman's knock.'

'Did you get kissed by the postman?'

'Yes. Every girl did, one at a time.'

'And when it was your turn, who was out in the hall pretending to be the postman?'

'I got picked twice and one time it was my dad and the second time it was Jimmy Webster. He lived right opposite to us.'

'And did they both kiss you?'

'Of course they did, it was a part of the game.'

'Do you remember how old Jimmy was?'

'Not really, but he couldn't have been more than eleven or twelve, though he was a lot taller than me. I remember he was very shy, didn't want to kiss me, said it was a silly game.'

'And when all the games were over, what happened next?'

'We were all hot and bothered and my mum and her friend made a drink for everybody.'

'What was there to drink?' Molly was being very patient, saying every sentence slowly and giving Paula plenty of time to think.

'All sorts – lemonade, orange squash, blackcurrant cordial.'

'And Paula, do you remember what you had to drink?'

Paula frowned, making deep lines in her forehead. 'My dad said he'd made a special drink for me.'

'And did he bring it over to you?'

'No, I remember he called me to come and sit on his lap because there weren't enough chairs and he gave me a glass and told me it was a special ginger drink. I didn't like it; it burned my throat.' Paula was lost in thought and her voice was wavering. It was as if she was reliving every moment of that afternoon.

'And then?' Molly gently prompted.

'My mother gave every child a small gift and they all went home.'

'But there were still a few adults there besides your parents?'

'Yes, there were, but they were all my father's relations. I never remember any of my mother's relations coming to the house.'

'I'll make us a sandwich,' Laura said as she patted Paula's shoulder, 'and Mum will mix us another drink.'

Paula's mind was in turmoil. It was as if they were delving into her mind, especially Molly. Oh, she knew full well it wasn't done for any wrong reasons. There was no malice in their thoughts or actions, they truly loved her, felt for her and would turn the whole thing on its head if they thought they could get some way towards finding the truth. She loved them both dearly, they were like family to her, and yet there *were* things that she remembered but could *never*, not in a million years, reveal even to them. They were not memories related to that fateful day but if she thought about it enough she could not truthfully swear that the two incidents could not be banded together. In both cases it was her father who figured so largely. Dimly aware that her own imagination was tormenting her even more cruelly than the truth might, she made herself sit up straight and take several deep breaths. She needed to regain some control. Molly and Laura had not said as much, but she sensed they believed it was her father who had raped her and made her pregnant. And hadn't that very same thought entered her own mind from the start? God knows she didn't want to believe it, but were she to reveal the way her father had acted towards her for as long as she could remember, that would put the cat among the pigeons. She knew if she carried on like this she was going to end up saying something she'd bitterly regret. In spite of her attempts to blot that period from her mind by focusing on her new job, however happy and safe she felt and however adorable the twins were, there were still times when it brought her no comfort. As she grew older the very thought of what her father used to do to her became more and more humiliating.

As a child, not a day had passed when her father didn't let her know that she was a burden that he would be glad to be rid of. But had that been really true?

He had always enjoyed torturing her mentally as well as physically; time and time again he subjected her to horrible torment, causing her no actual pain but total embarrassment. The things he did to her were for his own gratification. He would always lock her bedroom door, then order her to strip naked and for a while just sit and stare at her. After a while he would say it was exercise time and he would have her lay on the bed, moving her into numerous positions, arms above her head, both legs together held high in the air, kneeling on all fours like a dog, then flat on her back or face down on the bed, usually with her legs spread wide apart.

He would come close to her, sniffing her, saying he had to get rid of the evil that was in her blood. But he never actually touched her. When he said the time was up, he insisted that before he allowed her to put her clothes back on she must hug him, which she always did, although he must have sensed that she cringed as she put her arms around his bulky shoulders.

Molly came back into the front room carrying a tray which held three tall glasses. 'I've made hot toddies this time,' she said, grinning.

Laura was carrying a tray with a plate of sandwiches and a dish of hot sausage rolls. 'Yeah.' She grinned. 'Mum shoved the poker into the fire until it was red hot and then stuck it into the jug of whisky and ginger wine; she said it should warm the cockles of our hearts, whatever that means.'

It had occurred to Paula that what they were drinking was similar to what her father had given her to drink on her thirteenth birthday, and yet this drink was not burning her throat. It was warming and pleasant but then she supposed she had been a child then and now she was an adult.

It was while they were enjoying their late-night snack that Fred came home.

'Blimey, it's all right for some,' he said, smiling at the three of them, 'and you've got the cheek to begrudge me a pint or two an' a game of darts after a week of back-breaking hard work.'

The women looked from one to the other and burst out laughing. Fred was a postman!

Paula was more than grateful that the evening had ended on a much lighter note. Tomorrow was another day and Laura and her mother had promised to take her to either Tooting market or the much bigger market which was held at Brixton.

She was looking forward to spending some of her wages, which she had saved. It would be nice to be able to buy Molly and Laura a small present, something they would like, since they were being so good to her and she was pleased that for once she was in the position to repay them.

Later, when Paula was tucked up snugly in a narrow bed, Molly came in to see if she was all right. 'Paula, love, you said you had a paper you wanted us to see, did you forget?'

'Oh, yes, well I did bring it downstairs to show you, but I must have forgotten. It will still be in the pocket of my dressing gown.'

'All right, pet, you can show it to us tomorrow. You sleep well now. Goodnight, God bless,' she said as she tenderly planted a kiss on Paula's forehead.

Twelve

The following morning, having slept right through the night, Paula was feeling relieved that at least she had opened up her heart to Molly and to Laura.

'Honestly, I'm fine,' she told Laura when she came in bringing her a most welcome cup of tea.

'I think you had Mum worried last night,' Laura informed her. 'In fact she wasn't the only one. I too thought we had pushed you too far and I felt so guilty because to start I made it so obvious that I didn't believe you.'

'No need to apologize, Laura. I've told you over and over again, I have yet to meet the person who believes me when I say that I have no idea who it was that raped me. Now, I'm really touched that you both care so much, but for today may we please give it a rest and go out and enjoy ourselves?'

'We most certainly can. Fred's gone to work and the boys are eating their breakfast, then they're off to the Saturday-morning pictures down at Tooting Broadway.'

Feeling a joyous happy day stretching ahead, Paula asked, 'So what have you got lined up for us?'

'I'm not quite sure yet. Mum has to do the shopping for the weekend so would you mind if she tags along with us?'

Paula looked despondently at Laura. 'How can you even ask such a question? I wouldn't dream of leaving Molly out of our plans.'

Nineteen-year-old Alice Jackson lived with her family just three doors up from Molly's house. She had a good job as an usherette at the Mayfair Cinema in upper Tooting, a fact for which her parents were more than grateful. In their household the only other person who was working was her father and he was a tram driver, a good job and a steady wage but his pay packet did not go far. Helen, his wife, was good at making a shilling do the work of a half-crown. She made all her own bread, pies, pastry and great pots of stew, which was just as well because in all she had seven children to keep and feed as well as her great beefy-looking husband. There had only been eighteen months between the fifth child, who was a boy, and the twin girls who were now six years old.

Alice was behind the counter in the lobby of the cinema, serving the kiddies who were rushing to spend their Saturday penny. There was a sudden lull and Alice took the opportunity to come out from behind the counter and was tidying the packets of sweets and penny bars of Nestlé's chocolate when Molly, Laura and Paula came through the swing doors pushing Jack and young Ronnie before them.

'Hello, Mrs Owen. Hello Laura. You come to bring your tribe to see the pictures?' She grinned at her own joke, but was obviously really pleased to see her neighbours though she did glance questioningly at Paula.

'Don't tell me you don't recognize our Paula. It ain't that long since she's been around,' Molly sharply reminded Alice.

'No, it's not that, it's just she . . . well, she looks so different.' Quickly recovering, she said, 'It's nice to see yer, Paula. Yer look great! Yer really do an' I'm not just sayin' it. Yer 'air looks smashing.'

Laura looked at Paula and they both burst out laughing. It was Paula who recovered first and, remembering her manners quickly said, 'Thank you, Alice. You look pretty good yourself; the uniform suits you, shows off your lovely slim figure.' Meanwhile Laura was gazing at Paula's hair and she shook her own head in sheer disbelief. It was hard for her to imagine that Paula's beautiful rippling mass of hair had once been shorn so close to her scalp. But that was only one of the horrible things that must have happened to her while she had been away for all that time.

Poor Paula. If there was only some way in which they could make up for all the sufferings she'd had to endure. *We must always let her know how very much we do love her*, Laura vowed to herself. There was one thing in Paula's favour: her looks didn't pity her. Now at nearly twenty years old she still showed traces of the pretty girl she had always been, but the prettiness had been outgrown and her whole outlook had changed, transforming her into an elegant young lady. It was only sometimes when you caught her off-guard that one became aware of the suffering she'd had to bear and it was always her big green eyes that told of her sad, distressing memories.

'Come on then, Jack, and you, Ronnie, I've put the sweets yer Auntie Paula 'as bought you into a paper bag, 'ere you are, one each, in yer go cos the pictures will be starting soon.'

'We mustn't kiss them goodbye, not in public, Jack keeps warning me cos they're grown up now,' Molly told Paula, not attempting to smother her giggles.

'So you're off up to Brixton, Mum tells me,' Alice said as she let the long thick curtain drop back down after the boys had gone through into the cinema. 'I'm finished for the day when this morning session is over so I've 'ad me orders: I'm to collect our two girls and our Alan and your two boys and take them 'ome to me mum and she said t'tell you not to 'urry back cos she'll give your Jack and Ronnie their dinner when we 'ave ours.'

'She's one in a million is your mum. I'll bring her back a couple of bits from the market,' Molly thankfully told Alice, thinking that if Paula wasn't here it would be herself, the grandma, that would have had the job of looking after them. Not that she would normally mind, but it was going to be a nice change for her to have her lunch out today.

Laura also thanked Alice. 'You'll 'ave yer hands full, taking five of them 'ome when you finish 'ere, but I'll make it up t'yer – is there anything you want while we're out?'

'Not unless yer see any pound notes lying around. I wouldn't mind a few of those.'

'I'll keep me eyes peeled, love, but I reckon you've got as much chance as we 'ave of meeting the Queen doing her Saturday shopping while we're in Brixton Market.'

The three women got off the tram outside the Brixton Empire a little while later.

Laura glanced at her friend half anxiously, half enviously, as the tram conductor gave a long low whistle of approval as Paula hitched her skirt up an inch or two to enable her more easily to step down from the tram platform on to the road. Even Paula herself was grinning as she looked up at the conductor and he gave her a saucy wink as he called out, 'Bye Red.' Several of the passengers laughed. It seemed wherever Paula went her hair was always a focal point.

She was always good-tempered about it, even happy. Really she should have the world at her feet. Her life was now entirely different to what it had been when living with her parents. If only she could forget that awful period in her life. If only! But they were useless wishes because if wishes could be made to come true then even beggars would ride fine horses.

Paula was grinning to herself as she saw the uncertain sideways look Molly was giving the clothes that the models in the front windows of Morleys, the big departmental store, were wearing. There was a strong nip in the air so the store was pushing the sale of thick skirts, but they were mostly only knee-length and Molly did not approve; to her it made sense that a thick warm skirt should be a sensible length. The big bulky jumpers and cardigans did get Molly's vote of approval but not the price tags.

'Sheer robbery,' she exclaimed loudly. 'I could knit any one of them for a quarter of that ridiculous price.' And the truth of the matter was that Molly could and often did. Today she was wearing a tweed skirt that Laura knew she had swooped on with glee from a second-hand stall in the market and, over the top of a calico blouse, a long brown double-breasted cardigan with creamy-coloured cable stitching on both cuffs and the rolled collar. She had designed the pattern and had knitted it for herself. Her outfit had already brought several admiring glances and Paula thought Molly looked wonderful.

'Are we going to stand all day on this pavement just staring or are we going to go into the store and have a look around?' Laura, not waiting for a reply, was already on her way to the main entrance.

By twelve thirty it seemed they were all well satisfied. Molly had allowed Paula to buy her a knitting pattern and enough balls of wool to enable her to knit the elaborate twinset of which there was a photograph on the front of the pattern. In the same department Molly had discovered a huge basket full of dark-coloured skeins of wool being offered as 'discontinued colours' at very low cost. She had snatched up enough skeins to make a school jersey for both Jack and Ronnie and therefore she was very pleased.

Having found a chair outside the dressing rooms in the Ladies Outfitting department, Laura had sat her mother down and gone off with Paula to forage amongst the rails of dresses, skirts, blouses and costumes. After much wrangling Paula declared she just loved the emerald-green dress that was sedately trimmed with black braid and had agreed it would be very serviceable to wear of an evening at Ridgeway, but she wouldn't dream of treating herself to it, not unless Laura chose something for herself.

In the end Laura chose a winter weight skirt that had all the gorgeous colours of the autumn leaves woven into the tweedy material, and she gratefully allowed Paula to buy it for her.

Laden down with parcels they moved as one towards the stairs when suddenly Molly stood still and pointed to a sign that had an arrow pointing to the left and the one word: 'Restaurant'.

'I thought we were going to 'ave something to eat somewhere . . . I'm starving. Are we gonna eat in there?' she asked, nodding at the sign. 'Or we could 'ave fish an' chips in the market cafe.'

'You choose, Molly,' Paula said, hugging her warmly with her free arm.

'Hang on a minute,' Laura implored. 'We 'aven't given a thought to the weekend shopping yet. Mum, don't you think we should do all that before we eat?'

'No, I don't,' her mother answered forcefully. 'Me stomach already feels as if me throat's been cut, and besides, the later we leave it to get the meat and vegetables the cheaper it all will be. The barrow boys will be begging us to take the stuff 'ome for next to nothing if we leave it long enough.'

'All right, Mum, you're the boss,' Laura told her, making out she was a long-suffering, patient daughter.

Her mother pulled a face, which told Laura she wasn't a bit taken in by her air of gloom and hardship, but it was Paula she turned to face and she was smirking as she said, 'Don't suppose you get much fish an' chips living in that big posh house, do yer?'

Paula grinned to herself, thinking they often ate fish for their evening meal, always prepared by Joyce Pledger, but it didn't bare any comparison to fish-shop fish an' chips, but she was too well bred to make such a remark, besides it would be a nice welcome change. As a child she had simply loved to have a pennyworth of chips liberally sprinkled with salt and vinegar before being wrapped up in newspaper.

'No, we don't,' Paula answered kindly, 'and I really would love a plate of fish and chips, if that is all right with you, Molly.

Remember, it is my treat. No, no.' She held her hand up to stop Molly's protest. 'You're feeding me and giving me free board and if I am not allowed to pay my way I shall not feel able to come and stay with you again and that would be very sad for me. Very sad indeed.'

'Oh, pet. Don't talk like that. We've all of us told you to treat our house just as if it were yer second 'ome so don't let's 'ave no more argument.'

Laura quickened her pace. 'I take it we're gonna eat at the market cafe so let's get a move on cos if I don't get a cup of tea before long I shall die of bloody thirst.'

'Laura, there is no need to swear, just thank yer lucky stars that me 'ands are full otherwise, as big as you are, I'd be sorely tempted to box yer bloody ears.'

Laura and Paula could not contain their amusement but they each made sure they were out of Molly's reach before they let their laughter burst forth.

With a huge plate full of battered cod and chips in front of each of them and three large mugs of strong tea set down on the table it was Laura who skilfully controlled the conversation while they ate. Mainly she was telling Paula about her and Fred's hopes for their two boys and asking questions of Laura about Mr Lawson's two sons.

When her mother abruptly said, 'Paula, you said you were going to show me that slip of paper, something t'do with the place they locked you away in, wasn't it?'

In spite of the noise that was going on in that very large cafe, Paula felt she could have heard a pin drop. It was Laura who spoke up first.

'Mum, did you 'ave to bring all that up again right now? Didn't we delve into Paula's past deep enough last night?'

Molly was devastated. One look at Paula's face and she knew she had said the wrong thing. 'Paula, Paula, my love, I am so sorry. I just thought it wasn't much, just a slip of paper, and it was you that said you wanted me to see it.'

Paula's big green eyes instantly looked sad. 'It is all right, Molly, really it is; you just caught me unawares. The slip of paper I was going to show you was the only form of identification I was given while I was in that institution. It bore the number four-five-seven-four. Nothing else. Not even whether I was male or female.'

Laura was quiet, sitting next to her, not saying a word, not touching her, just waiting, but for the moment Paula wasn't even aware of her friend. Her expression was too controlled, too hurt and full of bitter, bleak despair.

Uncertainly, Laura still waited, instinct telling her not to speak, not to do anything and then just as suddenly as she had left them it appeared as if Paula came back to life. Blood surged through her veins, bringing colour back to her cheeks, and she seemed to focus on Molly. Reaching across the table she took her hand between both of her own and then she began apologizing.

They started to eat again, as though nothing had happened. Only now Laura was aware that the trauma which had struck her dear friend at such an early age had by no means gone away. The effects were still far-reaching and it was pitiful to watch as she sometimes struggled to remember and deal with what must have been a terrifying sequence of events.

Thirteen

All in all, Paula felt it had been a great weekend, a welcome break, but although she wouldn't admit it to Molly or to Laura she was really looking forward to seeing Peter and David. It had surprised her just how much she had missed the pair of them and she had missed the privacy of having her own large bed-sitting room.

Now she was standing on the doorstep waiting for Arthur Blackmore to fetch her and drive her back to Ridgeway. Arthur had arrived at least half an hour ago but he had been overwhelmed by the enthusiasm shown by Jack and Ronnie when he had allowed them both to climb in and sit in his car while Paula was saying her goodbyes. The crestfallen look on their faces when Paula had said it was time for them to get out of the car had touched Arthur.

'You're not in a great hurry, are you, Paula? Me and the missus are not travelling back to Devon until tomorrow so Mary and Joyce are both there seeing to the twins. What if I run these two little uns to their school before we set off?'

'Yes, yes,' came the cry from both lads.

'Try saying please,' their grandma rebuked them.

Arthur had been almost as excited as the boys as he let them each toot his hooter before they moved off.

'We're never gonna 'ear the last of this.' Laura grinned. 'They'll be made up in the playground and won't be able t'wait and tell their dad tonight that they were driven to school!'

The welcome that awaited Paula back at Ridgeway strengthened her belief that she had done the right thing in taking this job and becoming totally independent from her parents.

Both lads clambered for her attention and she did her best to scoop both of them up into her arms. 'My goodness, what have you been eating?' she cried in mock alarm. 'You are so heavy, it will soon be you that will be able to lift me up and not the other way round,' she said, laughing as they wriggled in her arms and Peter tugged at the strands of her hair.

Joyce came to her rescue, taking one of them from Paula as she said, 'You would not believe how many times a day Mrs Blackmore and myself have had to reassure them that you were only having a short holiday and that you would be coming back.'

'Well, it is nice to know that I was missed.'

'You most certainly were,' Mary Blackmore affirmed as she came in on the tail end of the conversation.

The next morning Joyce and Paula took the twins out to the driveway to say goodbye to their grandparents. Both Mr Blackmore and Mary had stated how pleased they were to be going back to Devon, but nevertheless it was plain that Mary would have liked to be closer to her son and her two grandsons.

Not much work was done in the house after Arthur's car had driven away. The twins wanted every bit of attention from Paula and as the morning went on their demands did not lessen. Turning to Joyce, Paula made a suggestion. 'How about if we get their coats and take them out for the day? We could go to the zoo, let them see the animals. What do you think?'

'I think it is a really good idea but a bit late in the day to start off now,' Joyce replied as she glanced at the clock on the kitchen wall. 'By the time we get there we wouldn't have long before we would have to start back.'

'Yes, you're right. I wasn't thinking. Well, have you got any suggestions?'

'Wimbledon Common isn't far. The twins could feed the ducks and we could take them into the hotel for a light lunch. It would be a nice treat and a bit different.'

'Great. And as it's not far, we won't bother about getting on the bus. No, I'll start getting Peter and David ready and you telephone for a cab to come in half an hour's time.'

'Good thinking, Paula. I know you were only away for the weekend, but it wasn't only the twins that missed, you know – I missed you too.'

The cabby was a cheerful chap and helpful with it. He put the folded perambulator into the boot, and then he held both Peter and David in his arms while Joyce and Paula settled themselves on the back sat of the taxi. For the next couple of minutes there was laughter and merriment as the boys managed to knock the cab-driver's peaked cap from his head and as he bent to retrieve it he pretended that he was going to drop them. The boys yelled, Paula stretched out her arm in a useless gesture to save them and Joyce said afterwards that her heart had beat against her ribs. However, his playful charade had gone down well with the boys and they were clamouring at the cabby to do it again as he handed them safely into Paula and Joyce, who quickly took a firm hold on each boy.

They got out of the cab within easy walking distance of the pond on Wimbledon Common and the hotel could be seen not too far away. Joyce asked the driver if he would pick them up for the return journey from the hotel entrance at three thirty.

'My pleasure, ma'am,' he said as Joyce gave him a half-crown tip. 'See you later, lads,' he called, and the boys stopped delving into the paper bag which Paula was holding. They were eager to go and feed the ducks on the pond.

'Hang on, I'm here,' Joyce called, striding across the grass. 'Which one are you hanging on to?

'I've got hold of Peter, if you can manage David,' Paula told her, thanking her lucky stars that she had Joyce with her to help with the twins.

Once all the bread had been given to the hungry ducks they had walked twice around the pond and by twelve thirty they were all in the ladies' restroom of the hotel where Paula and Joyce were giving the twins a quick wash and brush up before lunch. Their cheeks were glowing, their dark curly hair shining and with their outdoor coats removed they looked adorable in their short grey trousers and brilliant red jerseys. Heads certainly turned and voices murmured, 'Oh they're absolutely identical,' as the women carried the twins into the dining room.

'Ah, Paula, do come in,' Jeffrey Lawson beamed as Paula appeared at the door of the dining room. 'Did the boys go down all right?'

'Oh, yes. Out like a light as soon as their heads touched the pillows. I think they really enjoyed their day out.'

He sighed as he handed her a glass of sherry. 'It is when you have taken the twins out for a trip that I think even more about their mother. She was younger than me, you know, Paula. Only one year, but so full of life. I never thought our time together would have been cut so short.'

Paula nodded, trying to let him know that she understood. 'It is only natural that you miss her,' she said softly.

He raised his head and smiled at Paula and it was then that he saw the tears in her eyes.

'There, now I have upset you and after you have spent such a happy day,' he apologized, 'but I certainly didn't mean to do so.'

'No you haven't upset me,' Paula assured him, quickly reaching for her handkerchief and blowing her nose.

'You must be tired of hearing me talk so much about Sheila,' he murmured.

'No, I'm not,' Paula replied honestly. 'It surely must help to have such good memories.'

What would he say if he knew about her parents' marriage and how hard she had tried to love both of them? She knew she would never feel free to talk about them and certainly would never reveal what had happened to her as a child. The world that Jeffrey Lawson inhabited was entirely different to the one she had lived in with her parents before she had come to Ridgeway.

She had always found it difficult, impossible almost, to imagine her parents being in love. The ugliness with which they lived would be unbelievable to someone like Mr Lawson, and the guilt and shame over what she had been put through tormented her to this very day.

As she looked at him, Paula recognized how hard it must have been for him to have had to bring home two newborn babies, aware of his deep-rooted fear that if he failed to care for them the authorities might have taken them from him. Also, how painful it must be when every now and again memories of his wife stirred in his mind. Now, having on occasion heard him talk about his own suffering and his real feelings, she could understand him so much better.

'If you and Joyce feel like taking the boys further afield one day I want you both to feel free to take a cab whenever it suits you.' Jeffrey was quietly emphatic as he added, 'Don't let today be just a one-off.'

Bewildered, Paula did not quite know what to say. What Jeffrey had just said must surely mean that he really trusted his staff. It was a good feeling to know that he had so much faith in them.

They were both still standing, so Jeffrey said, 'Shall we sit down?

I think we should, as Joyce will be bringing our meal in any minute now.'

Paula immediately went to the chair she now normally occupied and Jeffrey took his seat at the head of the table.

'So, how did the boys behave today?' Jeffrey asked, and he wasn't just making conversation, she knew he genuinely was interested. His voice held a note of fatherly concern.

'Oh, both boys were fine, they got so many admiring glances as we entered the dining room at the hotel and I hesitate to say it but they knew full well they were being watched and admired and they play on it to the hilt.'

'Oh, for a moment I thought you were going to say like father like son.' He laughed uproariously and Paula felt her checks redden.

'Please, I am only teasing you. It is so good that you take the trouble each evening to tell me of the progress they're making. I don't get to see enough of them.'

Paula shook her head. 'You're the bread-winner. You leave early in the morning to go to the City and the boys are ready for bed when you arrive home, but as they get older all that will change.'

More's the pity, Paula said to herself, because if anything could cause her a problem, she rather thought that might be it. Grown lads would have no need for a nursemaid.

Sufficient unto the day, she chided herself.

Fourteen

December came soon enough, and Paula realized with some shock that it was almost a year since she had first come to Ridgeway, on a snowy day in January. Now her first Christmas was approaching.

This weekend there had been seven adults plus the twins to Sunday lunch: Hilda and Andy Burrows, who were regular visitors, and Aunt Helen and Aunt Julia, both sisters of Sheila, were included. The prospect of meeting relations of Jeffrey's dead wife had filled Paula with apprehension. Much to her relief, however, the meal had passed off well. Everyone seemed to fit in and the atmosphere was cheerful and happy.

'A trial run for Christmas,' Jeffrey had joked as he said goodnight to Paula at eleven thirty.

Mr Lawson was adamant that even when visitors were staying in the house they kept to the informal routine that was part and parcel of their everyday lives. This meant that once all the dishes were set on the table both Paula and Joyce sat down to eat with the visitors. There were times, especially during a normal working week, when Joyce would prefer to eat her evening meal in the kitchen on her own, her excuse being that she liked to see to whatever dessert she was serving. Paula always had her evening meal in the dining room with Jeffrey.

In the week following the lunch, Joyce was more than pleased because Mr Lawson had hired a firm to come into the house and thoroughly clean right through from top to bottom, including all the carpets. When everything was spic and span he had paid a visit to a local garden centre whose staff had been only too happy to advise and deliver all that he had chosen. His purchases had certainly put the finishing touches to the house and added to the festive atmosphere. The main hall was bright with poinsettias and branches of holly covered in red berries. In both the lounge and the dining room bowls of hyacinths and Christmas roses had been placed. When they came into full bloom the perfume would fill the air. A huge Christmas tree was being delivered on December twenty-first and Mr Lawson had said that although this was a busy time of the year for his firm he would finish work on the twenty-second and would not be returning to the City until the second week in January.

'All right for some,' Joyce had staged-whispered to Paula.

'Aren't you glad that he will be home with his sons, have the joy of helping them to decorate the tree?'

'Yes, of course I am. Just put it down to envy.'

'Envy?' Paula queried, wrinkling her forehead.

Joyce sniffed and dabbed at her eyes. 'I know I should count my blessings but I can't help wondering what my life would have been like if my Frank had come back from the war and we would have been married. I certainly wouldn't be living in Mr Lawson's house. Perhaps I should remind myself that there are thousands of women destined to live lonely lives because of that dreadful war.'

Momentarily Paula felt sad that she was often so full of her own problems that she hadn't given a thought to poor Joyce. *Please God, comfort Joyce*, she silently prayed. She had been about to say, 'At least you must have some wonderful memories of your intended,' but she scolded herself and had the good sense to remain silent.

Christmas of 1930, as well as being the best-ever weather, was for the most part a happy one at Ridgeway. Paula had spent the afternoon of Christmas Eve in the huge kitchen helping Joyce to put the finishing touches to the Christmas fayre. She had mixed boiled onions into a bowl of fine breadcrumbs then added fresh sage, flat-leafed parsley and fresh eggs and watched as Joyce had stuffed the large turkey. Joyce had allowed Paula to glaze the roast ham, a job she had felt a little apprehensive about tackling, but in the end was more than pleased with the end result.

'I'll just finish doing these parsnips and then all the vegetables will be ready for tomorrow morning,' Joyce sighed happily. 'I suppose it's time we took in the tea-trolley. I have put some mince pies in the oven, but, Paula would you mind taking some of this rubbish out to the dustbins first? It is getting a bit cluttered here in the kitchen.'

'Of course I will,' Paula replied, already stuffing vegetable peelings and empty cardboard boxes into a hessian sack. Both she and Joyce got a shock as she drew back the bolts on the back door and opened it wide. 'Ooh, there's a nip in the air tonight,' Joyce murmured as she shivered in the draught.

Paula had removed her working overall, washed her hands and combed her unruly thick hair into some kind of order before securing the loose strands with side-combs. Coming in from the frosty darkness outside to the bright warmth of the main hall she stood still for a moment, thrilled to the core to just stand and stare as Peter, David and their father were putting the last touches to the seven-foot-tall Christmas tree. Jeffrey Lawson caught sight of Paula and he grinned as he stepped back to view the effect.

'I think that's a bit of all right!' he declared. 'Though I say it myself as shouldn't. What do you think, Paula?'

'It is absolutely beautiful,' Paula agreed. 'You three have been really busy and you have made a really good job of it.'

Paula's heart was bursting with pride to see the children so contented with their father. She didn't dare look straight at Jeffrey's face because she knew what he would be thinking. *If only their mother could have been here . . .*

For her own part she wished, with a pang of remembrance, that her own mother could see her in this house now. She would surely approve and be happy that her daughter had made the right move. She had sent a gift of a bowl of Christmas flowers to her home address, writing on the card: 'Wishing you both a very Happy Christmas, with fond thoughts and love from your daughter'. That way her father could not say that she had excluded him. It would remind her mother that she did think about her, but she couldn't help but wish that she could have seen her mother at least once over the Christmas period.

Mary and Arthur Blackmore had arrived from Devon to spend the festive season at Ridgeway, and Arthur broke into Paula's thoughts as he stomped across the hall. 'I've sawed up enough logs to see us right through Christmas,' he said, 'though with a fire-place as big as that one we'll probably need a few more – but at least we'll have a real yule-log fire and there aren't many that can lay claim to that.'

Mary, having followed her husband in, shook her head. 'You've been doing too much, Arthur. You know you shouldn't overtire yourself.'

'I don't know where you get these tinpot ideas from; I'm one hundred per cent fit.'

Mary laid a hand on his arm. 'Just don't overdo it, love.' She didn't add what she was really thinking: that she had already lost her first husband . . .

Joyce came trundling in with a loaded tea trolley and Mary took it upon herself to be mother, pouring cups of tea for the adults and milk for the twins. The hot mince pies went down a treat. Joyce certainly made fairy-light puff pastry.

The evening meal was to be a light one of roast ham, salad and jacket potatoes with trifle and cheese and biscuits to follow. All of the rich food would be consumed on Christmas Day itself.

It had turned eight o'clock when Paula finished tidying the bathroom and went to see if the twins had settled down yet. She smiled to herself as she walked down the corridor.

As Paula entered the bedroom she noticed that both boys were still wide awake and showed no sign of being tired. She sat down and began to read them a story but had hardly begun before both boys began to close their eyes and soon they were fast asleep. Paula tucked the blankets around each child's shoulders, lightly placed her lips on their foreheads and kissed them both in turn before she crept from the room.

'Gave you a hard time, did they?' Jeffrey asked as Paula came into the lounge.

'They were both worn out but I soon got them to go to sleep,' she told him, laughing. 'They should sleep until morning now.'

On Christmas morning the whole household received an early-morning call as the boys awoke even earlier than usual. Paula thought they must sense the festive atmosphere although she knew there was little chance that at their young age they would understand about Christmas yet.

The adults later agreed that it was Peter and David who had made the day.

'Little uns are what make Christmas,' Arthur said, giving Paula a knowing wink.

'Well, I must get on,' Joyce said, picking up the wrapping paper that was lying around the room, and smoothing it out to be used again. 'What time do you suppose Mr and Mrs Burrows will arrive?'

'Andy said they'd be here by about twelve,' Jeffrey answered.

'Joyce, can't you slow down? You've hardly given yourself time to look at your presents.'

Paula had thought that Joyce looked flushed this morning, though whether it was from the heat of the kitchen or from the thought of spending the whole day with such an intimate family gathering, Paula was not sure.

'Nonsense! I'm thrilled with the presents I have opened, but I've left some to open later in the day. I've still got lots to do. The dinner won't cook itself. And I do so want everything to be just right.'

'I'll help you,' Paula offered.

'Indeed you won't!' Mary retorted. 'If anyone needs a break it's you, the boys had you up before five o'clock this morning.'

In the event, the Burrows arrived early, bringing their two lads who were laden with presents.

'I thought if we came in good time I could give a hand – and anyway our Freddie and Raymond can't wait to give the twins their presents. They'll play with them and help keep them amused,' Andy said, grinning.

Hilda quickly turned to Paula. 'I can help too if you show me what to do.'

Joyce was staring at Andy. 'Well, if you really mean it you could help Jeffrey to put an extra leaf into the dining table,' she said. 'Come along. I'll show you where it's kept.'

Freddie and Raymond Burrows were keen to allow the twins to find out how much more clever they were, but they were doing it in a very friendly way, showing great patience. As gifts for Peter and David, Hilda had chosen large-print story books with glorious coloured illustrations and books of black and while sketches to which she had added packets of coloured pencils. 'C is for Cat and D is for Dog,' Raymond chanted to Peter, although of course Peter was too young to be able to reply just yet.

With mixed feelings Paula sat back in her armchair watching the twins being taught parts of the alphabet. Time was going so swiftly, and once again she wondered how much longer Jeffrey Lawson would think his twin boys would have need of a nursemaid.

Then another thought flashed into her mind. She had sent and received cards and presents from Molly, Laura and Fred Wilson

and their two boys. Now, today, Hilda and Andy Burrows were
here with their two sons playing with Peter and David. That was
six boys – where were all the little girls? So many young men had
lost their lives between 1914 and 1918; was God evening the score
by giving parents more lads than lasses now?

After the huge Christmas dinner, when they had each pushed
their chairs back and Mary and Arthur had gone into the kitchen
to make coffee, Paula said, 'I'm going to wrap the twins up well
and take them for a walk. If I took them upstairs they wouldn't
rest and the fresh air will do me as much good as it will them.'

'What a jolly good idea,' Hilda agreed. 'Would you like some
company?'

'Why, yes I would, but what about Freddie and Raymond?'

'Boys, did you hear what Paula has suggested? Would you like
to bring your new football and we could go into the park and
maybe you can have a kick around?'

No sooner the word than the action.

Slippers were exchanged for boots, coats were buttoned up tightly,
woolly hats pulled down well over little pink ears. Long scarves
were wound around necks and gloves were put on the correct hand,
and then two ladies and four boys set out over the frosty driveway,
through Grayswood Gardens and into Barnes Lane. Surprise,
surprise! They were not the only ones who had forsaken the fireside to seek some fresh air. There were quite a few dads and big
brothers all keen to kick a ball with the youngsters of the families,
and everyone was welcome. Hilda and Paula sat themselves down
on a park bench with the twins and let the boys run riot. The
hooting, yelling and laughter told them that to bring their boys to
the park on this crisp Christmas afternoon had been a brilliant idea,
and Hilda's two lads were being very protective of the twins.

Seeing so many lads had Paula again thinking of Laura, promising herself that early in the new year she would spend another
weekend with the family. She had half hoped that in Laura's
Christmas card there might have been a message for her from her
own mother. *She must know that I would keep in touch with Laura.
She could have met Laura outside the school gates and asked her to pass
a message on to me. If only there had been just a few words from her. I
did think at Christmas there would be a word or two . . .*

* * *

It was just after midnight when Paula took her last look in at an exhausted Peter and David and then thankfully took herself off to bed.

Not hearing from her mother had been the only black spot on an otherwise perfect Christmas Day.

Fifteen

The first few months of 1931 brought so much work to Jeffrey Lawson's office that he often stayed the night in town and Paula felt he was missing so much of his sons' daily growth. Each and every day the boys established themselves as independent individuals and to her they were a joy to watch and to be with.

Without them realizing, June rolled around and with it Peter and David's second birthday. Since it was a perfect summer Sunday she and the boys were in the garden. Arthur and Mary had come up from North Devon and Jeffrey and Andy had taken them for a drive, promising to be back in time for the birthday tea. Hilda Burrows was there with her two boys and as she caught Paula's eye she gave a knowing wink.

'There's more to this drive that Jeffrey has suggested than meets the eye, don't you think?'

'Well, I did have my doubts that they would just up and go; I think they've gone somewhere to pick up a special present for the twins.'

Freddie and Raymond were gently pushing the twins on the swings. From the seat where she watched them Paula could smell the old-fashioned spicy clove scent of the border pinks and the headier perfume of the standard roses. Everything about this garden was beautiful, as was the house itself. How much she loved living here but even more so how very much she loved Peter and David. They had become the mainspring of her life, meaning more to her than anything in the world, and she so wanted the world to be perfect for them. She wanted to be around to see them grow into tall, handsome young men. But what if, as time went on, their father decided to dispense with her services? The thought came unbidden and very unwelcome into her mind, as it did all too often these days. She pushed it away. It had no place in this perfect June day.

From time to time she closed her eyes, trying to banish all such thoughts, letting the sun warm her body. So relaxed was she that she didn't notice when Joyce came towards her. It was only when her shadow blocked out the sun that she opened her eyes and looked up.

'Joyce,' she murmured, 'is anything wrong?'

'Quite the reverse,' Joyce told her, smiling.

At the same time as Paula got to her feet, the four boys saw their fathers and the twins' grandparents. 'Golly, look,' Freddie Burrows was the first to cry out as he grabbed Peter's hand and together they hurried across the lawn, leaving Raymond to follow with David.

Jeffrey Lawson was leading a Shetland pony!

'That for us?' Peter demanded as he stared disbelievingly at the small beautiful pony.

David, not to be outdone, had both of his hands buried deep within the thick shiny coat of the pony and his face was beaming.

Jeffrey drew Paula aside. 'This won't cause you any extra work, please believe me, Paula. I have come to an agreement with one of the young female grooms who works up at the local riding stables. Whenever the boys want to go out she will go with them – in fact I have been told that we may hire another pony at an hourly rate so that both Peter and David can ride at the same time – always with an adult with them, of course. And the pony will be stabled there, all its grooming and food will be taken care of, but the boys will have access whenever you take them to visit. I promise you, the arrangements will be cordial and informal.'

'Thank you for telling me. I was wondering how I was going to cope but obviously you have given a lot of thought to finer details.'

'Do I sense, Paula, that you think I have made the right choice, buying a pony for the twins' birthday present?'

'Oh, yes, absolutely! Just look at their faces – they will live to remember this day for the rest of their lives. Now, don't you think we'd better start thinking about this birthday tea? One thing is for sure: you'll not get any of the boys to go inside the house to eat. So if you agree, Hilda and I will give Joyce a hand to set it all up out here in the garden.'

'Well, as usual, Paula, you are right. Andy and I will set three tables together. That will give us all more room.'

Not long afterwards, the job of transferring all the food out to the garden completed, everyone took a seat and the festive birthday tea was allowed to commence, the new addition to the family being allowed to stand nearby.

Jeffrey explained to all four boys that the breed of this pony had originated in the Shetland Islands off the north coast of Scotland and the argument began as to what name he should be given. Amid much laughter and many rejections it was finally agreed that Shellie would be suitable, at least as a temporary measure.

When the boys started to yawn too much and the party broke up it was unanimously agreed that it had been a long time since such a boisterous and happy birthday party had been held in this garden.

August came around and brought with it some sweltering hot days. It was a quarter to eight one evening when Paula headed down the stairs having had to sit with the boys for a long time and they were still wide awake. They were restless, mainly because their father was staying in town and they missed him. She was looking forward to curling up in an armchair with a book.

As she headed down the stairs the telephone in the hall started to ring.

'It's all right, I'll get it,' Joyce said, coming into the hall wiping her hands on her apron before picking up the phone.

'Hello, Ridgeway Manor, Mrs Pledger speaking.'

'My name is Laura Wilson, I am a friend of Paula O'Brien's. Would it be possible to speak to her, please?' The voice coming down the line sounded very unsteady.

'Of course,' Joyce quickly assured Laura. 'Paula is right here, I'll hand her the phone.'

'Hello, Laura, it's me, Paula.'

'Is it all right for you to talk?' Laura hastily enquired.

'Yes, whatever it is, tell me.' Paula had an awful feeling that Laura was not phoning to give her good news.

True enough, Laura's first words were, 'I am so sorry, love, I 'ave some bad news for you, otherwise I wouldn't 'ave bothered you, yer know I wouldn't.'

Paula blinked, her mouth had gone dry and her heart was thumping against her ribs. 'Laura, whatever it is will you please tell me and try and speak a little more slowly?'

'I am ever so sorry t'be the one what has to tell you, but your mum has died. The police found her early this morning an' the news is already round the streets. The police 'aven't got round to us yet, but when they do I suppose I shall have to tell them where you are. Though Mum says you might wanna come 'ere before they do. We can put you up, glad t'ave you, you know that, don't suppose you want t'stay in that house with yer father, do yer? But my Fred said you'll 'ave t'come sooner or later cos the police will want t'ask you questions.'

'Stop! Stop!' Paula screamed down the phone. Then she did her best to take a deep breath before saying, 'Laura, please will you calm down and tell me exactly what has happened? How did my mother die? Was she taken ill? Why are the police involved?'

'I can't 'elp yer there, Paula, love. I only got the news from my mum and she heard about it when she was shopping down the market.'

'My mother isn't that old,' Paula muttered, more to herself, as she put a hand to her head because it seemed as if hammers were banging away inside of it. Eventually she managed to say, 'I am sorry, Laura, but I think I need a few minutes to gather my thoughts. I just can't take it in. May I call you back?'

'Well, love, I'm only in a phone box. I had quite a few coppers but I've only got tuppence left now; these boxes don't 'alf eat up the money. I know what, why don't you ring me at the Railway Arms later on this evening, say about nine o'clock? I'll walk up there with my Fred, the boys will be all right with me mum, and Tom Wainwright, he's the landlord, he won't mind taking the call though I can't give you the number just now cos I don't know it.'

'Don't worry, Laura; that's a very good idea of yours. I'll get the number of the Railway Arms from the operator. In the meantime please find out as much as you can about what happened to my mother and I will phone you dead on nine o'clock. That will give you time to warn the landlord that I shall be making the call. But before you go, Laura, have you any idea where my father is and how he is taking the news?'

'No, love. Ain't 'eard a dicky bird about him and no one seems to 'ave set eyes on him either.'

'All right, thanks, Laura, for taking the trouble to let me know. I'll speak to you later.'

Having replaced the receiver, Paula continued to stand there, staring at the phone. She couldn't believe her mother was dead. Even in her head she couldn't come to terms with it; it sounded so final. What should she do? What *could* she do? Where would she start? Were she to go home right now it would not be possible for her to see her mum, let alone talk to her. It was too late. That was the reality she had to face now. It had been eighteen months since she had walked out of their home, and that would turn out to be the last time she would ever set eyes on her mother. As she had walked up the hallway to get into the waiting taxi her mother had patted her shoulder. That had been the last physical contact between them. During the first weeks she had been at Ridgeway she had written several letters asking her mother to meet up with her. Paula hadn't really expected her to reply or want to meet. She was not sorry that she had continued to send letters, even though she was so afraid that her father would read them and make a terrible scene.

At Easter Paula had done as she had at Christmas, and had ordered flowers to be delivered to her parents. On the card that the florist supplied she had simply written on the back of it: '*Thinking of you both. Love, Paula.*' But she had never gone back. Never made the first move, and now she would have to live with that fact for the rest of her life.

By now she was so agitated that it took her a moment to realize that Joyce Pledger was hovering nearby. She wasn't sure how long she had stood there. It had to be shock, deadening her mind, but somehow she had to move from here and try to work out just what she could do about the awful news she had just been given.

Seeing that Paula was trembling, Joyce quickly came forward, grasped her by the arm and led her into the lounge. Helping her into one of the deep armchairs, Joyce looked at her helplessly. 'I am going to pour us both a very stiff brandy and then when you feel like it you can tell me how I can help.'

Paula started to answer, but the words would not come. She tried again, but the only sound that came out was a cry such as would come from a wounded animal.

Joyce turned her back on her, sensing that Paula needed a few minutes. Going to the cabinet she took out two balloon glasses and a bottle of brandy. Having poured a generous measure of the golden liquid into each glass Joyce seated herself in a chair opposite Paula and handed her a drink. For the next twenty minutes absolute silence lay between them but by then each of them had drunk at least half of their measure of brandy.

In her own time and of her own accord Paula started to tell Joyce the gist of the conversation she'd had with Laura. In a voice that was flat, devoid of all emotion, just as if she had switched her thoughts off for the moment, she ended by saying, 'I have promised to ring the Railway Arms at nine o'clock when Fred and Laura will be there and then I may get a clearer picture of what has happened to my mother.'

Then Paula burst into tears. Joyce went to her and held her tightly in her arms while she sobbed as though her heart would break.

It was a while before she was able to murmur, 'I'm sorry, so sorry.'

'Ssh, ssh, it's all right. Finish your drink and I'll get the number of the Railway Arms for you. Then after you have made your call we will decide what you must do, though, Paula, I have to warn you, I don't think there will be very much you can do, not tonight. You will have to phone Mr Lawson in the morning and by then the police will probably have tracked you down and will be wanting to interview you.'

Paula gasped! 'Why would they want to interview me?'

Joyce swallowed hard, and took a deep breath. 'To begin with they will be able to acquaint you with all the facts.'

In the end Paula did not have to call the Railway Arms, as the shrill ringing of the telephone once again echoed around the high-ceilinged hall. Joyce hurried to answer it, moments later calling, 'Paula, it is Mr Wilson, he wants to speak to you.'

As Paula took the receiver from Joyce and held it to her ear, Fred's familiar hearty voice came to her immediately. 'Hello, Paula dear. I am so sorry about your mum.'

'Thank you for taking the trouble to ring me, Fred. Have you learned any more as to how my mother died so suddenly?'

'Well, not really. The general supposition is that yer mum suffered a heart attack. Apparently no one discovered her until this afternoon. She was taken to the hospital and rumour has it that she was dead on arrival but we haven't been able to get any news from the police – or from anyone else come to that.'

Paula couldn't think of anything to say and a moment later Fred continued. 'Don't suppose there is much any of us can do at this time of the night but I think you should be prepared to come home to us in the morning or at least to ring the police and give them the address where you are.'

'Yes, Fred, you're right. I did ask Laura about my dad, but she said no one had seen him. Have you heard anything from him?'

'No, love, but then he's hardly likely to call round to our place, not since the last time when he went for my Laura because she wouldn't give him your address. I sought him out. Told him if he wanted any information to come to me, made meself very plain, I did, an' we ain't seen hair nor hide of him since and that was some months ago.'

'Fred,' Paula said, and there was a plea in her voice, 'I can't leave here tonight, not with Mr Lawson away from home, but as soon as he gets back he will advise me as to the best course of action I should take and then I shall probably come straight to you in the morning – that's if Molly won't mind.'

'Now, Paula, don't go talking all daft like, you know damn well Molly will welcome you with open arms. Given 'alf a chance she'd 'ave come an' got you 'erself tonight. So, never mind about letting us know you're coming, just turn up on the doorstep an' you'll see how glad we'll all be t'see yer. Especially the boys. Now I want yer to promise me that you'll do yer best t'get a good night's sleep – no need to telephone the Railway Arms – and I'll see yer in the morning.'

'I will, Fred, and thanks. I do appreciate what you are doing. Goodnight, see you tomorrow.' Very quietly Paula laid the receiver back on its hook and turned to face Joyce, who was hovering only feet away.

'I think it best if I give Mr Lawson a ring now,' Joyce said firmly. 'We have the telephone number of the place where he rooms when he has to stay in town. He always says if we have any sign of trouble or a problem we can't solve we are to get on to him immediately. He could be home in less than an hour.'

Paula was still dithering, which was so unlike her. 'But this is my mother who has died; why would he want to get involved?'

'Paula! I know this has been a tremendous shock to you, but please think carefully before you start making assumptions. You are in charge of Mr Lawson's boys, whether you like it or not you are going to have to leave them with me. If you don't go of your own accord I will lay you ten to one that the police will come and collect you.'

'How can you be so sure that the police will want to talk to me?'

'If, as you've been told, your father has disappeared, who next do you think they are going to contact? You are her daughter; you may even have to identify her body.' Seeing the look of horror on Paula's face, Joyce quickly added, 'I am sorry to be so blunt, but tonight, Paula, you are going to have to really grow up and face facts. I am sure, however, that Mr Lawson will give you all the help he can. I can't see him letting you go to the police on your own. Anyway, all this talking is beside the point. I am going to make that call and he can decide for himself what action he is going to take.' She was just about to walk back to the phone when she hesitated. 'Paula, don't try crossing your bridges until you come to them. We should be thankful, both of us, that we have such a good, understanding man as our employer. I'll see you are well looked after, never fear, and I'm sure he will be back in this house before midnight.'

Joyce Pledger was right.

Jeffrey Lawson had listened to the details Joyce had given to him over the telephone. After having enquired if Peter and David were all right, and been reassured by her answers, his own reply had been short and sharp: 'I will be there just as soon as I can.'

It was coming up to eleven o'clock when they heard his taxi drive up to the front door. Having first gone upstairs to check on his two sons, he went to his own bedroom, removed the jacket of his suit, rolled his shirt sleeves up to his elbows and took off his shoes, replacing them with a soft pair of moccasins before going downstairs.

Joyce had made a pot of coffee and placed a jug of hot milk on the tray with three cups and saucers, and she had also added an assortment of cheeses and biscuits. It didn't take long for Paula to relay to Jeffrey what had taken place, for as she remarked sorrowfully, 'My friends, Fred and Laura Wilson, have told me all they know, but it boils down to very little, and all we seem to know for certain is that my mother has died.'

Jeffrey knew he should be more than able to cope with this situation but somehow he felt at a loss. He was well aware of Paula's background, and of her unsuccessful attempts to meet up with her mother. Poor Paula: sudden death was always a shock but when two family members become estranged, it must be ten times worse, knowing that now there simply was no way of turning back the clock.

Having drunk his coffee and tucked into some cheese and biscuits, Jeffrey stood up, wiped his mouth on his serviette and briskly said, 'Come along, you two. Nothing to be gained by us sitting here all night. We should go to bed now and in the morning I have no doubt that the police will be descending on us bright and early.'

He got no answer. None seemed necessary.

Joyce placed the used cups, saucers and plates back on to the tray and headed for the kitchen. Left alone, Jeffrey remained standing but when he spoke again his voice was low and very gentle. 'Paula, you are not to worry about the twins. First thing in the morning I shall get on to Mrs Wright. Esmé will be more than willing to step into the breach; you do know that, don't you?'

Paula nodded her head.

'Well, that is a big worry off your shoulders for the time being. You will feel better knowing that both Peter and David are in safe hands and not being cared for by strangers.'

'Are you saying that I shall have to be away from here and the twins for some time?' she asked, sounding horrified at the prospect.

'Well, we have to face the truth. We don't have the facts yet so we must not jump to false conclusions but there will be a great deal of issues that will probably be left for you to deal with. However, I want to reassure you, Paula, that I will do everything I can to help. I am convinced that the police will make contact with you first thing in the morning but should I be wrong then I will drive you to the police station myself and stay with you until you get some satisfactory answers.'

'I feel that already I have imposed on you too much,' Paula started to protest.

'I would not be here if I didn't feel the need. Now then, no more worrying tonight, up you go and try to get some sleep.'

Paula thanked him again, called out goodnight to Joyce and wearily climbed the stairs. Once inside her bedroom she undressed, washed her face and hands and got into bed. She couldn't bring herself to lie down, so instead she piled the pillows high behind her head and shoulders and let her thoughts run riot. Her main feeling was one of utter frustration. She wanted to scream, but what good would that do? There were so many questions she still wanted to ask her mother. *Mum, you know the answers. I know you do, but you were always too afraid of Dad to take my side. Will I ever get to the truth now?* What a mess! Ridgeway was not her house or home. Never mind that she had been so happy here; it was still simply the place where she worked. Jeffrey Lawson was her employer. What did her future hold now?

Her mother was dead! She couldn't bear it, she just couldn't. From the day she had left home she had let herself believe that eventually she and her mother would meet up, they would he friends, they would talk and talk, tell each other how sorry they were. She had so wanted to explain to her mum why she had felt she had to get out of that house, away from her father. Now with her mother gone that was never going to happen.

Her mother had been the centre of her world until Paula's thirteenth birthday. Previous to that she had been the light in her mother's eye, and had always felt safe in the knowledge that her mother loved her dearly. To remember the year that had followed that birthday, the cruelty and the degradation she had been made to suffer. During the thirteen months that she had been kept segregated from the outside world, not once had she seen or heard from her parents.

All this reminiscing was doing her no good. She felt herself start to shake again, the memories filled her with such resentment and disgust that she had to press her hands to her head as though to stop it from bursting.

Sixteen

Next morning everybody was up and about early. Paula had the twins washed and dressed and sitting up to the table in their high chairs having their breakfast when their father put in an appearance looking very spruce in a charcoal-grey suit, crisp white shirt and a dark maroon-coloured tie.

Having made a fuss of both Peter and David he turned to Paula and said, 'I have already been in touch with Mr Wright and left a message for Esmé. I am sure she will either turn up here soon or at least telephone. Now as soon as breakfast is over I want you, Paula, to shut yourself away in my study and to feel free to use the telephone on my desk. I suggest you look up the telephone number of the Wimbledon police station and give them a ring. Explain who you are and give them this address as your permanent residence.'

Paula did know how to answer; just saying 'thank you' seemed inadequate, she thought. He was going out of his way to be kind to her.

Joyce, too, was showing concern. 'Did you manage to get any sleep at all?' she asked Paula.

'Yes, I did – in fact when I did go off to sleep I must have slept very heavily because I've woken up with a blinding headache.' She wasn't going to admit she'd had nightmares about her mother, and had woken up twice during the night, crying.

'Well, do as Mr Lawson has suggested. I'll see that the twins are kept amused.'

Paula was seated behind the big leather-topped desk, leafing through the telephone book when Joyce came back bringing her a fresh cup of tea and two aspirins.

'You'll be pleased to know that the cavalry has arrived,' she said, grinning widely. 'Esmé has just come in through the back door and the boys have shown her how pleased they are to see her by climbing all over her.'

Having drunk her tea and taken the aspirins, Paula picked up the phone and asked the operator for the number she had found for the police in Wimbledon. Inside her nerves were already starting to churn, making her wonder what kind of news she was about to be told. 'The number you have requested is engaged, please replace the receiver and try again later,' the crisp, formal voice of the operator informed her.

As Paula sat pondering on what her next move should be the telephone rang. 'Ridgeway Manor. Paula O'Brien speaking.'

'Eh, I am glad I've got straight through to you, Paula. I didn't want your Mr Lawson thinking I was becoming a nuisance.'

'Hello, Laura, you're up and about early this morning, aren't you?'

'Yes, I am, but don't get yer hopes up. I haven't any further news about yer mum, but last night when my Fred came back from the pub he was full of it about yer dad. He wouldn't let me go out to ring you last night, said it was too late and the news would keep until this morning.'

Paula was wishing her dear friend would come to the point but she didn't want to be rude and push her. 'So has my dad turned up then?' she asked finally, almost dreading the answer.

'I dunno that you could say he's turned up – not exactly. Somebody found your father . . . he was out for the count, lying by the River Wandle in Merton with blood oozing from a gash at the side of his head. Whoever it was that found him phoned the police.'

'You mean he was drunk?' Paula shot the question, utterly outraged.

'Well, I suppose so, love. Anyway, the police 'ave got him in custody according to what my Fred 'eard. But, Paula, I've got something else t'tell yer. Don't think yer gonna like it and I am sorry.'

'What can be worse than knowing that my mother is dead? Tell me, Laura, please.'

'Well, as you know everyone around 'ere knows you an' me 'ave always been bosom buddies, so when the police started knocking on doors, asking questions, they steered them in my direction. Me mum told them t'clear off – you should 'ave 'eard 'er!'

In spite of everything Paula found herself smiling. She could imagine it. She could almost hear some of the flowery words that

Molly Owen would have used when telling the police to get off her doorstep! She straightened her face and managed calmly to ask, 'So, what did the police want to know?'

'What children yer parents had. And apart from your father did I know who would be yer mother's next of kin and where did they live? All that kind of thing. I told them they only 'ad you and you had a live-in job but that I couldn't remember exactly where it was. I know they knew that I knew more than I was letting on. Of course they'll find out the truth sooner or later but I thought it would give you a bit of breathing space, you know, time to 'ave a bit of a think. Did I do right?'

Sighing heavily, Paula was wrangling with herself. Yes, she was grateful to Laura for her help, but it wasn't fair to drag her into this awkward situation. Forcing the words out she quietly said, 'Yes, of course you did right. Quick thinking that was. Thanks, Laura. Mr Lawson has already spoken to me at great length, he said to wait until I had spoken to you again, see if there had been any further development and if the police hadn't contacted me by then he was going to run me to the station. By the way, I assume they still have my father in custody? Do you know at which station they are holding him?'

'Well, me and me mum knew several of the coppers that were round 'ere knocking on doors and we knew they all came from the coppers' station at Amen Corner, top end of Mitcham Road in Tooting.'

'Thanks, that's useful to know. I know where that is. It is still quite likely that they will turn up here. It's inevitable that they will want to talk to me. If the police don't come here, Mr Lawson will take me to the station. In any case please keep in touch and I will see you as soon as I can. Give my love to the boys and to Fred and your mum.'

'Can't wait to see you,' Laura said, and Paula could hear the break in her voice. She was such a good friend. Laura had the last word. 'Bye for now. Bye, love.'

'Joyce has made some fresh coffee. Would you like a cup?' Jeffrey asked as Paula came into the kitchen.

'Yes, please.' She waited for him to pour, then took the cup from him and went to sit at the kitchen table.

'You'll be pleased to know that Esmé has taken the boys out for a walk.'

Paula nodded and managed a weak smile.

'So, did you get any more information from your friend Laura?' he asked.

'Yes, the police have found my father and he is now in their custody,' she said quietly. Silence settled between them as they both sipped their coffee until Paula felt it was only right to bring him up to date on what was happening.

'Laura was worried because she told the police mostly half-truths. She admitted I had a live-in job but did not disclose this address..'

'Well, it is only a matter of time before the police do discover where you are so I think it best if I make that call right now.'

Paula nodded thoughtfully, but made no comment.

Within the hour the police had arrived. Paula stood at the window and watched as the police car swept by the immaculately tended shrubs and the smooth lawn which lay in the centre of the circular drive. By the time the two officers had got out of the car Mr Lawson was standing with the front door wide open. He introduced himself and the officers produced their identification.

'Miss O'Brien is expecting you; she will be in the dining room by now. If you follow me I will show you the way.'

When Jeffrey had left they were all three still standing, so Paula said, 'Is it all right if we sit down?'

The tallest of the policemen said, 'I think we should.'

Paula immediately dropped into the chair at the head of the table and sat with her back held ramrod straight as the two policemen took a chair on either side of her. Both officers were big men, and the elder of the two had bushy grey hair, bright blue eyes and a smile that was meant to put her at ease. The younger one, however, looked very ill at ease. They introduced themselves, the young one calling himself PC Clarke and the older man stating he was Sergeant Gibson. It was PC Clarke who opened the conversation.

'Miss O'Brien, we are sorry to meet with you under such sad circumstances, but we do need to ask you some questions.'

'That's all right,' she answered dutifully, trying to stop her hands from trembling. She very quickly added, 'Are you going to tell me how and when my mother died?'

The constable coughed to clear his throat before he answered. 'We haven't yet received the coroner's report, but the duty doctor is pretty sure your mother suffered a heart attack.'

'Then you haven't charged my father with harming her in any way?' Paula asked, sounding annoyed.

'Miss O'Brien, are you suggesting that your father might have in some way hurt your mother?' It was the first time that the sergeant had spoken and his voice was deep and gruff.

Paula nodded her head. 'It wouldn't be the first time . . . his temper has always been a big problem. Do you know if there is going to be a post-mortem?'

'Yes, there will be, and all your questions will be answered,' he hastened to assure her.

'I hope so. Meanwhile, may I see my mother please? And I should like to know when I can begin making arrangements for her funeral.'

Sergeant Gibson leaned forward and took hold of Paula's hand. 'Try and be patient, my dear. Take time to grieve for your mother. It will be some time before her body will be released and it would be so much better if you wait until the undertakers receive permission to take her to their chapel of rest.'

Paula looked at him, her eyes full of fear. 'I know what you're saying is right, but it will be hard.'

For several minutes no one spoke, letting Paula's words resound around the room.

Then they began their questioning in earnest. How long since she had seen her mother? And what about her father? Had he ever visited her here in Raynes Park? Had they parted on amicable terms? What exactly had caused her to jump to the conclusion that her father might have harmed her mother enough to cause her death?

Paula felt intimidated. They made her life sound horrifying and her attitude towards her parents even worse. What if they knew the real reason why she had left home? But even then they would be entitled to query why she had returned to her parents' home after having been sent away for such a long period of time. God above, where was she supposed to have gone? She had only been fourteen years old! If they delved deep enough, would they question why she had continued living in that house for a further five years after what she'd been through?

Even she, herself, wouldn't have been able to answer those questions truthfully!

For some time after the officers had left she'd simply sat still at the table. Then the first sane thought came to her: she needed to see Peter and David. As she climbed the stairs to the playroom she was praying. *Please, God, don't let anything happen to take me away from this job. It has opened up another world to me, so different to what I came from. So full of love and kindness, two adorable babies each growing into strong, independent little boys. I couldn't bear to leave them, not now that they have become part and parcel of my life.*

The minute she opened the door to the playroom she felt a surge of panic. The room was so tidy and so quiet: the boys were not there. It was a long minute before she remembered that she'd been told Esmé was taking them out for a while. She began to busy herself, and taking a large ball of soft cotton wool from a glass jar that stood on the marble top of the washstand, she began wiping down all the hard surfaces, beginning with the trays the boys had used for their mid-morning drink. Then taking all the items from the airing rack she began to fold each article, smoothing the sleeves of the small jumpers, matching and folding into pairs the pile of small socks, the tiny shirts, one of which had a button hanging by a mere thread and she placed this shirt aside ready for sewing repairs when she sat down later that evening. She couldn't resist the urge to hold a couple of their vests up close to her cheek. The material was soft to the touch. She smelled the now familiar smell that she would always attach to the twins. She couldn't bear it if she were to be told she had to be parted from them.

Suddenly it was as if someone had thrown a switch and the whole house had become alive. The silence was shattered as two young clear voices rang out. 'Paula. Pauly, where are you?'

She almost fell over in her haste to get to the top of the staircase and show herself. 'I'm here, Peter. Did you have a good time, David? Where did Esmé take you?' She knew her words were all of a jumble and that she wasn't making much sense, but she didn't care. The twins were coming up the stairs and she was on her way down when the three of them met. The force with which they threw themselves at her made her topple over and they all ended up with a hard plunge on one of the stair treads. Arms and legs all seemed to be tangled together as they kissed and hugged their Paula.

'There is no need for either of you to worry,' she soothed. 'I shall have to leave you for a day or two but nothing is settled yet. I am still here and we are going to have a lovely lunch, all of us together – Joyce and Esmé too, because they took care of you for a little while when I was talking to the policemen, didn't they?'

Both boys still looked a trifle bewildered but as long as she held on to their hand, one each side of her as they walked, they seemed to accept that at least for the time being she was not going to desert them.

Seventeen

The following day, when Paula was extremely busy in the nursery trying to deal with both boys at once, Mr Lawson came in to talk to her.

'Good morning, Paula,' he said before going straight over to greet the boys as he usually did. 'I should begin by offering you my condolences. I should have done that a long time ago but somehow we got caught up in other matters. It was very remiss of me and I do apologize.'

'No need for an apology, really there isn't. I appreciate what you did, phoning the police and allowing me the use of the dining room.'

Jeffrey was shaking his head. 'Please think nothing of it. If you have to go away for a few days, to see your father or whatever, you will consider coming back, won't you?'

'Oh, Mr Lawson, whatever makes you think I wouldn't? Truly I have never been happier than in my position here as nursemaid to David and Peter.'

'Well, let me assure you I wouldn't know where to turn if you did decide to leave us. The boys really love you; it is so easy to tell. You are aware that in the first place I tried several so-called professional nannies and in the end I said to hell with the lot of them! Each and every one was a walking disaster. Strict rigid rules. No comforting cuddles were permitted and love never even came into the equation. To be honest, when I advertised for a caring, motherly person I expected a much older person to apply. You looked so young, but how I bless the day that you stepped into this house. Both Esmé and my mother urged me to give you a chance and never for one moment have I regretted my decision. You were made to order! And when Peter and David are older and we tell them how you came into our lives I am certain they will endorse my views in every respect.'

More pleased to hear his words than she wanted to show, Paula said, 'Thank you again. I will need a day or two off, and later on

I should want to attend my mother's funeral, of course, but other than that wild horses wouldn't drag me away from the twins.'

Jeffrey Lawson smiled, allowing her to see how relieved he felt. 'Joyce and Esmé between them will manage fine and if necessary I shall take time off from the office to be here – and if I do continue to work I shall make sure I am never away from here overnight so you need have no fears on that score. You make your arrangements, and please don't hesitate to talk to me, let me know what is going on and if I can help in any way whatsoever you only have to tell me.'

Paula swallowed hard and tried to focus on what he was saying but her chest was beginning to feel tight and she was having a job to keep a tight rein on her emotions. Realizing she was embarrassingly close to tears again, she dug around in her apron pocket for a handkerchief. 'I'm sorry,' she said. 'I just wish I'd been able to see her and talk to her before she died.'

'I think it is probably the same for everyone who has to go through the ordeal of a sudden death of a loved one, there are always going to be "if onlys".'

Hardly had Jeffrey finished speaking than the telephone in the hall rang and he went to answer it.

Paula busied herself clearing away the breakfast things. 'Boys, rinse your hands under the tap and use the roller towel to dry your hands,' she told them, making sure she kept her voice light and cheery. It was at that moment that Jeffrey came back and Paula's heart sank as she saw the look on his face.

'The police are sending a car for you, Paula. They insist they need to interview you down at the station. Would you like me to go with you?'

Paula hesitated. 'I don't see any reason why you should.'

'Paula, will you listen to what I say, please? I wasn't suggesting it was compulsory, just thought you might be glad of my support.'

'Oh, please, Mr Lawson, I didn't mean to sound ungrateful.'

'I know, Paula, you're moving in uncharted waters and I felt the need to ease the situation for you. However, I suggest you go with the constables when they arrive but if at any time during the interview you feel as if you are out of your depth I want you to call a halt to the interview and call me. I can be there in about half an hour. Will you promise to do that?'

'Yes, yes I will. I'd better go now and get myself ready.'

The police car arrived with two constables who were unknown to Paula. With their customary courtesy they eased her into the back of the car before she had realized that she hadn't said goodbye to the twins. Then she realized that was probably a good thing. She didn't want them upset all over again.

The outer office of the Amen Corner police station was a hive of industry, and Paula was slightly overwhelmed by so many uniformed police. 'Follow me, Miss O'Brien,' instructed the constable who had driven the car that had brought her here. Doing as she was told, she hastened along a long narrow corridor until he stopped at the end and threw open a door. 'This is the main waiting room,' he announced. 'Someone will be along to fetch you soon.'

Paula stepped in to find a room that was sunny and fresh, with white walls, pale blue curtains and several high-backed chairs. There was a single occupant facing the open window, standing with his back to her. Slowly he turned around and Paula gasped. It was Patrick O'Brien, her father's brother: her Uncle Paddy. Almost as enormous as her father yet far better-looking, quite a few years younger too, his bushy hair showed hardly any signs of turning grey.

As he stepped towards her, with arms outstretched, Paula started to tremble, and suddenly without a doubt she knew he was the dark figure who was always in the background of her nightmares. She hadn't set eyes on him for more than six years! As a child she remembered he had been a constant visitor to their house. When and why had his visits ceased? She had no idea. Soon after she had been freed from that lunatic asylum (always in her mind that was how she would describe that filthy place where she had been interned for more than a year) there had been a particularly dreadful argument between her mother and her father and all the while it had been going on her uncle had been sitting there beside the fire with a great grin on his face. The memory was now so clear! 'Not in front of Paula,' her mother had pleaded, but her father had been adamant, bawling and shouting loud enough to wake the dead that as long as he was master in his own house his brother would always be welcome.

With great haste her mother had ordered her to go upstairs to her room, walking right behind her, pushing her in the back to make her move more quickly and finally turning the key in the lock from the outside. A few minutes later her mother had tapped lightly on the door and quietly begged her to listen. 'Believe me please, Paula, you are better off out of this argument.' Try as she would now, she could not remember having set eyes on her Uncle Paddy from that day to this. Now, with him so close, it was impossible for her to look at him without wanting to remember why she was so frightened of him.

Even now, all these years later, it felt creepy just being in the same room as him. She shivered violently and immediately said to herself, 'Someone has just walked over my grave.'

'Paula,' Paddy O'Brien said, now reaching for her hand. 'How are you? I am so sad we meet like this; it is such a shame this bad accident your poor mother has suffered.'

'I'm very well, thank you,' she answered, sounding docile but trying not to flinch as he stroked her arm. 'But what makes you think my mother had an accident? Have the police told you more than they have told me?'

'No, I haven't spoken to the police yet; I'm just going on what my brother has told me. Your mum was hanging curtains, or trying to, went too far up the steps, which wobbled and crashed over, taking her with them, she fell backwards striking her head on the edge of the marble fire surround. She wouldn't have suffered; it was all over in minutes.'

'Oh, but I was told she'd had a heart attack! You know every little detail, by the sound of it. Were you there?'

'No, but by all the saints I wish I had been, might have been able to save her had I been. God rest her soul.'

'Well, I want to hear from someone who is in charge. Mostly I would like to speak to the doctor who first examined my mother. Someone who can give me some answers,' Paula cried.

'My dear Paula, you are becoming hysterical,' Paddy rebuked her in a high-pitched tone. 'And while you're about it keep your voice down, try and be a little more ladylike. I am not deaf.'

'Why?' she shouted at him. 'Afraid I might entice you to tell the truth?'

'Paula, I really do wish you'd accept that your mother has had a bad accident and that she is dead. Nothing more to say, no amount of discussion is going to bring her back. Even as a child you always had to make a drama out of even the smallest things. Now, why don't you leave things to me?'

Paula was totally shocked. 'You'll see to things? What about my father? He's still alive and he is the one married to my mother. Not you. After the police have spoken to me and hopefully have allowed me to see my mother then I'll know if we may contact an undertaker.' Paula was by now deeply troubled and was beginning to look flustered.

It was at that moment that Sergeant Gibson entered the room. Smiling gently at Paula he said, 'I think we have established that, after your father, you are your mother's next of kin, so will you please come with me? There are a few more questions we need to ask you.'

Patrick shook his head in disgust. 'You've got my brother banged up an' you're gonna let a slip of a girl like her manage his affairs?'

No one bothered to give Patrick an answer and he had to step aside to allow Paula to follow the sergeant. The fact that he was being ignored seemed to rile Patrick even further. He stood in the now open doorway and punched the air at the same time yelling, 'They never should have let that uppity bitch out of that bloody loony bin!'

What was puzzling Paula and hurting her at the same time was that her early memories of her Uncle Paddy were happy ones. He would pick her up, swing her high in the air, pretend to drop her and then catch her and hug her tightly. She had loved him then, was always excited when she came home from school and he was there having tea with her mother. In those days even her mother had liked him. What had caused the change in their feelings? What had happened to make her feel so different towards her uncle?

'Would you like a cup of tea?' Sergeant Gibson asked carefully as they entered a larger room and he waved her towards a sofa that was placed against a blank wall facing a window looking out on to a green field.

'No thanks, I'll be fine in a minute,' Paula assured him.

The sergeant nodded and sat himself down behind a desk which was positioned to the right of Paula.

For some reason Paula already felt more comfortable in this

room but was taken aback when the door opened and another policeman came into the room. He headed straight for Paula, held out his hand and said, 'I am Inspector Burrows. Sad business for you, young lady; please accept my condolences and be assured I and my colleagues will do everything we can to ease your grief over the death of your mother.'

Having shaken hands with Paula, Inspector Burrows had a quiet conversation with his sergeant and was just about to leave when a woman made an appearance.

Sergeant Gibson immediately stood up, and came around to the front of the desk to make the introductions. Patting Paula's shoulder he said, 'This is Mrs Sarah Jones. She is a social worker and she is a mine of information, I'm sure you will find her more than helpful in the days to come.'

Mrs Jones was a surprise to Paula; she looked too young to have such a position of authority. However, she was very nice-looking, well dressed but in a severe kind of way, Paula decided as they shook hands. Her eyes, her smile and her handshake all conveyed friendliness while her shoulder-length hair had them both grinning. It was auburn, only a few shades lighter than Paula's own thick tresses.

Paula began to feel comfortable with her, perhaps because she was the first woman she had been able to speak to who might be able to tell her the facts about her mother's death and also she needed to know what exactly were the procedures she would have to follow now.

'Let me begin by saying how sorry I am over the loss of your mother. She was no great age, was she? Sudden death is always the hardest to cope with. I ought to have made contact with you earlier on but I thought it better to wait until after the inquest. In the case of suspicious or accidental deaths the Crown decrees that a coroner should preside at an inquest. I am sure you will be relieved to hear that the formal verdict was death by misadventure.'

Paula knew she should be feeling relieved, but she wasn't; all her feelings were mixed up.

I'm sorry, she thought, *if only I could have made things different between us before you died, Mum*. She shuddered and brushed her hand across her eyes.

'You thought perhaps your father had injured your mother in some way?' Mrs Jones quietly asked.

'It wouldn't have been the first time, though to be honest it was usually verbal abuse. It was so easy for my father to intimidate my mother. He is such a huge man, while my mother was always slim, sprightly but gentle and graceful.'

'You don't live at home?'

This was a question Paula hadn't expected. 'No, not for over a year now,' she answered, feeling guilty. 'And no, before you ask, during all these months I haven't once seen my mother. My father forbade it. I have written to her on a regular basis, always suggesting we meet up somewhere. Even though I named places and times my mother never once wanted to – or couldn't – meet me.'

Even though Mrs Jones' eyebrows rose on hearing this information she didn't seem particularly surprised, but then earlier on she had paid a duty visit to Mr O'Brien and she hadn't got much thanks for her trouble!

'And how about your father? Did you not wish to meet with him?'

Paula shook her head. 'I think I've been a total disappointment to him. No matter how hard I tried, it never worked. He terrorized me.' Paula gave a shuddering sigh and quickly changed the subject. 'Are you able to tell me where my mother has been taken to?'

Mrs Jones had remained thoughtful. 'Oh, my dear, I should have told you straight off. Your mother has been taken to Cornford's, who are well-respected funeral directors. Their premises are not far from here and you can see her whenever you're ready. If you want to, that is. I know not everyone—'

'I want to, I have to,' Paula said tearfully.

'Would you like to go now? Or would you rather have something to eat first?'

'At the moment I don't think I could eat anything, so yes, please, I would like to go now.'

Becoming aware of just how nervous Paula was, Mrs Jones said, 'I am free for the whole morning so would you like me to come with you?'

Paula nodded. She would want to see her mother on her own but she would appreciate the company to and from the funeral parlour. Paula found she couldn't put her feelings into words, so letting it go for the moment she stood up and buttoned her coat. Mrs Jones was being so much kinder than her appearance had at first led Paula to believe she would be and she was glad.

The undertakers' office was about ten minutes' walk at the most, and it turned out to be a large corner premises at the end of the High Street. The reception area was empty as they walked in but within seconds a tall, well-built man in his early forties with neat dark hair wearing a well-cut dark grey suit emerged from a back office.

'Mr Cornford, this is Paula O'Brien,' Mrs Jones told him, then turning her head she explained to Paula, 'This is young Mr Cornford, we met yesterday when I gave all the necessary paper-work to his father.'

The younger member of the firm took Paula's hand in a firm grip. 'My condolences for your sad loss, Miss O'Brien. I'll take you through to our chapel of rest.'

'I could come with you,' Mrs Jones hastily offered, 'or would you prefer to be alone?'

Paula did her best to smile. 'Thank you. I'll go on my own, if you don't mind.'

As she walked at the side of Mr Cornford her heart was thumping nineteen to the dozen and she found herself wishing again that she had made sure to visit her mother when she was alive. It was an empty wish: it was never going to happen now.

As Mr Cornford held the door open for her she felt dizzy, unable to put one foot in front of the other. 'Oh no,' she muttered; she mustn't faint. *Get a grip*, she implored herself.

'Take as long as you like, Miss O'Brien; coffee will be ready when you come out,' Mr Cornford told her in a low voice that held both admiration and respect.

She was alone; she felt light-headed and had to force herself to move forward to where the coffin was resting on a long, low table. Trembling, she stood still and gazed at her mother. Oh, dear Jesus, she looked so peaceful, so beautiful, so utterly at peace. Paula sank to her knees, she hadn't meant to, and reached into the coffin to touch the hands that were clasped across her chest. Her mother had been dressed in a white gown and she looked like a sleeping bride.

'Mum – oh, Mummy,' she whispered despairingly. 'If only we could turn the clock back.' She wanted to remember her as the young woman who had taken her to school and met her every afternoon when it was home time. Who'd read her a bedtime story before tucking her up tight for the night. Who'd made her birthday cakes, always with candles. *Dear God, when and why had things changed?* Paula could barely see, her eyes were swimming with tears, and she pulled a handkerchief from her pocket and rubbed it roughly across her face. Leaning over now, looking straight into her mother's face, she gently smoothed her hair back from her forehead and asked, 'Mum, why did you never tell Dad that the things he was doing to me were wrong? Please, why did you never stand up for me?' She continued to stare, almost as though she was expecting a reply, yet she knew she was never going to get the answers now. She had for so long yearned to be told the truth, but now all chances had gone. It really was too late.

For the last few minutes her eyes had been clenched tight, but now she opened them and once again gazed down on that lovely face. Now, very quietly and very seriously, she whispered, 'Over the years, Mum, I have tried so hard to understand why you allowed the priests and the authorities to take me away and keep me locked up for a whole year. And now God has taken you! Why not my father? Please, wherever you are, watch over me; let me feel that that you did always love me.'

Paula staggered to her feet, straightened herself up and brushed her hands around her face to clear away the tears. Then, bending over the coffin once more, she kissed her mother twice, once on the forehead and once on her cheek. In a voice that was barely audible she said, 'God bless you, Mummy.'

Never had Paula been so grateful for the cup of coffee that Mrs Jones poured for her. Without saying a word she sat sipping the hot drink, quietly pondering over her last visit to her mother, but feeling thankful for this stranger's understanding.

'Paula, I have to ask you another question,' Mrs Jones said, sounding a bit anxious. 'Are you happy to let the funeral arrangements go ahead?'

Paula looked puzzled. 'I don't understand. Why wouldn't I be? In any case I don't have the money to pay all the costs.'

'Well, I have been made aware of the fact that your father has insurance cover and he has applied for the death certificate but since he is still in custody he has given his permission for his brother to act for him. However, after the inquest declared your mother's death due to misadventure, your father will soon be released without charge and will be able to attend to whatever is necessary himself.'

'Well, that is a relief.' Paula felt she might have exploded on hearing that Patrick might have been in charge of her mother's funeral, but for now she was going to leave her father to get on with it. She would attend, pay her respects, but that wasn't to say she wanted anything to do with her father ever again.

Eighteen

Having refused Mrs Jones' offer to drive her home, Paula walked to the railway station and bought a single ticket to Raynes Park. On her arrival she took a bus which dropped her off at the top of Wimbledon Hill. Walking at a leisurely pace it would take her no more than thirty minutes to reach Ridgeway. Mainly it was a fairly straight road, until she turned off down a narrow, winding lane that was bordered by high hedges and grassy banks for the last half-mile. Her mind was full of the coming funeral. Try as she would to concentrate on the beautiful surroundings she couldn't rid herself of the overriding fear of knowing that her father would be there. He had to be there, of course he did, she told herself sternly, but there would be other mourners, probably her father's Irish relations and neighbours. The dread of her having to attend on her own was building up to such a pitch inside her that she could feel herself starting to panic again. Once more she asked herself how was it that her mother had never seemed to show much concern when it came to her welfare. What about the time she had been locked away in the Hut, part of that big asylum in Church Lane, Tooting? Surely it would have been necessary for her mother to agree to have her taken away. Wouldn't she have had to put her signature on all sorts of forms? Or had her father been in complete control of her fate?

Fortunately she was brought back from all this morbid reminiscence as a lorry driver tooted, signalling for her to press into the side of the lane in order that he might drive past.

Coming to the end of the lane she stood still and this time as she breathed out she didn't sigh, but instead she whispered, 'Oh, my goodness, what a beautiful view.'

This had been a dark day with grey clouds in the sky yet it was still clear enough for her to appreciate the wonderful view. She was standing, not so many miles away from where she used to live, but the landscape which lay ahead suggested that this was a different world. She took a really deep breath and then slowly let it out. Already she was feeling a whole lot more calm.

Ten minutes later Ridgeway Manor came into view and immediately Paula sent up a prayer of thanks. She still wondered how this new life of hers had come about – how she had found the courage to go for it? What had Mr Lawson seen in her that he had entrusted his two baby boys into her care?

Less than an hour ago she had knelt beside her mother's coffin, lost in grief and shedding tears for what might have been. Now the anticipation of seeing both Peter and David filled her with such joy that she quickened her steps in order to get there sooner. She never remembered having so many mixed-up emotions as she was feeling now.

As she neared Ridgeway she told herself, *this house has a magic about it, with its ivy-clad walls, great stone steps leading up to a wide veranda and its massive oak front door.* 'Gorgeous,' she said aloud, staring at the shrubs, some of which were still flowering. She was going to have to make a more determined effort to put the past behind her, she vowed, as she walked round the side of the house and let herself in through the back door.

Joyce Pledger must have seen her coming, for she was halfway down the main staircase as Paula came through from the back of the house into the front entrance hall. Joyce leaned over the banisters and called, 'Glad to see you back, Paula. Are you all right?'

'Yes, thank you, Joyce, I'm fine, but what about the twins?'

'I've got them in the playroom, toys all over the place, but so far so peaceful. For how long? Well, your guess is as good as mine!'

Paula was unable to stop herself from breathing a sigh of relief. 'Thank God for that! You go back to them. Have you had lunch yet?'

'No, but I have fed Peter and David.'

'I'll make something for us and bring it up on a tray, will that do for now?'

'Perfectly, I'll get the dinner going later on, although there will only be us two. Mr Lawson phoned to say he is having dinner with a client, so it will be late when he gets home but he did say he will phone again before he leaves the office just to make sure you have returned safely.'

'Thanks, Joyce, I won't be long.' Paula made for the ground-floor cloakroom. *God, I feel dirty*, she thought, taking off her coat.

She washed her hands and splashed her face with hot water. Mitcham wasn't so far away, and yet it seemed so different, with so much traffic and so much noise – oh, she was so pleased to be back home! She looked in the mirror, which was fixed to the wall above the handbasin, and she grinned despite everything, telling herself she was taking too much for granted, thinking of Ridgeway as her home. God forbid that she was! Because if she ever had to leave, where would she go? True, Mr Lawson had assured her that she was needed here and for that she was more than grateful. Dragging a comb through her unruly hair she felt better now, having had the little tidy-up. A couple of sandwiches, a bit of salad and a pot of coffee then she would be free to play with her two boys. She knew they had grown so used to her being there twenty-four hours a day and because she had gone off so early this morning without saying goodbye to them they would be more than pleased to see her. For her part, she couldn't wait.

Joyce took the tray from her, leaving Paula to dash across the room, where one at a time she lifted the boys out of the playpen and on to the carpet. The next ten minutes were hilarious. Hugs and kisses, pushing cars along the floor, throwing balls, banging on drums; everything that came naturally to two small boys. They certainly showed their affection for Paula and let her know she had been missed. Settled now with two sets of building bricks, Paula left them building a castle and went to sit at the table opposite to Joyce, who had already poured out their coffee.

'So, did the interview go well? Did you get any more information?' Joyce asked.

'Better than I expected,' Paula replied. 'I went to see my mother in the chapel of rest.'

'That was brave of you. Most people shy away from that.'

'Well, I'll admit I was scared out of my wits when I first entered that room but I am so glad I went. My mum looked so peaceful, almost as if she had just fallen asleep.'

'I suppose not having seen your mother for well over a year it didn't hurt quite so much that she had died.'

'Then, Joyce, you suppose wrongly,' Paula hastily told her. 'It actually hurt even more and I feel so guilty,' she added, smiling a bitter smile. Joyce Pledger had become a good companion and the two of them worked well together, but each had their own distressing memories.

The dreaded day had arrived: the day her mother would be laid to rest.

Paula had been up since six o'clock. She had allowed the boys to play a while in the bath before getting them out, drying them and selecting suitable outfits for them to wear and finally giving them their breakfast of a boiled egg and soldiers. She had made the boys laugh when she had told them David's thin finger-shaped pieces of bread and butter were soldiers while those she had cut for Peter were ladies' fingers and gentlemen's thumbs. This announcement had caused an uproar, which was only settled when she gave half of Peter's bread to David and then did the reverse, taking from David to give to Paul. Peace at last and she was enjoying watching the twins expertly dip the fingers of bread into the rich yellow yolk of their eggs when the sound of voices reached her through the open window. She hoped it wasn't visitors; she had so much to get through this morning if she was to get away in time to attend her mother's funeral that afternoon.

She quickly glanced at the boys, who were doing fine. She ran downstairs. Spotting a lot of mail lying on the doormat she snatched it up, gathered it into a neat pile and turned to lay it on the hall table just as the front door opened. Mr Lawson and another man were in the porch before she had time to cross the hall and he was closing the heavy door behind them and then both men stepped into the vast hall.

Mr Lawson smiled at her. 'Good morning,' she gasped, trying to tidy her hair by running her fingers through the wavy strands.

'Good morning, Paula,' he responded in his deep, plummy, friendly voice that always made her smile. 'This is a colleague of mine, Martin Hamilton. He works alongside Andy Burrows. He is going to be our guest for the weekend.'

'How do you do?' Martin said, leaning forward to take her hand. 'I am very pleased to meet you.'

'Hello,' she said, knowing immediately that Jeffrey must have explained beforehand who she was and what she was doing at Ridgeway. All the same she felt a bit flustered. There was something about this Martin. He was neither as tall nor as well-built as Jeffrey Lawson, so maybe it was his jet-black hair and his big dark eyes and the casual way he was dressed. Casual clothes they may be; that they were expensive Paula could tell at a glance. All that was true but it was the way this Martin was looking and smiling at her that had her regretting how untidy she looked, although she knew this was absurd. What she looked like wouldn't matter one iota to him.

Seeming to realize that Paula needed some time to tidy herself, Jeffrey asked where Joyce was and then said it didn't matter; he would make some coffee himself.

Paula excused herself and as she passed him he put out a hand and rested it on her shoulder and gave her a squeeze before saying, 'They say the sun shines on the righteous, well the sun is shining for your mother and I do hope everything will go off well for you today.'

Paula looked toward the widow and smiled. 'It really is a glorious morning,' she said, aware of all the rich autumn colours of the trees and shrubs.

'What time are you aiming to leave here?' he asked.

'The funeral is at three fifteen, so if I may phone for a taxi to pick me up at two thirty, would that be all right?'

'Certainly not, I wouldn't hear of it. I thought you might have been going home first, travelling in the first car with your father. I would have offered sooner had I known you intended to go from here. I will drive you to the church and you may take a taxi back if you wish but I'm sure a member of your family will take you to the wake and bring you home later on.'

Paula didn't feel she could voice her thoughts aloud. Some things are best left unsaid. 'Please, Mr Lawson, I couldn't put you to all that trouble . . .'

'Stop, no argument. I shall bring my car round to the front door at two thirty,' he said firmly.

When Paula was out of earshot he turned to Michael and said, 'I can't believe she is intending to go to her mother's funeral entirely alone.'

Not knowing what to say, Martin walked on into the kitchen and started to take cups out of the cupboard. He couldn't help remembering how it had been here at Ridgeway when Sheila had been alive. One thing was for sure: this Paula had made a difference to Jeffrey's life. There had been a time when he and all their colleagues had believed there would be no alternative other than for the twins to be taken into care or even be adopted. *She's a bit young to be a nanny though*, he thought suddenly. *There must be more to this Paula than the eye could see.* But he certainly wasn't going to be the one to start rocking the boat!

In all the time that Paula had been at Ridgeway she had saved her earnings. There hadn't been anything she needed, since everything was provided for her. Most days she wore the plain uniforms that Mr Lawson had paid for, and Joyce had found her half a dozen decent white aprons in Kennedy's in Wimbledon. It was clothes to wear when she spent time with Laura that had not been so abundant. Today she was glad she had taken the advice that Joyce and Esmé had offered. Some months ago, they had persuaded her that a trip into Epsom while the sales were on would be well worthwhile.

It was two fifteen when Mr Lawson called out from downstairs.

'Almost ready,' Paula called back, taking another quick glance into the long mirror which was set into the door of the wardrobe; she was satisfied with what she saw. She was wearing a black cashmere twinset over a black slimline skirt that reached right down to her ankles, and the only jewellery she wore was a gold cameo brooch her mother had given her on her eighteenth birthday. Her high button boots were black, as were her silk stockings. Her outdoor coat was dark brown but she had sown a black armband on to the sleeve. The Windsmoor coat had been an absolute bargain, thanks to Esmé and Joyce. Joyce had also lent her a tight-fitting hat that was black with a small veil. The hat would certainly help to keep her abundance of thick auburn hair under control. She was wearing very little make-up and only a touch of a very pale lipstick because she didn't want to give her father the chance to show his disapproval.

She had tried hard to look her best for her mother.

'Thank you,' Paula said as Mr Lawson handed her into the passenger seat. By the time they arrived at the church there were a number of cars lined up in the road outside and a lot of people all dressed in black. Her Uncle Paddy made a beeline for her and she was in no position to avoid him. Mr Lawson had by then driven off.

Moments later the hearse arrived. The car which was following seemed at a glance to be carrying four or even five big men, one of whom Paula could see was her father. Forcing herself to remain placid she was glad to slip her hand through her uncle's arm as they walked through the church doors and on down the aisle, following behind the first mourners. The front pew was soon filled and Patrick and she slipped into the second row.

Paula kept her eyes lowered and instantly sank to her knees and began to pray. When she felt ready she straightened up and took a seat next to her uncle. She didn't look around but she could hear people rustling their clothing and moving their feet. Who were all these people? Why had they never visited their house when she had been growing up? Were they here because they knew and loved her mother or were they here on her father's say-so?

The coffin was now positioned directly in front of her, raised high, covered with the most beautiful flowers, the heavy scent of which was filling the church. All she could think was that her mother had gone and she herself had not remembered to buy any flowers for her. Too late now, for even as she struggled to accept that, it was as if a blackness was closing over her. Summoning all the strength she could muster she made a silent promise. *Mum, I will come back when all these crowds are not around and I will bring you flowers, not a wreath but a pretty posy and I will talk to you, light a candle for you and there will just be me and you on our own.*

She never got an answer but then she had never expected one. If only she could feel the closeness of her mother, but even the warmth of that emotion eluded her.

Surrounded by all these people, all she felt now was loneliness and despair.

Her Uncle Patrick made to hold her hand but she moved away from him and stayed that way throughout the service. Although Paula listened to the sermon, sang the hymns, closed her eyes and gave the right answers to the prayers that the priest recited, she really wasn't there in spirit and by the end she was starting to feel light-headed.

Before she knew it the coffin-bearers were lining up ready to take her mother out to the graveyard. Paula had been gripping her hands so tightly together that her fingernails had dug into the back of her hands. She lifted her hands to her face, she felt her uncle's arm go round her shoulders and she felt powerless to resist his attention.

By the time they were all filing out of the church, Paula had herself under control, at least to a certain degree. The priest acknowledged her as if he knew her and, making the sign of the cross in front of her, he said, 'Bless you, my child.'

Patrick had a firm hold of her arm as they walked slowly allowing several of the mourners to walk pass them until she said, 'I am sorry, Uncle Paddy, but I need to find a toilet.'

'We know where it is, just off to the left of the porch.' Two middle-aged ladies smiled at her. 'We're going there. Come along with us.'

Paula needed no second invitation, and she accompanied these friendly souls. After she had used the toilet, she told a white lie. 'I need to go back into the church to light a candle,' she said, her voice little more than a whisper.

'Will you be all right on your own, or would you like us to come with you?' the elder of the two ladies asked, showing friendly concern.

'I shall be fine. I won't be long; I'll soon catch up with you.' Paula did her best to sound convincing.

When they left her, Paula sat in one of the now empty pews where she waited for a while before leaving by another door.

The sky was greying and she knew that before long it would be dark. Where would she find a telephone booth? She needed to phone for a taxi, she was telling herself when she heard a child's voice cry out, 'There she is, Mum, look – there's Auntie Paula.'

Oh, dear Jesus, what a good friend she had in Laura!

Laura was running down Blackshaw Road, holding tightly on to the hands of her two boys, Jack and Ronnie. Jack, the eldest boy, broke free from his mother's grasp and flung himself at Paula. She wrapped her arms tightly around him and held him close. Oh, it felt so good to be wanted. Jack raised his head and held it back until he knew she could see his face, then he said, 'We thought you'd gone off in one of them big black cars; we didn't wanna miss yer cos me gran is getting tea ready for you.'

'Oh, Jack,' was all that Paula could mumble because Laura had by now wrapped her arms around the two of them and Ronnie was complaining that he was being ignored. All cuddled up together in a mass of twisting arms, Paula felt this kind of a welcome was exactly what she had needed. She couldn't think why she hadn't arranged to go to the funeral with Laura in the first place. Eventually they sorted themselves out and with the two boys in the centre and Paula and Laura at either end they all held hands and started to walk.

Soon Paula said, 'Thanks so much for coming along today.'

'Of course! The notice about the funeral was in the local paper so I took a chance. Mum and me thought you might be in need of a friend.'

'Oh, you darling girl. Never more so, believe me.' Paula sniffed, doing her best to wipe away the tears that were streaming down her face.

Laura stood still, then stepped back and looked into Paula's tired face, and it was then that she sensed what an ordeal all this had been for her. 'Come on, my love, let's get you back. What you need is a good strong cup of tea.'

'I was thinking of going straight back to Ridgeway . . .' Paula said hesitantly.

'Is that what you want, or do you just feel it is your duty?'

Neither . . . Oh, I don't know,' Paula said, doing her best to smile. 'Mr Lawson kind of guessed that I wouldn't want to go to the wake and he told me if I came to you and wanted to stay the night that was fine by him.'

'Well, there you are then.'

'I will have to phone him, to let him know that I am all right.'

'Of course, but you can do that later. Come on, boys, best foot forward, let's get yer auntie home.'

Nineteen

Molly Owen had been on tenterhooks for the past hour. She worried about Paula O'Brien just as much as if she were one of her own. Poor kid, she hadn't had much of a life even when she was at school. Her mother had married beneath her – even a blind man would be able to tell that. Dainty and ladylike was how she would have described Frances O'Brien – Frances Stevenson that was. She had been born to upper-class parents, brought up in a posh detached house in the Fishbourne Road area where the lady of the house paid other women to clean their doorsteps and polish their brass door-knockers. How on earth had their daughter ever come down to marrying a bloke like Mick O'Brien? A great hulk of a man who could put the fear of God into you with just a look. All the neighbours knew that Frances was terrified of him, and it was common knowledge she'd walk barefooted on burning coals if he told her to. But that was her choice, her own business, but the way that man treated their only child was criminal and no mother worth her salt would have stood by all these years and let him get away with it.

Molly was getting impatient. 'They should be back here by now,' she murmured, fearing the worst. She got up from her chair, went to the window and looked up the street. Where on earth were they? Her Laura was a good girl, the kind of daughter that anyone would thank the Lord for. This morning she'd been undecided as to whether or not she should go to the church.

'Mum, I won't interfere,' she'd protested when Molly did her best to persuade her not to go anywhere near the funeral. Molly had told her that Mick and Paddy O'Brien and all their Irish relations would be there, that it would be like being near a time bomb, but she wouldn't budge. Laura had gone her own way and she'd taken the kids with her to boot! 'I'll stay in the background. I promise I will, Mum, till I see what's 'appening, but I have to let Paula know that we are there if she needs us.'

That's what she'd promised. *But what if a rumpus should break out?* Molly wondered. *My Laura an' me two grandchildren, what could they do?*

Glancing at the clock Molly saw it was a quarter to five. *They'll all be frozen to death if they stay out much longer. I'll go an' open the front door,* she decided, walking up the passageway like a cat on a hot tin roof. She hadn't quite got there when the letterbox rattled and a small hand came through the opening, caught at the length of string that held the key and pulled it through. Never had she been so thankful to hear her grandsons arguing as to who was going to turn the key in the lock! Suddenly the door burst open and there they all were, presumably safe and sound. 'Thank the Lord for that,' Molly murmured.

'Gran, Gran, we found Auntie Paula and we made her come 'ome with us cos we told 'er you was going to 'ave tea ready for all of us.'

'You did right an' all, you clever pair.' Molly showed her appreciation and her relief by swamping the boys in her arms and smothering them with kisses.

'Oh, leave it out, Gran!' Jack protested loudly. 'Yer can kiss Ronnie all yer like cos he's only little but I'm too big for all that silly stuff.' Laura and Paula were just coming through the door and they heard Jack's comments.

All three women couldn't help but laugh.

It was a delicious tea that Molly had laid on, with corned-beef sandwiches, some egg and cress and some fish paste, but it was the big trifle that the boys had their eyes on.

'Bread first,' their gran warned. 'After that you can have trifle and then if you've any room left I've got all sorts of cakes in me larder.'

There was a solemn mood as the women watched the boys eat and drink their home-made lemonade.

Watching Paula, Molly was troubled. This grown-up young lady looked so sad, which of course was understandable given that she'd just been to her mother's funeral. How she wished she could grab hold of her, take her in her arms and cuddle her as she would do with her Laura from time to time. Paula had just lost her own mother and she had no family, at least not on her mother's side.

The silence was broken by a quick rat-a-tat-tat on the front door. 'Who the 'ell would be using our door-knocker?' Laura cried. 'I was just about to talk to Paula about her mum's funeral, so Mum, we don't want any neighbours coming in now.'

'I wasn't thinking of inviting them, whoever it is. You give the boys their trifle while I go to the door.'

There was much laughter as Laura ladled trifle into two bowls and Jack and Freddie began to quarrel over who had got most of the chocolate bits off the top.

Loud voices could be heard, so Paula raised her head and Laura told the boys to be quiet so that they could listen.

'And I am saying you *are not* stepping over my threshold, not the state you are in. Look at you, you're drunk an' you're only here to make trouble, but let me tell you, Paddy O'Brien, it's not gonna 'appen, not t'day an' certainly not in my house!'

The conversation had been clearly heard and Paula made to rise.

'Stay where you are,' Laura ordered sharply. 'My mum is well able to sort that one out.'

'How did he know where to find me?' Paula asked with a sob in her throat.

'Come off it, Paula, everyone knows we've always been the best of friends and that my mum 'as always treated you as one of 'er own. Your dad came 'ere asking for your address but Mum saw him off with a flea in his ear. Think about it, love; this would be the first place your dad would tell him t'look.'

'Yes, I suppose you're right. I shall have to make sure that no one follows me back to Raynes Park. I wouldn't want my father causing a conflict at Ridgeway. Mr Lawson would send me packing and then where would I be?'

Laura was flabbergasted. 'Christ, Paula, you ain't got much faith in the bloke you work for if you can sit there and say he'd send you packing. It would be a lot more likely that he'd see yer ole man off so quick his bloody feet wouldn't touch the ground. Your Mr Lawson knows the law, doesn't he? And from what you tell us he's good t'you and that's because he appreciates the way you take care of his boys.'

Laura's outburst was cut short. The front door was slammed with such vengeance it seemed as if the whole house shook.

'I wish your Fred had been here,' Molly said to Laura, huffing and puffing as she came back into the kitchen. 'That Paddy

O'Brien's temper will land him in a load of trouble one of these days. I remember him as a young man and he always was a bad lot, a real hothead. How your mother ever came to be tied up with that family beats me. A proper lady, Frances was, you could tell by the way she talked and she made sure you always spoke nicely, didn't she, Paula?'

'So 'ave yer got rid of him?' Laura shouted, not giving Paula a chance to reply.

'Well, yes, for the time being at least.'

'Molly, did he say what he wanted?' Paula asked, and the pleading note in her voice was noticeable.

'Obvious, ain't it, my love? He thinks you ought to 'ave gone back to the 'ouse with yer dad. All his family are there and seems they 'ave been asking about you. I told him that if that had been what you wanted you'd be there now. You're over twenty-one and old enough t'make yer own decisions.'

'Thanks, Molly. I am sorry to have brought all this trouble to your house.'

'Now that's enough of that sort of talk. How many times do we 'ave to tell yer that this is yer home whenever yer feel the need? I am sorry that yer mum has died, but at least it has given us the pleasure of seeing you. I know yer mum would be pleased that you came to us. Don't you think so?'

'Oh, Molly, thank you for that. Yes, I know she would be happy knowing that I am with you, but it seems as if I am forever having to say thank you for all that you do for me.'

'Then, lass, for Christ's sake, stop saying it and treat us as if we are bloody family. Have yer got that?'

For a moment Paula was shocked and she just stared at Molly, for this was the first time she had ever raised her voice to her.

Molly wasn't finished. Still with her voice high, she said, 'I asked you if you 'ad got that? And I want to know if you 'ave.'

'Yes,' Paula answered meekly.

'There's a good girl, and t'prove yer mean what you say I'm gonna let you make a nice fresh pot of tea.'

Laura raised her eyebrows and with a grin she said, 'You might live to regret that you've been initiated to being a fully fledged member of this family.'

That little incident had set Molly thinking. Paula had bucked up courage, broken away and found a new life for herself, but she was going to find it a lot harder to end her relationship with her father for once and for all. Especially now, with his wife gone, he'd be looking for Paula to come back home and keep house for him. She'd be a damn fool if she even considered it, Molly declared silently to herself.

The tea things all cleared away and now with a chenille tablecloth in place the three women sat with the boys and they played Snakes and Ladders and Ludo and when they tired of those games Molly produced a couple of packs of cards. Beat Your Neighbours Out of Doors was a popular game and from there they went on to Snap. However, the game of Snap turned out to be a bit boisterous as the boys threw their cards in the air if one of them shouted 'snap!' more often than his brother. At last Laura said the boys must soon start to get ready for bed but promised they could stay up until their father came home in order that they might say goodnight to him.

It was almost seven o'clock when Fred walked in, surprised but pleased that Paula was still there. Laura explained that Paula had been on the phone to Mr Lawson and he had been in full agreement that Paula should stay overnight with her friends.

Paula affirmed that she felt confident enough to leave the twins because Esmé Wright had offered to spend the night at Ridgeway. 'Peter and David both love Esmé; it's not like she is a stranger and besides she'll be company for Joyce,' Paula said, making sure that Fred knew she hadn't just deserted the boys.

'And did the funeral go well?' Fred asked, showing his concern.

'As well as these things can go, yes. I suppose I should say it all went well.'

'Until that bugger Patrick O'Brien decided to come knocking on our front door looking for Paula, would you believe?'

'What! Paddy O'Brien came here?'

'I just said so, didn't I?' Molly answered back quickly.

'Well, all I can say is I wish I'd been here!'

'Well, I think it's just as well that you weren't,' his wife piped up. 'Mum said he was blind drunk, could 'ardly stand up but she saw 'im off good an' proper without any help from us.'

Fred didn't want this conversation to be continued in front of his two lads. There would be enough gossip going on tomorrow, outside the school gates and then up the market, with all the O'Briens' dirty washing being done in public.

'Come on then, boys, it's up the wooden hill to Bedfordshire.' Stooping low he added, 'Climb up on to me shoulders, Ronnie, an' we'll gallop up those stairs. I'll come back for you, Jack, in about ten minutes.'

There followed noisy goodnights to his parents, grandma and Auntie Paula. Then all was repeated when Jack's turn came except that he needed to be reassured that Paula would still be there when he woke up in the morning.

Molly always served dinner at seven thirty sharp. Tonight it was a quarter of an hour late and she was getting flustered, even though she knew her lamb casserole wasn't coming to any harm. Since midday it had been slowly simmering away in the oven which was set at the side of the fire-grate. She had mashed the pot of boiled potatoes and transferred them into a vegetable tureen, so she only had to strain the cabbage and the peas. The other vegetables had been added to the big black casserole earlier in the day.

Molly had removed her tie-around pinafore, washed her hands and face, combed her hair and was now ready to feed her family. With everything set out on the table and the adults seated around the table she said, 'I hope you like braised lamb, Paula.'

Paula had been lost in thought but was startled out of it by Molly's question. 'Love it,' she said hurriedly. 'My mum used to cook it often, but I haven't had it for a very long time.'

They ate in a companionable silence, for they had to do justice to Molly's cooking. Paula was the last to finish eating and she grinned as she scraped up the last of the vegetables from her plate. 'That was so good, Molly, the meat just fell off the bones.'

'You 'ad better have saved enough space for some pudding.' Molly laughed. 'While the oven was going I made a bread and butter pudding an' I threw in loads of sultanas.'

'I'll make room,' Paula said, patting her tummy.

'It's good to see you eating so well; you look good,' Laura told her.

'Well, I don't go short of anything at Ridgeway. Joyce Pledger is a good cook.'

'I thought when you first went there you said Joyce was the housekeeper?'

'Yes, she was when Mrs Lawson was alive, they employed Joyce before the twins were born. They also employed a cook in those days. Now though Joyce does anything and everything – she helps me with the two boys and I help her wherever she needs me. Esmé Wright comes in three or four times a week. She does the cleaning, but she is always willing to step in if needed. Because of Esmé I can have some time off from time to time. Joyce wouldn't want to be left in sole charge of the boys.'

'It's good to know you've got a bit of adult company,' Molly remarked.

'It works both ways. Poor Joyce, there was a time when she was planning to get married, but her fiancé was killed in France, and she still gets upset because his body is lying in a grave so far away.'

'That is sad,' Molly agreed, 'but there must be hundreds of women who lost their men in the war and now face a life of loneliness.'

Doesn't make it any easier on Joyce, Paula was thinking, but she kept that thought to herself.

The bread and butter pudding went down a treat and Fred said he wouldn't hear of the women doing the washing up, and said it was the least he could do.

'Peace at last,' Laura sighed as they settled down in the front parlour each with a strong cup of tea in front of them. Fred drank his tea almost straight down, got to his feet and said, 'Well, you three ladies seem well and truly settled and no doubt you've got more than enough to talk about so I'm off down to the pub. Game of darts and a pint or two works wonders for a bloke that's been slogging his guts out all day.'

Laura looked up at him, raised her eyebrows and said simply, 'Fred!'

Twenty

Molly didn't even bother to switch the wireless on because Paula had complained that her head was aching. She had given her a Beecham's powder to take with her coffee and told her to lay back in the armchair and have a good rest. Poor Paula. It certainly had been a tough day for the lass and Paddy O'Brien turning up here had been the last straw. True, she hadn't let him in to see Paula but it just went to show how determined that family was to find out where Paula was living. Paula was sitting with her hands screwed tightly into balls and her head hung low. Molly was watching her not daring to even think about what was going through her mind.

'I guess today has brought memories rushing back from the past,' Molly ventured.

Molly's suggestion had startled Paula, but she quickly said, 'Lots that I would rather forget all together, but seeing my father today and my Uncle Paddy has stirred the whole episode up again. It's as I've told you before, Molly; no matter how many times I go over and over in my mind as to what exactly happened to me I cannot bring to mind the order in which things took place. I know it was a long time ago, yet I am still convinced that the whole affair was unjust. Today has only served to remind me that I am not over it. I still feel bitter because not once, before or since, have I ever been given a chance to defend myself. My mother could have given me answers, had she chosen to. Now she never can.

'Would it help to talk about it?' Molly asked cautiously.

'Oh, I don't know!' Paula answered, more abruptly than she should have. 'I'm sorry, Molly,' she quickly went on. 'At home my year-long absence was never allowed to be talked about. I was convicted of being immoral, wayward and unpredictable, not by any court of law but by the priests that my father had such faith in. God knows I tried often enough to get my mother to discuss it with me, and now, well, I don't even have that straw to clutch at, do I?'

Laura and her mother gazed at each other, longing to offer comfort to Paula yet not knowing how to begin. It was a while before anyone spoke again and when Paula finally did, the tone of her voice was enough to pull at Molly's heart strings.

'I know I shouldn't be raking this all up again but today has brought it all surging back through my mind. Some time after I had turned fourteen I was released from the asylum I'd been sent to and was allowed to return home. I promised my mother that I would not delve too deeply into the whys and wherefores of how I came to be sent away. I've kept that promise until now but only because I knew she was afraid – but I didn't and still don't know exactly why. Sadly my mother has gone now, but it means that promise no longer applies and I can openly ask why was she so afraid of the truth. My father must be involved because my mother was absolutely terrified of what he might do if she did talk to me. It was the same for me. If I ever dared to ask a question and my dad was around, he only had to look at me and I would be petrified. Truly, Molly, I am not exaggerating. At times he frightened me so much I swear my blood ran cold.'

'You don't have to tell us anything if you don't want to, Paula. We are not asking for an explanation, only trying to help you in any way we can. You've 'ad this 'anging over you since you were fourteen years old and if you ask me it's about time the truth was brought out into the open.'

'Since I was thirteen, actually,' Paula muttered. 'All the time I was in that hell hole it was like a pain inside me, because it was not my fault that I came to be pregnant and I knew it was so unjust that I was sent away. Out of sight and out of mind – at least that's how it always seemed to me. And, Molly, you wouldn't believe how many times since I have needed to talk to someone about it. It seems so easy to say, "Wipe the slate clean and start again." That's what they told me when I left the asylum. But how can I when what was on that slate is still such a mystery?'

Laura felt it was time she brought herself into this conversation. She had loved Paula since she was a small girl, couldn't love her more if she'd been her blood sister, and it was making her heart ache to see her so troubled. This affair should have been sorted out years ago instead of letting it drag on, eating away at Paula like some stinking disease. No matter how bad the truth

turned out to be it couldn't be worse than all this torment that
Paula was being put through. It wasn't as if there was an end in
sight. It had dragged on now for over eight years and it was time
someone helped Paula finally to get at the truth. Maybe, with
Paula's mother gone, this might just turn out to be the perfect
time. At least Frances O'Brien wouldn't have to fear her husband's
intimidation any more. What a shame the poor woman wasn't able
to speak from the grave!

The three of them sat staring into the fire. Paula was still
grasping her coffee cup with both hands when Laura spoke up. 'If
you're so sure it will help you to dig up what happened to you,
then fire away. I promise you, Paula, and I mean it, nothing of
what you tell us will go outside of this room.'

Molly Owen sat up straight in her chair nodding her head vigor-
ously. 'And what my Laura 'as just said goes for me too, believe
me, you can rely on that.' She said it with such determination that
it made Paula jump.

'I do believe you, Molly, but will you still think so highly of
me when I tell you what I remember? Will you still be happy to
have me in your house?'

Molly grabbed the poker and started to jab away at the fire.
'Dammit, Paula, do you think so little of me to even think that I
might turn on yer?'

Paula rose from her chair and crossed the room to kneel at her
friend's feet. Placing her hands on Molly's knees, she stayed still,
remembering how kind this woman had always been to her, and
how often she had turned up at this house crying and frightened.
It had never bothered Molly Owen. No questions asked. Just drew
her into her arms, soothed her and made sure she knew how
welcome she was. She stayed still for a while, feeling the joy of
Molly's hand pacifying her as she stroked her long hair and from
time to time patted her back.

Reluctantly Paula got to her feet, went back to sit in her chair
and after a few moments she drew her handkerchief from the
pocket of her cardigan, wiped it roughly around her face and then
blew her nose. 'Well, although from time to time I have told both
of you bits and pieces of what I remember, this time I think I shall
start at the very beginning.

'You already know about the party that my mother held on my

thirteenth birthday, where we played some games and my father made me what he called a special ginger drink . . .'

'Yes, go on,' Laura urged.

'I didn't like the drink. There was a lot of it and it burned my throat. My dad got angry, said he could never do anything right for me and that I was ungrateful and that I was never loving enough towards him . . .'

Silence dragged on for a full minute before Laura asked, 'So then what happened?'

'I drank all of it.'

'May God above preserve us all!' Molly exclaimed fiercely.

Laura was thankful, because by the look on her mother's face she had thought she'd been about to let rip with a few choice four-letter words.

'Paula, love, have you remembered yet what happened next?' Molly asked, sounding a lot more composed than she actually was.

'No, only that after we had played more games, I was very tired and all my friends were getting ready to go home. I think it was my mum who suggested my dad should carry me up to bed . . .'

'Christ Almighty, you were thirteen years old! Who in hell's name would think of carrying you up to bed?' Molly's voice was a roar and her cheeks were bright red.

'Calm down, Mum, you look as if you're going to explode. Please let Paula finish what she has to say,' Laura almost begged.

'It will take a long time for me to tell you everything, but already I feel better. It is as if I have opened the door to the cage but I am still not sure if I can come right out of it. Do you want to bear with me?' Paula asked sounding for the first time as if she were in control of her own feelings.

'Yeah, you carry on, love; you're doing well,' Molly quickly declared.

'Well, as I told you, I woke up next morning bleeding and sore. I knew it couldn't have been my time of the month because I'd had one only ten days before. My mother was furious, yelling at me to get moving and wash myself and tidy up my bedroom.

'So as you know, about a month after the party I started to feel queasy in the morning and had to run to the bathroom to be sick. It was about that time that my parents started to row like cat and dog and my father hit me, hurt me really badly, and that was the first time he had ever hurt me. I've told you before about the weird things he'd done to me, things that my mother wouldn't talk about except to say that he was my father and he had the right to check on how my body was developing.'

Paula stopped talking again, Molly covered her face with both of her hands and Laura was visibly trembling.

Taking a shuddering breath but tilting her head defiantly, Paula started talking again. 'The next couple of weeks were horrible, both my mum and dad said it was my fault, and he called me a "bloody little whore".'

It tore at Molly's heart but she had to ask, 'Did you realize you were pregnant?'

'Of course I didn't! It was 1924. I barely knew the facts of life because no one ever talked about such things and if they did it was only in whispers. All I got from my parents was that I was wicked, sinful, and that what had happened to me was my own fault. My father had never been one for fun and laughter but he had, until now, shown a weird kind of indulgence towards me, even professing from time to time that he really loved me. From that day on though he made my life intolerable, a fact which seemed to add fuel to the flames of my mother's growing hostility. "Please tell me what I have done wrong," I would plead, as day after day I was confined to the house – no school, no outings, not even a walk around the block – and as their resentment towards me grew the way they looked at me was awful, so full of hatred. I kept out of their way as much as possible but it was very hard.

'The confinement to the house didn't last too long. Very late one night when I was in bed my mother came upstairs and told me to get dressed. I asked so many questions but my mother wouldn't answer any of them. They both kept up a stony silence. Then two officials came with a car and I was to be taken away. Can you imagine it? I cried, yelled at them, even tried kicking my dad as he pushed me towards the front door. Neither my mother nor my father raised a finger to prevent me going and needless to say no goodbyes were said.' Paula stopped talking, too choked to continue.

Molly hesitated. All this was tearing Paula apart. It must have been simmering for years. Now the death of her mother had brought it all back and by the look of it was turning Paula into a quivering wreck. Something had to be done. But what? She wiped the tears from her eyes with the corner of her apron. 'It doesn't bear thinking about,' she loudly declared.

Paula ran her tongue round her dry lips.

'Go on, Paula,' Laura prompted gently as Paula seemed to be wavering. All this was very difficult and painful for her but surely it was better to have it all out in the open.

'It seemed to me that everything was happening in the middle of the night. The car stopped and the two gentlemen walked, one each side of me, leading me into a huge church. I had no idea where we were, only that the interior of this church was so vast and intimidating that it was enough to scare the wits out of any child. To me, to have been brought there under cover of darkness by two men I had never seen before, believe me I didn't know what to do or who to call on to help me; I was absolutely terrified. I was led up to the high altar, told to kneel down and a heavily built priest laid his hands on my head, gave a blessing and prayed that our Good Lord would see fit to forgive my sins.

'I was then told to go and sit in the front pew. I did and from where I was sitting I could hear most of the whispered conversation that took place between the priest and the two men that had brought me here. The priest was explaining that since war had been declared in 1914 the Tooting Bec Asylum had been taken over by the London County Council and was now home to mentally ill patients and young women who had fallen by the wayside. The board of guardians for the Tooting military hospital had decided their premises were to become a home for the poor. They, too, had discovered since the war had been started, many unmarried mothers were in need of shelter and many young women had consequently found themselves locked away within these walls and forced to earn their keep.

'It turned out that it would be at least a month before a place in the military hospital could be offered to me. Yes, "offered" was the word used by the priest! As if I had a choice. I had to spend a whole month in that asylum.'

Molly shuddered. 'Paula, that's enough for now. You, my darling girl, are in need of a strong drink, and now I come to think of it, that's what we all need. Come on, Laura, move yerself and come and help me make three hot toddies.'

Laura stood up, patted Paula's shoulder and muttered, 'Best idea my mum's 'ad for a long time! Neither of us are going to disagree with that decision, are we?'

Twenty-One

Laura came back into the front room to see Paula once more seated on the floor, leaning backwards with her back against her mother's legs. Molly was stroking Paula's lovely auburn hair. Paula's eyes were closed and for the first time since she had started to talk she looked peaceful. Laura had been going to complain that her mother had supposedly been going to help her make the toddies but she hadn't the heart to disturb the pair of them.

Setting the tray down on a side table Laura poured a good measure of whisky into each glass, added a heaped spoonful of brown sugar and then from the small tin kettle that she had quickly boiled on the gas stove she added the hot water and gave each glass a thorough stir.

'Here you are,' Laura said, holding out a glass and interrupting Paula's troublesome thoughts.

The three of them sipped away at their drink, each deep in thought, and it was Molly who finally broke the silence. 'Paula, do you feel you want to carry on?' she asked, distress still obvious in her tone of voice.

'Yes, Molly, if you're willing to listen; there isn't much more left to tell, but the facts will speak for themselves.'

'You do feel better for having started to speak out, don't you?' Laura asked warily.

'Yes, thank you, Laura, and I'm ready to carry on.' Paula drank the last drop of her hot toddy, wiped her lips with her handkerchief and told herself she felt better for having had that drink.

'From that church I was taken to the asylum and I was kept there for four weeks. An experience I wouldn't want to have to go through ever again. I won't even begin to describe the noise, the cold, the dampness and the smell of that place but the memory will stay with me for ever. I just never came to terms with why I was there. It was as if the whole world had turned its back on me and no one would tell me why. Such a mixture of human beings! There were huge brutish looking men that scared the living daylights out of me and there were also women so ragged and thin they looked like skeletons, but worst of all were the young-sters, many of whom would mess themselves and the excrement was left sticking to the backs of their thin legs.

'I think for me it was the loneliness that wore me down. I tried hard to make friends but when I attempted to speak and be friendly the females of all ages jeered. "La-de-dah" and "posh bitch" were the nicest names they called me. Mostly the young women appeared to be real Cockneys, and no matter what the warders threw at them they courageously faced each day as it came.

'During the time I was there I was examined by two different doctors and told I was twelve weeks pregnant. Over and over again I was questioned by social workers who practically begged me – and some who would have gladly used force – to name the father of the child I was carrying. There wasn't one person who ever said they believed me when I said that I was totally unaware as to the identity of the father. I really wish I did know; it would stop all of my suppositions.'

Molly latched on to that straight away. 'Oh, so you *do* have an idea as to who it might have been?'

Paula sighed heavily before she answered. 'I'd be lying if I said different. Don't you think over the years I haven't lain awake at night asking myself that same question? I'm grown up now and I am not in any way simple – or at least I hope I'm not. I was sitting next to my father when he gave me that drink so he must have put a drug of some kind into that glass and it knocked me out good and truly.'

As Paula lowered her eyes Molly continued to look at her, sensing again what was going through her mind now, but deciding she'd let her be the one to say it.

'I know what you and Laura have been thinking and I don't blame you in the least. Of course I have considered the possibility that it could have been my own father who raped me. But I shy away from that thought every time, because I think I would want to die if it were true.'

Paula had spoken so softly it had been hard to catch all of her words.

Laura felt that someone should ease the tension that was growing by the minute. 'Maybe the truth really is not as horrible as you fear. Do you remember if there were any teenage boys at that party?'

'Yes, like I told you before, there were a couple, and we played some games together . . .'

'Paula are you sure your father never touched you, you know, in a sexual way . . .?'

'No, Laura. I've told you about the weird way he made me strip off my clothes but . . .' Paula couldn't go on. Her cheeks were flaming and big tears were rolling down her cheeks.

Molly was on her feet in seconds and her arms were flung around Paula. 'Ssh, ssh, love, we're gonna stop this right now. We'll always be 'ere if you do want to continue with this, but enough is enough for one day.' Turning to her daughter she said, 'You, my gal, 'ave gone too far – those kind of questions are none of your damn business.'

Relief had unfurled some of the knots in Paula's head, but now they were tightening again because she felt awful causing friction between her best friend and her mother. 'Please, Molly, and Laura, you've both been wonderful to me. I should never have been able to get through today without you two being there for me. Laura, the least I can do is be candid with you. My father would often say I needed to be chastised "good and proper", was how he put it, whenever I had said or done something that displeased him, but no, apart from locking me in my bedroom and sitting there staring at me naked when I was growing up, he never once abused me, not sexually anyway . . . Now, shall I carry on?'

'Only if you're sure you are up to it,' Molly said gently.

Paula did her best to smile as she nodded her head. 'After four weeks I was transferred to the military hospital, my stay there was for only two weeks and then again I was consigned to a place known as the Hut, which had recently been built in the grounds of the hospital. At least it didn't smell so horrible and the patients, as we were known, were mostly sane and were able to work – and believe you me,' Paula said, glancing at Molly, 'we did have to work, sometimes eighteen hours a day and on very little rations of food. I used to think that the days of Dickens were long gone. How wrong I was!'

'Why did you have to stay in that place for so long? Wouldn't your parents have you home?' Laura was finding it hard to believe what she was hearing.

Paula's laugh was hollow.

'I had to pay back for my keep. It was backdated from the day those two men delivered me. I owed the authorities for my bed and board.'

'I can't take all this in. Anyone would think you were a criminal,' Laura said harshly. 'Were there other girls in there with you?'

'Lord, yes, some were younger than me, a lot were older, not all were pregnant – some were what they called "loose women", others were serving a sentence for having repeatedly been caught thieving.'

'You never said it was a prison!' Laura sounded more shocked by the minute.

'It wasn't. The powers that be apparently convinced the magistrates of their benevolence. All wayward women who entered their doors would be helped to see the errors of their ways and hopefully when discharged they would become pillars of the community.'

'So all of you had to work, did you?'

'You did if you knew what was good for you. But please, Laura, don't ask me to give you a description of the jobs we were told to do, you would be physically sick, really you would.'

'What about the conditions, were you looked after and fed well?' Laura asked.

Paula could not resist; she gave a cynical sneer. 'Oh yes.' Then quickly she added, 'On the days when we were allowed to work in the Hut, it was bearable. We sewed calico dresses, uniforms for the inmates and were given a big bowl of soup and two thick slices of bread for our dinner. It was the smell I just couldn't get used to. I stank. I knew I did but there was nothing I could do about it. On the first day I was there my hair had been cut so short, they had all but shaved my head and I was so upset. Later on I was glad they had. Hygiene wasn't a priority in that place. There wasn't a night I didn't long for a bath. And always the noise, so many people squashed into small spaces, coming and going, you couldn't count them all. Worse of all was the clanging of all the metal doors.

'The worst time of all was when the baby was about to be born.'

As Paula made that last statement there was no mistaking the sob in her voice and Molly herself felt choked just looking at her. She was such a lovely girl, gentle, kind and considerate. Why oh why had life dealt her such a terrible hand? The shocking, traumatic things she had had to endure for months on end would have been enough to send any young girl mad, yet Paula had come home and for six years she had lived entirely under her father's thumb. Never allowed to live her own life. Mick O'Brien had most days even walked her to and from the job she got at Boots the Chemist. It had taken time, nearly six years, but that lass had shown that even a worm will turn!

'Mum, are you all right?' Laura was tapping her mum's arm.

'What . . .? Oh, yes, of course I am.' Molly shook her head, telling herself to pay attention to what Paula was saying and to stop thinking about what might have been.

'Carry on, Paula,' Laura hastened to say. 'Me mum was just doing a bit of daydreaming.'

'I was going to tell you about when I went into labour. Not one person had told me what to expect, and I had never felt so alone. I got no help and certainly no sympathy.' By now Paula was visibly shaking and neither Molly or Laura said a word. After giving her nose another good blow she got up from her chair and started to pace the floor.

'It was a boy,' she finally said. 'They took him away, right there and then. I never even got a glimpse of him. Still, I couldn't have looked after him; I had no milk and I was so weak. By the time I was able to get out of bed and go back to work, the baby was gone. I had no say in the matter; he'd just been taken away. I did ask if he had been adopted but no one in the whole place, not even the doctors, would answer my questions.'

Molly Owen was an easy-going woman. She liked a contented life and rarely did she lose her temper. But once in a while, when she felt strongly about something, she'd put her foot down very firmly and all her family knew she meant what she said. There was no arguing with Molly when her mouth was set in a firm line and her jaw stuck out.

'Bastards – 'aven't these people got any feelings at all? All that bloody secrecy, didn't it bother you? It must 'ave felt like you were getting shot of him.'

'In a way that is exactly how I did feel. I didn't want him. I was relieved that there'd been no milk in my breasts for him. That way I never bonded with him at all.' When Paula saw the look that Molly was giving her, she quickly added, 'I prayed that good people would have adopted him and learned to love him dearly. I didn't even want to hold him – how could I when no one to this day is willing to admit that at least one man raped me? Maybe there was more than one . . .'

Paula was leaning forward, her face to the wall, her gorgeous red hair hanging down loosely over her face and shoulders and she was sobbing her heart out, great sobs that were racking her slim frame.

Molly too had tears streaming down her weather-beaten old cheeks. 'Oh, you poor lass, you poor lonely child. Come 'ere, come on, turn around and let me hold you.'

Paula did as she was told. 'One way or another you've certainly 'ad one helluva day. I've put a stone hot-water bottle in yer bed, and the boys are staying in my room for the night so you've got their room.'

Twenty-Two

Paula was seated at the kitchen table watching the twins eat their breakfast.

Yesterday, the minute she had put foot inside the house, her heart had soared. On her arrival back at Ridgeway she found Jeffrey Lawson had already left to go to the City but a welcome-home party of Esmé, Joyce, Peter and David was more than enough to convince her that she had been missed.

Oh, how glad she was to be back at Ridgeway! The pleasure of having had the boys swarming all over her during the day, an hilarious bath time, then into bed and a story to be read followed by hugs and kisses and 'goodnight' repeated several times because the boys were reluctant to let her go. She hadn't realized just how much she had missed them.

Too busy feeling sorry for yourself and raking up old and frightening memories, she chided herself. However, she had firmly made her mind up and there was nothing going to stop her, no matter what it took. One way or another she was finally going to forget her fears and do her best to unearth the truth. With her mother gone, the fact that in her efforts to discover the truth she might discover some really devastating details involving her father no longer seemed to matter. Having made that resolution she wasn't about to let the shameful events of her past cloud the fact that she now had a wonderful life, here and now, where every day she felt wanted, needed and loved. No, she would not let anything spoil all of that.

Over the past two weeks, since her mother had died, thoughts of her father had re-entered her mind unbidden. Suddenly, though, with all the questioning and unveiling of events that had taken place so long ago, she had become aware that her own imagination was tormenting her, possibly even more than the truth would. Did she really believe that? One thing was for sure: she needed to take control, set things in motion if she were ever going to get to the real facts of what had happened to her all those years ago. If she didn't – if she just let all the memories lie – she was going to live to regret not having persevered enough. A sudden thought crossed her mind: she might even pluck up enough courage to ask Mr Lawson's advice. After all, he was a barrister, but – yes, always there had to be a but – wouldn't that mean she would have to reveal to him all of her sordid past? Probably. Well, *that* she could never bring herself to do. To even think about doing so made her feel dirty. Whatever would he think of her? He had put his faith in her, trusted his two boys into her care. How could she even contemplate disclosing the raw facts of how she had been put away for a whole year for being pregnant when she had been only thirteen years old?

Finally accepting that no answers were going to drop into her lap, she decided she would wait a while, let the dust settle again, enjoy where she was and what she was doing here and now. In other words, for the moment, she meant just to live for the day.

A happy, uneventful week had passed. The weather today was bright but really cold. Nevertheless Paula had decided some fresh air was essential for her and the twins and her suggestion to spend some time in the park had been greeted with much lively enthusiasm. They made a colourful trio as they set off, well wrapped up in heavy coats and strong little boots on the feet of the twins, they were all wearing woolly hats and long scarves. The twins' scarves were wrapped once around their necks, crossed over their chests and tied behind their backs. Paula's scarf was knotted under her chin. Peter's hat and scarf were bright red, David's royal blue and her own woolly set was purple. They would be easy to spot in a crowd!

The twins soon found little playmates and Paula was talking to a trio of mothers when she saw Patrick O'Brien coming quickly towards her. Breaking away from her companions she excused herself and with great trepidation walked towards her uncle.

'At last I've caught up with you,' he harked as he approached her.

'Uncle Paddy,' she said, nodding her head and feeling as disturbed by the fact that Peter and David were riding on the roundabout nearby as she was that he had found her.

'Paula, at last, your father and I cannot understand why you should want to avoid us. All we want is what's best for you, and to do that you have t'put the past behind you, come and visit your father and be friends with the family. If you don't, well . . .'

The tone of his voice, so threatening as he uttered that last unfinished sentence, had her remembering that occasionally he forgot himself and showed what a vile temper he had. She answered him, sounding much shakier than she would have liked.

'Uncle Paddy, I've got a whole new life now. I'm old enough to make my own decisions, I can—'

His hand came up, palm flat, fingers spread wide, and she thought he was going to slap her. He must have thought better of it for he dropped his arm to his side and loudly said, 'Paula, you're not listening to me. If you don't stop all this stuff and nonsense we shall have to take strides to stop you. It's not what we want to do, but if you force us, well, so be it. I promise you, you won't like it.' He finished the sentence on a high note, shook his head hard and glared at her.

Paula was shocked. She couldn't believe it. He was threatening her! Which could only mean one thing: he and perhaps other members of the family must have something to hide. Anger such as she had never known before and didn't know how to control was rising up in her. To stalk her like this, to openly make threats. Why? Merely to reunite her with her father? To make her part of the family once more? Why suddenly was her uncle mixed up in this at all? What the hell was it to do with him? She just wanted to run, get away from him before her own temper got the better of her. This was something she had to seriously think about later, when she had managed to calm down.

The roundabout had come to a halt. One of the mothers was helping the twins to climb down.

Be friends with the family. Why now? Her father had visited Ireland from time to time but as far as she was aware her mother had never gone with him. Thank God she'd left home when she had, otherwise as things stood now she'd have been left alone in that house with her father and she didn't even want to think about what might have happened then.

'Paula, Paula,' the boys cried, running towards her. 'May we go on the swings now?' they yelled.

Paula summed up every ounce of her courage. 'Get out of my

way, Uncle Paddy; I have to see to the twins,' she said, pushing past him and breaking into a run.

'I understand why you're angry,' he called after her, 'but you don't have to work looking after somebody else's children, your father will welcome you home with open arms.'

'I bet he would,' Paula muttered as she caught hold of David, swept him up in to her arms and twirled him round and round.

'Swings, swings, please, Pauly!' Peter was impatient.

Setting David down she took hold of Peter's hand and walked with him to the swings, lifted him into the chair-like seat and made sure he was secure.

'Me next,' David demanded irritably.

'How about asking nicely and saying please?' Paula quickly reprimanded him.

'Oh, sorry Paula, please may I have a turn on the swings?'

Again she lifted him up and hugged him tightly. 'Of course you may, David,' she said, settling him in the swing next to his brother. She stood back a few paces, watching. They were strong enough now to propel themselves backwards and forwards, and even though they were not able to reach any great height they seemed well pleased. She sighed softly, no longer feeling quite so angry. Oh, she loved the pair of them so much; there wasn't a thing she wouldn't do for these two darling boys.

'Paula, I'll be in touch. Your father wants to see you, he needs you.' From yards away Paddy was shouting at the top of his voice.

Later, when she was giving the boys a drink from the fountain and then making ready to return home, she lifted her head and looked around. Thankfully there was no sign of her uncle.

'Paula, why was that man shouting at you before?' Peter quietly asked as he slipped his hand into hers.

'Yes, I heard him too, I thought he was nasty man, did you know him?' David didn't want to be missed out.

Faced with such innocence she had little choice but to tell the truth.

'That man was my uncle.'

'Then why was he shouting at you?' Peter asked, his voice sounding very fearful.

'He isn't a very nice man, so he and I don't get along, but it was a long time since I had seen him until we met again at my mother's funeral.'

'And did you find out that you still didn't like him?' David piped up again, determined not to be outdone by his brother.

Paula found herself smiling; the children's simplicity was amazing. Between them the twins had summed up the incident so well. 'Yes, David, something like that.'

Later that evening the boys had had their early supper and were ready for bed. The usual ten-minute romp with their father was in progress when Peter, out of the blue, said, 'Daddy, when we were in the park today Paula's uncle came to see her, but she didn't like him.'

Before their father had a chance to form an answer, David said, 'I didn't like him either, he shouted and got angry and Paula was upset.'

'Well, you both brought Paula home safely, didn't you? And that's good, you are two brave little soldiers and you can see that Paula is all right now, so come on, up to bed, say goodnight to Joyce and Paula will be up to tuck you both in as soon as I come down.' He pulled his sons toward him and ruffled their hair before saying, 'I bet I can beat both of you up the stairs.'

The rush to get to the staircase turned into a stampede, and toys and books they were meant to be taking upstairs ending up scattered all over the floor.

Left on her own, Paula felt dazed. The twins between them had certainly opened a can of worms. Now what? Jeffrey would surely have questions to ask and, more to the point, he would be looking for explanations.

She never had expected this!

Obviously the truth, as far as she knew it, would have to be told. Probably, if she were honest, it was long overdue. Would she be told to pack her bags and leave straight away? She had to act normally. As soon as their father came down she would have to go upstairs and read a story to the twins.

And then what?

Would Jeffrey Lawson want a showdown before they sat down to dinner or would he wait until after they had eaten their evening meal?

Either way, what difference would it make?

Having read the twins their story and seen them settled down for the night, Paula went into her own bed-sitting room. She took off her blouse and skirt and had a wash before pulling a grey tailor-made dress from her wardrobe. The dress had straight lines with a v-shaped neck and long sleeves. It also had a small slit at the side that reached up from the hem of the dress to just below her knee. Sitting on a stool in front of her dressing-table mirror she applied a light coating of make-up, sprayed a little perfume behind her ears, and then spent a considerable amount of time doing her hair. When she had the sides swept up to her satisfaction she wound the rest of her hair into a wide knot on top of her head and secured it safely with a huge tortoiseshell comb with an edging of small imitation diamonds. For the finishing touch she took a long emerald-green chiffon scarf from her drawer, wound it round her neck and tucked the ends into the neckline of her dress. The emerald green served to highlight her green eyes, showing them to be very attractive. Emerald was a colour that suited redheads perfectly, one thing she had learned from her mother a long time a go. She felt better for having taken pains while deciding what she should wear for this evening.

God alone knows how this day will end, she thought as she made her way down the wide staircase. If her feeling of foreboding was anything to go by she could well be on her way to the railway station before the night was out. She wouldn't be able to blame Jeffrey Lawson, whatever his decision. She hadn't lied to him but then neither had she told him the truth.

'Joyce is ready to serve dinner, so shall we eat and talk later?' Jeffrey asked as she walked into the dining room. Paula nodded her agreement, thankful that he had made the decision for her. She was also grateful that Joyce was eating with them tonight; it would save a lot of strained silences.

Roast leg of lamb with an assortment of vegetables was followed by blackberry and apple pie served with cream. Jeffrey passed on the dessert and Joyce went to the kitchen to fetch cheese and biscuits for him. Joyce rarely drank coffee at night, as it tended to keep her awake, but as if she had sensed a strained atmosphere this evening, she quietly queried, 'Where would you like your coffee?'

'Oh, in the lounge I think, Joyce, but I'll come to the kitchen and fetch our tray. Are you sure you won't join us?'

'No, thank you,' she sensibly answered. 'I'll clear the dishes away and then I'm going to have an early night. I have a new book which I am going to start.'

'Well, if you're sure,' Jeffrey said, 'I'll say goodnight now, Joyce. It was as always an excellent meal, thank you.'

'You're more than welcome, sir. Goodnight.'

Jeffrey often wished he could persuade both Joyce and Paula to stop referring to him as 'sir', but then again it was a very unusual set-up in this household, even so he was forever grateful that things had worked out the way they had. Normally staff would not eat and associate with their employers quite so casually. However, he needed no reminding that these two women, and also Esmé Wright, had all come to his rescue when he had badly needed so much help. He *still* needed their help, probably more so. Between these three women, their help had enabled him to keep his baby sons under his own roof, to watch them grow unto delightful little boys, to be able to check for himself that they were well fed and clothed and, most importantly of all, to ensure that they were both happy and that they felt loved. And if all of that caused him to relax all the known rules, even to socialize with his employees, then he was more than happy to do so. In fact he counted himself extremely lucky. His home was well run. His washing and ironing done to perfection, well-cooked meals were always served and if business kept him in London overnight he had no worries as to how his boys were faring. All in all he felt he had much to thank the Lord for.

'Goodnight then, Joyce,' he said once more as he picked up the tray that now held coffee for two and made his way into the lounge.

He had felt the tension, even anxiety that Paula was feeling and as much as he wanted to hear the reason why she had been accosted by her uncle he too felt there had to be an underlying motive in his sudden appearance.

Paula poured the coffee, then passed the cup and saucer to him and he set it down on an occasional table that was positioned beside his armchair. He was wearing a navy blazer, an immaculate white shirt, very smart grey trousers and he looked very handsome.

He leaned forward to look at her and then started the ball

rolling. 'I want to ask you something,' he said cautiously, 'and if you don't want to talk about it, then I promise we shall leave the matter there.'

Paula made no attempt to speak; she was anxious to hear the question.

'Can you tell me why you were so upset when your uncle apparently turned up out of the blue today?'

Having already gone through this with Molly and Laura, Paula had already decided she was going to seek advice and now to keep Mr Lawson in the dark any longer would not only be unfair, it would be totally wrong.

She took a deep breath and slowly let it out before saying, 'If you can spare the time, Mr Lawson, I would like to tell you quite a few details about my life before I came to work here. I know many of the disclosures that I am about to make I should have told you about when you first interviewed me. I held back for many reasons, the main one being I badly wanted you to give me this job.

'So, I should tell you that for the previous six years before I came here I had been unhappy living at home . . . and for the year prior to that, which was 1924, I had spent four months in an asylum for the mentally ill and then for a further ten months I was detained in what had been a military hospital during the war. As soon as the Armistice had been signed a Board of Guardians had decreed this hospital should be used as a punishment block for misguided loose women, thieves and female vagabonds . . .'

Paula felt she had said enough – in fact she was getting tired of hearing her own voice. It was less than a week since she had gone through these sordid details with Molly and Laura.

Jeffrey sat quietly for a moment, absorbing what Paula had said. To say he was shocked would have been an understatement. He had listened to every word intently, nodded several times, but had not yet asked any of the questions that were crowding in his mind.

Just looking at him, Paula decided he was an amazing man.

The house suddenly felt strangely quiet after they had listened to Joyce going upstairs. 'Well, that was quite a revelation,' Jeffrey said as he placed his coffee cup down on to the tray. 'I certainly didn't expect that kind of news, and I cannot begin to understand how that awful fate fell upon you any more than I can begin to visualize what a traumatic experience it must have been for you, especially as you couldn't have been much more than a child. How old you were you, Paula, at the time when you were held in these dreadful institutions?'

'I was thirteen years old,' she stated, her voice little more than a whisper.

Jeffrey was shocked at what he was hearing and genuinely bewildered. 'Would you mind if I ask you to tell me what all of this had to do with your uncle unexpectedly turning up in the park today? Apparently you were not at all pleased to see him.'

'What happened to me began on the day I reached thirteen. Since my mother's death and her funeral I have had the opportunity to speak with my dear friend Laura Wilson and her mother, Molly Owen, who live quite near to my family home and who have always been there for me when I needed a friend. They knew I had been sent away for a year, and they had missed me, but they had not known *why* I was sent away because even I have no memory, not even the slightest recollection of what happened to me . . .'

'Paula, why are you trembling? What is worrying you so much?' Jeffrey Lawson had never felt so out of his depth. He did not need telling that this girl's story was one of sheer horror. He couldn't have said why or how it had come about but he believed that anything she chose to relate to him would be the truth.

'Please, Paula, for the moment let's leave the past alone. Tell me, at this moment, what is worrying you the most?'

She looked at him and his kindness was her undoing. She covered her face with her hands and began to cry. The crying turned to sobs, sobs wracked her whole slim body. He rose from his chair and came to kneel in front of her. He took hold of one of her hands, placed his own big white handkerchief into it and told her to wipe her face. With only a slight degree of hesitation she did as he asked.

'Now, it appears to me that you have reached the end of your tether, so please will you just answer that one question. Right now, at this very moment, what is worrying you the most?'

It took a few seconds for Paula to form an answer and she waited until Jeffrey stood up and went back to sit in his chair. When finally she spoke the words came shakily from her mouth.

'The fact that I shall have to leave here now, leave the twins and probably never be allowed to see them again.'

Looking extremely serious he leaned forward and waved one hand through the air as if to wipe away her fears, then lightly he said, 'I guessed as much. Now, young lady, you listen to me. Have you judged me so harshly that you think I would turn you away from this household without a very good reason? It is not so long ago, when you left to go to your mother's funeral, that I had the same fears of you deciding you didn't want to return to us. Did I not convey those fears to you at the time? Did I not reassure you that we would not know how to manage should you decide to leave us? Come on, Paula, wipe away your tears and take note of what I am saying. Enough has been said for tonight; you and I will have a drink and then I want you to get a good night's sleep. Then tomorrow, I suggest you use one of the boy's exercise books and you write down the series of events that began when you were thirteen years old. It will be less harrowing for you and not nearly as embarrassing as having to relate your thoughts aloud to me. Tomorrow evening I shall carefully read them and I will offer you my advice. It will be up to you as to whether or not you take that advice, but I shall be here and will help in any way possible.

'Meanwhile, Paula, will you please try and remember that this is your *home*. Peter and David need you, I need you, and even Joyce would be lost without you – and come to think of it even Esmé would sorely miss you. Now, do we have a deal?'

Paula looked up him. He was smiling and slowly she smiled too.

'Deal?' he asked once more, holding out his hand.

'Deal, and thank you,' she replied taking his hand.

While growing up, Paula had never been allowed to be demonstrative but as relief surged through her she felt the impulse to throw her arms around Jeffrey Lawson and kiss him.

She was hard put to resist the temptation.

Twenty-Three

Alone in her bedroom Paula was delving through to the back of her wardrobe where she had stacked several items when she first came to Ridgeway. What she was actually looking for was a cardboard box that held some mementoes of her early childhood. She moved aside her attaché case. 'It wouldn't be in there,' she murmured, but smiled when her hand dropped on to a canvas bag that was closed with a long zip fastener. The box wasn't hard to locate; it was sitting on top of a pile of Girl Guide magazines in the base of the bag. Removing it she tipped the contents out and spread them over her bed. Every single item held a memory for her. Early birthday cards, hair slides and Alice bands, a certificate for having swum a whole length of the Balham Baths when she was six years old. 'Ooh,' she sighed as she lifted out a lace handkerchief that her mother had embroidered with the capital letter 'P'. She held the slip of white linen to her face. It wasn't her imagination; it did still smell of lavender, a smell she would always associate with her mother.

A narrow book that resembled a diary but wasn't. That was what she was looking for. When Jeffrey had suggested she make notes of what she needed to tell him the thought of this book had come to her. If she could find it, it would probably be exactly what Jeffrey was asking for. It wasn't among the bits and bobs that she had tipped out of the box and she was disappointed, but then she picked up the box in order to replace everything and there it was, lying flat in the bottom of that precious old cardboard box.

Soon after she had been released from that military hospital and started work at the age of fourteen and a half, the idea had occurred to her. She should make a catalogue and , to the best of her ability, record each and every incident that had taken place from the time she was taken away from home until the day she had been allowed to return. At the time she hadn't given a thought to the significance such a record might have in the future. Why had it taken so long for her to remember all these entries she'd made in this slim book? Never mind, she had it now and who knows, something might be written in there that she had forgotten all about. She wasn't going to start to read through it tonight though. Today had thrown up enough shocks for one day. She would do as Jeffrey had advised, and have a good night's sleep.

She was undressed and ready to get into bed when the temptation became too great. Just a peep, she promised herself as she slid in between the bedclothes, propped her pillows up, made herself comfortable and opened the book at the first page.

> *On the order of the priest I was taken to an asylum where I would he held for four weeks until a vacancy would become available in the military hospital.*
>
> *I cannot say which struck me as being worse: the noise, the dirt, or the inmates, who were really frightening.*
>
> *I didn't think I would be able to cope. I wanted my mum. Why had I been sent there? Told I had to see two doctors. Horror, because I couldn't believe what they were doing to me, but then they told me. Twelve weeks pregnant. I was going to have a baby. That wasn't the worst. They did everything they could to make me reveal who the father was. How could I tell what I didn't know? I explained how I had woken up the morning after my birthday party to find the bed sheets were bloody and I was so sore it was painful to walk. Body covered in bruises . . .*

Paula flinched, quickly closed the book and placed it under her pillow. In the daylight tomorrow perhaps it wouldn't make such horrific reading.

As it turned out it was a thoroughly miserable day, overcast with dark clouds, not at all suitable for taking the twins out. With breakfast out of the way Paula took them to the playroom and suggested that they all sit up at the table and do some drawing.

Brilliant idea, Paula congratulated herself as she left the two happy little boys with their crayons. Walking to the other end of the table she set her own writing materials out, sat down and opened her slim book on the second page.

Glancing quickly at the boys she sighed softly. She must read her own writing swiftly, not linger over it or even try to analyse any part of it; there had been too much of that going on in her head since she had lost her mother. She was doing this because Jeffrey had asked her to. Just the facts were all that he needed to know, then he would make up his own mind as to whether or not he was in a position to help her.

In that first long month I had hoped against hope that conditions in the military hospital would be much better. In some respect they were. All the inmates were female. Many were Cockneys and they kept the rest of us cheerful no matter what.

Work was harder and the hours much longer. Food was much the same as in the asylum. Monotonous and sparse. Breakfast: bowl of gruel, so thin it would have been easier to drink it rather than eat it. Midday meal: bowl of soup and a large hunk of bread, never with any butter. Dinner: one sausage and boiled potatoes, or cold corned beef, same potatoes, sometimes a kipper. We scrubbed floors, corridors and walls, we worked in the laundry and we sewed yards and yards of calico.

As the time for me to give birth drew nearer I became ill. A doctor said I had influenza. I was in a bad way. I didn't know what to expect. One morning my bed was sopping wet, girls told me my waters had broken, then came unbearable pain, soon told I was in labour. I was given no help, no advice and certainly no sympathy. It was hell. I wanted to die. I wanted my mum. The girls told me it was a boy. The people in charge took him away. I never saw him. Just as well. I had no milk. I asked if he had been adopted. Nobody would answer my questions.

Silly me, I had deluded myself that once the baby was born I would be allowed to return home. I had to stay and work for a further six months in order to cover the cost of board and lodging and to pay for the medical care I had received during my stay. In total I was kept in custody for fourteen months.

Paula closed the last page and leaned back in her chair.

It wasn't much of a chronicle – it didn't come anywhere near to revealing the heartache and the degradation she had been made to suffer – but it would suffice to give Mr Lawson the bare outlines of her story.

It was at that precise moment that Joyce put her head around the door and called, 'Who's ready for a mid-morning drink?'

The boys got down from their chairs and ran to Joyce. Peter said, speaking for the both of them, 'Hot chocolate!'

Joyce was by now standing beside Paula and as she looked into her face she felt alarm bells ringing in her head. 'My God, Paula, are you all right? You look absolutely drained.'

Paula thought drained was a very apt description; it was certainly the way she was feeling. 'I'll be fine once I've had a cup of coffee. I'll come downstairs with you and I'll make the chocolate for Peter and David.'

'You'll do no such thing,' Joyce answered quickly. 'You may come downstairs into the lounge where the fire is burning brightly and put your feet up for a while, and perhaps I'll toast a teacake for each of us.'

Two little hands shot into the air. The boys were clearly excited about the prospect of this unusual treat.

'All right then, come along with me. We'll leave Paula to clear up all this paper and pencils, shall we?'

'Yes, you both go along with Joyce and we'll leave all of this paperwork spread out on the table for now. Then later on when we come back you can show me your drawings.'

Paula's head was throbbing and she was never more in need of a coffee. Delving into the past was becoming far too much of a habit for her liking, she decided as she followed the others down the stairs.

Some time later Paula remembered that she had left her thin book lying on the table in the playroom. Making sure the twins were occupied she almost ran upstairs. It wouldn't do for Joyce or Esmé to find that book lying about!

The very thought made her shudder. If only her Uncle Paddy hadn't traced her, come into the park yesterday and upset everything for her. It wasn't Peter's or David's fault they had told their father of the strange man who had shouted at her because with their childlike faith they had thought their father capable of putting everything to rights. And of course she had so much to be grateful for: Jeffrey had shown her great consideration, he hadn't jumped to any hasty conclusions but had, without any hesitation, offered his help.

After he had read her diminished account, which would only give him the bare outline of the sordid details of her past, would he be of the same mind?

Inside the playroom Paula snatched up the slim manual and with great haste flew back downstairs and let herself into Mr Lawson's study. From a pigeonhole in his desk she took an envelope and slipped the book inside, sealed the flap and turned the envelope over, picked up a pen and addressed it to 'Mr J. Lawson'. As she left his study she stopped a moment and looked back: the envelope was lying on the blotter. He couldn't fail to see it.

As much as she longed to know the answer to so many questions and at this moment was grateful that Mr Lawson had offered his advice, she felt her mouth go dry and her heart quicken its beat. It was one thing to tell Molly and Laura all her intimate secrets, but Mr Lawson was her employer. Her whole future rested in his hands. Would he read what she had written and still want to help her?

She was ashamed to admit, even to herself, that she was afraid.

Tonight the course of her entire life might be decided. It may well mean that she would have to leave here and never see the twins again. Rejection was what she dreaded most. She had made so many friends within the bounds of this new life and Peter and David were the centre of her world. She gave herself a mental shake. She must simply be patient and wait until Mr Lawson had read her notes, then good or bad she would know what the outcome was going to be.

Twenty-Four

How am I ever going to get through this day? Paula repeatedly asked herself. Time and again she was tempted to remove the envelope with its cruel and revealing contents from where it was lying ready to be read by Mr Lawson.

The matter, however, suddenly was taken out of her hands.

Joyce, Paula and the two boys were sitting in the kitchen eating their lunch when Jeffrey Lawson walked in and with him was Esmé Wright. Excitement got the better of both Peter and David, they flung themselves at their father and then Esmé was given the same treatment.

Joyce got to her feet, all flustered. 'Oh dear, I haven't any lunch prepared for you, sir, is there anything in particular you would like? It won't take me long to rustle something up.'

Leading the boys back to the table Jeffrey was laughing at the concern his unexpected arrival had caused. 'Joyce, will you please sit down and finish your lunch? And as for you two lads, I know you are surprised and pleased to see me at this time of day but you are well aware that you should not have left the table without first having asked Paula's permission, so apologize to Paula and then get on with your lunch.' Turning back to Joyce he said, 'I met Esmé trudging up the hill carrying a large parcel so I stopped and gave her a lift, and now in return she is going to make us both a sandwich.'

'First I've heard of it,' Esmé chuckled, 'but your request is my command.' Still shaking with laughter she took off her coat and went to hang it in the hall cupboard. Jeffrey filled the kettle and to Joyce's dismay he set out two cups and saucers and prepared to make a pot of tea while Esmé, now back in the kitchen, was rummaging in the larder. For all Esmé's weight she moved lightly on her feet and the snack she had quickly concocted looked both delicious and appetizing.

Soon what had been four having lunch around the kitchen table had become six, and it was an enjoyable time once everyone had settled down. Paula was so deep in thought that she didn't at first hear Esmé speak. It was only when the boys said, 'Is that all right with you, Paula?' that she realized she had missed something.

Esmé touched her arm. 'Paula, I have just offered to take the boys up to Wimbledon Common for an hour or so; they can bring some stale bread and we'll fed the ducks.'

'Oh, no, there's no need for you to do that,' she answered hurriedly, getting to her feet. Then she caught the glance that had shot between Mr Lawson and Esmé and the penny dropped. It was no coincidence that Esmé was walking up the hill and he'd stopped to give her a lift. Neither was it by chance that he'd left his office and come back home in the middle of a working day. Between them it had been prearranged, as had been the offer from Esmé to take care of the twins for the afternoon. Mr Lawson had come home with the sole intention of reading her notes and taking the opportunity to discuss the matter freely with her without the boys around to ask awkward questions.

She looked at Esmé and managed a smile. 'Well, if you're sure, there are a number of things I could be getting on with.' Her voice faltered and she knew her cheeks had turned red.

Mr Lawson stayed where he was, watching her, still saying nothing.

As she helped Joyce to clear the table she was aware that today it would be make-or-break time. Mr Lawson was about to find out that she wasn't the good, clean-cut young lady he had assumed she was. He had taken her into his home, given her full charge of his young sons and now every single part of her wretched past was going to be made known to him.

Having placed the dirty china into the sink she turned back to face him, and caught a response as their eyes met. Was it sympathy that she saw? And even if it was, how long would it last when he knew the truth?

'Did you manage to do as I asked?' His voice was low and he actually smiled.

'Not exactly,' she answered. 'I remembered that some years ago I wrote a kind of a diary – or perhaps a record would be a better word, because it was a brief account of what happened to me in the order that I remembered certain things having taken place.'

'And did you bring this journal with you when you left home?'

'I wasn't sure at first, then last night I sought out an old box of mementoes and the book was at the bottom of the box.'

'And you are going to allow me to read it?'

'I've put it in an envelope and it is lying on your desk.'

He started to move and Paula was almost on the point of blurting out that he shouldn't read it after all. Not sure whether she wanted to laugh or cry she chided herself for being so ridiculous.

He saved the moment. 'On my desk, you said? I'll go through and read it in my study.' Then he added, 'Paula, if I call you when I have finished reading your notes, will you come into the study and join me, please? We won't be disturbed there.'

As he looked at her, waiting for an answer, she felt the heat flaring up in her cheeks again. 'Yes, certainly,' she said. 'Thank you.'

Well aware that it wouldn't take him long to read her notes, Paula remained in the kitchen, wretched with anxiety. The course of her entire life might be decided within the next hour. If Mr Lawson's attitude changed, how would she be able to cope? She would just have to try and brazen things out and pretend it didn't matter if he asked her to leave.

But the truth is finally out. I will never be allowed to carry on here as if nothing has happened.

Paula was still seated at the kitchen table, staring into space and torturing herself with so many negative thoughts, when she heard the door to the study open and his footsteps coming across the hall. Her heart was thudding, her thoughts still racing in too many directions.

'Paula, would you like to come and join me?' His voice sounded deadly quiet.

'Oh, my God!' she gasped, putting a hand to her mouth.

'Please, Paula, calm down and come with me.'

She couldn't look up, didn't want to meet his eyes, fearing what she might see. She didn't want this to be happening, but it was too late to stop it now. He finally knew the truth about her. 'I can't listen to what you have to say, I just can't.' She lifted her head and her lovely face was ravaged with tears and so much pain.

'Paula, I understand how you must be feeling . . .' The very sight of her made his heart melt. 'You've been brave enough to get this far. Please, let's talk.'

The dread of what he must surely be about to say made her feel sick. How could she have let this happen? Living such a pack of lies, as she had been doing for such a long time now, had been like living on the edge of a volcano. If only she had faced the truth at the beginning! How could she have been such a fool? Letting Mr Lawson read all the horrific details of her early life, what had she thought it would achieve?

'Paula, please.' He reached out and gently touched her cheek and it was then that something melted inside her and Paula recognized her own vulnerability. She so badly wanted him to tell her that he could make all the bad things go away and for him to say that she could stay here and continue to look after the twins.

Never having felt so helpless, Paula stood up and followed him into his study.

Having seen her comfortably seated in an armchair, Jeffrey took a chair and pulled it round until he was facing her. Without any hesitation he said, 'I have read your short version of events and I fully realize that they only touch the tip of the matter. I instinctively know there is so much conspiracy and manipulation behind these facts. It is absolutely appalling that for all this time you have had to deal with these matters entirely on your own.'

His voice rang with such sincerity that Paula's heart lifted. Was she dreaming? Might he even believe that she was telling the truth?

'Paula, if I am to help you I must ask you some questions, is that going to be all right with you?'

She pressed a hand over her mouth and tried to force herself to think straight. It took a few seconds for her to get the words out. 'I'll do my best,' she eventually said, nodding her head for emphasis.

'Your written exercise only begins when you were taken from your home; may I ask if you can recall the events which led up to that awful day?'

Paula sighed softly as she began to tell him of the party her parents had held for her on her thirteenth birthday. She didn't have to ferret through her mind to bring out all the details: each one was itemized in her memory. Jeffrey Lawson was listening intently. Sometimes he shuddered, another time he hung his head so low it was almost resting on his knees, but not once did he interrupt her and not one word did he utter. It was only after she related the part about her father having made her a special ginger drink and had pressed her to drink it that she stopped speaking.

Silence hung heavy between them until Paula said sharply, 'I was young and gullible and, yes, I worked it out for myself that my own father drugged me! I do remember that having drunk the ginger wine we played a few more games until I became very tired, but after that . . . nothing. If you were to offer me a king's ransom I could not tell you what happened to me after that.'

Still Jeffrey Lawson made no comment.

Coming to the morning after the party, Paula was embarrassed but she kept going, telling how her mother had ordered her to wash herself well, while she stripped the bed of the sheets that were badly stained with blood.

'Battered and bruised as I was, life in our house continued as normal for the next four weeks. Then I was cursed with morning sickness, although I didn't know it at the time, and the whole atmosphere changed. Even my mother turned on me, and my father said I had asked for it, that I was a little more than a whore in his opinion.'

More time elapsed as Jeffrey sat in silence, taking this in. Paula continued, 'That's about it. The rest you've already read about. I will add one more thing, although there is little chance of you believing me . . .'

'Hey, Paula, let's get one thing straight.' Jeffrey was holding up his hand and challenging her with his voice raised to full volume. His aggressive interruption had shaken her.

'Paula, you have to stop jumping to the conclusion that because other folk have expressed their disbelief in what you say happened to you that I shall be exactly the same. Now go on with what you were about to say and leave me to make my own decisions.'

Paula took a deep breath before she felt able to continue.

'At that time I had no idea that I had been raped and certainly had not realized that I was pregnant. You can say that no girl could have been that innocent, that I was naive and foolish, or you can resort to what my fellow inmates in the military hospital used to say about me: that I was wet behind the ears, green as grass, and too righteous for my own good, although they never said these things quite so politely.'

Jeffrey straightened himself up in his chair but it was still some minutes before he could bring himself to look at her, never mind voice his thoughts. Eventually he said, 'Paula, I am not going to offer you my sympathy, that never does anybody any good, but I will tell you I do believe every single word you have told me and I do feel for you and the despair which at times must have persisted. However, I don't intend to offer you false hope.' There was a long pause, then she heard the anguish in his voice as he said, 'I will help you, and that is a promise that I intend to keep. There must be records and such like regarding your detention and luckily enough I am in a position to gain access to them.'

'Thank you, I don't know what else I can say,' she responded softly.

'I hope we're able to produce some facts so you can finally understand what happened to you all those years ago, but in the meantime I do have a few more questions I need to put to you.'

'I understand,' Paula said in as firm a voice as she could muster. She felt bowled over and, although she would still carry the mental scars that the doctors and officials had inflicted, at this moment her anger and sense of injustice had been mollified by Mr Lawson.

'Did you never discuss this matter with your mother?' Jeffrey asked. 'Surely she must have known?'

'You'd think so, wouldn't you? She probably did, but she would never talk about it with me.'

Jeffrey frowned, apparently bemused by that.

'My mother and I were very close while I was growing up, but then everything changed after what happened on my thirteenth birthday. From the day she suspected I was pregnant she drew away from me. I knew how terrified she was of my father but I kept waiting and hoping that soon she would help me, tell me it wasn't my fault . . .'

Having said that Paula realized that she had never told Mr Lawson about the strange things her father had made her do from a very young age. Thankful that she had made that omission, she still felt her cheeks redden, for wild horses couldn't drag from her those memories. Telling Molly Owen had been one thing, but not Jeffrey Lawson – never him!

Jeffrey was looking vaguely bewildered and somewhat hesitant. 'I know what I am about to say will be horrible . . .' He paused and coughed to clear his throat before saying, 'Paula, it is indisputable that a man clearly had intercourse with you that night and I fully understand your need, even after all this time, to find out who that man was. I think we have established without a doubt that your father persuaded you to drink a glass of ginger wine that had been heavily drugged. Now I have to ask you, Paula, has it never crossed your mind that the man who raped you could have been your own father?'

Paula sighed and gave a bitter laugh. She looked straight into his eyes as she said, 'More times than you would believe, but I always try to tell myself that not even he would do such a thing.'

'Have you ever asked yourself why your mother became so disapproving of you?' Jeffrey persisted.

'I think she knew more than she ever admitted. I know it was my choice to leave home but I tried very hard to keep in touch with her, I truly did.' Paula met his gaze, pleading with him to believe her. 'She died before I could make it up with her, let alone get any answers from her.'

Again there was a long silence between them before Jeffrey reluctantly asked, 'Do you ever think about meeting your father, face to face, to ask all your questions?'

'Is that what you think I should do?' Paula asked, sounding doubtful.

'Oh, my dear Paula, that's not up to me. I know it would cause you a lot of pain but it might be worth it in the long run.'

Paula shrugged her shoulders. 'Well, we'll see,' she murmured. The very thought appalled her. But did she have any option if she really was determined to find out who raped her and why she was imprisoned for so long?

Watching the emotion showing on Paula's face, Jeffrey smiled. As yet he had no idea as to how he was going to proceed with this matter, yet he was determined not to let the matter drop. He was going to do his utmost to help in any way possible.

Seeming to realize that Paula needed a moment to collect herself, Jeffrey got to his feet and stepped towards her, saying, 'I don't know about you, Paula, but I think we have both earned ourselves a drink. Would you like something from my cabinet or shall we go and make ourselves a nice pot of tea?'

As Paula saw that he was smiling brightly, she smiled too. 'Tea would be fine, thank you, or as our Esmé would say, "I could murder a cuppa".'

As they walked side by side across the vast hall Paula reminded herself that this was her life now, this beautiful home and the twins, and she must hope and pray that she would be allowed to hold on to them. Her mother had gone. She couldn't come back to answer questions, but now, suddenly, it felt as if a great weight had been lifted from her shoulders and she didn't feel anywhere near so lonely or despairing.

Twenty-Five

It was Friday, the end of another week. Paula had told Peter and David that very soon now she was going to take them to a swimming baths and at that suggestion both boys fell into a fit of giggles.

'When Esmé comes in later on we'll ask her about it. All her children are good swimmers, or so she tells me, and I think it's to Mitcham Baths that they regularly go.' Their discussion was interrupted by a loud rap on the front door.

Joyce had just come down from upstairs and she quickly moved to open the door, had her usual word about the weather with the postman before taking the pile of letters from his hand.

'Quite a lot of mail this morning,' Joyce observed as she sorted through it on her way to Mr Lawson's study where she would leave it for him to deal with later. Abruptly, however, she stopped sorting and stood still. 'Paula,' she called, 'there's a letter here for you.'

'Letter?' Paula was instantly distracted and the look on her face became wary. She'd stopped watching for the post ages ago. Laura didn't write much, since Esmé covered for her and she was able to have regular time off and visit her friends. As for expecting or looking forward to hearing from her mother, even that anticipation was denied to her now. Now she felt tension rise in her as Joyce walked towards her and handed her the letter. 'It's postmarked London,' Joyce remarked. 'It looks very businesslike.'

Paula said nothing. The envelope was long and not very wide. Was that good or bad? She was hoping against hope that it was not from her father or from any member of the O'Brien family because, when she came to think about it, she knew surprisingly little about any of them. She turned the envelope over in her hands, and now it was her turn to study the postmark. Finally she thrust it straight into her pocket. She knew it would burn a hole there until she had a chance to read it. Whoever it was from she felt it was essential that she be alone when she did.

The dark clouds had persisted and by mid-morning the skies

had opened up and the rain was falling in torrents. Paula was watching the boys, who were in a mischievous mood today and she was in a quandary as to how to keep them occupied. Joyce sensed what was going through Paula's mind and she came to the rescue.

'I thought after lunch I might spend the afternoon baking; I could make all sorts of nice things to eat over the weekend when your daddy will be home and I'm fairly certain I heard him say that your Auntie Hilda and Uncle Andy would be coming so that means you will be seeing Freddie and Raymond.'

Joyce never got so much as a glimmer of enthusiasm, the twins were so engrossed with their toys, until she forced out a sigh and in a woeful tone murmured, 'I don't think I shall bother to attempt gingerbread men or brandy snaps or even chocolate fingers, they're all hard for one person on their own to make. Other things like fairy cakes are all right but you do need help to do those specialities.'

'We'll help,' chorused the twins, climbing all over their toys to get to Joyce and wrap their arms around her. Paula watched them and laughed, but above their heads she winked at Joyce and mouthed the words 'thank you'.

With lunch over and the boys settled happily in the kitchen with Joyce, Paula decided now was as good a time as any to go to her room and to read her letter.

Turning the letter over in her hands she was trying to decipher what she supposed was the name of the person or firm that had sent it. Unfortunately the franking machine had smudged the lettering and it was impossible to make it out. She set the envelope on her dressing table then climbed on to her bed, wrapped her arms around her knees, and looked at it, asking herself why was she being so daft. Why was she afraid to open it?

Paula slipped from the bed and picked it up, turning it round in her fingers, again studying the postmark, which still told her nothing except that it came from the London area. Sitting back on the bed, she slit it open with her finger, removed a single sheet of thick paper and swiftly read the letter-heading. It was from a firm of solicitors called Griffith & Perkins with a W1 London postal code, and at the bottom of the page there was a signature: Jonathan Griffith.

Paula blinked, took a breath and started to read the typewritten lines. She frowned over the legal jargon then the substance of the letter became clear. This legal firm had drawn up her mother's will and Jonathan Griffith was one of her two named executors. He pointed out that he was charged with calling in all her mother's assets, settling all liabilities and distributing all the monies to the benefactors. The next line had her sitting up straight. She, Paula Veronica O'Brien, was the main recipient.

A new paragraph also stated that the said Jonathan Griffith was charged by Frances O'Brien to deliver a letter into the hand of Paula O'Brien. The said letter was in their safe awaiting her attendance at the above offices. At her convenience would she please telephone, make an appointment to come into the office, where the matter would be discussed in further detail, a copy of the will would be made available for her to scrutinize and the said letter would be handed to her.

Well! That was a turn up for the books!

Paula folded the letter, placed it back into its envelope and laid it back down on the dressing table. Later she would give it to Mr Lawson to read. Meanwhile her head was buzzing with more unanswered questions. Why on earth had her mother left a letter for her at the solicitors' legal chambers? Come to think of it, the letter she had received today had been posted to Ridgeway, so how had they known her address? Her mother must have given it to them. So why leave a letter with strangers when she could have posted it?

Suddenly, for the first time since the postman had called this morning, Paula felt a surge of hope run through her. What if her mother had left behind answers to all of the questions she had been seeking for so long? Where she was now her mother had no need to fear the wrath of her father. Had she looked ahead and felt this was a way of speaking from the grave? Whatever, she could not wait to have Jeffrey's opinion on her letter and, after he had read it, hopefully tonight, she would telephone and make an appointment to go to London.

Meanwhile, not many miles away in Milner Road, the two brothers, Michael and Patrick O'Brien, were steadfastly drinking their way through a bottle of Irish whiskey. Only that morning Mike had received a letter from a London solicitor. The following result had left Mike O'Brien in a very bad temper.

And as the morning had worn on his mood had got even worse. It seemed Griffith & Perkins had also sent a similar letter to Paula. That the content of Paula's letter was far more advantageous than his own had been was like a red rag to a bull. The main recipient of Frances's will was Paula Veronica O'Brien!

More than a month had gone by now since Frances's death, and they hadn't heard a word from Paula or seen her since the day Patrick had accosted her in the park. Mike had known Paula would pay no attention to whatever his brother had to say and she most certainly wouldn't heed the fact that he'd asked her to meet up with the family. She was an ungrateful little bitch. Sneaking out of the house while he was at work, getting herself a job looking after some posh bloke's two brats. Especially now, her place should be with him. She knew he'd never cope on his own, yet had she visited to see how he was faring? Had she hell! Going on for almost two years and she'd never once been home. She had a new home, new friends and sod them that had cared for her, fed her and clothed her all those years since she'd been born.

She didn't understand what he had done for her – or for her mother come to that. Saved the Stevenson family a load of humiliation, that's what. It would never have done for it to be known that the daughter of posh city banker Stuart Stevenson was carrying a bastard. Oh no, the stigma would have been too much for a man like him. Losing face was something he'd never cope with. Over the years Frances seemed conveniently to have forgotten that she was four months' pregnant when he had married her – and it wasn't even his child she was carrying. Oh no, he'd barely been allowed to kiss Miss Prissy Frances Stevenson before their wedding day, let alone find out if his wedding tackle would fit. And what thanks had he received? A few hundred quid and a house! Marvellous!

Frances was an intelligent woman; she'd known what she was doing. The man she was engaged to, the man who hadn't waited to put a ring on her finger before he'd made her pregnant, had been killed in a railway crash in 1911. Mick had got to know Frances when she'd been kept a prisoner in the house, out of sight of neighbours' disapproving looks and their wagging tongues.

He and his brother had been doing some building work on the back of their large family home. Daft sod that he was, he'd felt sorry for her. Her father had taken him for a right mug, so he had.

But it hadn't all been bad. He'd come to love that baby girl. Frances just didn't understand how much. She'd never given him his own child: was it the Lord's will? Hard to tell. Frances would never discuss matters like that.

According to this blasted letter from the solicitors, his wife had left Paula not only the house and a considerable sum of money – apparently she'd had thousands of pounds tucked away ever since her grandmother had died, the deceitful cow – but to crown that lot she'd left letters, one for him and one for her daughter. Christ Almighty, what muck had she raked up in them?

Had she thought it all out, spoken from the dead and told his Paula the truth? If she had she was more spiteful than he'd even believed. She had promised she would never speak out. Suppose now that promise was abolished. And if so, what could he do about it? 'Bugger all,' he raved, as he tipped more whiskey into his glass and tossed it down his throat.

Paula had momentarily forgotten that she had confessed to Jeffrey Lawson everything that had happened to her during the year she had been incarcerated. Now, what with this surprise from the solicitors, her heart had nearly stopped in shock. Would she . . . could she bring herself to go to him again? Ask for more advice; ask for time off to go to London. Did she have any choice?

Dinner had passed off quite well that evening; the two boys were tucked up in bed and Paula was thinking, *it's now or never* as she tapped on Mr Lawson's study door.

Answering his call of 'come in' she turned the handle and walked towards where he was seated behind his desk.

Immediately he got to his feet and the same thought came to him as he had experienced during dinner. Tonight Paula looked even younger than usual, and perhaps more glamorous. She was certainly a beautiful young lady. Her eyes were bright, her smile wide, and both conveyed a generous amount of warmth, while her long, wavy hair appeared to be even more shiny than usual and she'd got it under control this evening by the use of a wide black velvet band. Her clothes were rather more colourful, but then perhaps she had decided not to wear mourning clothes any longer.

'Have you given any thought as to what you want to do?' he asked, coming round from behind his desk and walking to the door, which Paula had left ajar, and firmly closing it.

'Actually, I received this today,' Paula answered, pulling her letter out of the pocket of her long skirt. 'I thought if you could spare the time you might like to read it.'

He took the envelope. 'Would you like a drink?' he asked cheerily, waving her towards the big old sofa which was placed near the huge fireplace.

'No, I'm fine, thank you,' Paula told him.

'Paula, just for once do you think you might relax? Surely you know by now that I don't bite.'

Paula felt the colour rising in her cheeks again. Why did she go all sloppy as soon as she was left alone in his company? She didn't answer, she couldn't; she was tongue-tied.

Jeffrey moved across to his drinks cabinet and opened the double doors. 'Now then, Paula, I would like a drink but it would be very remiss of me to drink alone while I have you for company, so please will you join me?'

Paula nodded and sat down. 'Yes, please may I have a dry sherry?' Then looking around she told herself this study was probably typical of a successful barrister who brought a lot of his work home with him. It was a large room with a lofty high ceiling. Some of the soft furniture was slightly shabby but the office furniture was old, well kept and probably would be classed as valuable antiques, passed down from his grandparents she guessed. Against one wall two piles of files were stacked, each one tied with pink tape, and row upon row of books could be seen through the leaded glass doors of another huge cabinet. The rich heavy curtains had been pulled but Paula was aware of the gorgeous garden which lay beyond. She turned her gaze to where Jeffrey kept a cluster of framed photographs, recording all ages of the twins. Oh, and they did look so bonny! One very formal photograph had been there when she had first arrived and it remained today in the same place. It was of beautiful Sheila Lawson, Jeffrey's young wife. Beside it stood another photograph of Sheila dressed ready for a game of tennis. Paula sighed. Sheila had died far too young.

For some reason Paula felt comfortable here, and as Jeffrey handed her a glass of sherry she didn't feel in any way out of place. The room had an atmosphere that was rather like Mr Lawson himself, friendly but in need of a little help. She herself was feeling almost on top of the world tonight – optimistic, was that the right word? The solicitor's letter had buoyed up her hopes. The letter, written by her mother, now lay locked away in legal offices some-where in London. Was that going to give her the answers she had for so long been seeking?

'Cheers,' Mr Lawson said, breaking into her thoughts as he raised his glass of whisky and soda.

'Cheers,' Paula answered, raising her glass.

Jeffrey went back behind his desk and sat down. Still facing Paula he took a few sips from his drink and then set his glass down and withdrew Paula's letter from the envelope.

'Is it all right with you, Paula, if I read through this now?' he asked, holding the letter up in the air.

'Of course,' she answered quickly, settling herself comfortably in the corner of the big squashy sofa. She watched the expressions on his face change and even though at one point he raised his eyebrows, he didn't seem particularly surprised. He came to the end of the letter, laid it down on his desk, and looked up at Paula. 'As I understand it you have not been in touch with your mother, not seen her nor spoken to her, in all the time you have lived here.'

'That wasn't my choice – truly, I wrote regularly, asked her to meet me, but my mother chose not to come to any of my prearranged meetings.'

'So, no news of her in all this time?'

Paula shook her head. 'I did from time to time ask my friend Laura if she had seen or met up with my mother, but other than that I had nobody to talk to about her.'

'This letter,' he said, indicating it lying on his desk, 'was deliv-ered here to this address this morning?'

'Yes, it was.'

'Yet as far as you can tell nobody was aware of where you were living?'

'Well, none of the O'Briens were, they made that clear when I met my uncle at the funeral. Patrick must have followed me at some point; I don't for one moment think he came across me and the twins purely by chance.'

'I'm sure you're right, Paula. I also think your mother must have been a very astute lady. She has used a well known and respected legal firm not only to write her will but to be her executors. She also may well have used a private detective to discover your address. Before she would have been granted permission to leave any letters or articles in the safe of Griffith & Perkins she would have had to produce evidence supporting the fact that she was a person of stability and that she had assets.'

Paula looked perplexed by that. 'Is that what you think she did?'

'I certainly think it is a feasible explanation. Now why don't we drink our drinks while I sort out in my mind the best way for you to deal with this?'

Now Paula had to smother her laughter. He'd got everything so cut and dried and all without moving out of his chair or seemingly making any effort, but as he sipped at his drink he did look as if he were deep in thought.

Paula had drained her glass and was about to stand up and take her leave when Jeffrey became all businesslike again.

'What I propose we do is this: I will make a few telephone calls – I know *of* Jonathan Griffith but we have never met, however Anthony Perkins is an old friend, as were his father and mine, so that will enable us to be able to pull a few strings. We will then get in touch with Esmé, see if she is able to come in for the whole day on Monday instead of just the half day. If you agree you could travel up to town with me on Monday morning and I will see that you arrive at the appropriate offices safe and sound, then you will be able to conduct your own business. How does that sound to you?'

Paula was feeling slightly dazed. She nodded her head and smiled her thanks.

It was going to take a while for her to realize just how profound an effect this was going to have on her. *Dear God above, had her mother really left her some answers? And if she had, please give her the strength and understanding to deal with it all.*

Twenty-Six

Jeffrey was gazing at his sons lovingly. 'I confess I wasn't really keen to bring them to the swimming baths this afternoon,' he told Andy as he watched him climb out of the water and brush strands of wet hair away from his face.

'Best entertainment you can find for the lads, especially now that the best of the weather has gone,' Andy responded. 'I was just remarking to Hilda that your boys have taken to it like a duck to water. And as for having someone in the water to watch over them, you're dead lucky. Paula is a strong swimmer, isn't she? Even the lifeguards have been commenting on how good she is.'

Jeffrey flinched; he had seen the lifeguards watching Paula and he felt sure it wasn't only her swimming strokes that they were admiring. How badly he was regretting not being able to swim. And not for the first time he realized just how good Paula was for his boys in so many different ways.

Jeffrey called to Paula, 'I'm going to find an attendant, hire a bathrobe if I can, then I'll come back and help dry the boys and get them dressed.'

Andy Burrows was already out of the water and was waiting, ready to lift his youngest son Raymond out and up on to the side of the pool.

'Tell you what,' Hilda piped up. 'As soon as all of us are dressed, who's for going down to the Fair Green?'

Peter turned to Raymond with a puzzled look on his face. 'What's the Fair Green?'

Raymond splashed water at his older brother and laughing he said, 'You tell them, Freddie.'

'Just about the best fish an' chips in the whole world – that's right, isn't it, Mum?' Freddie said, gloating at his own cleverness.

'Absolutely, bar none,' his mother confirmed, 'so come on, you lot, get out of that water before you all begin to look like shrivelled up old prunes and we'll see about a high tea for all of us.'

Jeffrey came back, wrapped in a heavy white towelling robe

and his feet were bare. 'I got the tail end of that conversation,' he remarked to Andy. 'Are we included in this high tea?'

'Both of you are,' Hilda shouted at them. 'We need you to pay the bill!'

All four boys cheered, Hilda looked at Paula and winked, while the two men gave an exaggerated sigh.

It took a good half-hour before everybody was dried and dressed. As they came out of the main entrance there was a smile in Paula's voice as she said, 'We had a great time, didn't we?'

A whole chorus of voices agreed with her as they all sorted themselves out and clambered into the two cars.

The cars having been parked near to the Three Kings' Pond, they separated into groups, and all holding hands they crossed the road to the famous Hutchinson's seafood restaurant. They received a great welcome as they were led to a table for eight.

Paula felt she would long remember this day. It was like a family outing where everyone was happy and contented and very pleased to have each other's company. She felt totally at ease, part of the gathering and not just someone on the outside looking in.

As they left the restaurant Andy said they would do the swimming bit a whole lot more often in the future and Jeffrey asked if everyone had enjoyed their fish an' chips. Again the answer was unanimous, but the twins seemed anxious about saying goodbye to their friends, Paula thought, perhaps after they had helped Joyce bake so many cakes the day before.

Jeffrey came to the rescue. 'But of course they are all coming to tea. Don't worry, Peter, you won't have to eat all the gingerbread men yourself.'

Amid a great deal of laughter, another set of goodbyes were said and at last they went their separate ways, the Burrows promising to arrive about three o'clock tomorrow afternoon.

It had been one of the most enjoyable weekends that Paula could remember. Now on this Monday morning as she looked around at her fellow passengers on the train that was taking them up to London she was thinking that this was an entirely different world. Two thirds of the travellers were male. All wore dark suits, shirts that were mostly white and a sober-looking tie. Each carried a briefcase, some had a rolled umbrella and many wore a bowler hat, which they had removed on entering the carriage, placing it high up on the luggage rack. Many of the men were preoccupied with their daily newspaper, others had removed official-looking papers from their briefcases and were caught up in what Paula supposed was work. For these City-type gentlemen the day started early.

Soon after the train had pulled out of Raynes Park station the lovely scenery Paula had been staring at changed drastically. The wide open green fields disappeared, giving way to housing estates, shops and tall buildings. The nearer to London the worse the outlook became. Great blocks of flats, almost every balcony festooned with lines of washing, huge factories, the walls of which were blackened by dirt and soot from the frequent passing of the trains. By the time the train pulled into Victoria, Paula was feeling grateful that she didn't live within the bounds of London.

'I'm sorry I don't have time to come with you, Paula,' Jeffrey was saying as she struggled to keep up with his long strides. Everybody seemed in such a hurry – were they all so anxious to get to work? She kept glancing sideways, suddenly realizing he was taller than she had thought, and Paula felt proud to be with him. He was very good-looking. His face lean and strong, with his thick dark hair brushed back from his brow. He looked extremely smart, but then he always did. She chuckled to herself as she said under her breath, 'I'm glad he doesn't wear a bowler!'

'Paula, I shall see you safely into a cab and give the driver the address to which you are going. Also, after some time has elapsed, I shall put a telephone call through to Jonathan Griffith requesting that he ring me when your interview is over. Whether or not I will be able to come and fetch you remains to be seen. I do have a heavy schedule to deal with today.'

Paula stopped walking and Jeffrey turned his head in surprise when he noticed she was no longer by his side. She stared at him as he retraced his steps, closing the small distance between them. 'Whatever is the matter, Paula? This meeting is what you have been waiting for; you have to be brave. There are people ready to help you now, me included, but you have to be prepared to let them into your life. You have to learn to trust. Not everyone will let you down or disbelieve when you state the true facts.'

Paula stayed silent, for a long moment she didn't attempt to answer him. People were rushing by, the noise was deafening but suddenly she wanted to laugh out loud. Finally she managed to say, 'Mr Lawson, I am twenty-one years old. London does seem strange to me but I do have a tongue in my head and when my meeting with Mr Griffith is over I shall be quite capable of making my way back here to the station, getting on to the right train and going back home. Oh, and by the way, yes, you did give me my return ticket and yes I do have money enough for taxis, so will you please attend to your own daily grind and stop worrying about me.'

Jeffrey's jaw had dropped by the time she had finished speaking. He placed his briefcase down between his feet and placed his hands on to her shoulders and pulled her close. Then, lowering his head, he said, 'Paula O'Brien you never cease to amaze me!' And with that said he placed his lips on hers and kissed her. If he hadn't retained hold on her Paula would have fallen, she was that shaken. It was a moment before he did release his hold on her, then bending down he picked up his briefcase, took hold of her elbow and firmly said, 'Right, Miss Independent, I shall show you where the taxi-rank is and leave you to get on with it.'

Jonathan Griffith turned out to be something of a surprise to Paula, for she had imagined an older and perhaps stuffier elderly gentleman. But he was certainly a pleasant-looking man and only in his early forties she guessed as they shook hands and he led her into his large but very orderly and officious-looking office. He smiled and his handshake had conveyed a certain amount of warmth, all of which served somewhat to put Paula at her ease, but not entirely. She had known in advance that there would be tension, and she was aware that it was absurd, but that didn't stop her feeling keyed up and very anxious because at this moment she had no idea as to what the outcome of this meeting would turn out to be.

'You must have travelled on a very early train,' he said, following her in and closing the door.

Paula smiled her agreement. She didn't see the need for words and it was too early for her to let down her defences. First she wanted to hear what he had to say and find out just how much he knew about her.

'Would you like some coffee?' he asked politely, waving her to be seated on an upright chair which faced his leather-topped desk.

'No, I'm fine, thank you,' Paula replied.

The office was much more sophisticated then Jeffrey's study and it was light and airy too. The window behind Mr Griffith's desk looked out on to a small courtyard where benches were positioned under trees, and an ornamental pond in the centre completed a lovely setting. Paula still felt terrified at the thought of what her mother's letter might reveal, yet somewhere beyond the bewilderment she had felt ever since the letter had arrived on Friday morning, she was aware of feeling buoyed up by the very fact that at long last she might be given the chance to unearth the truth.

'Thank you for your letter and I appreciated you sending your condolences,' she said. 'May I ask how you knew where to contact me and if you have ever met my mother?'

Jonathan Griffith was relieved that this young client had opened the conversation. He had met Mrs O'Brien on three separate occasions, had admired her immensely but had found her affairs to be complicated. She had not asked for his advice and he had offered none; he had however consulted with his senior partner, Anthony Perkins and had consequently carried out Mrs O'Brien's orders to the very letter.

He raised his eyebrows as he replied, 'Yes, I met your mother more than once and in the written instructions that were handed to me by Mrs Frances O'Brien were contact details appertaining to where you were employed and apparently the same location was your permanent residence. I was also given to understand that neither of you had been in touch with each other for some time.'

'Not since I left home,' Paula replied hastily. 'But it was not by choice, at least not on my part.'

'Please, Miss O'Brien, don't distress yourself, your mother implied that the fault was entirely of her own making. She felt it was for your benefit.'

'Was she afraid of my father?' Paula immediately regretted saying those words; it was wrong to try and implicate this young man in her family quarrels.

Mr Griffith shook his head. 'Apart from business details your father's name never got mentioned.'

Paula looked puzzled by that. 'So you don't really know much about my father?'

'The need never arose. We were, and still are, acting solely on behalf of your mother. I have to confess that I was not involved in the writing of her first will; it was drawn up quite a few years ago. I first became an associate when she came to this office in order to change her will, which was approximately six months ago.'

'Did she give a reason for wanting it changed?' Paula asked.

Mr Griffith nodded sadly. 'She had been in hospital for a spell; she'd suffered a stroke. She wanted everything to be set out clearly and to be in order should anything happen to her. Mainly for you.'

Paula felt her heart miss a beat and the colour drain from her face. Why oh why had no one thought to tell her that her mother had been so ill? Laura must not have known, or she would have told her, Paula knew. Her father must have kept her mother's illness a secret. Tears were pricking behind her eyelids and she had to swallow hard before she was able to say, 'Why ever didn't you let me know she was so ill?'

'Please believe me, Miss O'Brien, I wanted to. I did suggest it, but your mother wouldn't hear of it. I don't have the right to go against a client's wishes.'

Paula was trembling; her hands were gripping the sides of the chair so tightly that her knuckles had turned white. 'She was my mother,' she whispered. 'The hospital should have notified me.'

'You were not her next of kin,' Mr Griffith explained as gently as he could. 'The hospital would have left that to your father.'

And that bastard deliberately kept that information to himself!

Realizing she was letting her thoughts and her temper get the better of her, Paula pulled a handkerchief from her coat pocket. 'I am sorry,' she said. 'It's just that . . . it wouldn't have hurt him, he could have told friends of mine that my mother was so ill, they would have contacted me like a shot. I just wish . . . Oh, what the hell – it's too late for wishing now, isn't it?' She blew her nose, and took a deep breath.

'Something happened to me a long time ago,' Paula found herself saying. 'Only my mother could have given me answers that would have helped to solve the problem and now I'll never have the chance to get at the truth.'

Mr Griffith was looking very concerned as he said, 'I think,

Miss O'Brien, you may be wrong in that assumption. There are two reasons why you are here today. One is for me to give you a copy of your mother's will; it will take some time for it to go through probate to establish the validity of it, but rest assured it is one hundred per cent watertight, and you are the main beneficiary. The second reason is the letter your mother instructed me was to be placed into your hands. From the little that she disclosed to me I have the feeling this letter may well hold the answers you are seeking.'

Having said that, he opened a drawer to the left of where he was sitting, removed a bunch of keys and got to his feet. 'I am going into the main office to collect your letter from the safe. It won't take me many minutes providing there is a senior member of staff on hand; it takes two keys to open that particular safe, you see.'

Paula was feeling slightly dizzy, and all she managed to say was, 'Thank you.'

It was no more than ten minutes before Mr Griffith returned yet it had seemed like ages to Paula. Grateful for the reassurance he had given her, she was conscious of her need to try and stay practical and not to let her mind be overtaken by her emotions.

'Here we are then, Miss O'Brien,' Mr Griffith said, laying a bulky envelope down on his desk and sounding a whole lot more optimistic than he felt. 'I do need your signature on this release form, if you wouldn't mind.'

He laid a small form down in front of her, handed her a pen and using his forefinger indicated the line along which she was required to sign her name. There wasn't much to read, his explanation had said it all. Paula took the pen and quickly wrote her name. The exchange was made and Paula was holding her mother's letter in her hand. It felt strange as she pressed the envelope close to her chest and it was only from a long way off that she heard Mr Griffith ask, 'Are you all right, Miss O'Brien?'

Paula just about managed to nod her head, still clutching the letter tightly.

'I think a cup of sweet tea might be in order,' he said, more to himself than to Paula as he picked up the receiver of his telephone and spoke into it. 'Miss Barclay, would you please bring a tray of tea for two into my office and something in the way of a tasty morsel? Thank you.' He replaced the receiver and, turning to Paula, said, 'I feared for a moment you were going to faint. A cup of tea and perhaps a biscuit or two will help you to decide whether you would like to remain on these premises while you read your mother's letter. We can certainly put a private room at your disposal if you so wish.'

Far too hastily Paula shook her head and again it felt to her that the room was beginning to swirl around her.

Providence came to the rescue, as a tap sounded on the door and Miss Barclay came in bearing a loaded tea tray. 'Here, set it down on my desk please. I'll see to it if you would be so kind as to take Miss O'Brien to our ladies' cloakroom. I rather fancy she will feel better if she is allowed to splash some cold water on her hands and face.' Even Mr Griffith sounded a little flustered.

Paula gave a soft sigh of relief as she got to her feet and felt Miss Barclay take hold of her arm. Walking side by side slowly down a corridor, Miss Barclay remarked, 'Very kind and thoughtful is our Mr Griffith.'

Paula couldn't have agreed more. 'I am grateful,' she murmured.

'Oh well, a nice hot cup of tea usually works wonders,' Miss Barclay responded.

A little while later when a refreshed Paula was now safely seated in an armchair this time, Mr Griffith handed her a small lap tray that held a cup of black tea, a small jug of milk, a sugar bowl, a glass dish of fresh lemon slices and a plate of dainty savoury biscuits. 'I wasn't sure if you took milk or lemon in your tea.' And for the first time he actually laughed. It certainly eased the tense situation.

They drank their tea and nibbled several biscuits, all in good companionable silence, until he enquired, 'Are you going to read your letter while you are here?'

The question as to whether it had been her father who had made her pregnant had been a horrible suspicion that had haunted her for so many years. Would her mother's letter reveal that she had been right all along? If it were so, did she want that fact to think about all the way on the journey home? No, she'd much rather read what her mother had to say in the privacy of her own bedroom. For the moment she would continue to give her father the benefit of the doubt . . .

Twenty-Seven

It was the sound of the rain lashing against the windowpanes that finally woke Paula. It had been three o'clock this morning when she had finally switched her bedside light off and she was surprised that she had finally been able to drop off. The last few days seemed to have passed in a blur. She had taken the twins to the park, and another day they had gone on a shopping spree, for once again the shops were displaying their Christmas stock. The boys had, with her help, written a note to Father Christmas. The main thing both Peter and David had requested that Father Christmas bring them was some building blocks – they were easily pleased. Having dropped their letters into the huge red pillar box the store had provided she had taken them to the new, rather posh restaurant that had opened in Wimbledon High Street, where they had enjoyed a lovely meal with delicious ice-cream to follow.

The purpose of all this activity was to keep herself active and not to dwell on the revelations of her mother's letter. She was keenly aware that she couldn't keep the lid on any of these disclosures, not for much longer anyway, and yet she didn't want to go barging in where even angels would fear to tread. *Think and then think again before you even attempt to act*, is what she kept warning herself over and over again.

And she hadn't even allowed herself to think more about the kiss that had passed between herself and Mr Lawson! To do so would be to open too many cans of worms, and she didn't think she could bear that at the moment.

Every evening she had spoken with Mr Lawson and he had advised caution. He had also promised to speak to the officer in charge at the Probate office to see if it were possible to speed things along. With Mr Lawson she hadn't discussed the letter at any great length; to tell the truth she felt too embarrassed. Having already involved him she felt she had no option but to allow him to read it in full and she had paid close attention to his advice, but his remarks on the subject had been few; for the moment at least, he was keeping his opinions to himself.

Tomorrow was to be her half-day off and Paula felt more inclined to discuss her affairs with Molly and Laura, even though the support of her dear friends would not help ease the devastating facts her mother had laid open to her. She had to keep reminding herself it had all happened a very long time ago, she must keep her mind on the present, just survive day by day, because she knew without any telling that should she take the steps that she so badly wanted to, it would be like putting a match to a tinderbox.

'OK, what's been happening?' was Laura's usual way of starting their conversation when they met up, but it was always asked with her cheeky look of mischief.

Paula smiled, knowing that Laura was a good friend and she was always so happy to see her. Laura didn't have a jealous bone in her body, even when times were hard. She cared about her family and Paula knew that included her. She never spoke about money or the advantages that her boys did or didn't have. Paula had always believed that Laura showed so much love and generosity to her family and friends because she was so happy with her husband, Fred, loved her mum and her boys dearly and all in all was clearly satisfied with her own little world.

On the other hand, over the years Laura had spent many a sleepless night worrying about Paula. Right from early childhood Paula's life had been so different from her own, and there wasn't a neighbour who wouldn't agree that the O'Briens' house held so many dark secrets.

Laura's eyes were now twinkling with merriment as she giggled and then asked, 'How's your Mr Lawson then?'

Paula grinned before answering. 'I don't see a great deal of him and when he is at home I don't have much spare time; the twins keep me busy.'

'Oh come off it,' Laura scoffed. 'Don't you eat your evening meal together? You know, after the boys are in bed?'

'Now, you're being downright nosy,' Paula said firmly, but smiling at the same time. 'I'm there to work, and Mr Lawson is not remotely interested in me in any other way. You have to remember he was knocked for six when his wife died and he's done his best to pick up the pieces.'

'That was all a long time ago and you've said before that you thought he was lonely.'

'I dare say he is from time to time,' Paula said suddenly, remembering their kiss at Victoria Station and feeling her cheeks begin to burn. But it had only been a brotherly gesture, he hadn't meant anything by it – had he? Oh dear, this conversation was getting out of hand. She had to admit that just lately she had found it very pleasant to be in Jeffrey's company but she told herself to be sensible. She really did like her job. She felt secure and happy, Mr Lawson treated her with respect and that was how she liked it. She appreciated the life she had now and, come what may, she didn't want any complications.

Laura was still looking at her, not satisfied with the answer she'd been given.

'You don't understand, Laura. I don't have the time or the interest to sort Mr Lawson's life out. I get paid to be a nursemaid to his two sons and that's all.'

'That don't mean yer can't 'ave a little fun, too,' Laura said, only meaning to tease her.

Fun, with Mr Lawson! Or with any man come to that! The very thought had Paula cringing. It sent shivers down her spine and the colour immediately drained from her face.

Laura knew immediately what was wrong: her silly remark had brought Paula's darkest memories flying back. It was a terrible shame really, because Paula's past nightmares were stopping her thinking about or even talking about the future.

Paula's thoughts had gone a whole lot deeper than that. She had scanned through her mother's letter, twice actually, but she had kept her emotions under strict control. Now at this moment she knew what she had to do. She had to be entirely on her own, and slowly and carefully read each and every line that her mother had written. Never mind that the words turned her stomach and made her wish that she had never been born; she had to do it and for her to digest every single detail she needed to be alone.

'What time will Molly be back?' Paula asked, looking at her watch.

'Any minute now; she's only popped to the corner shop for

another couple of pints of milk. She's spent the whole of the morning baking all your favourites. Why did you look at your watch? Do you have to be back early or something?'

'Of course not, Laura. I wouldn't miss my evening dinner with you and Molly for the world. I know your mum goes to the very limits making sure I have a good feed. It's just that if you and Molly don't mind I'm not going to stay late tonight and play cards; when we've eaten I'll ask Fred to walk me to the taxi-rank and I'll get a cab back. Peter has a chesty cold and I know Esmé will see to him all right but I don't think he'll settle down all that well until I've been in to say goodnight.'

Paula had said all of that with one hand in the pocket of her cardigan and her fingers tightly crossed, so she was now asking God to forgive her for her little white lie. It was a spur of the moment untruth about Peter, but that sudden urge to reread her mother's letter had become urgent. Funny thing though – and it was a matter she couldn't quite understand – suddenly she didn't feel capable of letting Laura and Molly have access to her mother's letter, let alone discuss the contents with them. She didn't even feel she was ready to disclose the fact that she had received such a letter. Once she admitted that much it would lead to how the letter had come into her possession and from that moment their questions would be numerous.

For one thing it was very personal, some facts very much more so than others. She wasn't exactly familiar with all the details herself yet. Having skimmed through paragraphs that had turned her stomach over she now knew the time had come for her to read it properly, take in every gory detail, and only then would she be able to deal with this matter and hopefully set the past to rest once and for all. The fact that she had already allowed Mr Lawson to read the letter was not the same thing at all. His legal qualifications set him apart. And it was only now that Paula realized he also had the ability and the potential not only to offer advice but to open doors to which she herself would never be able to gain access. At that thought Paula allowed herself to smile a little. The first thing she was going to ask Mr Lawson was how to go about obtaining a copy of her birth certificate.

The slamming of the front door heralded the fact that Molly had returned. 'Hello, love, ain't that lazy daughter of mine got the kettle on yet?' she shouted as she crossed the room and enfolded her plump arms around Paula, tugging her close to her ample bosom.

'What was the good of making the tea when you said we hadn't got any milk an' you'd gone to fetch some?' Laura crossly asked her mother, annoyed that she had referred to her as being lazy.

'No, love, I never said we 'adn't got any milk, I just said we needed extra cos I've made apple dumplings and no one wants to eat them without lashings of custard, do they?' Quickly she added, 'Especially your Jack and young Ronnie, kick up bloody 'ell they would if they didn't get their custard.'

Laura got to her feet, laughing at her mother who had an answer for everything. 'Sit yerself down, Mother, stay there an' talk to Paula. I'll make the tea since you suggested so nicely that I should.'

And that was just the beginning of a humorous, entertaining afternoon, with Molly and her side-splitting jokes and Laura being just as comical as they cracked one jibe after another and they all drank numerous cups of tea. Dead on three thirty the front door slammed open again and Paula wondered how the walls of the passageway had remained standing all these years when everyone that came in or out seemed to slam the front door back against the wall.

'Auntie Paula!' came the boisterous greeting from two grubby but healthy-looking little boys. 'Did that man what's got a car bring you?' Jack urgently needed to know. 'When we come out of school at a quarter past three on the day that I know you are coming to visit I always look cos he was a nice man and he took us to school so he knows which school we go to.'

'I'm sure he does,' Paula agreed, taking the matter seriously because it obviously meant so much to Jack. 'That gentleman's name is Arthur Blackmore, he lives miles away in North Devon but it won't be too long now before he brings his wife to see their grandchildren, that's the two little boys that I take care of, and when they do come to stay I will ask him to make sure that he takes you and Ronnie for a nice long ride in his car, would you like that?'

'Course we would. He's a nice man and his car was a good un too.'

Paula glanced across at Laura and they grinned at each other.

'Let yerself in for it good an' proper now, you 'ave,' Laura quietly said. 'He won't let you forget a promise like that in a hurry.'

'I wouldn't want to forget it. I think it's great that your boys remember incidents like that.'

Five o'clock and Fred Wilson was home and once more Paula was heartily greeted; this time strong arms were wrapped around her and then Fred held her at arms' length as he studied her. 'My God, gal, you've always had a fabulous head of hair but it gets even better each time I see you. Is it really that colour all the time or do you touch it up from a bottle?'

Paula looked astounded as she touched her head. Today her hair was twisted into a rope and piled on top of her head, secured as usual by two giant combs.

'Oi you, Fred, don't be so blasted rude,' Laura shouted from the other side of the room. 'Our Paula 'as always 'ad red hair for as long as I've known her. Colour it from a bottle indeed, serve yer right if she never talks t'you again. What you just said is bloody insulting.'

Fred looked sheepish as he took hold of Paula's arm. 'You know I wasn't insulting you, don't you? It's just almost unbelievable; you really do 'ave a wonderful head of hair.'

'I forgive you for your first suggestion, Fred. Your apology and your compliments have more than made it up to me.' Paula smiled as she spoke, but all the same she was annoyed that anyone would dare to think she dyed her hair. Giving vent to her bad temper she said, 'Anyway, my hair is not red, it is dark auburn and this is the first time anyone has even hinted that I dye it.'

'Well, that's me told,' he muttered, thinking he should have known better and not make comments about women's hair. God alone knows they spend enough money and time on it and his Laura was forever changing the colour of her hair. Paula must be the exception to the rule, he decided.

'Right, move yerselves; some of yer lay the table, and you boys can get the glasses out of the cabinet and fill a glass jug with water.' Nobody saw fit to argue with Molly and by six o'clock they were all seated around the table with a meal fit for a king in front of them. Slices of belly of pork, slowly roasted until the meat was tender, and so many vegetable tureens, which Paula was aware had been brought to the table in her honour. Roast and boiled

potatoes, roast parsnips, swede mashed until it looked liked rich
cream, cauliflower, cabbage and carrots, sage and onion stuffing,
apple sauce and rich dark gravy. At last everybody had got a serving
of everything and the meal could begin.

Few words were said as they tucked into the delicious food,
and Paula was pleased as it gave her the chance to enjoy her meal
and to feel the love of the company that surrounded her. They
weren't many leftovers, which pleased Molly and had her feeling
that all the preparations had been worthwhile.

Having helped to stack the plates Paula made to stand ready to
take the pile of dirty dishes and plates out into the scullery. 'Sit
down, Paula, you're our guest, and besides, this is your afternoon
off, you don't come 'ere t'work, you come here to get a well
deserved bit of spoiling. We love 'aving yer. Now, are yer ready
for yer apple dumpling and custard?'

'Cor, 'ave we really got apple dumplings an' custard?' Ronnie
asked, only half believing.

'Course we 'ave,' Jack piped up. 'Good old Gran always does
something special on the days that Auntie Paula comes. You ought
t'know that by now.'

Out of the mouths of babes and sucklings, Paula smiled to herself,
at the same time thinking how very lucky she was to have this
family take her as one of their own and make sure she knew she
was always welcome in their home.

It was just turned nine o'clock when the taxi drew up in the
driveway of Ridgeway. The driver moved swiftly and was out of
his cab and holding the door open for Paula before she had even
gathered up her purse.

'Thank you, Miss Paula,' he said, as he took the tip she offered.
'Will I be taking you and the twins anywhere this week? This is
my last day on nights; I start daytime shifts as from tomorrow,'
he informed her pleasantly because she was a regular customer of
their firm and a very popular one at that.

'More than likely,' she told him, 'we shall see what the weather
is like.'

'OK, miss, I'll wait here till you've gone up those steep stone
steps, see you safely indoors.'

'Thank you.' She smiled her thanks. 'Goodnight John.'

Her key was ready in her hand as she reached the big oak door. She turned to signal to the cab-driver that she was safe, then turning the key in the lock she opened the door and breathed a happy sigh as she walked across the vast entrance hall. It was nice to have regular time off but she always felt the same sense of relief as she returned to this beautiful house.

She found Joyce in the kitchen. 'I was just making myself a hot drink, can I get you anything?'

'No thanks, Joyce, I'm fine. Have the boys been all right?'

'Yes, Esmé is still upstairs, she's reading, said she would wait until you were home seeing as how Mr Lawson phoned to say he was staying in town for the night.'

'What time did he phone?'

'Soon after you had left.'

'I am so glad I've come home a bit earlier tonight; I'll go straight upstairs and relieve Esmé. It was so good of her to stay on.' Paula was feeling a bit guilty but she couldn't have said why. After all, she wasn't to have known that Mr Lawson wouldn't be coming home.

Joyce too was feeling awkward. 'I did tell Esmé there was no need for her to stay; I would have sat with the twins until you came home, but Esmé insisted.'

'It's all right, Joyce, I'll come down again when I've seen the boys are all right, to say goodnight to you and maybe I'll have a drink with you then.'

David was fast asleep but Peter raised his head from the pillow as soon as he heard Paula's footsteps. She grinned at Esmé, but made straight for Peter's single bed. Leaning over low she put her finger to her lips and whispered, 'Ssh, we don't want to wake David. Are you all right, Peter?' she asked, smoothing his hair over his forehead. 'I'll just thank Esmé and let her get off home and then I'll come back and give you a cuddle before I tuck you in for the night.'

Esmé was struggling into her coat by the time Paula turned to her. 'Thank you so much, Esmé, for staying on so late, it was really good of you,' she said, meaning every word.

'Think nothing of it, me love. Glad I was here to do it. Joyce does tend to fluff a bit if things don't go exactly right, but all's well that ends well. See you in the morning.' Then, turning to see

Peter was watching, raised up from the bed by leaning on his elbows, Esmé retraced her steps. 'All right are you now, young Peter?' she said, tickling him beneath his chin.

'Well, Paula is here now, so I'm going home, but I will see you in the morning. Will you give me a hug before I go?'

He held out both of his arms for a hug, but still seemed as if he felt he'd been hard done by.

Paula spent some time reassuring Peter that she was going to bed herself soon and that he knew she was only in the room next door. When she bent over him to give a last look his breathing was regular and his eyelids had dropped. She softly laid her lips to his forehead before leaving the room. Walking down the corridor Paula felt her conscience prick her. Poor old Joyce, she was so willing, always ready to step in when help was needed, but she did like to be praised for her actions. *My letter can wait a while longer; in fact I might even leave it until tomorrow now since it is getting late and I really must keep my promise and go down to say goodnight to Joyce.*

Paula knew all this talking to herself was just her way of making excuses for putting off the rereading of that wretched letter. A sudden thought came to her: was she pleased or sorry that her mother had seen fit to write this enlightening letter before she had died?

There was no way she could answer that. Not yet anyway. She'd have to wait and see the outcome of it all first.

Finally Paula and Joyce were sitting at the kitchen table and they were on their second glass of sherry. By now Joyce was feeling pleased with herself; she'd wondered how she was going to tell Paula her *little secret* and now she had.

Paula could scarcely take in what Joyce was saying. 'Honestly, Paula, he is a really nice man. His name is Stan, Stanley Tompson, he came to read the electric meter about two weeks ago and twice since then he's been back, I suspected he was making excuses for calling but I couldn't be sure. Then this afternoon he admitted he came back just to see me, because I had been kind and made him a cup of tea. He told me he is fifty-five years old, a widower without any children, and I think he's lonely. Anyway, he's asked me to go to the theatre with him this weekend. Do you think I should?'

Paula did a quick calculation; her guess put Joyce's age at around thirty-five. She really had to check herself: it would be so easy to laugh but so cruel. She sternly told herself to feel happy for Joyce. A woman who had made up her mind that she was destined to be left on the shelf, to be an old maid, and all because of the dreadful war. Maybe now she was being offered a second chance. She felt she should warn Joyce to find out a little more about this man – were his intentions honourable? But then who was she to burst the bubble? During the telling Paula felt in all the time she'd known Joyce she had never once seen so much happiness on her face. So she reached out across the table and grabbed hold of both Joyce's hands and said, 'Joyce, I couldn't be more pleased for you. You deserve some happiness and yes, I think you should accept his invitation and see how things progress from there.'

In her haste Joyce almost sent her chair flying, round the table she came, grabbed Paula to her and kissed her on the cheek. 'Oh, Paula, thank you, thank you for your approval. I just hope I am doing the right thing.'

So do I! Paula had the sense to say this to herself. 'Anyway, this seems to have been quite a day for each of us, one way and another. We'd better wash these glasses and take ourselves off to bed.'

They parted at the top of the stairs. Paula took one more look at Peter and David and then alone in her bedroom she plonked herself down on to the bed, kicked her shoes off and out loud she declared, 'I need to get a good night's sleep. I'll need a clear head before I can begin to go through my mother's letter once again.'

So, she decided, *it will just have to wait until tomorrow*.

Twenty-Eight

Most unusually, Jeffrey Lawson had to stay in town for the second night. On the telephone he had made his apologies to Paula and she in turn had assured him that everything at Ridgeway was running smoothly and that both the boys were in fine fettle. He had asked to speak to his sons and each in turn had had a short conversation with their father, spiced with laughter and even a spat of giggling from David. Final goodbyes were called down the line and Paula had replaced the receiver.

For the whole of the day Paula had, to the best of her ability, kept the boys active. Two hours of the afternoon had been spent up playing with their pony since it was such a fine day to be outdoors. After supper she had given them extra time in the bath, playing with them, splashing them and in return getting herself thoroughly soaked.

It was now seven o'clock, and both boys were in their beds. Having cleaned up the mess in the bathroom Paula put her head around the bedroom door and shook her head in disbelief at the two angelic-looking little boys. Their damp hair was curly, causing them to look even more like their father, and the looks on their faces said that butter wouldn't melt in their mouths. There was many a time when she knew different but at this moment the very sight of them tugged at her heart and she knew she loved the very bones of each of them.

'I'm going down now to have my dinner with Joyce and when I come back upstairs I expect to see you both settled down so that I may put out the light.'

Peter and David looked at each other and by the look on their grinning faces it was quite apparent that they had no intention of settling down just yet. 'I mean it, I shall be less than an hour, and then I shall be back to say goodnight.'

She and Joyce enjoyed a light meal of salmon served with salad and a jacket potato, which they ate in the kitchen, followed by biscuits and cheese. It was only when Mr Lawson stayed in town that Joyce didn't bother to make a dessert.

They were both now standing at the sink, Joyce washing the dishes and Paula drying them.

'I've got quite a bit of sewing I need to get on with,' Joyce said, sounding almost apologetic. 'Do you mind if I do it in my room?'

'No, of course not. I have a few letters I need to write, so I'll see you in the morning,' Paula said, laying down the last plate and hanging her tea towel up to dry over the kitchen range.

She went upstairs to look in on the boys, and was amazed to see they were fast asleep. She picked up their toys, most of which were scattered on the floor, tucked a teddy bear closer inside the covers of David's bed and put Scamp, Peter's favourite fluffy dog, across the foot of his bed. Having kissed the tops of their heads she paused a moment inside the doorway and sighed softly. *David and Peter*, she murmured, shaking her head before she switched off the light. *Whatever would I do without you?*

Back in her own room she gave herself a good talking to. She really couldn't put off reading her mother's letter any longer. Quickly she undressed, put on her nightdress and dressing-gown. From the top shelf inside of her wardrobe she retrieved the thick letter, sat on the bed and having piled three pillows behind her head and shoulders she leaned back, stretched her legs out in front of her and took from the envelope the handwritten sheets of notepaper.

My darling Paula,

I haven't been at all well for some time now and my every instinct tells me to write this letter to you and to leave it in safe hands for you to read when I am gone. You will be perfectly entitled to judge me and you will no doubt condemn me for never having revealed these facts to you years ago.

I shall begin in the year of 1910. I was engaged to be married to an officer in the Royal Horse Guards, one of the regiments of the Royal Household Cavalry. His name was Alexander Gerard Grantham. I first met him at Windsor on a ceremonial occasion in the early part of 1910. We were to have been married at Easter of 1911. It was because of our natural affection and love for each other that we made love soon after we met. I make no apology for having done so. Fate can be so cruel. I never discovered I was pregnant until after Alex had been killed in a train crash.

I was devastated. My father was adamant. He would disown me unless I agreed to have the baby adopted. I wanted my baby, boy or girl. I loved Alex so much and the baby was all I had left of him. Then Michael O'Brien and his brother Patrick came to do some work on my father's house. I was not included in any discussion. My father paid Michael to marry me and he provided us with a house. Thereafter he washed his hands of me.

At least you now know Mike O'Brien is not your father. I was wicked and sinful but I truly loved your father and he truly loved me. Believe that, Paula. Please.

Over the years I have been neglectful of you. In many ways this is true, but always for the best of reasons. One thing has to be said: Mike O'Brien adored you from the day you were born. When I complained about how much time he spent alone with you in your bedroom, he threatened me both mentally and physically. I came to realize before long that he was sick in the head.

If at any time he had hurt you I swear I would have killed him.

I struggled so often with my conscience. When sober he was a good father. Never a good husband, he took great delight in being cruel towards me and if I complained about the ill treatment his everlasting threat was that he would tell you that you were a bastard and that I was a whore. He was so possessive of you because he had it fixed in his warped mind that he had bought and paid for you before you were even born.

To skip the years and come to 1924: never in my wildest nightmare could I have envisaged that he would have sunk so low as to allow his own brother to have intercourse with you. His excuse was that his brother would have, or so he thought, gently 'broken you in'! I still cannot imagine that he expected me to believe that. Nor can I ask you to believe that, until I saw the bloody sheets the next morning, I did not know anything about what had happened to you. But that is the truth. They drugged me too, although the drug did not have such a hold on me as it did on you and the next day I recollected hearing Michael congratulating Patrick on 'a job well done'.

As to what you were made to suffer in the year that followed, it was perversion on the part of both Mike and Paddy. Why did I not go to the police? Why did I not tell what I knew to the Catholic priests? Why didn't I kill them both? Because between them they *almost killed me. That wouldn't have bothered me. In fact there were days when I wished they would. Patrick beat and kicked me on many occasions. Michael burnt my breast with his cigarettes and when the burns weren't big enough for his liking he used a red-hot poker on me. I wasn't allowed out of the house for six months. I would have gladly died but for one thing: I had to live to see you come home, to be there for you, even if I were useless as a mother and even worse as a protector. Without me Mike would probably have locked you up for ever. Kept you for himself. His one aim in life was to make sure that you never found out who your real father was. He had truly convinced himself, was one hundred per cent sure, that he was your father.*

What can I say, my darling? I tried my best for you but it was not nearly enough.

As her mother's despair seemed to fill the pages Paula's heart was breaking. There was only half a page left to read; she wiped away the tears that had slowly been streaming down her cheeks, rubbed her eyes and finally blew her nose.

She continued reading.

It is my only consolation that you finally broke free. I easily found out the address where you were employed. Money speaks all languages. You will never know how badly I longed to meet up with you. I needed to be assured that you were now happy and leading a normal life. I did follow you, just one time. I watched you with those two little boys and I would have given the earth to have been able to hold you in my arms, even held the babies, but that would have been selfish. I wouldn't have been able to hide my happiness, Mike would have guessed and he would have punished me in so many ways until at last I would have given in and revealed your address. And then what? Much better that I stayed away, stayed quiet. But I cared. Please, my dearest Paula, believe that I did care. I miss you and I love you so very much.

On an otherwise blank sheet of paper there were just a few lines.

Michael was not that clever. My grandmother felt my parents had treated me much too harshly. She left me a huge sum of money and a rather nice property which has been sold and all the money is invested in your name. You have so much to forgive me for, Paula, so I beg you, please believe that I acted as I thought best at the time.

Anthony Perkins has been dealing with your affairs. I promise you, darling, you may trust him. Enjoy what is rightfully yours and may the rest of your life give you all the happiness you deserve.

Always with my love,

Mum

Having leapt to her feet in sheer frustration, Paula was pacing the floor and tugging at her hair, letting it fall free down over her shoulders. How could it have happened? *Why* had it happened? Her whole life had been one great big lie, starting even before she had been born. How was she supposed to cope with that fact? She felt like screaming but the only thing that stopped her was the thought that if she started she might never be able to stop.

There was one fact that stood out and she was going to shout it from the rooftops, inform anyone that cared to listen: *Michael O'Brien is not my father!*

The things he had done to her. What had given him the right? It was unthinkable that she had been imprisoned in that hellhole for more than a year and all because Mike O'Brien had allowed his own brother to rape her. That man had made himself a self-appointed father to an unborn baby and later professed a great love for a young child. Didn't that make the deed ten times worse?

So, now I've read the letter properly do I feel better or worse? Sorry for my mother, yes, but why on earth couldn't she have done something? Anything. Gone to the police. Told a priest that her husband and his brother had abused her only daughter. Too late now. Far too late.

As she paced the room Paula was all the while muttering to herself. 'At this moment I could cheerfully have a go at strangling them both.' It had made loathsome reading. It was a disgusting affair, thought up by two filthy-minded men. *And who had paid the price? Me, me, me, all along the line it was just me.*

Paula felt she couldn't take much more. She had cramps in her stomach that were hurting so badly and the bile that kept rising in her throat was awful, she had to get to a toilet but she couldn't use the bathroom which was so near to the boys' bedroom.

Disturbing them was the last thing she wanted to do. She ran down the stairs, half blinded by tears that just wouldn't stop falling. Inside the cloakroom she fell on to her knees and raised the seat of the toilet. She remained there for several minutes.

For years she had felt guilty because she had let herself half believe that it was her father who had made her pregnant. It wasn't him: it had been her Uncle Patrick and he had paid money to his brother for the privilege of doing so! She had been used. The very thought of the pair of them touching her, invading her young body, filled her with loathing. Over the years she had locked away so many distressing memories and now her mother's letter had brought it all back so vividly. It wasn't fair. How was she ever going to rid her mind of all this filth and be able to feel herself clean again?

Her hands gripped the cold china of the sides of the lavatory pan and she began to retch until the vomit spewed out of her, over and over again, until she collapsed backwards and was left lying on the floor heaving great dry sobs. It took a while before she felt able to move. She longed for a drink of water but wasn't yet capable of getting up on to her feet. Instead she wiped some paper around her mouth, even trying to wipe the remains of vomit from her tongue.

The enormity of what she had read had by now sunk in. For one moment she took pleasure in the fact that her real father had been a gentleman. Oh, she was certainly going to find out more about him now. Was she entitled to use his surname? But all of that would come later; for now she had to get herself up off this floor, get upstairs, have a bath and go to bed.

Eventually she had managed to do all of that and as she lay in her nice clean bed, wearing a clean nightgown, her last thought before she fell asleep brought her some degree of comfort.

That warped, evil bastard is not my father.

Twenty-Nine

The following morning Paula was up and about soon after seven o'clock. She had decided to make this a restful day, for the boys as well as for herself. There was no point in going over and over the information her mother had revealed, at least not until Mr Lawson was back in his usual routine and she was able to discuss her options with him on a level-headed basis. She went about her usual routine, washing and dressing the twins, cleaning the bathroom and making the beds, but there was no mistaking the fact that her bout of sickness and her show of bad temper last night had taken its toll on her. She had a severe headache and just a glance in the mirror told her that her eyes looked bleary and her face was pale.

Breakfast was over and Joyce came from the kitchen into the hall carrying her shopping basket. She was humming and Paula had to stop herself from asking what she was so happy about, but then she remembered Joyce telling her about Stanley Tompson. She spared a few moments to be happy for Joyce. She truly hoped things might work out between Joyce and Stanley. *God knows Joyce deserved a break – at least where men were concerned.*

For her own part Joyce had, these last few weeks, become aware of a difference in both Paula and Mr Lawson and she was in a position better than anyone to be the judge of that. Paula and she had become good friends; they played cards together of an evening, sometimes confiding in each other about their hopes and dreams and fears for the future. Joyce felt that in the time Paula had been living here, taking care of the twins, she had in many ways become a different person. The Paula who, when she had first arrived, had been scared of her own shadow had for the most part vanished.

The same could be said of Jeffrey Lawson, which pleased Joyce greatly. Before the arrival of Paula there had been days when she had despaired for him. The tragic loss of his wife had hit him hard and he had struggled with his conscience as to what was in the best interest of his two baby sons. Left to the social workers they would have had him signing adoption papers and he would have lived to regret that decision. These days he looked and acted younger and was definitely more relaxed.

As for Paula herself, she was more than pleased that Joyce and she had become friends. There had been times when she would have liked to share more with Joyce, talked about her own particular situation, but she hadn't dared. Her secrets were enormous, and after having read her mother's letter she would have to say they were dark, evil secrets, and that meant even more so that she had no right to tell them to anybody that was not involved. Of course, Mr Lawson was the exception.

'I feel like a walk this morning,' Joyce declared cheerily. 'I thought instead of phoning my order through to Warren Brothers I'd have a change. Go to the small local shops, see what they've got on offer, anyone care to join me?'

Paula heaved a thankful sigh; she'd been wondering how she was going to keep the boys occupied this morning. 'I'd love to come, thank you, Joyce. Let me just find where the boys are and see how they feel.'

The suggestion was met with wholehearted approval and twenty minutes later it was a happy foursome that set off to the shops. Their first port of call was to the greengrocer's, next a visit to the ironmonger's because Joyce said they were almost out of tapers, matches and firelighters. Then to Mr O'Grady's butcher's shop, where Joyce pondered a while before making her decision. Braising steak and kidney for a pie was a must because it was an obvious favourite, but whether to have a leg of lamb or a nice plump roasting chicken for tomorrow when their father would be home was soon resolved by both boys shouting, 'Chicken, please!'

The butcher raised his straw boater hat to the ladies and thanked them for their custom. By now each of then had a parcel to carry and Joyce said they only had the baker's shop left to visit. Paula whispered something in Joyce's ear; they looked at each other and burst out laughing. Both Peter and David were clamouring to be told the joke but were told to be patient and wait and see. No amount of pleading was going to alter that decision.

As Joyce pushed open the heavy glass door to the bakery they were overcome by the delicious smells: numerous pastries, cakes and tarts but most of all by the smell of freshly baked bread. Joyce often made bread and rolls but never in this quantity and the different shapes and sizes that were laid out in wooden racks at the back of the shop were wonderful to look at.

'Now, shall we go through and have ourselves a little treat?' Joyce asked Paula and the boys. The suggestion was met with wild enthusiasm.

It was a merry little group that sat around the table and there were shouts of delight when the waitress, having first brought their four drinks, went away and returned with four side plates and four silver cake forks.

Peter's face beamed as the waitress returned yet again, this time carrying a large dish that held four delicious-looking cakes, all of which were wolfed down with great gusto and little talking.

'Did you enjoy that, boys?' Paula asked later, as she helped them on with their coats.

'Yes, yes,' they heartily agreed.

'Then don't you think you should thank Joyce? It was her idea for us all to come out, otherwise we wouldn't have been able to enjoy that lovely treat.'

Peter and David didn't hesitate to show their gratitude, even if their hugging of Joyce was a bit boisterous.

As they trooped out of the shop the admiring glances and the cheery goodbyes made a pleasant end to their coffee break.

The high street was busy: delivery vans were parked along the kerbside, shoppers were out in force, the postman was bent low, and having unlocked the door of the big red pillar box he was removing the heap of mail, transferring it all into his sack. A huge horse-drawn coal cart was partially blocking the entrance to a side road and Paula and Joyce had to wait a moment before they were able to dodge round it. All of this was imprinted on Paula's mind as just for a few seconds she lost sight of the twins.

Then the fierce barking of a dog filled the air and immediately Paula broke into a run. For ever after she would remember the premonition that engulfed her at that moment. Forcing her way past people who were merely dawdling she did her best to run toward the ferocious sound of the dog barking. She broke through to where a cluster of people were standing and she took in the situation at a glance. Peter was standing alone, his head bent low, staring at his brother who was lying flat on his back on the pavement, being guarded by this big, savage-looking dog. By now the noise of its barking was deafening and its great fangs terrified her. For what seemed an eternity she cowered there not knowing what to do, she was so frightened. All her limbs were trembling. She reached out to grab Peter; he too was shaking like a leaf, great sobs were wracking his body and his face was a deathly grey colour.

'Down! Down, I say, and stop that blasted racket!' With this voice of authority came a burly policeman and the crowd parted to let him through. Unafraid, he stepped right up to the dog who was baring his teeth and still ruthlessly snarling. 'Down, down I say,' the policeman repeated, this time with his head so low it was within a foot or two of the dog's face. Miraculously the dog dropped down on to his belly, its four legs spread wide and its barking turned into a whimper.

'Who is the owner of this dog?' the policeman asked and a middle-aged lady gingerly stepped forward, a dog's leash dangling from her hand. Taking the lead from her the officer clipped it to the dog's collar then handed the end of it back to her.

Paula sighed with relief.

'Keep a tight hold on that leash, take him away, go and stand over by that wall. I need to get to this injured child but don't move far because I shall need a statement from you.' The policeman had soon taken charge of the situation.

As all this was being carried out Paula had her arm protectively around Peter but when the dog was removed and her gaze fell upon the pool of blood that lay to the side of David's head it took every inch of her strength to stay upright.

The policeman ran across to the nearby police box to make a telephone call to the local station, and returned swiftly to the scene of the accident. Lifting one of David's hands the officer began to stroke the back of it. 'Can you tell me your name, son? No, don't feel like talking? Well, don't worry I am going to stay right here beside you until an ambulance arrives.'

Not a murmur from David; his eyes were closed and the colour of his face was a dirty grey. Blood was still oozing from the side of his head. This small crumpled heap that was David seemed so small as the big policeman continued to hold his hand and to talk to him. 'Are you the boy's mother?' The policeman had raised his head and was staring up at Paula.

She shook her head. 'No, but I have full-time charge of them.'
She indicated Peter, whom she was still hugging close to her side.
'This is Peter, he and David are twins.' There was no more time
for explanations as the clanging of the ambulance's bell preceded
its arrival by only minutes. The officer was up on his feet, waving
back the small crowd that had gathered and two men in navy-blue
uniforms with bright green armbands were soon on either side of
David, attending to him with such gentleness and talking softly to
him all the while. Soon David's head was swathed in bandages and
over the top was placed a soft-looking kind of helmet with straps
that went under his chin. It made his head look exceptionally large.

Suddenly Joyce broke through the crowd and sank down beside
Paula. With Peter squashed between them and their arms around
each other they all gave way to their tears. One man had gone
back to the ambulance and quickly returned carrying a stretcher.
They lifted David from the ground, laid him out on a stretcher
and wrapped him in a big red blanket before proceeding to place
him inside the ambulance.

'Is anyone going to come with David?' they asked, looking at
the woe-begotten trio. 'We shall be taking him to the Wilson
Hospital.'

'May we all come?' Paula timidly asked.

'Sorry, my love, we might need to work on the lad on the way
and there's not much room in the vehicle. One of you ladies get
in, and I suggest if you don't want to be parted the other lady
and the boy follow on in a taxi.'

Joyce was trying to take hold of Peter. He was resisting, loath
to let go of Paula. There was no time for Paula to console him,
however. Her arms were being held firmly as the men helped her
up into the ambulance. 'Peter, Joyce will bring you along, you
won't be far behind,' she called down to him.

No more talk: the doors were slammed shut, the warning bell
switched on and they were racing through the streets.

Paula was full of disbelief and still in shock when they arrived
at the hospital a few minutes later. They had had such an enjoyable morning; how in heaven's name had this nightmare begun!
She wanted to get nearer to David, to touch him, to make herself
believe that he was going to be all right. He still hadn't opened
his eyes and his little face was such an awful colour. *Dear God, he*

hasn't done anything to deserve this. He must have been petrified when that dog came at him. It seemed ages since she had been shown into this waiting room – where were Joyce and Peter?

After the last few days, with the worry of all those disclosures her mother had made in her letter, Paula had thought she couldn't feel more wretched. Well, she was wrong. She walked about this dreary waiting room. Picked up an old newspaper then put it down, exchanged it for a magazine. Tried looking out of the window but all there was to look at was a high brick wall. *Please, please, let David be all right!*

At last the door opened and Peter rushed into her arms. One look at Joyce told her that she was just as worried as herself.

'Let's leave the door open,' Joyce suggested. The reception area was buzzing with activity. Joyce pointed to the little café on the other side of the room. 'Peter would you like to fetch a bar of chocolate from that cafe? I'll give you some pennies.'

'No, thank you, Joyce.' He turned his big dark eyes towards Paula and in a voice that trembled with fear, he asked, 'Will they be keeping David in this hospital?'

Paula sat down on a chair and pulled Peter to stand between her knees, thus making his face on a level with her own. 'I think they will, Peter, but it's all right; they have doctors here who will be able to attend to David, they will know exactly what to do and then nurses will put him into a nice clean bed and he will have a nice long sleep and when he wakes up he will be feeling a whole lot better.' All this was said by Paula with her fingers tightly crossed behind her back.

'Paula, I don't feel well,' Peter said, his voice little more than a whisper.

'Want a cuddle, do you?' she offered, sensing his need to be comforted as she pulled him on to her lap. Pulling a clean handkerchief from the pocket of her coat she allowed her compassion for poor Peter to show. She wiped the tears from his eyes and began to rock him gently as she had done since he was only a few months old. She held him lightly to her but for all that her mind was in turmoil and not the least of her worries was that very soon now she would have to make a telephone call to his father. Whatever was she going to say to Mr Lawson?

She was saved the immediate problem of having to answer her

own question by the arrival of a man dressed in a white coat. 'Which one of you is the mother of David?' he asked quietly, holding out his hand to Joyce. 'I am the doctor who will be in charge of the boy. Doctor William Harvey.'

Joyce looked flustered, she felt it too, and her words came out in a proper tumble. 'David and the little lad sitting there on my friend's lap are twins.' Lowering her voice she added, 'Their mother died when they were born. I am Joyce Pledger, their father's house-keeper, and the young lady there is Paula O'Brien. She is a full-time nanny to the twins, whose names are Peter and David Lawson.'

During the introductions Paula had set Peter down on his feet and was standing beside him, still holding on to his hand. It was then that Peter found his own voice, looking up at this portly doctor who had a red face, bushy hair on his upper lip, and a kindly smile. 'Please may I see David? He is my brother.'

Dr Harvey was six foot tall; he bent his knees and spoke kindly to Peter. 'I have been given to understand that you and David are very special brothers, is that right?'

'Yes sir, we have the same birthdays and Daddy says people sometimes cannot tell us apart because we are . . .' He paused and looked to Paula who slowly mouthed the word 'identical'. 'Identical twins,' Peter finished with a flourish.

'Well, young man, that makes you both very special and because I appreciate that I am going to make sure you are given prefer-ential treatment. Right now David is fast asleep; we have patched his head up, stopped it bleeding and given him a sedative, so now he is asleep and quiet. But tomorrow you may come and visit him and we'll see how he goes on from there. For now though I will take you up to the ward that they have put David in and you will be able to see for yourself that he is doing fine.'

Dr Harvey led the way to the lift and pressed the 'going-up' button on the wall. While they were waiting for the lift to come down to the ground floor he drew Paula to one side. 'I need you to give me a few details before you leave the hospital, like where and when we can make contact with the boy's father.'

Paula didn't like the sound of that. She needed desperately to be the first to speak to Mr Lawson. The lift had arrived, the doors were pulled open and three nurses came out of the lift, each one acknowledging Dr Harvey as they passed.

Two floors up and within minutes they were at David's bedside.

It was heart-wrenching for Paula to stand there and see that little boy in such a big bed and the sight of blood being dripped into his arm was deplorable for Peter to stand and stare at.

'That blood is doing a great deal of good for your brother,' Dr Harvey patiently explained. 'It is replacing all the blood that your brother lost when his head hit the road surface so hard.'

'He fell cos that big dog jumped up at him,' Peter remarked, tears rolling slowly down his cheeks.

'We know, the policeman told us how brave you both were. If either of you had tried to run that dog would have been after you and probably would have bitten one of you. But come closer to the side of the bed, Peter. I'll lift you up and you can lean over and see that David is really asleep.'

Paula felt Dr Harvey was bending over backwards to keep Peter calm and she was truly grateful as she watched him lift Peter up in his arms and hold him out over the bed. Minutes later he set him down and suggested that Joyce take him off to the cafe for a drink while he spoke to Paula and got her to sign a few papers.

'I'll come and find you,' Paula said to Joyce, but Peter needed more assurance than that. 'I promise I am not going anywhere. Look.' Paula opened her bag, took some money from her purse and held it out to Peter. 'You be a big boy, Joyce will order what she would like to drink and a cup of tea for me; you can have orange juice, milk or whatever takes your fancy and then you give the cashier the note I've just given to you. Make sure you put the change safely in your pocket and by the time you're sitting up at the table I shall be there with you.'

Paula's heart was breaking as she looked at the little boy's sad face. *This is the very first time that he and David have ever been separated.* She'd have trouble getting him to sleep tonight in their bedroom all on his own.

You, my girl, have worse things to worry about than where is Peter going to sleep tonight, she was chiding herself. *You have to get on the end of a telephone and let Mr Lawson know that one of his sons is in hospital with a head wound.* Right now she had to have this interview with Dr Harvey, who said he needed information from her. Well, it works both ways. Good or bad she needed to be in possession of the full facts as to what damage that dog, and

David's consequent fall, had done that was so bad he had to be hospitalized.

Dear God, give me strength, she prayed. Yesterday her problems had seemed enormous. Some parts utterly revolting. Yet today the fact that David might have been badly injured, put everything into perspective and her own troubles paled beside that fact.

'This way, Miss O'Brien,' Dr Harvey said, holding open a door to a rather large office. Winter sunshine was pouring in through double glass doors that looked out on to very pleasant and neatly kept grounds. The walls of the office were wood panelled, the furniture large and solid looking. The doctor indicated that Paula should be seated in a leather armchair that stood facing a huge desk; he walked around the desk, settling himself in a similar chair directly facing her.

'Would you mind if I ask you to fill me in with the details as to how you became to be in complete charge of two small boys?'

'Not at all, Dr Harvey, but first I would like to thank you for being tactful in front of Peter. Mrs Lawson died giving birth to the twins.'

'Oh, I am sorry. How long have you been taking care of them?'

'They were seven months old when Mr Lawson first employed me, that's almost two years ago.'

'So, you have complete charge.' Without waiting for an answer he murmured, 'I must say you look very young.' He could have added, 'You are truly beautiful and that glorious mass of red hair doesn't seem to sit well with being a nanny,' but in his profession he hard learned the hard way: silence is more often than not better than speaking one's mind.

Paula sighed; she had an inkling as to what he was thinking. 'Mr Lawson had tried many avenues; two newly born babies were quite a problem for a man on his own. Several professional nurses came and went, and he was advised to think about adoption. Mr Lawson's mother then suggested he placed an advertisement in the local paper for a young, caring person rather than a stiff, starched qualified person. I answered the advert. Mr Lawson offered me a month's trial.'

Dr Harvey gave a hearty laugh. 'I apologize for doubting you, Miss O'Brien. Are you able to contact their father?'

'Very easily. I put off making the call until you had spoken with me. Mr Lawson is at home almost every night and he is always home from Friday evening until Monday morning. I can give you his business address and a telephone number but I would ask that you allow me to speak to him first, unless of course you have something drastic you need to discuss with him . . .'

'No, Miss O'Brien, but I do insist that you notify Mr Lawson without delay. If you will leave the details at reception I will have a word with Mr Lawson myself later on this morning. Meanwhile, let me put your mind at rest. We need to keep young David in hospital for the time being, we need to monitor him and keep him under strict observation for at least twenty-four hours. That was a nasty bang he suffered to his head.'

Paula felt a lump so large in her throat she thought she might choke. 'Please, Doctor, tell me, is David going to be all right?'

His sigh was so heavy that Paula thought the worst. She had to dig her fingernails into the palms of her hands to keep herself from fainting. The thought that there might even be the slightest chance that David would die sent her reeling.

All thoughts of her father and his horrible, disgusting brother and what revenge she wanted to vent on them was wiped out. She had to get back to Peter, hug him tight, reassure him, if that were possible. She would call a taxi, she decided. Get home as quickly as possible, for there was no reason for her to put it off any longer. She had to telephone Jeffrey Lawson.

Thirty

'Thanks, Joyce,' Paula said, accepting a cup of coffee, stirring it thoughtfully.

'Well, don't take too much time drinking it; you can't put off making the call for much longer.'

'I know, but . . .'

'But what?' Joyce prompted gently.

'I was wondering whether or not I should call Mrs Blackmore, you know she is Mr Lawson's mother and grandma to the twins.'

Joyce gave a small, hopeless shrug. 'You're being silly, and clutching at straws. Mr and Mrs Blackmore will be told in good time and if it turns out to be necessary they will be here in no time. Right now you've no option; you've delayed long enough so pick up the receiver and get through to Mr Lawson. I'm going to see about preparing our evening meal. I know neither of us will feel like eating but we have Peter to think about. We'll sit up to the table this evening and have a proper dinner together and who knows, Mr Lawson may well be home by then. Surprise me if he isn't.'

Paula drained the remains of her coffee, set the cup back down on its saucer and walked out into the hall, knowing she could no longer put off making the call. She picked up the receiver and spoke into the mouthpiece, giving the London number to the operator. Joyce was standing a few feet away.

'This is the first time I've ever had to ring Mr Lawson. I know he often rings us, but now it's a bit scary not knowing what he will say.'

'Don't be silly, Paula, he's not going to blame you; what happened to David was an awful accident,' Joyce said, doing her best to show support.

'*I am sorry caller, the number you require is engaged, please replace the receiver and try again later,*' the clipped voice of the operator informed her. Paula somehow forced herself to stay calm, but as she sat down on a chair near to the phone she was feeling so anxious and nervous that she was actually afraid to try again. In the end she forced herself, and this time having given the number to the operator once again, she managed to get through.

'Mr Lawson's office, how may I help?' asked a lady with a soft, polite voice.

'I urgently need to speak to Mr Lawson please.'

'May I have you name, please, caller?'

'Oh, I'm sorry, Paula O'Brien, I am . . .'

'It's all right, Miss O'Brien, I know who you are. My orders are should you ever have cause to ring Mr Lawson here at his office I am to contact him wherever he is. Hold the line please. It may take a while depending whether he is still in court or not.'

'I'll hold,' Paula assured her, feeling a horrible fit of nerves beginning again as she waited for Jeffrey to come to the phone.

'Hello, Paula,' he said, coming on to the line. 'So what's happened? Tell me, I need to know.'

Paula took a breath, then, knowing she had no choice but to go through with it, she braced herself and said, 'David has been admitted to the Wilson Hospital. There was an incident with a very large dog this morning. I think he is going to be all right . . .'

'You *think* he's he is going to be all right, or you are certain? *Which?*' he asked sharply. 'Tell me. Tell me what happened.'

Paula flinched at his harshness. 'This morning Joyce decided to do her shopping locally. I got the boys ready and we all went together. We had a lovely walk, visited several shops and ended up having a hot drink and a pastry in the Olde Bakery. The boys were really enjoying themselves and every customer there thought the twins were enchanting – you know yourself how appealing they can be when it suits them.'

She heard Mr Lawson utter a sigh of annoyance and quickly she got back to what she was supposed to be telling him. 'When we left the bakery the boys were in high spirits, they broke into a run and were a few yards in front of Joyce and myself. I called to them to hold each other's hand and to walk, not run. The High Street appeared to be very busy this morning, a horse-drawn cart was trying to come out of a side alleyway, inching its way forward, and for a few moments it blocked my view; I lost sight of the boys. Then I heard a dog barking, really ferocious it was. I can't explain what my feelings were at that moment, I just knew I had to get by everything and everyone that was in my way.' She stopped talking suddenly, feeling such a weariness descend on her that for a moment she wasn't sure she had it in her to tell him any more.

'Paula, are you all right? Answer me, please.' He was calling as he heard the phone drop down on to the floor. Joyce too had heard the disturbance; she rushed over, gave a quick glance to Paula and picked up the telephone receiver. 'Are you still there, Mr Lawson? It's me, Joyce.'

'Can you tell me what happened, Joyce?' His voice held a note of alarm.

Joyce was thrown off balance by his question: did he mean what had happened this minute or did he need to have more details about David? Nervously she said, 'I think Paula felt giddy, she fell down but she has opened her eyes so I'm sure she will be all right. As to David, I only know what Paula has told me. She was the one who got the details from Dr Harvey. I do know that the dog knocked David to the ground and in doing so he banged his head, pretty hard I should imagine. Before we left the hospital we were allowed to see David; his head was bandaged but he was sleeping peacefully. Dr Harvey said they would telephone Paula if she was needed otherwise we could go to see David tomorrow morning, but Paula is insisting that as soon as she has reassured Peter that David will be all right she is going straight back to the hospital to check on the boy.'

'Hang on, Joyce, my secretary is signalling that I have a call from the hospital on my other line. Tell Paula I am not laying blame on her; no person can keep an eye on children at all times. I'll take this call and then I shall be leaving the office as soon as I possibly can. I shall go straight to the hospital but I will be home later tonight.'

Joyce looked at the receiver in amazement; all she could hear now was a buzzing. Mr Lawson didn't hang about; he had cut the line dead. She replaced the phone on to the hook and knelt down beside of Paula. 'My God, you look awful, Paula, whatever happened to you?'

'My head was hurting fit to bust and then the room seemed to be swinging round and round. I am sorry.'

'No, don't be sorry. I finished your call with Mr Lawson; he said to tell you not to take all the blame on yourself – he as good as said you need eyes on the back of your head when looking after children.'

'Where is Peter?' Paula was anxious to know as she struggled to get up from the floor.

'He's in the kitchen, but he is not on his own. Mr Tompson called in to see if I was going to be free this afternoon; he was going to suggest that he take me for a drive. I don't know if I told you he has bought himself a small motor car. He was shocked to hear about David but sad also to see how upset Peter is. Right now he is playing snakes and ladders with him. He said it's best to keep the boy occupied.'

'Right, I'm up on my feet now,' Paula said, stretching her shoulders back hard and extending her arms out straight in front of her. 'Let's go and see how they are getting on.'

Joyce came into the kitchen first, but she got no response to her cheery greeting. But Paula had hardly set a foot inside of the room when Peter was running across the room and flinging himself at her.

'Have you been talking to my daddy? Is he coming home? Can I see David soon?'

Paula was worried. Never before had she seen Peter show such agitation. He had got down from his chair and came towards her all right, but now suddenly he was rocking on his feet, tossing and shaking his head. 'Come here, Peter, come to me.' She stood stock-still, arms spread wide. Peter made no move to comply with her order; he was now really trembling and suddenly Paula was afraid: was he in the throes of a convulsion?

Rushing to the sink she grabbed a cloth and held it under a running cold-water tap, then with the wet cloth in one hand and a large dry towel draped over her arm she came up behind Peter. Wrapping her arm around his waist she pulled him backwards until his back was resting flat against her thighs. 'Ssh, Peter, David is going to be fine. If you make one big effort to stand perfectly still I will make us a drink and then I will take you back to the hospital. You may not be allowed to go into his room but I am sure the nurses will let you peep round the door to David's room. Peter, I can only promise to do this if you will make a big effort to stand perfectly still for one minute while I place this damp cloth on your forehead.'

A few seconds dragged by and then Paula felt it. One long

shiver and then he totally relaxed – or maybe sagged would have been a better world as he remained leaning heavily against her and she was still holding him tight.

Gently she guided Peter to a chair; twisting him round she managed to get him seated. A minute or two passed and Paula was worried sick. 'Thank God,' she murmured when Peter's eyelids fluttered; it was as if he were just waking up from having been asleep. 'Paula, may we go soon? If David wakes up and I am not there he will be frightened.' Those two sentences had come from Peter almost reluctantly. It was obvious either it hurt him to speak or he was having great difficulty in forming the words.

'Listen to me, Peter, I am going to heat some milk for you. I want you to drink it and to eat something. I know I know,' she said, as he shook his head at the suggestion. 'How about some cheese and crackers? If you do as I ask I will take you straight back to the hospital, so do we have a deal?'

The poor little lad did his best to smile at Paula's suggestion of a deal. Somehow he still didn't seem to want to talk.

Joyce had been watching the whole time and had done her best to help. Coming up alongside Paula she said, 'I've heated some milk and I have stirred quite a bit of sugar into it. You hold this glass while I fetch a small table to put beside him.' Before moving away Joyce lowered her head so that her face was in the line of Peter's vision. 'Hey, young man, could you eat a gingerbread man with your hot milk?' she playfully asked, yet feeling far from happy; she was as worried as was Paula.

Peter shook his head and Paula wondered what it would take to get him to speak properly again. Why oh why were so many bad things happening today?

It took rather longer than usual to get themselves ready to go out again and Paula was more than grateful when Stanley Tompson suggested he run them to the hospital in his car. 'Would you like to come along for the ride?' he hesitantly asked Joyce.

'Yes, please, I would like that but I have to come straight back because I must have a proper dinner ready for this evening. Mr Lawson said quite firmly that he would be home.'

'That's all right. We'll see Paula and Peter safely into the hospital and then I will drive you home again. How about you, Paula? How will you get home?'

'Please, Mr Tompson, don't worry about Peter and myself. We'll stay a while, let Peter know that David is being well looked after and when we are ready to come home I will phone the cab firm we always use, and they will come out and fetch us home.'

Joyce sat in the front of the car with Mr Thompson driving. Paula was in the back seat with Peter snuggled up close to her. Why were they going back to the hospital? Was it purely to set Peter's mind at rest? Since his funny turn he'd hardly said a word – surely to God he hadn't lost the power of his speech. *Dear, oh dear*, she sighed; this morning had started out so well. Now it was as if a sinister cloud had slipped into a clear blue sky, threatening everybody, and all she wanted to do was to make it go away.

As if sensing Paula's thoughts, Joyce turned her head and said, 'Try not to think about what happened this morning; it was truly unfortunate that dog happened to be there the same time as we were. Just try and remember David is in the best possible place at the moment, so you worrying yourself sick isn't going to change anything.'

'I know, Joyce, and I do thank you for your concern. Maybe I'm as bad as Peter here. We don't like being parted, one from the other, so we'll have another quick look, satisfy ourselves that David is still sleeping peacefully and we'll be able to come back home. Won't we, Peter?' Paula asked, giving him a little squeeze. She felt well rewarded and so utterly relieved when he raised his head, smiled at her and simply said, 'Yes, see David.'

The trip had been well worthwhile. It seemed as if just being told that he wasn't going to have to wait until tomorrow to see his brother had jerked some new life back into Peter. It was almost four o'clock in the afternoon when Paula, holding tightly on to Peter's hand, stepped out of the lift and they made their way down the corridor towards the single room in which David had been placed. It was much more peaceful, with less hectic rushing around. Coming to a room where the door was slightly ajar and Paula could hear soft voices she stopped, sat Peter on a chair against the wall, put her finger to her lips and whispered, 'Ssh, Peter, I am going to pop my head around that door, see if I can get permission for you to have a peep at your brother. Stay quite and stay still, all right?'

Peter couldn't bring himself to speak, but he nodded his head eagerly.

A light tap on the door and Paula showed her head. For a moment she felt intimidated. One nurse and the matron were both standing looking at some forms that were spread out over a desk. The matron was older and her uniform was entirely different to that of the nurses. It certainly sat well on this kindly faced woman and it gave her an air of authority.

Paula was amazed when she received a smile. 'Can we help you?' the matron asked.

Paula had expected a reprimand for just being there.

She began a tangled tale of how David had been admitted as a patient this morning, was a twin to Peter who was at the moment sitting outside in the corridor; she'd had to bring Peter back because he had become so agitated, it being the first time the brothers had ever been parted.

The matron held up her hand, palm outward, and gently said, 'My dear, I understand perfectly. Dr Harvey has been in touch with me and I have been kept up to date about David's progress.' She lowered her voice. 'There aren't any doctors about at the moment; their regimental rules are all right in the right place and at the right time. Come along, let's see you settled.'

Paula hadn't noticed that the nurse had left the room but her eyebrows shot up on seeing her sitting next to Peter and talking very quietly to him. Peter, she was thankful to see, was not showing any signs of fear, in fact he looked up at Paula and softly told her, 'The nurse is going to let us sit for a while beside David's bed.'

It was pitch dark outside now. Long since the nurse had drawn the curtains at every window. Peter sat still. Now and again he rested his elbows on the edge of David's bed and let his chin rest in his cupped hands. His eyes remained open as he gazed at the still form of his brother lying flat in what seemed an enormous bed.

It was when Paula felt she was beginning to nod off that the nurse gently tapped her on the shoulder and whispered for her to bring Peter out into the corridor.

Strangely Peter raised no objection when Paula took hold of his hand and led him away from the side of the bed. Outside, away from the ward, the nurse drew Paula to one side and told her that

Mr Lawson was on his way up. Peter hadn't been told. Hand in hand they stood, both of them looking slightly lost. Footsteps echoed down the uncarpeted corridor. Mr Lawson came into view, a big man still wearing his dark suit and white shirt with a silver-grey tie. He had come almost directly from having been in court, his heavy unbuttoned Crombie overcoat flapped as he walked.

Paula was about to nudge Peter but she was too late. He had seen his father and was off like the wind.

Jeffrey would forever remember that moment. He stood still, arms spread wide, watching his son racing towards him as fast as his little legs would carry him. Not a word was spoken by father nor son. Peter was swept up high into his father's arms and Jeffrey Lawson, if asked, would not have been ashamed to admit that as he held his son close his own tears were dripping down on to Peter's head.

Still holding Peter in his arms Jeffrey Lawson looked into Paula's eyes and even at this stressful time he was aware just how green and beautiful they were.

'Hello, Paula. I've had quite a chat with Dr Harvey. He admires the way you have coped, but how are you really?'

Relieved at the intimate tone of his voice, she said, 'I'm fine. How are you?'

'Better now that I have spoken to Dr Harvey. The train journey seemed endless and at times like this we don't seem to be able to control our imagination, do we? I hear you and Peter have been sitting beside David's bed for a couple of hours or more; you haven't been bottling things up, have you?'

'Not really, just wishing to God that I had never let the boys go ahead of me.'

'Paula, my dear, the twins aren't babies any more, they are separate individuals. You have done a marvellous job in bringing them up so well but you cannot keep them tied to your side for ever, any more than you can now use self-incrimination as a stick with which to beat yourself.'

Paula's heart turned over. She wished he had never made those comments!

She struggled to pull herself together. 'The nurse told me there is a cafeteria downstairs. I know you will want to go and sit beside David and Peter is not going to relinquish his hold on you, so I'll go and have a drink.' *The toilet was going to be her first port of call but she kept that fact to herself.* 'I'll bring you back a coffee – what would you like, Peter?'

There was a moment before he was able to say, 'Orange juice please, Paula.' Still being held tightly in his father's arms he was able to manage a smile.

Suddenly there was an uncomfortable silence hanging between them and Paula hesitated about walking away. She looked at Jeffrey and she was shocked. What she would have dearly liked to do was to hug him, but she felt it wouldn't have been appropriate.

'Mr Lawson, don't cry. Please don't.'

'I'm not,' he said, but she felt sure he was.

Knowing how close to tears she was herself, she said, 'Did Dr Harvey tell you how long David would have to remain in hospital?'

'Not exactly, but he was optimistic, said he would be able to tell me more after twenty-four hours.' He shifted the weight of Peter to his other arm before adding, 'I always knew it was more than a stroke of luck the day you applied for the job of looking after the twins.'

More tears welled up in her eyes. 'I've been the lucky one,' she said brokenly, hurrying away to save herself more embarrassment.

Downstairs she found the toilet and, having washed her hands, powdered her nose and combed the font of her hair (the length at the back was still secured tightly into a French pleat) she wandered into the cafe. There were about a dozen nurses chatting amicably amongst themselves and she couldn't help but think what a wonderful job they did – but how, she wondered, did they cope with the sadness of death?

She ordered a cup of hot chocolate and a bun because she realized she hadn't eaten anything since they had been in the Olde Bakery this morning. Having drunk at least half of her hot drink she sat tight-lipped, staring at the bun. She didn't feel in the least like eating it. What Jeffrey had hinted at had shattered her world. To say that she was perturbed would be putting it mildly. In a nutshell he had hinted that her job as a nanny to his boys was almost over. Just like that, without a hint of warning.

Think carefully, she chided herself, *exactly what had he been insinuating?* Or, more to the point, what exactly had he said?

He had pointed out that the boys were no longer babies. Well nobody was more aware of that fact than herself. 'You have *done* a marvellous job' – not that she was *doing* a marvellous job. It was very hurtful. But perhaps she had misread his meaning.

She finished her drink, stood up, leaving her bun untouched on the plate, and returned to the serving counter. 'Please may I have a coffee and an orange juice to take away?' Paula politely asked the young lady who was serving behind the counter.

'How far have you to go?' the assistant asked.

'Oh.' For a second Paula was confused. 'I am only taking the drinks to a ward on the second floor,' she explained, opening her purse and taking out some coins.

'I thought you might be travelling. I was going to pack the drinks in a cardboard box for you.'

'That was very considerate of you,' Paula said, smiling her thanks as the young lady passed over a small tray to her which now held the drinks for Peter and his father.

As Paula came out of the lift there didn't appear to be anyone about. Tiptoeing into the ward she had to smile. David didn't look as if he had moved a muscle, he was still sound asleep. Peter's fears must have diminished, for he was settled on his father's lap, cradled against his broad chest, and he too was fast asleep. Jeffrey looked up as he sensed Paula's nearness and he smiled broadly.

'So, how are you feeling now you've seen David?' Paula asked.

Jeffrey's eyes closed as he took a deep breath. 'When I arrived at this hospital I was as nervous as hell,' he confessed. 'Now I feel I ought to go to church and thank God.'

'If you stand up I'll take your place and you can place Peter into my arms while you drink your coffee.'

There was not a whimper from Peter as she settled him on her lap. Jeffrey seemed as if he were stretching every limb, arms above his head, shoulders well back. Finally he must have felt he'd loosened up enough, for he smiled as he said, 'I wish I had your stamina, Paula; you've spent the best part of today in this hospital and you still are not complaining.'

'Drink your coffee. I have just seen a nurse pop her head round the door and she tapped her watch. I think she's signalling that it's time we went home.'

'Right,' he said, taking a few swigs of what by now must be his lukewarm coffee. 'I'll carry Peter if you would bring my overcoat and briefcase; they're over there on that chair. When we get down into reception I'll ask one of the porters to call us a cab. My mind is certainly a whole lot easier now than it was when I arrived. How about you, Paula? Been a rough old day for you, hasn't it?'

'I'll admit I do feel different now that you are here,' she answered him quietly. 'To be honest I was terrified of having to face you.'

'Really, Paula, am I that much of a terror?'

Jeffrey was now bending low, his face almost touching hers, as he made to lift Peter from her lap up into his arms. Peter whimpered and jerked a little as they did the transfer but soon settled as he must have realized it was his father that was holding him.

Paula gathered up Jeffrey's belongings – she was glad of something to do. It had saved her from having to answer his question. Placing his overcoat and briefcase near to the door she went to the head of the bed, leaned over far enough so that she was able to hear the soft murmur of David's breathing. Oh, what she would have given for this never to have happened. He looked such a tiny mite, she longed to pick him up, cradle him in her arms; instead she gently smoothed one corner of his pillow which had become crumpled, kissed the tips of two of her fingers and then very lightly she let those two fingers brush across his forehead. 'Goodnight, David,' she faintly whispered, 'sleep well and in the morning I will be here hoping to see you smiling. God bless you.'

Now standing beside Jeffrey in the lift she was considering how awkward the evening could have been with so much tension between them. It somehow had managed to pass quite smoothly, though she was horribly aware how different the outcome might have been if David's injuries had been worse.

She was hoping against hope that tomorrow might bring good news that David was on the road to recovery.

Thirty-One

It was Joyce coming into her bedroom, bringing her a cup of tea, that finally woke Paula the next morning. She had lain awake more than half the night and when she had finally drifted off she had apparently overslept. It took her a moment to gather her thoughts. As the events of yesterday came back to her she could only wish that she had never taken the boys in to the village. Then she remembered that she owed Joyce an apology for failing to go back downstairs when she had called her to say that she was serving dinner. She had given Peter his supper, not that he had eaten much, helped him to undress and seen him into his bath. Poor Peter, he had been really crotchety, hadn't wanted to be left on his own, and in the end she had dozed off herself sitting at the side of his bed.

'Thanks for the tea, Joyce. Sorry I didn't make it for dinner last night.'

'Don't let it worry you, Paula. I understood and so did Mr Lawson. Peter is up and about; I've been seeing to him this morning but he keeps asking for you.'

'Oh my goodness!' She drank the last few drops of her tea, pushed back the bedclothes and swung her feet to the floor.

For one alarming moment she thought she was going to faint, and quickly she dropped her head between her knees.

'I know exactly what is wrong with you, Paula,' Joyce ventured to sound harsh but the words didn't quite come out right. 'You've had virtually nothing to eat since that pastry yesterday morning.'

'I know, Joyce, but please, don't start worrying about me. I don't feel particularly hungry now.'

'All right, it's up to you but it won't look good if you're going back to the hospital with Mr Lawson and as soon as you get there you black out. Take your time, sort yourself out and then come downstairs. I'll boil you a couple of eggs and make you some nice hot buttered toast.'

'And you'll stand over me while I eat it all, is that the idea?' Paula had the grace to smile as she spoke.

'Yes, if that's what it takes. Now get up slowly and get yourself ready, I'm going to see what Peter is up to.'

It took about half an hour before Paula decided she looked presentable enough to face the day. Mr Lawson was still seated at the kitchen table reading his newspaper when she came into the room. 'Morning,' she said, wishing she had spent more time doing her hair.

'Morning,' he answered in his deep plummy voice. 'Joyce tells me you haven't had a very good night and that you don't feel one hundred per cent this morning.'

'Joyce shouldn't be worrying over me. I shall be fine once I have something to eat. Have you phoned the hospital yet?'

'Yes, I rang through at seven o'clock this morning and the night nurses were still on duty. They hadn't much information to offer me. All I got was that David had had a peaceful night apart from one short episode. He had woken in the early hours and, not being used to hospital surroundings, he had felt frightened. Medically there was nothing to report. Doctors' rounds begin at ten thirty, so I was advised to phone again around midday.'

Paula pressed a hand to her mouth imagining David waking up in a strange environment. He must have been petrified. Glancing at the kitchen clock she saw it was half past nine, about three hours before they could learn how David was doing. 'Did they tell you what hours we are allowed to visit?'

'Not exactly but I did read the notice in the corridor while I was there; two until four on Wednesdays and Saturdays and two until five on Sundays. Evening visits six to seven every other day.'

'Good Lord, are you saying we can't see David until two o'clock today?'

'No, I'm saying no such thing. As soon as you've had a good breakfast, get yourself and Peter ready and we'll go to the hospital. Always better to go straight to the fountain's head if you badly need a drink.'

Oh, a great philosopher was Jeffrey Lawson, but even he didn't look quite so sprightly this morning. She would be one of the first to admit that normally there was something about him; those big brown eyes of his would certainly set most women's pulses racing. But today he looked as if he had the worries of the world on his shoulders.

'Paula, sit down.' Peter had his head tilted to one side as he gave out these important instructions. 'I am going to have some toast,' he quickly added.

Silently Paula walked to the end of the long table and took her seat. Even now she wasn't sure whether or not she had been rebuked by Peter.

'Do you think David will get something nice for his breakfast?' His sweet dear face was turned upwards and the very sight of him had Paula wanting to cry.

'I'm sure the nurses will see that David is given a really nice breakfast. Anyway, you will be able to ask him for yourself soon because your daddy is taking you and me to see that brother of yours.'

Silence hung heavy for a moment as Joyce brought their eggs and toast to the table. 'I hope David has woken up by the time we get there and will know that I'm there.'

Those few words whispered by a little boy had summed up the feelings of the three adults that were in the room.

As Paula made herself and Peter ready for the hospital visit the echo of Jeffrey's words from yesterday were still with her. Had she understood their meaning? Had Jeffrey definitely stated that Peter and David would soon be attending a school and would no longer be in need of a nanny? If so where did that leave her? Since the death of her mother the knowledge that from now on she would be financially independent should be making her feel a whole lot better. It wasn't. Where would she go? She could have a house of her own now, but who would live in it with her? Her heart felt so heavy, worried sick about David, blaming herself for having let the twins run off on their own. When David did come home she might have to pack her bags and leave. She'd have to make sure that the boys were not in the house on that day. How was she ever going to be able to bring herself to say goodbye to each of them? Except on the rare occasion when she had stayed with Molly and Laura for a few nights she had never been parted from them since they were seven months old.

Mr Lawson was well within his rights to dispense with her services; she could understand his reasoning. No father would want his sons being mollycoddled by a nanny once they were old enough to attend school. But God alone knew how much she would miss them. They hadn't become part of her life, they were her *whole* life. A tap on her door put a stop to her remorseful thoughts.

'Paula, may I come in?'

'Yes of course, Peter.' The words were scarcely said when he was across the room, flinging his arms about her. 'I bet David doesn't like being in hospital on his own. Wish I was there too.'

What could she say in answer to such devotion? Nothing.

'Peter . . .' Her breath caught on a sob, and she pulled him closer and kissed the top of his head.

'Are you two hiding from me?' The voice came from the doorway and as she looked up Paula wondered how long Mr Lawson had been standing there.

In actual fact he had been right behind Peter and had heard and seen every word and action. Paula and his two boys. He couldn't seem to focus on them separately: it was always her and the twins. The events of yesterday had brought it home to him that together they were everything in the world that mattered to him. He found himself remembering his wife and the time when she had been carrying Peter and David; he had never been able to get enough of looking at her. Even swollen by her pregnancy she had looked so lovely. It had been so unfair. Sheila had not lived long enough to even hold her babies. The cruel part had been the first six months of their young lives. Do-gooders had driven him up the wall. Ridiculous suggestions from all sides. Frigid professional nursemaids. What had they cared? It had been people like Esmé Wright with her down—to-earth common sense that had saved his reason.

His own mother had been shocked at the way the experts had badgered him to put the babies up for adoption and it had been she who had made the suggestion that he placed an advertisement in the local paper for a younger person to live in and take care of Peter and David. How many times since had he blessed his mother and thanked God for having sent Paula O'Brien to him?

Unlike so many men he'd never wanted his boys to be seen but not heard. They were a gift from Sheila, the very centre of his life; they were what gave it meaning and purpose. Yesterday fear had churned his insides to jelly when he had been told that David was in hospital.

Paula whispered something to Peter and he laughed, broke away from her arms and went towards his father. 'Daddy, are you going to take Paula and me to see David?'

That brought Jeffrey out from his contemplative mood with a jolt. He ruffled Peter's hair and said, 'I actually came to tell you both that I have got the car out of the garage and have brought it round to the front of the house, so when you two have finished canoodling your carriage awaits you,' he finished with a flourish.

Paula and Peter were seated in the busy reception area of the hospital; Jeffrey had gained an audience with Dr Harvey. If Paula had thought that yesterday had been a scene of activity then today the hospital looked like a battlefield. Men and women hobbling about on crutches, small toddlers screaming – mainly from fright, Paula supposed – elderly couples holding hands: were they fearing that their loved one was suffering from an incurable disease? Oh, she thought, they weren't doing any good sitting here; the people and the surroundings were making her feel very morbid.

She was about to suggest to Peter that they go outside and take a walk, though she knew it would take a lot of persuading to get Peter away from the bounds of the hospital. The sight of Jeffrey Lawson striding towards her with a big smile on his face had her sending up a prayer of heartfelt thanks.

'Daddy, what's happening? Are we going to see David now?'

'Don't be in such a hurry, son, that's two questions you've asked without waiting for me to reply. Come along, hold my hand, we are going to the cafeteria and once we are sitting down I will explain what is happening to David.'

Having found an empty table set in a corner of the cafe Jeffrey felt obliged to buy something. 'Stay with Paula,' he ordered as Peter made to trail behind him.

In no time he was back with two cups of tea and a glass of milk. 'Dr Harvey's report is not bad, much better than I expected,' he said, noticing that Paula was making no effort to drink her tea. 'Paula, are you all right?' he asked, showing great concern.

Paula nodded, though she knew that the strain must show in her face. There had been no more communication between them since she had allowed him to glance at her mother's letter. In any case she wasn't even sure what it was she wanted him to say or do. She realized that the anxiety of David's accident had probably

driven all thoughts of her worries from his mind and she understood that, but it was still upsetting her and it hadn't helped that
he had as good as said that her live-in job at Ridgeway would soon
come to an end. Try as she might the dread of that day was building
up inside her. In the end she raised her cup and took several sips
of the hot tea to appease him.

'What was your opinion of Dr Harvey? Did you like him?'
Jeffrey asked, and Paula couldn't work out why he was smiling so
broadly. 'I am asking you because he is going to join us as soon as
he is free; he wants to renew his acquaintance with young Peter
here.' Having given that as an explanation, he winked at Peter.

'My assessment of Dr Harvey?' For a moment Paula mulled
over that question. 'Well, he's a jovial, middle-aged, well-dressed,
intelligent gentleman who takes pride in his work. Has a great
deal of patience, especially with young children, but I imagine he
could be sharp-tongued should the occasion arise.'

Jeffrey was taken aback at such a sharp, concise characteriza-
tion. He however had no time to ponder over her definition, as
the man himself was approaching.

'Miss O'Brien, how very nice to see you again – and as for you,
young man,' Dr Harvey turned to face Peter, 'I've been given to
understand that unless I allowed your brother to go home with you
today, you yourself will move into this hospital and stay with your
brother until he is well enough to be taken home. Is that correct?'

Peter shot a worried look at his father, who merely shrugged
his shoulders. Quickly he reached out to take hold of Paula's hand.
'Will you stay here with me and David, please, Paula?' he implored
her as tears trickled down his cheeks.

Paula's mouth was so dry and her throat so tight that she couldn't
form an answer. In desperation she looked at Jeffrey.

His eyes seemed to focus on hers as though guessing how bewildered she was feeling. In a voice that made her relax a little, he
said, 'Let's all sit down. Dr Harvey has kindly offered to spare a
little time and bring us up to date on how David is doing.'

There didn't seem to be a need to form an answer so Paula just
nodded.

'Excellent, but I've got a better idea.' The doctor smiled, holding
out his hand to Peter. 'Would you like to come along to my office?
We'll all be more comfortable there.'

After glancing again at Paula, who gave his arm a reassuring squeeze, Peter put his hand into that of the doctor's and walked with him along a carpeted hall towards his office. Jeffrey seemed more relaxed as he and Paula followed on behind. But suddenly he startled Paula by pulling her close to his side and giving her a mighty hug before announcing, 'I just do not know what I would do without you, Paula, and as for Peter and David, should you ever decide to leave, move on or whatever, I am pretty sure that they would both demand that you take them with you. And as for me . . .'

He left that remark unfinished, but the tender look he gave her had her heart thumping against her ribs. She felt utterly stunned.

Only yesterday he had as good as said it was about time she thought of moving on, that the boys were becoming too grown up to be in need of a nanny. Now he had just declared that not only did his boys need her, but he himself did too. Inside she almost glowed at the thought. She'd be lying to herself if she hadn't often had the odd romantic thought about Jeffrey Lawson, but never once had she allowed these thoughts to prevail. Why? Because she loved her job and didn't want to jeopardize it by acting foolishly. Now her life had been turned around. As soon as David was on the road to recovery she must make an appointment and go to the solicitors' again, get matters sorted out officially, but none of that meant that she didn't want to continue with her job. *God above!* She scolded herself. *Get one set of problems sorted out before you create more complications!* And to do that she needed to have a proper talk with Mr Lawson, find out exactly where she stood as regards her employment.

Once inside Dr Harvey's office there were comfortable chairs for everyone and Paula, when seated, found she was facing a large picture window which looked out on to a beautiful lawn and carefully tended flowerbeds. At least the view was helping her to relax; she was breathing deeply and slowly but she was still remembering the way Jeffrey had hugged her close and the look that had been in his eyes.

'Well, Miss O'Brien, I understand you have been a substitute mother to Mr Lawson's twin sons since they were seven months old.' Dr Harvey certainly believed in being forthright.

Paula was struck dumb. No one had ever referred to her as the boys' mother, substitute or not. It would be madness to think she would ever be referred to as such.

Dr Harvey had remained standing. Not having received an answer from Paula, he pressed on. 'So, it would seem that these boys do not like being apart.'

'No, I miss David,' Peter interjected.

'Be quiet, Peter, and listen,' his father admonished him.

Ignoring the interruption, the doctor continued. 'We have taken X-rays and are pleased to tell you that the wound to his head was mainly superficial. We did need to put in quite a few stitches, which means he has had a very nasty headache and he probably won't feel on top of the world for some time to come. However, I and my team of doctors are of the opinion that nothing can be gained by us keeping him here in this hospital.' He paused, delighted and moved by the looks of sheer love and contentment that Peter bestowed on both his father and on to Paula. It wasn't his place to work out what the relationship was between this obviously well-off City gentleman and this beautiful young lady he supposedly employed as a nanny to his twin boys. Needless to say the boys adored her. The nurses had written in their report that during the night their patient, David Lawson, had constantly called out for Paula. As for the young lady, she appeared to be utterly devoted to the pair of them.

Dr Harvey pulled himself up sharply. *None of your business*, he reminded himself.

Peter looked up at him and his eyes were pleading as he asked, 'Please, Doctor, are you saying we may take David home with us?'

'Mmm,' he said thoughtfully. 'You would have to promise not to let your brother get excited, to make sure you will be very quiet when you are with him because as I have told you he will still have a very nasty headache. You will also have to promise me that you will bring him back to see me in one week's time so that I may remove the stitches from his head. Peter, do you think you can remember all of that?'

'I'm not sure,' Peter said truthfully and he sounded almost heartbroken. Then a smile crossed his face and his eyes lit up.

Jeffrey Lawson had learned a lot in these last two days. A wave of emotion came over him and he respectfully asked, 'Are you sure I won't be asking too much of you, Paula? If we take

David home today a lot more responsibility will fall on your shoulders.'

It was the way that Peter looked at her that tore at her heart, as if he was beseeching her to wave away his father's objection and take David home.

'I wouldn't have it any other way, Mr Lawson; even I shall sleep more soundly knowing that David is back in his own bed.'

In turn the doctor was still having thoughts of his own. *If I were in the father's shoes I'd have had that young lady up the aisle long before this. But then again, some folk are so busy looking for the grass to be greener on the other side of the road that they never see what good things are in their own backyard.*

'Come along, young Peter, I am going to let your nanny take you up to the ward to see your brother, because I need to have a chat with your father. You won't let David get excited, will you?'

A serious-faced little boy was trying so hard not to smile as he said, 'Can I tell him he can come home with us?'

'No, not straight away, as I have said I need to talk to your father first. You have a nice visit with him and later on we'll decide if and when David will be discharged. Is that all right with you, Peter?'

'Could you hurry up and decide?' But he quickly added, 'Please?'

Paula didn't dare look at Jeffrey; her own laughter was a job to conceal as she grabbed Peter's hand and made for the door.

Thirty-Two

Six days had passed since David had been brought home from hospital and Paula was feeling as wretched as she looked. She had accepted Joyce's offer to take Peter with her to the local church where there was to be a coffee morning plus a bazaar, hopefully to raise funds to help with the cost of badly needed roof repairs to the church.

Joyce had reminded her that she wouldn't be able to stay out too long as Mr and Mrs Blackmore were expected some time that afternoon, which meant there would be seven for dinner that evening and she hadn't as yet started on the preparations.

Yes, she had been relieved when Jeffrey had told her that his mother had made the suggestion that she and her husband would like to come up to Surrey and stay a while. It would enable her to see for herself how David was doing and also give her a chance to pamper her grandsons a little.

Every evening since Jeffrey had informed his mother about David having been admitted to hospital Mrs Blackmore had phoned for news of her grandson's progress. The call always came just after six o'clock, an hour before Jeffrey arrived home. There were times when Paula hadn't known what to say to her. Mary was an extremely nice lady and it was only natural that she was concerned for David. However, there was only so much to say about a little boy who was in pain and who most of the time was feeling sorry for himself. Paula herself was fraught with worry. To be honest she wasn't at all sure that she was dealing with the situation as well as she should be. David never wanted her to leave his side and Peter wasn't taking too kindly to the fact that he was not getting as much attention as his brother was. Had she been over optimistic when saying she could cope? She hadn't reckoned on being called to David's beside almost hourly throughout each night. Having slept so badly, tormenting herself with all kinds of horrors in the early hours, only then to drift off as the daylight came.

These last few days she'd been feeling oddly remote, as though the death of her mother and the communication she had written and left with the firm of solicitors unearthing dark secrets, which sooner or later she was going to have to deal with, was a bad dream she couldn't quite shake off. It was all perfectly real though, she was well aware of that, but with her emotions so muddled up and she so exhausted from her sleepless nights she'd barely managed to keep both Peter and David happy this morning. Admittedly, it was on her shoulders that the full force of caring for David had fallen; Mr Lawson had not missed one day of going to the City but he was going to have to take a day off tomorrow, as there was no way she could cope with the responsibility of taking David to have his check-up with Dr Harvey. His father had to be there.

To make matters worse, yesterday morning she had received a letter from Jonathan Griffith stating that both Michael and Patrick O'Brien were attempting to contest parts of her mother's will. What it had to do with Patrick was beyond her. She was also anxious about the fact that at some point she was would have to meet face to face with Michael O'Brien, who from the day she was born had passed himself off as her father. The very thought sent shivers of fright up and down her spine, yet she knew only too well she wouldn't be able to put the meeting off for much longer.

Glancing up at the clock, she wondered if it was too early to telephone Mr Griffith. She'd try anyway, and if he wasn't in his office perhaps his secretary would be and she'd be able to leave a message.

After two attempts when the operator informed her that the line was engaged and she should try again later, Paula did just that, thinking that the City of London started work early. She was feeling frustrated; there were so many pressing questions that she needed to have answers to. Right now she had to go back upstairs and check on David.

'Oh, bless him,' she murmured out loud. He was fast asleep, lying on his side, one cheek resting on the palm of his hand. The side of his head that was uppermost showed the quite large patch of baldness where the doctors had shaved his hair and put stitches into place. It had been just seven o'clock this morning when she'd had David in the bath, removed the gauze, gently creamed the wound and put into place a fresh clean dressing. David had been contrary whilst eating his breakfast, annoyed that she had buttered Peter's toast before his. Now he looked so peaceful and she longed to lie down on the bed beside him and sink into a deep sleep herself. These past few days he had cried a lot, didn't seem to want to move from his bed and that fact alone worried Paula. It was not a bit like either of the twins. Several of the times when he'd been disagreeable she had asked if he had any pain and always he had said yes but apart from his head wound he had never indicated anywhere else.

She walked across the room and stood gazing out of the window into the garden. It was a dreary morning, with leaves still being blown from the branches of the trees, and now rain was falling on to heaps of sodden leaves that were already lying in untidy heaps on the lawn. The shrill ring of the telephone broke into her thoughts. Paula half ran down the stairs knowing she was running a risk of breaking a leg because the staircase was steep and winding. She unhooked the hearing trumpet and placed it to her ear. 'Ridgeway Manor,' she said breathlessly.

She heard button 'A' being pressed and the two pennies dropping down into the tin money box which was placed at the bottom of all pay phones in telephone kiosks.

'Is that you, Paula, my dear?' Arthur's broad Devonian accent came down the line.

'Yes, Arthur, how is the journey going?'

'We should be with you by about three. We broke off at Exeter and had a bite to eat. Everything all right with you, is it?'

'Will be better once you and Mrs Blackmore arrive,' Paula told him, and he heard the thankful relief in her voice.

'Well, you just get that kettle on an' we'll be with you in no time at all. I'll say goodbye now my dear, won't be long afore we get there.' The line went dead and Paula replaced the receiver. *I might as well try Mr Griffith again while I'm here*, she told herself, once more picking up the phone. This time she was connected without delay. Having stated her purpose she was informed that she was speaking to Miss Gibson, Mr Griffith's secretary. 'Mr Griffith will not be in the office at all today. May I be of help to you, Miss O'Brien?' The offer was kindly and politely made.

'I have had a letter from Mr Griffith asking me to make an appointment to see him,' Paula explained.

'That is no problem; I have his desk diary here. When would be convenient for you?'

Paula had to think quickly. It would mean that she would have to be away a whole day if she were going to his London office, not a good idea with David being so poorly. Then it came to her that Mrs Blackmore would be staying for a while.

'Sorry to keep you waiting, Miss Gibson. Almost any day of next week would be fine if Mr Griffith is free.'

'Late Tuesday morning he has an open slot or—'

'No need to look any further, Miss Gibson. Tuesday morning will be fine, but what exactly does late morning mean?'

'Mr Griffith is free from eleven o'clock until twelve thirty.'

'Thank you, I'm sure I shan't take up that much of his time, but I will be on an early train and at your office by half past eleven on Tuesday morning.'

'I'm pencilling that in his diary now. Lovely to talk to you, Miss O'Brien.'

'And you, Miss Gibson. Thank you for your help.'

Once again Paula replaced the receiver, this time deep in thought. Would Mrs Blackmore object to her taking a whole day off? And was it going to be possible for her to have a long talk with Mr Lawson before she travelled up to London? Oh dear, her life was suddenly becoming complicated; would this visit to the solicitors' be beneficial to her or would it once again be like opening an old can of worms? She had many decisions to make and a whole lot of wrongs that she was determined to put right.

It wasn't the usual lively evening meal but Mary Blackmore assured herself that it had been the right decision for her and Arthur to travel up from Devon.

She'd make allowances for Peter and David; they had each suffered a terrible shock. It must have been hellish for Peter to have to stand by and see a huge dog knock his brother down, and as for David, one look at the bald patch covered by a large dressing and she was holding him gently in her arms, her lips repeatedly placing gentle kisses on the rest of his dark curly hair.

She was annoyed at her son; having learned that he had gone to work every day as usual since David had been discharged from the hospital she could see why Paula was looking so worn out. To cope with two little boys at the best of times was a job most young women wouldn't have wanted to take on. She was well aware that over this long period of time Paula had coped admirably. She had been an absolute godsend to Jeffrey but now he was taking too much for granted and in the morning when they had all hopefully had a good night's rest she was going to have words with him. It was wonderful to watch her husband doing his best to amuse Peter; he had him on his knee and was reading him a story, patiently describing the meaning of every illustration as they came to them. Oh yes, she was a happy and well-contented lady. Jeffrey's father had sadly died too young. Arthur was always telling her that the journey he'd made to London, the occasion when he had first been introduced to her, had been a very lucky day for him. *Well, it works both ways*, she said, smiling to herself. Maybe the passionate fires of yesteryear didn't burn so brightly, but oh the companionship, the joy of having another person to say goodnight to and good morning the minute you woke next day, the fact that that someone cared enough to give you a hug for no other reason than they felt like it. All this loving companionship was beyond price.

For her part Paula couldn't help but feel that a whole weight had been lifted from her shoulders with the arrival of Mary and Arthur Blackmore.

The following morning, having only had to get up and attend to David twice during the night, Paula was feeling almost human again, though perhaps a little groggy, but then she hadn't long woken up.

'Honestly, I'm fine,' she told Mary when she came into the bathroom just as Paula was cleaning the bath.

'You slept a little better than you have been?'

'Yes, yes I did. Mind you the two glasses of scrumpy that Arthur insisted that I drank might have had something to do with it.'

'Well, he does tend to boast that the scrumpy he makes himself acts as a magic potion and it definitely seems to have done the trick where you are concerned,' Mary told her, looking most pleased with herself because it was she who had suggested he coaxed Paula into trying his scrumpy. 'You had me worried the minute I walked into this house; you looked absolutely worn out and I wanted to have a go at my son last night but Arthur stopped me.'

'Why would you blame Jeffrey? It isn't only David's accident that has given me sleepless nights. I have had so much on my mind since my mother died.'

'Well, yes, that's as may be but he shouldn't have left you to cope with David all on your own.'

'Please, Mrs Blackmore, I offered. Mr Lawson did try to contact Esmé, but her own mother is ill and she has taken her youngest two children and gone to look after her. Besides, I have had Joyce here with me, and she takes care of all meals for the twins. I never have to give a second thought as to what we are going to eat; Joyce is a fantastic cook as you well know.'

'But not that good at handling children.'

'Oh, Mrs Blackmore, I never said that!'

'I am not implying that you did, my dear, I have known from the day they were born that Joyce would never want to accept the responsibility of looking after them.'

'Joyce does her best – she helps me out whenever I ask it of her and the boys are fond of her. After all, I don't help her much in the kitchen, but having said that we have become good friends. Perhaps now is as good as a time as any to tell you Joyce has a gentleman friend.'

'Really!'

'Yes,' Paula smiled. 'Don't look so surprised. His name is Mr Tompson, Stanley Tompson; he works for the Electricity Board, a widower with no children'

'By the sound of it you approve.'

'Yes, I'm happy for both of them. I think Joyce was resigned to the fact that she would become an old maid. Her fiancé, like thousands of young men, was killed in 1917. She looks on this as a second chance.'

'Yes, I knew about Joyce; she and her young man had made wedding plans before he was killed. Thank you for warning me, Paula, does my son know?'

'Yes, he does. It was through Mr Lawson that Joyce met him. He was here in the house reading the meter and Mr Lawson told us in advance that Mr Tompson could be trusted.'

'Oh, that's all right then.'

Paula allowed herself to smile. She had heard the relief in Mrs Blackmore's voice once she knew her son had given his approval to the liaison.

'So what are you going to do about today?' Mary Blackmore hurriedly changed the subject.

'I'm not sure yet. It would be a whole lot easier if Peter would stay here with you, but I doubt that he's going to agree to do that.'

'Does that mean you are glad that I'm here?'

'You'll never know, Mrs Blackmore, just how grateful I am to you and to your husband. I was almost at my wits' end before you arrived.'

'In that case, will you please try and call me Mary and my husband Arthur?'

Paula made no answer; she wouldn't feel comfortable with that arrangement.

Not long after they had finished their conversation Jeffrey called out to say that he was bringing the car round to the front and that they should be leaving within ten minutes.

It was a scramble and it was twenty minutes before Jeffrey settled himself in the driver's seat, his mother seated beside him with David on her lap and Paula alone in the back of the car. They set off to make the short journey to the hospital.

Peter hadn't needed too much persuasion to stay behind with his grandfather, Paula was sure the bribe that Arthur must have offered was a good one. At the very last minute as Paula had handed David in to the car he had needed reassurance that David was coming back home as soon as the stitches had been removed from the wound in his head.

They had been sitting in the waiting area for half an hour when Mary decided to complain. 'Jeffrey, why are we being kept waiting so long?' Mary's feet had been tapping impatiently almost from the minute they'd sat down and now her loud irritation had woken David, who until now had been sleeping peacefully in his grandmother's arms.

'Paula, Paula,' David was quietly murmuring as he wriggled to free himself from Mary's arms. It was at that moment that the door to Dr Harvey's consulting room opened and a nurse was ushering out parents and their children.

'The doctor will see you now, Mr Lawson.'

Mary was on her feet in a flash; still holding on tightly to David she gave a sweet smile to the nurse and walked past her into the office.

Paula's face tightened as she looked at Jeffrey. He sighed and shrugged his shoulders. The door closed behind him and there was silence.

Silence that told Paula she was only an employee. No relation whatsoever to the patient. She sat perfectly still, allowing herself to remember how insecure her whole life had been and contemplate how insecure it still was.

Her thoughts were interrupted by the door being opened with a considerable amount of force. Mary Blackmore's face was like thunder. 'I hope that doctor knows what he's doing,' she said in a long-suffering tone.

Resisting the urge to ask what had happened, Paula sat still and waited.

'He suggests that as it is you who has full charge of David on a day-to-day basis it had better be you that sits in on today's consultation.'

There was a moment of astonished silence before Paula said, 'Are you saying Dr Harvey asked for me to go in? Are you sure?'

'Of course I'm sure. What's the matter with you?'

'I'm sorry, Mrs Blackmore, I just needed to be sure.'

'No Paula, it is me who should be apologizing. I am sorry but I feel hurt. That is my grandson in there. But never mind, we will have to discuss this matter . . .'

'We will, but not right now, eh?'

'No, you're right, the doctor has asked for you, so in you go.'

Paula sat in the chair that the nurse indicated and in a second David had climbed down from his father's knee and was clambering up on to Paula's lap. Settling himself comfortably he gave a soft, contented sigh.

The conversation from then on seemed to be on a one-to-one between Paula and Dr Harvey. He fired questions at Paula and she did her best to give a straight answer.

'So you are convinced that it is only his head wound that has made him irritable?'

'I never said that.' Paula was adamant that she had stuck to the facts. 'I have on numerous occasions asked David if he felt pain in his limbs. He always shakes his head and answers no.'

'You say he is not eating at all well.'

'He isn't, but I think that is understandable. He enjoys soft, smooth things such as mashed potatoes and creamy rice pudding, fruit and custard. Anything that requires chewing bothers him and I can see why.'

'Yes, the jaws moving.' Dr Harvey tut-tutted.

David spoke for the first time. 'Joyce makes me nice puddings, doesn't she, Paula?'

'Yes, David, she tries very hard to tempt you and you are eating something at each meal now, aren't you?'

'Can we go home now? Why is Peter not here?'

Paula felt guilty. 'I asked Peter to stay and be company for your grandad; they will both be waiting for you.'

'All right,' he said firmly, 'let's go.'

Jeffrey and the doctor exchanged glances, almost asking who was going to tell the lad that before they went any further he had to have the stitches removed from his head.

All the persuasion in the world wasn't going to stop David from crying. The nurses had offered him sweeties. One had pinned a badge to his jumper which said 'I am a brave boy'. His father had tried to take him in his arms, but no luck. Everyone who came near him was an enemy, with the exception of Paula.

Finally the job was done, a fresh dressing was put into place and with his hand in Paula's David was making for the door. 'Aren't you going to say goodbye to the nurses and to Dr Harvey?'

David's head was hanging low, he was looking at the floor but Paula caught his determined answer: 'No.'

His father was shaking hands and making his apologies.

'We got off lightly today,' the senior nurse assured him. 'We very often get a kick in the shins or even a bite on the arm.'

Arriving back home all three adults made for the kitchen and breathed a sigh of relief when they smelled the coffee Joyce was just brewing.

David made for the lounge where he got a boisterous welcome from his grandad and his brother. 'The wounded soldier returns,' Arthur shouted, lifting David up in his arm and hugging him close.

'Grandad bought us twelve soldiers; I haven't taken them out of the box yet. You can choose which six you want,' Peter told him as he too put his arms around his twin and gently hugged him.

Arthur Blackmore reckoned he was a tough old bird but seeing the two little lads standing there with their arms around each other had him sniffing and fishing in his pocket for a handkerchief.

Thirty-Three

'Mr Lawson,' Paula called, hurrying to catch him on his own as he strode across the hall. 'Would you have time to spare this evening? I would like to speak to you and I do need to ask for a day off next week if you could arrange it, please.'

'Paula, I owe you an apology; our discussion is long overdue but we will talk tonight, I promise. After dinner I'll ask Joyce to serve our coffee in my study and I'll leave Arthur to pour drinks and to keep my mother occupied in the lounge.'

Paula felt it was against her better judgement to force the issue but the sooner she started to sort matters out the quicker she would know just where she stood. For the rest of the day the hours dragged; she so badly wanted to get some answers from Mr Lawson and to listen to his advice if he were willing to give it. She was grateful when at last it was time to give Peter and David their supper and to see them safely into bed.

Mrs Blackmore came up trumps. 'I'll help with the boys if you like and I'll watch out for them while you and Jeffrey are having your talk.'

First off Paula had been annoyed that Jeffrey had told his mother of their arrangement but then Mary had explained a few things and now she was feeling grateful towards her. Even so it was eight thirty before she was seated in Jeffrey's big soft armchair, which he had pulled around in front of his desk.

Now she was sitting facing him as he said, 'Who's going to start the ball rolling?'

Paula hesitated.

'Very well. I think we should deal with the events of this past week first and then come back to deal with the letter your mother left you. Is that all right with you, Paula?'

'Yes . . .' She was still in a quandary as to how she should address this man under whose roof she had lived for so long.

'Paula, first off I must thank you for the loving care and attention you have provided for David while he has been under the weather. I must also apologize for having taken you so much for granted. It is no excuse, but I have been involved in a pretty important court case, and had I not had you to rely on I would have had to declare myself as unfit to continue. Instead I put my own needs first knowing full well that the twins could not have been in better hands. However, my mother has pointed out that I have driven you too hard and she suggests that you take a fortnight's paid holiday. She was absolutely astounded when I told her you had never taken a holiday in all the time you have been here, only the odd weekend. So now, whilst my mother and Arthur are here, seems to be a good time, what do you think?'

'I'd be a bit doubtful about leaving Peter and David, especially as David is a bit touchy at the moment which is more than understandable, but on the other hand I do have an appointment with Mr Griffith for next Tuesday. He also tells me I must sometime soon meet with the probate officer. Then there is my so-called family. I certainly do have to deal with the O'Briens.'

Hoping and praying that she hadn't accepted the holiday too readily she stopped talking, quickly sat up straight and reached for her cup of coffee.

'Here, take this pen and notepad,' he said, handing them across his desk. 'A lot of what you have just said I am in a position to help you with. First, make a note to ask Jonathan Griffith if your mother mentioned your birth certificate. If not, at a later date I shall take you to Somerset House and we'll apply for a copy. It also may be possible for me to deal with the probate officer for you; check that with Jonathan. Have you any preference as to where you would like to stay for two weeks? A family-type hotel will probably suit you the most. Do you want to stay in London?'

'Oh, no, certainly not London; I would be like a fish out of water. In fact I don't fancy staying in a hotel on my own one little bit. I would be so lonely. I'm sure my friend Molly Owen will be only too glad to have me stay with her and her family. I always feel most welcome whenever I do go there.'

Inwardly Jeffrey Lawson was sighing heavily. Just sitting here gazing at Paula was making him wish it were under very different circumstances. He hadn't been a saint since his Sheila had died and he knew that women found him attractive but he had never met anyone that he had wished to take out for a second time.

Paula O'Brien was different. For a quick moment he was smiling inwardly, thinking that this truly beautiful girl would not be using that surname much longer. Once she got started there would be no stopping her. Surely she'd been given that shock of red hair for a purpose! There had been many a time when he would have loved to ask her to accompany him to various dinners he was duty bound to attend, but always he told himself he was much older than she was. And she had never seen life. Not as it should have been. It made his blood boil just trying to imagine what she had suffered.

If only he had the right to make it up to her. Paula felt she would have given a lot to know what Mr Lawson was thinking about; he looked as if he was miles away but there was one more thing she had to get settled before she left this room.

'Mr Lawson, I would like to raise another point with you if I may.'

'Please, Paula, fire away and if I can help you know I will.'

'It was the first night you came to the hospital, you reminded me that the twins weren't babies any more. You praised me for having done a marvellous job in bringing them up but you also warned me that you couldn't allow me to keep them tied to my apron strings for ever.'

'Paula, Paula, stop!' He looked dumbfounded. 'What are you trying to say to me?'

'What I was going to suggest is that as you have so kindly said I may have two weeks' holiday we use this to make the break. With your mother being here the twins won't notice my going so much.'

It was like watching slow motion as he got up from his seat slowly and came to stand directly in front of her. He leant over her, placed his hands under her armpits and lifted her to her feet. She was tall but he was taller, and they stood silently, looking into each other's eyes.

'I could cheerfully strangle you.' It was said in such a low voice that Paula scarcely heard the words. It didn't matter. He lowered his head and brought his lips to cover hers. How long they stood like that neither was able to say. All the pent-up, constrained years of Paula's life melted into the background. All she wanted was to stay like this, his arms enfolding her, the gorgeous manly smell of him wrapping her in close while his soft lips moved over her face and back to her lips.

Jeffrey came up for air. Now was not the right time. He had acted on impulse.

He had thought about this young woman for so long yet he had respected her to the point where he had banished her from his head his heart and his mind. He was too old for her; she had a lot of living to do before she settled down; she would never look at a stuffed shirt such as he had become. But now, she was in his arms!

Now was not the time for declarations, not while his mother was staying in the house and certainly not until Paula had set about putting her life in order. But of one thing he was absolutely sure: before long Paula O'Brien would get her wish, and she would be using the surname of her real father, something she was legally entitled to do. He'd tried to imagine how she must be feeling to have learned that Mike O'Brien was not her father. It shouldn't be too hard to prove the legitimacy of what her mother had disclosed.

He tightened his hold on her, let his head rest on her glorious soft hair and inwardly he sighed sadly. *What could he say to her? When would the time be right?*

It was Paula who broke free from his arms; she needed to find a handkerchief because her eyes were brimming with tears. Quickly he removed a large white one from his pocket and handed it to her.

'Sit down again, Paula; we need to get a few things straight. I am so sorry if I misled you about staying with David and Peter. Can you even begin to imagine what my life would be like were I even to suggest that you were going to leave this house and not come back? I know at some point you will need to think about your own future – as you have so wisely pointed out, you do have a great deal that needs to be put to rights – but in the meantime let me assure you that if and when you should ever come to the conclusion, for any reason whatsoever, that you must leave me and the twins then it will be your own decision, not mine. Am I making myself clear?'

Paula could only nod her head. Her eyes were so bright, still brimming with unshed tears, but they were now tears of happiness.

'I can't believe that on top of everything else you have been labouring under the misapprehension that I no longer thought Peter and David needed you. All I can do is apologize again.' He had stumbled to find the right words and would dearly have liked to add the fact that *he* would missed her more than words could say. 'Am I forgiven?'

Paula wanted to throw her arms around him again, but instead she nodded, smiling, and said, 'I take it I am still to have my two weeks' holiday?'

'Reluctantly I am saying yes. You not only *need* a break, you damn well deserve one. I cannot believe I have been so thoughtless where you are concerned. It took my mother to point out the error of my ways. But, Paula, I guarantee it will not only be Peter and David that will miss you . . .' He left that sentence unfinished.

He didn't want to wait but in fairness to Paula he would. He was trying desperately to put these feelings into words.

Paula would have none of it. 'Thank you for being so honest. There is so much going on in my head that I do need to get sorted.' She gave him a saucy grin as she tossed her long red hair over one shoulder. 'I was about to address you as Mr Lawson.'

They looked directly at each before they burst out laughing. He recovered first and declared, 'Well, thank the Lord for that! At last, one thing has got settled this evening, hasn't it?'

'Jeffrey, I rather think it has.'

'Good, then no more of the "Mr Lawson"?'

'Jeffrey,' she said and suddenly the name held such a very different meaning. 'Jeffrey, I would find it hard to put into words what I am feeling at this moment, but please believe me, I do not remember *ever* feeling so happy, so wanted or so loved. However, as you have so rightly pointed out, I have to get my past life sorted out before I can grab all this happiness. It won't hurt to wait; not now I know what I might be able to look forward to in the future.'

Jeffrey knew differently.

It would hurt like hell!

But he needed no telling: the wait would be well worthwhile.

Thirty-Four

The wheels of Arthur Blackmore's car had barely stopped turning when Molly Owen had the front door open and was almost running down the short path, with Jack and Ronnie Wilson hard on her heels. Paula was only half out of the car when Molly had her plump arms around her.

'Jesus wept, lass, but you're a sight for sore eyes! Why the 'ell you 'ave t'leave it so long between visits I'll never know.'

'Mr Blackmore, Mum 'as let us 'ave the morning off from school so you can give us a ride in your car.' Young Ronnie was thrilled to have got in first with his information.

'Has she now? Well, I'll have to be 'aving words with your mum. You'll never get to be the prime minister of England if you don't go to school and get a proper education.'

Jack was about to say that neither he nor his brother fancied being a prime minister as they were both going to work at the post office with their dad when they grew up.

Arthur beat him to it. 'I know my last visit was a long time ago, but I thought we'd agreed that both of you would be calling me Uncle Arthur, is that still all right?'

Jack took charge. 'Suits us fine, Uncle Arthur. Are we gonna get a ride in your car?'

'You're more likely to get a box round the ears if you don't remember yer manners and stop pestering the man the minute he's got here.' It was the harsh voice of their mother calling from the doorway that silenced Jack.

'Mr Blackmore, nice to see you again and thanks for bringing Paula to us. Will you come inside and have a cup of tea with us?' Laura's tone of voice had softened.

Arthur Blackmore had never been inside one of these small terraced houses and he was curious. He turned to look at Paula but she was busy helping Molly to remove her luggage from the back seat of his car and he found himself smiling as he listened to Molly ranting on. 'I know you said yer was coming to stay for a fortnight, but Christ, by the look of it you've got enough clothes with yer to last six bloody months!'

'Molly, are you saying you don't want me to outstay my welcome?'

'Course not, yer silly cow, I'm only joking. Come 'ere, give me another hug just so as I know you really are with us again.'

'Would somebody please tell me how much longer we're all going to stand about on this pavement giving these neighbours of ours a good eyeful? And by the way, don't I get a look in when it comes to saying welcome to me best friend?'

Paula dropped the suitcase she had just dragged out of the car and flung her arms around Laura, who had by now joined them out on the street.

'I don't mean to interrupt this mutual admiration society.' Arthur grinned. 'But didn't I hear Laura offer me a cup of tea?'

'Oh, whatever must you think of us all? Please, Mr Blackmore, come in. I did put the kettle on so I won't be long making the tea.'

'If me blessed kettle ain't boiled dry,' Molly mumbled, while Paula and Laura exchanged amused glances.

Arthur was pleasantly surprised. He had been born in a small cottage in Coombe Martin in North Devon, which hadn't had many amenities, not even the advantage of running water. He had loved his home, still did. That cottage, now modernized, he rented out to summer holidaymakers. He was a self-made man and proud of it and he was more than grateful that he and Mary had met up, been given a second chance as it were, because money might buy objects that were considered to be materially essential but it certainly did not buy happiness. This family glowed with cheeriness and contentment and from the little he had seen of the inside of this house the occupants had turned it into a real home.

The tea was good, hot and strong, the company stimulating even though it had been exhausting. *The trouble with you, my lad, is you're feeling your age*, Arthur sternly told himself after he had taken the boys for a ride and then taken them back to school in time for their afternoon session. Now he was more than ready to return to the peace and quiet of Ridgeway. He had forgotten that he had just deposited Paula here with her friends for a fortnight's holiday.

Who, now, was supposed to keep Peter and David amused? He laughed and quickly thrust that thought aside.

'Ah, there you are,' Molly said, looking up from the evening newspaper she'd been reading. 'So what on earth have you been doing upstairs all this time?'

'Well I wanted to spend some time with Ronnie and Jack and then I've been putting my clothes away. By the way, thanks for all the coat-hangers you put out for me.'

'I knew you'd be needing then; different now to when you first left home. You've some really nice clothes now.'

'Well, I don't have much else to spend my wages on: everything is provided for me at Ridgeway,' Paula said, taking a cup of tea that Laura was holding out for her.

Laura frowned. 'Paula, are you feeling all right? I'm asking because, to be honest, you look thoroughly washed out.'

'I'm fine. Or rather I will be when I have a few days' rest and get my breath back. So much has happened since I last saw you – just after my mother's funeral, wasn't it? I haven't known whether I've been on my head or my heels.'

Laura smiled, though she still appeared concerned. 'I see you've put some bottles on the dresser; are things that bad that you're hoping to get tipsy while you tell us all the news?'

It was Paula's turn to smile. 'The brandy and the whisky are for us all to share; the bottle of rum is for Fred.'

'Oh, he'll be made up, sorry he had to leave as soon as we'd finished dinner, he's on nights for the next couple of weeks.' Laura laughed as she watched her mother open the bottle of whisky.

'So what shall we drink to?' Molly asked. Having poured a measure of whisky into three glasses she handed the two girls a glass and kept the third one for herself.

'To us,' Paula said decisively as they clinked glasses, then she poured her tot into her tea.

'You said you have to go to London next Tuesday – will you be all right travelling on your own?' Laura hadn't lost the habit of caring for her young friend.

'Of course I will. Though I have to phone once I've made the arrangements, it's just possible that I will be travelling up on the early train with Mr Lawson.'

'Hmm, like that is it?' Laura had her head tilted to one side and there was a big grin on her face. 'I wasn't meaning to pry but you went all girlish for a moment.'

Paula chose to ignore that remark and Molly saved her bacon by saying, 'It's getting a bit late for you to go in to too many details tonight but you've got to start at some point cos as Laura has already pointed out you look as if you're carrying a whole heap of trouble on those shoulders of yours, Paula. And you know what they say: a trouble shared is a trouble halved.'

Paula looked at her, then sighing heavily she stared down into her teacup and wondered where to begin. In the end it didn't prove too difficult, for she was soon confiding everything. The fact that her mother had been engaged to an officer in the Royal Horse Guards, how they had met at Windsor during a ceremonial occasion and how he had been killed in a railway accident leaving her to discover she was pregnant in 1910.

She told them about her mother's father. 'My grandfather, I'm glad I never met him. The pompous, arrogant, bombastic so and so!' Nothing was too awful to say about a man who had literally paid an Irishman to take away his daughter and his unborn grandchild and to make sure he never had to hear from them or see them ever again.

'Some grandfather he would have made!' Laura was heard to mutter.

Now Paula told them that she would in future be financially secure due to a legacy left to her by a grandmother she'd never known, but she emphasized the money was insignificant against the loss of a family.

Paula had stopped talking; she was lost in thought. Laura was worried by the look on Paula's face; it was as if she had just woken up from a bad dream.

Laura gazed at her mother and mouthed silently, 'Have I got it right?'

Molly nodded her head but turned her gaze back on to Paula. Oh my God! What a life this poor lass had been called upon to live. It was just one nightmare after another. Surely it was a miracle that over the years Paula had remained sane.

Laura screwed up every ounce of her courage to be able to ask, 'Paula, are you saying that Mike O'Brien is not your father?'

Paula raised her head and gave Laura such a sweet, sad smile that it brought tears to Laura's eyes. 'That is exactly what I am saying. He is not my father, he never has been, and he never will be in the future.'

Laura blinked; she was having a job taking all of this in. How much worse it must be for Paula – no wonder the poor girl looked as though she was recovering from a nightmare. That wretched father of hers needed seeing to! Paula's life story was even more unbelievable now the truth was out – and all along he'd had no legal rights. Why had her mother always sided with him? She supposed that in 1910 it was really not done to have a child out of wedlock. Even today, twenty-one years later, illegitimacy still carried the same stigma and always gave the neighbours plenty to gossip about.

Paula herself had thought the same; many times over these past days she had felt such pity for her poor mother trying to picture the scene when her mother would have had to face up to her father. It must have been terrible, even terrifying, but to sell his own daughter to a man who was wholly unsuitable, cast her and her unborn child aside, never to see them or to make contact with them ever again. It was incredible – to any normal father it would be unthinkable.

'Paula, no wonder you look washed out, it must have been very hard for you to make sense of it all. You said you were going to London soon – what's going to happen, do you know?'

'Not really, with David having been in hospital and him being a bit tetchy since he's been home I've put my own affairs on hold. To be honest I was pleased when Mr and Mrs Blackmore said they were coming up to stay for a while, I never thought I would say it but it was a relief to get away for a while.'

'I should think so too,' Molly declared sharply. 'But it's an ill wind that blows nobody any good; at least we've got you to ourselves for a nice long time.'

Molly felt so sorry for her. Paula's whole life had been one disaster after another but there was nothing she could do to alter the past; it was all far too late for that. Molly thought her eyes looked so sad as she sat there, and something about her made her heart ache. Still, her mother had done her best to put things right by writing the facts down before she had died. From now on events would have to take their course, though Frances O'Brien had given them a good shove the day she had put pen to paper. She couldn't help but wonder how it would all work out. Right now what Paula needed was a few good nights' uninterrupted sleep. Once she felt less tired she'd get her confidence back and she'd bet her last shilling Paula wouldn't let the grass grow under her feet where that bugger Mike O'Brien was concerned!

'You must be exhausted if you've been up two or three times a night seeing to young David,' Laura remarked quietly. 'I know what it was like when Freddie broke his wrist; they want yer full attention twenty-four hours a day, but I had Mum here to help me and I must say Fred did help when the thought struck him. Didn't that Joyce help at all?'

'Oh, yes she did, but Joyce isn't the mothering type.'

'And you are?' Laura was grinning from ear to ear. 'You're what, twenty-one? Never really seen the best side of life, but you're entirely wrapped up in those two little boys. Take it from me, Paula, when you've got things sorted an' you've money behind you it's about time you started to live a little, begin to think of yerself for a change.'

'Yeah, yeah, Miss Clever Clogs, good at giving advice, aren't you? It's getting on for midnight and the poor lass is almost asleep sitting there. So, let's be having you. Tomorrow's another day; let's wait and see what turns up then, shall we?' Molly's words were uttered quite firmly for she did like to let the girls know she was still capable of taking charge!

'You do looked whacked out,' Laura said, looking again with concern at Paula. 'Would you like another drink or anything else to eat before you go upstairs?'

'Actually I do feel worn out,' Paula confessed. 'I appreciate the offer but I have had more than enough to eat and drink, thanks, Laura. All right with you if I go on up, Molly?'

'Oh, lass, don't start all that nonsense, asking permission before you do anything. How many times d'yer need telling? This time you're 'ere for a long stay so for God's sake treat this 'ouse as if it is yer 'ome an' then we'll all feel a whole lot more comfortable.'

'Thanks, Molly,' Paula said, and went over to where Molly was sitting to put her arms around her neck and kiss her cheek. 'Goodnight, see you in the morning.'

'Goodnight, lass. God bless you and just remember we're all glad t'ave yer home 'ere with us.'

Upstairs, in her makeshift bedroom, Paula started to take her clothes off. She really was dog-tired yet her mind was still active. For the moment she was left guessing as to how things were going to turn out. Of course she was pleased her mother had written the letter but some passages were printed on her mind. For years she had half believed that Mike O'Brien had been the man who had raped her, made her pregnant. Was finding out that it was her Uncle Paddy and not her so-called father any easier to bear? The two brothers were as horrible as each other. Between them they had put her and her mother through the worst hell anyone could imagine. Would it have been better had she never learned the truth?

With all these conflicting thoughts running through her head she so badly wanted to drive the disgust and horror from her mind and be done with it. It had all happened so long ago. Did that make it any better? Or any easier to deal with now? No, it did not. She had the means with which to put some things right and for that fact she owed a debt of gratitude to her dead mother. There were, however, things which were imprinted on her mind that nothing would ever erase. The filth of the rape had been bad enough but the year that had followed had been a living hell.

And what about the priests? Had their involvement been down to Mike O'Brien? They were supposed to have been God-fearing men. *Well they had certainly put the fear of Christ into me*, she stormed as she got off the bed and began pacing the room.

Right up to the day that she had left home all the men in her life had caused her to be afraid of them. During those awful months she had been shut away she had been terrified of every single doctor who had examined her. If you weren't mad when you entered that place you most certainly were not wholly sane when you were released.

Paula felt she was living proof of that. True, her nightmares had diminished since she had been living at Ridgeway but there was always the thought at the back of her mind of how she had ever landed up in such a place and who was entirely responsible for her being imprisoned there in the first place.

Paula shuddered at the memories.

No matter what else was brought to light once she started to confront people, she had to make sure that one very relevant fact was brought right out into the open.

Michael O'Brien was *not* her father.

Stop it! Paula silently rebuked herself. *Do as dear Molly had suggested, and get a good night's sleep.* That was good advice, because as much as she kept telling herself it was all behind her now, she knew in her heart she had a long way to before that would become true.

Thirty-Five

Paula was sitting opposite Jeffrey Lawson on the train that was due to arrive at Victoria Station at five minutes past nine. At the moment Jeffrey was showing a serious frown but whenever their eyes met she gazed at his infectious smile.

She had been staying with Molly and her family for four days now and she did feel a whole heap better for the change in her lifestyle. She missed the twins, of course she did, but it was a wonderful change to be able to relax in such easy-going company as Molly and Laura provided. She had been shopping with them, not just to ordinary shops but to buy from the several stalls that made up the local markets. She enjoyed the smell of fresh-baked bread mingled with the odours of fresh fish and cheeses and loads of ripening fruit. To hear the barrow-boys calling out their wares, and the housewives bargaining with them really amused her. Cups of strong dark tea and a jam doughnut was a regular routine, it seemed, in the steamy market cafe where everyone had a bit of news to pass on.

'No need to buy a newspaper,' Molly had laughingly told Paula. 'If you don't hear it down the market then it ain't worth the likes of us bothering our heads about it.'

Jeffrey turned the pages of *The Financial Times* and ran his finger-nail along the edge of the page before folding it in half again. Very different he looked in his business suit this morning, Paula decided, as she eyed him from top to toe, and his actions were almost fastidious. Inwardly she was comparing her two different ways of life.

Life at Ridgeway had carried along practically undisturbed and she had loved every minute of it. Life in Blackshaw Road was totally different.

Noisy, but jolly, with neighbours popping in and out, endless cups of tea and fish and chips for dinner every Friday night. Having said that, she knew these hard-working men and women took a great pride in their homes. Anyone who found themselves in trouble didn't have to look far for help and for the most part Paula would say they all had hearts of gold. Their children did not always speak good English but then neither did their parents, most of whom had left school at the age of twelve, but when it came to good manners they hardly ever stepped out of line.

Jeffrey was closing his briefcase. Paula stared out of the window as the train approached Victoria Station. The passengers on the train, mainly men in dark suits, were standing, buttoning up their overcoats, putting on their gloves. Another working day was about to begin, another way of life for a different type of person. It certainly seemed to take all sorts to make up this world.

Once they had disembarked, Jeffrey turned to face her and with a very stern look on his face said, 'I'll put you into a cab as I did on your previous visit but when your interview with Jonathan Griffith is over I want you to promise you will not leave his office, but you'll wait there until I come and fetch you.'

'Shall I phone you?'

'No, Paula, I have spoken to Jonathan and he will ring me when you are ready to leave, then depending on what advice he gives you we shall have lunch before we do anything else.'

'Are you saying that you are going to chaperone me everywhere I have to go?' Paula asked, sounding quite cheeky.

'I most certainly am. Letting loose a country mouse such as yourself in this big bad city is not something I am willing to risk. Come along now, you'll have to queue for a cab but don't forget what I have just told you.'

'Right, sir.' Paula gave him a mock salute, but secretly she was thrilled that he was taking charge of her.

'Sorry to keep you waiting,' a young good-looking man said, popping his head round an office door. 'Are you Miss O'Brien, here to see Mr Griffith?'

'Yes I am,' Paula replied softly, thinking to herself, *Not for much longer; the quicker I get rid of that hateful name the better I shall feel.*

'Mr Griffith is tied up with a technical problem, but he shouldn't be long.'

'No hurry,' Paula assured him.

The young man opened the door wider. 'Why don't you come in here? I'll fetch you a coffee and let Mr Griffith know that you've arrived; it's not very comfortable out there in the reception area.'

Twenty minutes later and Paula was back in Mr Griffith's office.

'Some good news and some bad,' he said to open the conversation, having gone through the usual routine of asking after her health. 'Yesterday after I had spoken with the probate officer I was given yet more bad news, as it seems your father not only intends to contest your mother's will but he is insisting that he *is* your natural father.'

It tore Paula apart to hear Mike O'Brien still being referred to as her father and the thought of all the unnecessary legal procedures he was planning had her fuming.

'I understand that you have taken Mr Lawson into your confidence and that is good. He will be in a position to open a good many doors on your behalf. I am sorry Mr O'Brien has seen fit to cause so much trouble.' Jonathan Griffith knew the whole story now, and was able to say, 'Obviously it was a shock, your mother leaving you a letter laying out all the facts, and a pretty profound one no doubt, but Michael O'Brien has no choice but to get over it. He won't win and in the process he won't like the procedures that will follow. Once again, Miss O'Brien, I have to warn you these matters will take time; there is no way one is able to hurry legal transactions.'

Paula was gazing at the floor and it was only when Mr Griffith spoke again that she raised her head. 'I see you flinch each time I use the name of O'Brien and I know it will be a big confidence boost when you are able to use your true surname. To change your name by deed poll would be a far quicker course of action, but that isn't what you want, is it?'

Paula was shaking her head as though baffled and she gave a dry laugh. 'No, what I really want is to make it happen legally. Shout it from the rooftops; let everyone know who I really am. Paula Grantham.'

Jonathan laughed; he was imagining this truly beautiful, amazing young lady with this gorgeous head of auburn hair standing on a rooftop. She would certainly stop traffic! It was a wonderful thought.

'I am so afraid that somehow he will be able to dispute what my mother has stated.' Paula's eyes reflected the apprehension she was feeling.

'I have explained, Miss O'Brien, that if he has legal represen-
tation his solicitor will most probably use every delaying method
known, but in the end we shall produce all the evidence that will
be needed to substantiate your mother's facts. You have to trust
me,' he chided.

Paula nodded slowly as she considered that, and when she let
her eyes meet his she slowly smiled.

'Would you like to know what I think? Off the record for once,
because I don't usually get so personally involved with a client's
affairs. I think you should have your holiday and then go back to
Ridgeway Manor where I've been given to understand you have
been very happy. Mr Lawson tells me his young sons adore you
and he is more than willing to provide you with sanctuary even
if it is only while you sort yourself out.'

Paula sighed softly, suddenly feeling very lonely, thinking of the
twins.

'It's a nice thought,' she said. 'And God knows I need to do
that – I want to do that – besides, where else would I go?' Then,
after a pause, 'I have to be honest, though, I don't think I can go
on using the name of O'Brien. And I do know that sooner or later
I am going to have to come face to face with more than one
member of the O'Brien family and that is a matter that I truly
dread.'

'There's no rush,' Mr Griffith reminded her. 'You are a wealthy
young lady now, so you can travel if you wish, go where you like,
see the world.'

'I don't want to do anything like that,' she responded grimly,
but she didn't add that all she really wanted to do was to go back
and take care of Peter and David and see how things would develop
between herself and Jeffrey. Was that asking too much? She sincerely
hoped not.

Jonathan was regarding her curiously. 'I hope you're not planning to confront the O'Brien family in person. Think before you
act; the last thing we want is for them to bring a lawsuit against
you.'

Paula smiled. 'I have always regarded myself as a peacemaker,
never a vengeful sort of person, but just lately I dream of revenge.
When it comes right down to it I have so many scores to settle
with that family. They intruded into my life so intensely that it is

hard just to wipe away all the sadness, the hurt and the brutality that I was made to suffer over the years. Then again I can't begin to imagine just what would settle the score. The wounds have penetrated far too deeply to be easily healed.'

'I need your signature on a couple of forms before I phone Mr Lawson to come and pick you up,' he said, quickly changing the subject; he was beginning to feel very protective towards this young lady and that wouldn't do at all. Sorting through a pile of papers that lay on the desk in front of him, he kept his head low.

'Will it still be legal for me to sign Paula O'Brien?' she asked, sounding somewhat doubtful.

'You could legally carry on using the same name for the rest of your life if you wanted to,' he replied. 'You'll be in a better position to decide after you've made your visit to Somerset House. I gather Mr Lawson is taking you there today while you're in town.'

Paula did not respond to this; she had too many thoughts going round in her head.

'Can I get you another coffee while you're waiting?'

'No thanks, I'm fine,' Paula told him, struggling to hide her excitement.

Mr Griffith left the room to make a call to Mr Lawson, so he said, but there was a telephone on his desk and she wondered why he hadn't used that one. Perhaps he wanted a private conversation. The moment he was back his attitude altered as he passed several papers to her and indicated just where she should sign. 'Two of these are merely consent forms, which give me the right to delve into your late mother's affairs and even into archives that are appertaining to sections of her will. In a few days' time I shall have a much clearer picture as to how we may approach the points that Mr O'Brien is choosing to contest.

'I'm sure we shall have cause to meet again in the near future,' he added as he helped Paula on with her coat. 'I hope you are successful at Somerset House.'

He held out his hand and Paula shyly took it. This man knew so much about her, a complete stranger and yet he knew her history almost from the day she had been born, thanks to her late mother. Mr Griffith walked her to the front of the building just as a cab drew into the kerb and Jeffrey Lawson almost leaped out. The two men greeted each other heartily and stood in earnest conversation while Paula climbed into the back seat of the cab. After a short while Jeffrey tucked his briefcase under his arm, nodded briefly as he turned towards the cab, saying, 'There's always one fly in the ointment. Thanks, Jonathan, for keeping me posted.'

Even the burly London cabby was struck by the couple who were now his passengers. The gent was obviously in the legal profession; he had picked him up in the Inner Temple. Apart from the expensive dark suit, which was almost a uniform for these lawyers and barristers, his dark hair was turning silvery-grey above his ears, which served to give him an even more distinguished look.

But boy, the young lady who was now with him was a proper eyeful: tall, figure like an egg-timer and legs that went right up to her hips, but it was that head of hair that really made her stand out. Flaming Nora, fancy waking up and finding that all spread out on the pillow beside of you! He'd lay ten to one she didn't go to bed with a load of tin Dinkie curlers in her hair like his old woman did!

Twisting round, the cabby slid the glass partition back and asked, 'Where to now, Guv?'

'Covent Garden, please, driver,' Jeffrey said, barely taking his eyes from Paula.

'Righto, guv,' the cabby replied, an envious look on his face.

'I thought we might do a bit of slumming, have our lunch some-where different. Do you know much about Covent Garden, Paula?' Jeffrey asked, smiling mischievously.

'I know it is famous for wholesale selling of fruit and vegeta-bles and more recently I did hear they also deal in imported flowers from all over the world, but I have never been there.'

'It is not only flowers from foreign parts that come to the market now, many are from parts of England and in the spring all the daffodils and such like are brought up to there from Cornwall. Look,' he said, and touched her elbow, 'we are just passing the Abbey of Westminster.'

Jeffrey was obviously no stranger to this district; he indicated exactly where he wanted to be dropped, which was outside of a busy, prosperous-looking cafe. He paid the cabby and must have tipped him well because he was brightly told, 'You're a toff, thanks, guv.'

Leaning well forward the cabby caught Paula's eye. 'You enjoy yer lunch, miss; you could travel a damn sight further but take it from me you ain't gonna find a better load of grub than you can get in there.' He said this with a broad grin and finished with a saucy wink.

He was rewarded by a flash of Paula's big green eyes and a smile the like of which she didn't very often show to a stranger.

The cabby must have appreciated it for as he made to drive away he called out, 'Gawd bless yer, luv.'

Paula was enthralled as she watched the biggest chef she had ever seen carving an enormous joint of steaming hot salt beef. The man must have been well over six foot tall yet he wore a tall white hat and a gigantic white apron which would have wrapped around Paula almost a half dozen times.

They both decided to have the house speciality of salt beef. The meal in itself was a unique experience, one which they both heartily enjoyed, and the same went for the surrounding company, which mainly consisted of broad-shouldered tough market porters. Yet for all his outward appearance Jeffrey looked every inch at home and from some of the greetings and remarks that were shouted at him it was obvious that neither he nor his colleagues were strangers to this establishment.

Paula left that cafe with Cockney humour ringing in her ears and as soon as she stopped laughing she told herself, *Well, that's another facet of the human race that I had never met up with before*, though maybe Molly and her family came a close second.

'Would you like a walk around the market, before we set off to Somerset House?' Jeffrey asked, pointing to where the wholesale stalls were laid out.

'Yes, please, I would,' Paula answered, smiling.

The sight of so many exotic blooms had Paula in raptures and moving on to the vegetable section she was amazed; there were some weird and wonderful shapes, colours and sizes and many that she couldn't put a name to.

Suddenly Jeffrey took hold of her arm and linked it through his own, pulling her close to his side as they walked. He was smiling his most winning smile and it secretly melted Paula's heart.

'Well, time to get down to business. What did you make of the fact that Mr O'Brien has declared his intent to contest your mother's will?'

Up until now Paula had been making a conscious effort to put that to the back of her mind. The more she thought about what Mr Griffith had said, the more upset she became. The facts laid out in her mother's letter had been explicit and he had done his best to reassure her that they could and would produce proof. Just the same she had been stunned to think that her so-called father was willing to put her through the ordeal of having to sit in a court of law and listen to him spout a load of lies. It was not the money, that didn't bother her, but that he would even think about challenging her parentage when her mother had set out the truth in such detail made her blood boil.

'I think I shall go to see him, face to face. I might be able to talk some sense into him,' she murmured as if talking to herself.

'You aim to confront him?' Jeffrey was astounded.

Paula laughed. 'I promise I won't take a gun.'

'You most certainly won't because you won't be going anywhere near him – or any member of the O'Brien family come to that.'

Paula had the sense to keep her thoughts to herself.

Jeffrey knew he had to act sensibly; this was not the time to start feeling pity for her. He took a deep breath and as they turned out of Covent Garden he hailed a taxi.

'Where to, sir?' a baby-faced driver asked.

'Somerset House, please,' Jeffrey said as he handed Paula into the cab.

'I've got yer, sir, it's where yer register births, deaths an' marriages, right?'

Both Paula and Jeffrey were laughing as the cab drew away from the kerb and Paula had shelved her worries and was smiling broadly now because Jeffrey was holding her hand between both of his.

What a building! Paula was bewildered; there were so many different departments and so many different clerks to be dealt with. Jeffrey took charge and it was funny how staff reacted to his voice of authority. He very quickly established that yes, the young lady could obtain a copy of her birth certificate. The fee for the search would be two guineas and it would take about seven days. There were, however, two forms that first needed to be filled in. The clerk slipped the forms across the counter and Jeffrey picked them up and looked around the already crowded vestibule.

Sensing his frustration the elderly clerk quickly said, 'Sorry sir, please come to the end of the counter and I will unlock the door and allow you to come through.'

That accomplished, Jeffrey and Paula were shown to a small anteroom where there was a table and two chairs.

Thank God Jeffrey is with me, Paula thought. She doubted she would have received the same preferential treatment had she been on her own.

Paula answered the questions as Jeffrey read them out to her and he unscrewed his own fountain pen and filled in each one of the forms. 'I wonder why your mother never left your birth certificate along with the letter she lodged at the solicitors' office,' Jeffrey mused quietly.

'That's easily answered: because it wouldn't have been in the house. If my mother had had it in the house all these years you may be sure that my father would have found it . . . Oh! I mean Mike O'Brien.'

Jeffrey patted her hand. 'I know exactly what you mean, Paula; it will take a while to shake off that name. However, the fact that your mother did not see fit to keep your birth certificate in the house gives me hope. If at the time of your birth she registered your father as being Alexander Gerard Grantham; occupation, officer in the Royal Horse Guards, now deceased, she would not have wanted Mr O'Brien finding it – that's what you're saying, isn't it?'

Paula's eyes were glistening and her smile was brilliant as she answered a question with one of her own. 'Is that how *you* think it might have been?'

'Paula, how I wish I could say yes. Just remember your mother went to great lengths to tell you who your real father was and to put all her estate in custody for you. I have great hopes and as hard as it will be, all we can do for the present is to wait and see.'

Jeffrey thanked the clerk for his courtesy and was told on which floor he would find the Registrars of Wills and Probate. This part of their mission was not so easily completed. It was an elderly lady this time who came forward as Jeffrey pressed the bell. Paula was standing well back, leaving the talking to

Elizabeth Waite

Jeffrey. Whether he and the clerk were already acquainted or whether they were merely being polite Paula couldn't tell as she watched them cordially shake hands. It was some time before Jeffrey came back to stand by Paula and explain that this office was holding the official copy of her mother's will, together with the certificate of its having been approved to establish the validity by probate, but as the will was now being contested it would most likely have to go before a probate court, which would exercise jurisdiction.

This was all legal jargon to Paula, but she had got the gist of it. Nothing at the moment could be classified as straightforward because Mike O'Brien had seen fit to oppose her mother's wishes.

'Cheer up,' Jeffrey urged as they came out of Somerset House and walked towards the Strand. 'Come on, I'll treat you to afternoon tea in one of Joey Lyon's Corner Houses.'

This was a treat that she wouldn't have missed for the world, Paula said to herself as she let her eyes wander all over the place. There was a Lyon's tea shop at Wimbledon and another at Tooting Broadway, where it was possible to have a freshly made cup of tea for tuppence and a chocolate cupcake for another penny. She had often taken Peter and David in there for refreshments. This establishment was part and parcel of the same firm, but this was the west end of London where you sat at a table and waited to be served, as Jeffrey informed Paula.

Soft music was playing, the bone china was exquisite, and the toasted teacakes came served in a hot dish with a lid on to make sure they stayed hot. Just as Paula was deciding she could not eat another morsel their waitress came back with a two-tiered cake stand that held an assortment of delicious-looking fresh cream cakes.

'Do you often bring ladies here for tea?' Paula couldn't resist asking.

Jeffrey grinned. 'No, only when they are young, have the most beautiful head of red hair and live under the same roof as I do.'

Paula felt herself blushing and very quickly she asked, 'Isn't there a famous toyshop near here?'

'Yes there is, Hamleys on Regent Street, quite near to Oxford Circus. Why do you ask, as if I can't guess?'

'Let me hear your guess,' she said, purposely tantalizing him.

'You wish to buy a present each for Peter and David.'

'I did think it would be nice; you could give it to them and it will help them to know that while I am staying with Molly for a while I am still thinking of them both.'

Jeffrey Lawson was not one to show his emotions in public but at that moment he was having a hard job to restrain himself from leaning across the table and planting a kiss on her glowing cheeks. Paula was so young, and had become vivid and lively since she had been at Ridgeway. It was criminal the way she had been made to suffer during her early years.

'How about I buy them both a red London bus?' Paula asked, breaking into his thoughts.

'Funny, I was just thinking the same thing. Their mother, my Sheila, used to love to ride on the top of a bus through London.'

Paula looked at him and the sadness in his eyes would have frightened her at one time but suddenly it didn't. 'Maybe things happen in life for a reason,' she said and was immediately sorry. 'Oh I didn't mean . . .' She smiled sadly at him.

'Don't be sorry,' he said generously. 'I bless the day when you came into my life and as for the boys, well, you need no telling that I sometimes think they'd miss you more than they would miss me.'

'It works both ways you know; the boys are my whole life,' she said kindly, not realizing exactly what she had just said.

'That's a sweet thing to say,' he said gently, wondering if she would ever bring herself to include him in that statement. She seemed suddenly so different. And without saying another word to her, he slid slowly closer and gently kissed her soft lips.

'Oh dear,' he murmured as he watched her cheeks flame up. She had so many personal problems that needed sorting out, and he didn't want to add to them, he just wanted to let her know that it wasn't only his two sons who would be lost without her. When she had first come to take care of his boys she had seemed so very young, only nineteen and he had turned thirty. Those eleven years might as well have been fifty. Now she was different. No longer afraid of her own shadow, no longer ruled by that domineering Michael O'Brien, very much more self-assured and now the difference in their ages seemed less important.

'Shouldn't we be making a move?' she suggested. 'Would you

mind taking me to Hamleys? Oh, and I meant to ask before now: do you have to go back to the office today?'

'No, I'm all right, I cleared up what was outstanding this morning so let's buy two buses or whatever takes your fancy and then get the train home; we can't do any more by staying in town today.'

Paula was laughing at the idea of buying two buses.

Jeffrey was thinking, *She isn't coming home with me, she still has at least ten days left of her holiday.*

It would be a long ten days for him!

Thirty-Six

For the next three days Paula did her best to live for the moment. No one could have been kinder than Molly, who watched over her like a hawk, cooked special dishes that she knew would delight her and generally made her feel more than welcome. Laura was a laugh a minute; she joked with everyone from the milkman to the postman but especially with the barrow boys down the market. Life couldn't have been easy for Laura and Fred; being a postman was considered a good, safe job but the wages weren't much and with two growing lads to feed and clothe at times it must be quite a struggle for them to make ends meet.

The fact that they lived with Laura's mother was a benefit for all of them in so many ways. Paula had been shocked when she had unintentionally learned that Molly's sole income was her widow's pension, often shillings a week which she supplemented by taking in washing and it was Laura who did all the ironing and of course Fred paid the rent. Despite the shortage of money there was always a good fire burning and a substantial meal on the table every day. Paula felt she had no way of knowing just how they did manage on such a low income. She had great admiration for all of them because no one grumbled; indeed they were a really happy family and she felt privileged to have them as her friends.

It was only lately she had fully realized what a terribly miserable life her mother and Mike O'Brien had lived all those years. Quietly she vowed that as soon as her own affairs were put into order she was going to see if she could in some way make life easier financially for Molly and her family without in any way causing them embarrassment.

Paula's own peace of mind was shattered by the arrival of a package from the firm of Perkins & Griffith, Attorneys at Law. So many frightening documents!

She turned a page and continued to read. Her heart missed a beat. Mike O'Brien really was going ahead with his claim that he was her natural father! Was he saying that he had made her mother pregnant before he had married her? Well, yes, that was exactly what he was saying, and he had listed the dates when he claimed they had had intercourse and the date, place and time of the day when he had married Frances Stevenson, and she had become Mrs O'Brien.

Paula lowered the pages and stared out of the window. Why hadn't her mother brought all of this out into the open while she was still alive? But Paula knew the answer to her own question. Her mother had been absolutely terrified of her husband. *Oh, my poor mother, what a terrible life she had been forced to live.* And yet, thinking back now, and with the knowledge that she had revealed, it became obvious her early life must have started out so well.

As a young woman, the moment she had found herself pregnant had probably been a time of joy. Then had come the heartbreak of hearing that her handsome young officer had been killed and there would be no wedding.

In 1910, the stigma of an illegitimate child was unbearable but surely her own family should have stood by her! The scene at the time must have been terrible, devastating for her mother as her father cast her out without so much as a second thought. Her horrible father had even paid a great hulk of a man to marry his daughter and take her anywhere, just so long as he never had to set eyes on her and her unborn child in the future. And all those terrible years that had followed and the brutality Mike O'Brien had used towards her gentle mother – it didn't bear thinking about.

If Mike had been so dead set on being a father to Frances's unborn baby, why had his behaviour been so bizarre?

Why in God's name had he been obsessed with staring at my naked body when I'd only been a little girl? Oh, dear Jesus, she hadn't allowed these thoughts into her mind for years and now he had brought it all back. Would this all be brought out into the open if it did come to a court case? Mike O'Brien himself certainly wouldn't make that disclosure. Would she want all of that laid bare for everybody to hear about?

Paula was finding it hard to breathe. Please God, it wouldn't get as far as that. It couldn't. It was unthinkable.

Paula paused in her remorseless reflections when a sudden thought hit her.

If Mike O'Brien was not her father, then neither was Patrick O'Brien her uncle!

God above, this was becoming so confusing; there had to be a way in which she could sort it out. She couldn't live for weeks on end with all this uncertainty hanging over her. She just had to find a way to do something about it.

She was pacing the floor, raging at herself for having let things get so out of hand, but until now what could she have done?

'Hey, hey, slow down and calm down,' Laura implored. 'I left you alone in here to read your papers quietly and now I find you crying buckets an' tearing yer bloody hair out. Come on, come through to the scullery and wash yer face while I put the kettle on and then you can tell me what it is that is sending you over the edge.'

Paula had washed her face but the cold water had done little to calm her down.

After all these years she now knew it was Patrick who had made her pregnant, but it was that warped, evil bastard who wanted everyone to believe he was her legitimate father, it was he who had drugged her and taken money off his own brother for the privilege of being the first man to ravish his daughter on the day she reached the age of just thirteen.

If that wasn't abnormal perversion, then what in heaven's name was it?

All these horrible thoughts and memories had lain dormant once she had settled in to the good life at Ridgeway. Now, after all this time, rage was making her blood boil. She had to make someone accountable for what she had suffered, if ever she was going to settle down and lead a good peaceful life someone had to admit to the crimes that were committed against her. Never mind all the warnings to keep away; she was going to confront Mike O'Brien and that repugnant brother of his.

'And where do you think you're going to?' Laura asked as she came into the living room bringing a loaded tea tray.

Paula already had her arms in the sleeves of her coat and was about to button it up. She stared at Laura and her friend knew straight off there would be no stopping her; determination was showing in every line of her face.

'Paula, I asked you a question, where are you thinking of going?'

'Laura, I've finished thinking. I've done nothing else for the past eight years and it's got me nowhere. There have been times when I have thought I'd managed to put the nightmares behind me but every so often it all pops up again and old wounds are reopened. Since the day my mother died it has been just one thing after another and I've had a gut full of it all. I need to get some true answers and believe me, Laura, this time I will, if I have to stand outside that house in Milner Road and shout my head off for the whole world to hear, then I will.'

'Don't be so daft; you'll get yourself locked up!' Laura pleaded.

'Well, that won't be the first time, will it?' Paula said spitefully. 'But at least this time I shall be fully aware of what I've done.'

'Look, love, just let me pour our tea out and if by the time we've drunk it you are still bent on going to face the lion in his den then I'm coming with you.'

'Don't make a joke of it, Laura, because I have never been more serious in the whole of my life. Those two O'Brien brothers think they have got away with so much but even that is not enough for either of them. They want to tarnish my mother's memory and they want all the dirt that they made brought out into the open and my life will be laid bare for everyone to talk about. My life will be in ruins; I'd never be able to go back to caring for the twins. No, I've stood more than enough and before I let them do this to me I will see them dead first.'

'Well, if you're that determined I'm definitely coming with you.'

They walked the length of Blackshaw Road in silence, then crossing the main road they only had a few minutes to wait before a bus came along. They got off the bus in Wimbledon and from there it was a matter of yards and they were in Milner Road. It was only Paula's temper that was keeping her going, yet as she stood outside of the house in which she had been brought up she was admitting to herself that the outside of the house looked spic and span; the windows were clean and the white lace curtains that hung from the downstairs bay windows and the upper-floor bedroom windows were crisp and white as snow. This couldn't be the work of Mike, but she remembered that there had been a number of females in the O'Brien family, though they had very rarely visited when her mother had been alive. Perhaps one or more had taken pity on Mike and had moved in with him.

It was Laura who strode up the short garden path and lifted the door knocker, letting it fall heavily three times. She glanced over her shoulder at Paula, who was trembling, and she felt sorry for her, but there was nothing she could do now. Far better to let her have her say, get it all out in the open and let events take their course.

Neither the walk nor the short bus ride had lessened Paula's determination or subdued her temper. If anything her fury intensified as they waited and no one came to open the door, even though both of them had seen the lace curtains twitch and a female had stared out at them. Paula nudged Laura aside and she banged hard with her fist on what had been her mother's front door.

'For goodness' sake, do you really need to make such a racket?' Patrick O'Brien shouted, pulling the door wide open.

'Is my father in?' Paula asked, putting the emphasis on the word 'father' but keeping a reign on her temper.

'Yes he is, but he does not want to see you.'

'Oh really? Well things have changed, haven't they? When I lived here he couldn't get to see enough of me, and at my mother's funeral you said his dearest wish was to see me again.'

'That was before he found out that your mother had written a pack of lies and left the letter with a solicitor.'

'Oh really? Well, let's get one thing straight right away: I have no intention of leaving here until I have been given some answers and to do that I need to see him face to face.'

'Well, Paula, my dear girl, I'm afraid you're in for a long wait, your father is not well. He is upstairs lying down and he certainly won't come down to see you, so you might just as well turn round now and go away.'

Paula was grinding her teeth together by the time he had delivered his message. 'Patrick O'Brien, you have just made three mistakes in your swift delivery. One, I am not your dear girl; two the man upstairs who you say is unwell is *not* my father; and three I have no intention of waiting around. But before I leave here your brother will not only have met me face to face but he will have listened to what I have to say. Now, I don't intend to argue the toss with you out here on the doorstep, so get out of my way,'

Paula finally snapped, and shoving him aside she grabbed hold of
Laura and practically yanked her into the hall.

'Where are you, you great bully? Come downstairs and tell me
face to face just what you are intending to do.' Paula had her head
thrown back and was shouting from the foot of the stairs.

'You've no right to come barging in here,' Patrick snarled from
behind her. 'I won't have it.'

'*You* won't have it!' Paula practically spat the words at him. 'You
didn't mind barging in when I was a young girl – and how about
the night of my thirteenth birthday party? You did a little more
than barge in that night, didn't you, *Uncle Patrick*? You bloody well
raped me good an' proper. And you made me pregnant. And even
that wasn't enough for your rotten, twisted mind; you connived
to have me put away in a mental institution for thirteen months.
Yes, *Uncle Patrick*. I am now going to tell my side of the story for
a change.'

Patrick's face had turned green. 'Come into the sitting room;
we need to talk.'

Paula was shaking from head to foot, and he was as white as a
ghost. Laura decided it was time she put in her two pennyworth.

'I think Paula has made it plain what she thinks of you, Mr
O'Brien, but it was yer brother that she came to see, the one who
reckons he can go into an open court of law and prove beyond
doubt that he is her real father. I promise you we shan't be leaving
here, not until that brave man 'as shown his face. Oh, an' another
thing, if he ain't come down them stairs in two minutes I shall
open that bloody front door and shout out for all the neighbours
to 'ear just why we've come 'ere today.'

'You wouldn't; this has got nothing to do with you,' Patrick
hissed at Laura.

'Wouldn't I? Given half the chance I'll go up and down the
street knocking on doors, an' for your information every bit of
this is ter do with me. Paula is part of my family now and I think
the damage you lot did to her – well, the whole bloody lot of yer
ought to be inside.'

'Paula,' Mike O'Brien called from the top of the stairs, 'I will
come down and talk to you but only if you promise to calm down
and send that friend of yours home. This has nothing at all to do
with her or her bloody mother.'

Laura span round and only fury kept her from running up the stairs and having a go at him. 'Oh, it's Mike O'Brien, the big man! You don't like my mother cos she sussed you out years ago; she knew why you got on to the priests and with their help you had your little girl locked away in a nuthouse. Only thing you didn't tell them was that you had been acting in a creepy, unnatural way towards Paula probably from the day she was born. An' another thing, did yer tell them priests who was the father of the baby this thirteen-year-old girl was carrying? You bet your rotten life you never did! No, you dirty, rotten sod. You and this filthy brother of yours wormed yer way out of it by suggesting it might 'ave been some young lads that was up 'ere on holiday and got to know Paula when they'd been helping the local milkman out for a few days. But I can go up to the Catholic Church and tell them for yer if yer like. Even after all these years I'm sure they'd be more than pleased to find out about the truth.' Laura had been screaming at the top of her voice and it was only shortage of breath that brought her tirade to an end.

Paula was staring at her friend, her eyes wide with amazement. After a short while, during which the silence was almost deafening, she said, 'Laura, are you suggesting that the local priests were led to believe that I had had sex with a young man unknown to my parents?'

'No Paula, love, I'm suggesting nothing; I'm merely telling you what more than likely really happened.'

Paula sighed and in a strange voice she murmured, 'Laura, why didn't you tell me this years ago?'

'If only I could 'ave, love, but we never knew for certain. It was my mum who sussed it out the minute she gathered that you'd given birth to a baby. She tried to 'ave it out with your father a few times, he knew she'd guessed the truth and that's why he hates her.'

Poor Paula, she looked utterly stricken. 'Time and time again I was questioned, by doctors, by social workers – even by the priests themselves – and not one of them would believe me, no matter how many times I tried telling them that I knew nothing about men or sex. Good God, now you tell me they had all been led to believe that I had no morals, was a girl of easy virtue and that I slept around with any Tom, Dick or Harry!'

Paula's sudden change was startling. It was as if a time bomb had at last gone off in her head and she was feeling the heat of utter humiliation. Patrick was the nearest and she just flew at him. He didn't even have time to cover his face with his hands before he felt Paula's fingernails dig deep into his flesh and rake down his cheeks.

Laura was the nervous one now. She had never imagined that Paula had it in her; this was definitely not how she had imagined this visit turning out. Blood was oozing between Patrick's fingers and trickling down the front of his shirt.

'You rotten little bitch! What d'yer wanna go an' do that t'me brother for?' Mike's voice was so full of disbelief as he stormed down the stairs that it made Paula want to laugh. She was however sensible enough to know that this was just nervous laughter, but the urge to turn and shriek at her so-called father and to do even worse to him was too hard to suppress.

'For the same reason that I'd like to kill you, you lying, hateful man!' As Mike reached the lower step she kicked at his shin bone and hit him hard between the legs. When Paula finally stopped Mike fell backwards, squirming in agony and yelling like a wounded animal.

'Jesus wept! Paula, whatever's got into you?' This was so out of character for Paula that Laura wondered if she had seen correctly and she found herself asking, 'Where on earth did you learn t'do a trick like that?'

'I suddenly remembered a few of the lessons I learned while I was shut away. You have to remember it wasn't exactly a finishing school for young ladies; you learned to watch out for yourself, or you just didn't survive,' Paula told her, but she wasn't yet ready to smile.

'Paula, please, bring your friend and come into the sitting room,' Patrick persisted, as he threw his bloodied handkerchief on to the hall table.

'Don't touch me!' she hissed, jerking away as he tried to take her arm. 'I've let the pair of you get away with so much, mostly because I was afraid of how you might retaliate towards my mother. Well, she's out of harm's way now, but I'm still here and believe you me, what I have heard today has changed me considerably. I can promise neither of you will like the change. First thing I am going to do when I leave here is apply for an audience with the Holy Fathers of the Catholic Church where you two so regularly attend mass. Then . . . well, we'll take it from there, shall we?'

Mike O'Brien was now down in the hall but he was having a job to stand up straight. 'Paula dear, this show of bad temper isn't going to get us anywhere. Go on, do as Patrick has asked; come in to the sitting room and let my sister bring us in a nice pot of tea.'

'I don't know how to address you,' Paula said scathingly. 'What I have discovered this afternoon is unbelievable. Don't you have *any* understanding of what you put me through? Doesn't it make both of you feel ashamed? Even if the priests had agreed to me being sent away until after the baby was born, if I had been believed when I told them the truth that I had no idea what had happened to me I would have been given an easier time in that hell of a prison. But no, you two filthy-minded buggers fed them the story that I was little more than a whore, a prostitute and a liar. Consequently the priests decided I deserved every bit of punishment they could throw at me. I suffered for thirteen months, and for all these years since, just so that you two rotten men could keep your reputations. Well! It's my turn now and, believe me, I shall enjoy watching the pair of you squirm. Come on, Laura, I think we're about finished here. I cannot thank you enough for the way you have opened my eyes today. I just can't believe that the truth never struck me before. But then I was just a child. Wait till we get home. I shall say a prayer to our Blessed Lady solely for Molly; I always knew there wasn't much that got by her but all this time and it was only she who had worked out how devious these two brothers must have been.'

'Paula, if you'd only listen to me—' Mike O'Brien's eyes were still watering.

'You think I want to hear any more of your lies?' It was a very different Paula who almost spat the words at him. 'No, today has turned out one hundred per cent better than I could have ever hoped for. I'll see you two rotters at Mass on Sunday morning and after that, if you've still got the guts for it, I shall look forward to seeing you both in court.'

'Come on – I was going to say Paula O'Brien,' Laura said, and then she let out a great belly laugh as she flung the street door wide open. They linked arms and practically danced their way down Milner Road.

'As God is my judge, Paula, I never thought you 'ad it in yer! Whatever 'appened to turn you into a cow?'

'You don't need to know and I am not about to tell you. You and I have both learned a lot today and let's make sure we make the most of it.'

'Right, well let's get on that bus an' hope that me mum's got the kettle on cos I'm bloody parched.'

'Well, Patrick did offer us tea.'

'Oh yeah! And like we were going to accept an' sit around all cosy like after what you did to the pair of them.'

Their laughter could be heard the length of Milner Road, except that the occupants of number twenty-one were not rejoicing, they were busy licking their wounds.

Thirty-Seven

Molly Owen lifted the corner of her apron and wiped away the tears that were brimming over and running down her cheeks. 'On my life, I ain't laughed so much in years. God, what wouldn't I 'ave given to 'ave been there, just to see that great fat slob in such pain. Good on yer, gal, but t' be 'onest, if my Laura hadn't been there to vouch for the truth of all this I'd say you were dreaming. Christ Almighty, I didn't think yer were anywhere near capable of tackling him, never mind practically crippling the man.'

'Well, Molly, as they say, you live and learn. It was a school of hard knocks I was locked away in but I have to say never in all the years since my release have I had cause to bring forth some of the ways in which I learned how to defend myself. That is until today! I was so shattered when Laura told me your version of what happened to me. Why in God's name did it never dawn on me? If I could have spoken up in my own defence, all those wretched months of my life would have been made so much easier. With hindsight it is so easy to realize why all the doctors and priests saw me as an out and out liar. Even when the priests questioned me over and over again, always repeating that I would feel so much better if I made a full confession, what did I have to confess? I was as green as grass; I had only had two periods and each time I thought I was bleeding to death. On the night I was raped my so-called father doped me so heavily I never knew what happened to me, let alone who had committed the act.'

'I'm only sorry I never came up with it before now,' Molly said, sounding really upset. 'Though I never 'ad nothing to go on really. Just pure instinct and knowing what deceitful bastards Mike and his brother were. Also knowing what a dear little innocent girl you were. God above, lying to the priests! They'll not get a good night's sleep till they find out what you're going t'do about it.'

Laura had been busying herself with making the tea while Paula had been relaying to Molly what had gone on in Milner Road; she had already poured the milk into the cups but she hesitated before lifting the teapot.

'And what *are* yer gonna do about it, Paula?' Laura asked with a grin on her face that spread from ear to ear. 'Whatever it is, I bloody well want t'be there!'

Paula stood up and opened her arms wide. Laura forgot about the tea as she flew across the room to be encircled in a tight grasp. The two of them stood rocking on the spot; there was no need for words. The love and the relief were enough. Paula felt that at last the unseen shackles that had bound her for so long had suddenly been cut away. She now had the means to exonerate herself in the eyes of so many people.

Minutes ticked away, both young women were crying softly, almost as if the release from so much guilt was too good to be true.

Molly decided she wasn't going to let a good pot of tea go to waste; she filled her own cup and took it with her out into the scullery. Paula was a good girl, she hadn't deserved what had happened to her, and now she was hoping that it was all going to be turned around and Paula would be able to live her life without having to remember all those horrible black parts. And she would be able to start using her rightful surname. That would give the O'Briens something else to cringe over!

Paula had made two telephone calls from the phone box at the corner of Blackshaw Road. One had been to her old school and the other call had been for a cab.

'Would you like me to come with you? It won't take me long to get myself ready,' Laura offered.

'No, it's all right, Laura, but thanks for offering.' The two of them were standing looking out of the window, watching for the taxi to arrive. 'I was surprised to hear that Mother Theresa is still there but then I remembered when I first started there I must have been three years old and Mother Juliet was there for a few years and then she retired, so I suppose it is not that long that Mother Theresa has been there.'

The sound of the cab driver tooting his horn made them both laugh. 'Does he think he's invisible?' Laura suggested.

'Probably not, but he can't tell that we were watching for

him from behind the lace curtains. Come on, come out and see me off.'

Once inside the cab Paula twisted round to wave to Laura, half wishing that she had brought her friend with her. Her tummy was rumbling; it was a long time since she'd had an audience with a Mother Superior. Within half an hour Paula was pushing open the huge iron gates of the convent school, walking up the long path that was bordered by leafy shrubs, climbing the flight of stone steps and tugging at the bell rope.

While she waited Paula thought she couldn't remember ever having entered this building by the main front door. The entrance to the school was to the rear of the building. The opening of a slide panel startled her as she found herself looking into the sweet face of a very young-looking nun.

'My name is Paula O'Brien, I have an appointment with Mother Theresa,' Paula found herself whispering, though for the life 'of her she didn't know why.

She received no word of reply but the panel was slid back into place and the door was finally opened. Paula entered and was immediately drawn back in time. The familiar fragrant fumes of incense. The crucifix on which Our Dear Lord Jesus hung and the beautiful picture of Our Blessed Lady, Holy Mary, Mother of our Dear Lord Jesus Christ were both still in place, as were many more pictures of the saints. She had spent ten years attending this school, some of the happiest hours of her life. The quietness and the tranquillity washed over her and she had such regrets that her life within these walls had been so drastically and so cruelly cut short. Maybe today's visit here would bring about the retribution she so badly needed. She wasn't seeking revenge; what she needed was for the truth to be told and for herself to be exonerated from all the evil deeds she had supposedly committed.

The sound of their footsteps as she followed the young sister down the tiled corridor was loud enough to wake the dead. The room she was shown into was still recognizable even after all this time. She had sat in here waiting for the Mother Superior to inform her how well she had performed at exam time. This time two large wooden panels were both slid back and Mother Theresa was smiling at her from the room beyond.

Paula jumped to her feet and curtsied. 'Good morning, Reverent Mother, thank you for seeing me.'

'Good morning, Paula; it is always pleasant to see an old pupil. Now, my child, how can I be of help to you?'

'I can't answer that question. Mother Superior, what I would like to do is tell you why I suddenly was removed from attending school here when I reached the age of thirteen.'

'Take your time, Paula; this is a subject that worried me for some time. At the time it seemed as if you had been spirited away.'

Paula heaved a deep breath and sent up a prayer for guidance.

It was to Paula as if God *was* guiding her. She started at the birthday party and then somehow she coordinated every single nauseating, offensive detail of the thirteen months that she had been impounded in that mental hospital. The only time she had stammered and become tongue-tied was when giving the relevant details of the birth of her baby.

Reaching the story of how she was released, Paula felt drained. She slumped in the chair and let her shoulders sag, then she remembered and, quickly straightening herself up, she quietly told of her mother's recent death and of the letter she had left with a firm of solicitors, but only very briefly outlining the contents.

'My dear child, I must confess I know a little more about what has happened to you these past few years than I have made known, but nothing of the horrendous year you have just described. I have been given to understand that for the past two and a half years you have not been living with your parents, is that correct?'

'Yes, Reverent Mother.' Then as an afterthought Paula added, 'I have with me the letter my mother wrote before she died, which might help you to decide if you are in any way able to help me or even advise me.' Paula opened her handbag, withdrew the letter and placed the envelope unopened on her knees.

The Reverent Mother was silent for some time, then she smiled and it was such a sweet smile it brought a lump into Paula's throat. 'Paula, I am going to send Sister Marie to take you down to the dining room where you will be served a nice tea, you'll be able to have a chat with some of the pupils and there are still at least three sisters here that taught you when you attended day school here. Would you like that?'

'Very much, thank you.'

At that moment Paula felt as if she were six years old. What happened next was all done in complete silence.

The wooden panels were slid into place by unseen hands and Mother Superior disappeared from view. Two nuns entered the room where Paula was sitting. One picked up the letter from Paula's knees and the other one smiled and beckoned for Paula to follow her.

Paula really did feel as if time had been turned back as she took her place at the long tea table. How young all the pupils looked, but how smart and clean. Each girl wore the school uniform, their drill slip emblazoned with a badge of the Scared Heart. Three nuns stood at the head of the table and Paula felt so pleased that she could not only recognize two of them but she also could recall their names. Sister Celia and Sister Madeleine. Prayers were said, a blessing given and a few words of welcome offered to an old pupil.

Paula accepted a sandwich and she smiled; the crusts had all been cut off. Nothing had changed much here. As they ate in silence Paula's thoughts were turning over and over. Why had no one ever told her some of the things that could possibly have made such a difference to her life? She involuntarily shuddered as she thought of how her so-called father, his brother Patrick and indeed the whole of the O'Brien family would be acting once they became aware of the action she was taking. When their lies were brought to light they would hate the disgrace that she was bringing on this God-fearing family. She hardened her heart. It might be terrible, even terrifying, for Michael and Patrick, but they were grown men and the lies and deceit they had perpetuated over the years were unforgivable. How very different her poor mother's life might have been if only Alexander Grantham had not been killed, but he had been and there was no altering that fact.

But now she was attempting to deal with so many different aspects of her past when all she really wanted to do was face an entirely different future. At times it was all so unbelievable, almost as if her entire life had collapsed. She forced herself to eat and at the same time to look around this peaceful room. If only she had been allowed to stay on here, finish her education and go forth into the world a clean-cut, good-living young lady. All right to say 'if only' but it didn't get one anywhere. Because of Patrick

O'Brien's lecherous, wanton behaviour she could never be classed as a clean-cut, good-living young lady. The one good thing her mother's letter had revealed was the fact that Mike O'Brien had not fathered her and today she had handed the communication which dealt with so many other facets of her life to Mother Superior. What she and the Holy Fathers did with the information was no longer her problem. For the whole year that she had been locked away people had treated her badly but no one had sinned as much or as atrociously as the O'Brien brothers had. They had been and still were vicious, revolting men.

A hand rested lightly on Paula's shoulder and a soft voice asked, 'Are you well, my child?'

Paula turned her head to gaze into the soft grey eyes of Sister Celia and she envied the peace and tranquillity she saw there; time had not withered her sweet face.

'Yes, thank you, Sister Celia, I am very well.'

Sister Celia removed her hands from where they had been tucked in the sleeves of her robes and held out a manilla envelope. 'Mother Superior is returning your mother's letter; she asks that you keep it in a safe place. She also wishes you to know that Father Donnelly has made a note of the contents. When you have finished your tea I will escort you to the main entrance.'

Those few words brought Paula back to the present with a bump. This building was set apart from the outside world and although she had been allowed a glimpse of it this afternoon she was being made aware that it was an entirely different way of life to that which she now led. She shook her head to clear it of all the disjointed, complicated thoughts that had haphazardly come to her from the minute she had set foot in this sanctuary. Slowly she rose to her feet and said, 'Thank you, Sister Celia, I am ready to leave now.'

Paula decided a walk would do her good. Deep in thought she passed through Tooting, on over Longley Road bridge towards Colliers Wood Underground station and it was only as she neared South Wimbledon that she realized she was in the vicinity of Milner Road and the last thing she wanted was to come face to face with any member of the O'Brien family. Her mind was on so many other things that she hadn't noticed she had walked too far; she shouldn't be going back to Raynes Park because she was still staying with Molly and her family. Quickly she crossed the main road, turned around and started to retrace her steps.

Laura was at the gate watching for her. 'Thank the Lord for that,' she called out as Paula came nearer. 'I was beginning to think they might 'ave preyed on yer to stay in that convent and join them.'

'It isn't a convent as such,' Paula explained, as Laura held the gate open for her. 'And to be truthful they wouldn't have needed much persuasion: it was so peaceful in there.'

'Well, if it's peace and quiet you're looking for you'd better turn around an' go straight back cos the boys are home from school early cos a water pipe 'as burst in the main part of the building and they've brought Billy and Tom Cresswell with them cos their mum don't finish work till four an' there's nobody in their house.'

Paula found herself chuckling. Laura was the only one she knew who could state so many facts in one long sentence without ever pausing to take a breath.

Molly was seated at the kitchen table playing cards with the four boys. She raised her head as Paula came in, gave her a cheery grin and said, 'How did things go, love? Are them priests gonna sort the O'Briens out? And more to the point, did you get an apology from them for what they did to you?'

'I never got to see any priests, only Mother Superior. She read my mother's letter and returned it to me. She did say she was aware of what I had suffered but other than that she made no comment and no promises. However, for what it's worth I did get the feeling that she thought retribution was long overdue.'

'So is our cup of tea, ain't it, boys?' Molly said sharply as she threw her cards down. 'My Laura's spent the last 'alf an hour standing out there on that doorstep looking for you.'

'I'll make the tea,' Paula quickly volunteered. 'What would you boys like?' She waved a packet of chocolate biscuits she had bought when she walked past Tooting Broadway Market.

'Cor, if we're going to get choccy biscuits I'll have tea please, Paula,' Jack was quick to decide.

'So will I, please,' Ronnie hastened to get in while their two friends just looked at Paula in disbelief.

'Is the same all right for you, Billy and Tom?' Paula asked, grinning.

'Yes, please, miss,' they answered in unison.

The surroundings and the atmosphere were extremely different from where Paula had spent the earlier part of the afternoon, yet when Fred Wilson came home and offered to walk the Cresswell boys home, Paula would have been one of the first to agree that she had thoroughly enjoyed the last noisy hour she had spent with these four boys.

The rest of Paula's fourteen-day break just flew by. So much had happened and yet nothing specific and certainly nothing explicit had been decided in regards to Paula's affairs. Until the morning of her last day.

It was barely ten o'clock, the boys were safely away to school and Molly, Laura and Paula had finished a leisurely breakfast when there was a loud knocking on the front door. Molly was the nearest and she rose, curious to see who it was that hadn't just used the key on the end of the string and let themselves in; only strangers bothered to knock. It was some minutes before she returned and as she entered the kitchen she held out a padded envelope to Paula.

'It was Arthur Blackmore,' she stated, sounding very important. 'He said this arrived at nine o'clock this morning and although you are due back at Ridgeway tomorrow Mr Lawson said it might be better for you to have this straight away so he offered to bring it to you. Wouldn't come in, said he was taking his missus shopping today, sends his love an' says they're all looking forward to seeing you tomorrow.'

Paula turned the packet over several times in her hands before picking up a clean knife from the table and using it to slit the envelope open. When she withdrew the one sheet it appeared that the parchment was coloured in places and had quite a lot of straight lines of writing. Paula appeared to read it several times before she silently handed it to Molly and as Molly took it from her Paula put her arms down on to the table and rested her head on to them and began to cry as if her heart was about to break.

Molly took a while to decipher what the document actually was. Meanwhile, Laura was in a fix as to what she could do to comfort Paula since she had no idea what had upset her so badly.

'Leave her be; she'll tell yer in a minute she's crying cos she's really, really happy.' Molly made this statement with the biggest smile set on her face. 'Jesus, this will be the day that girl will feel she's been born again. No one, not the O'Briens, not even a church full of priests, will ever be able to wipe this minute away. God knows she's been deceived all these years but from now on she can hold her head high and, Paula, if you can hear me, I'm telling yer, your mother is dancing with the angels today.'

Paula raised her head, her face streaked with lines of tears, and smiled at Molly. 'Bless you, Molly; I will never forget that you said that.'

Laura looked from one to the other, flabbergasted. 'Would one of you please, for Christ's sake, tell *me* what is going on here? One of you is crying your heart out and the other one is practically dancing for joy.'

Paula took her arms from the table, sat up straight and sniffed while she searched in her pocket for a handkerchief. 'Please, Molly, will you pass my original birth certificate to Laura?'

'Here you are, love, sorry about the delay. I just 'ad t'read it over and over again.'

Laura took one look and although she was handling the certificate with care she started to read it aloud. 'Sex of child: female. Mother: Frances Margaret Stevenson. Father: Alexander Gerard Grantham; occupation: Officer in The Royal Horse Guards, now deceased.'

Laura didn't bother to read any more. All the dates and times were there but Paula's mother had been crafty or clever, whichever way you wanted to look at it. She had registered the birth of her baby daughter as she was duty bound to. Like a wise old owl she had probably disposed of the original birth certificate because she had registered the true facts, not those which Michael O'Brien would have preferred her to commit to paper. And she had never kept a copy in the house for him to find. The fact that she had attended a solicitors' office before her premature death had been a wise thing to do. Leaving a document giving all the details as to how and when she herself had become Mrs O'Brien and her daughter had been brought up to believe she was the daughter of one Michael O'Brien had indeed been a very wise move.

More tears welled up in Paula's eyes. 'Never again will I have to acknowledge Michael O'Brien as my father.' And she began to cry again with more heartache than she'd ever felt before.

'For God's sake, Laura, move yerself and make a fresh pot of tea and bring the whisky bottle in as well, cos if this don't call for a celebration I'm damned if I know what does,' Molly declared, getting to her feet and reaching down three glasses from the dresser.

Paula also stood up and wiped away her tears but her eyes were shining as she moved to kiss Molly.

'I suppose you'll have to practise your new signature,' Molly said and as Paula let out a laugh Molly wrapped her arms around her. 'When Laura comes in with that bottle I think the toast today should be to new beginnings.'

No one was going to argue with that!

Thirty-Eight

Paula had lain awake all that night, tossing and turning, filled with conflicting emotions, telling herself how very different her life would be now she no longer had to use the surname of O'Brien.

It was seven o'clock when she heard Molly get up, her footsteps slow as she crept downstairs. A few minutes later Paula got herself out of bed and by a quarter past eight everyone was in the kitchen with the exception of Fred who had left the house at five thirty to go on an early shift. Breakfast was a jolly time. Jack and Ronnie were chatty, telling her about the sports field their school had bought because it ran alongside their school building. 'We'll have our own football field soon,' Jack told her gleefully.

Jack wanted to know if Paula would be a different person now that she had a new surname. 'Would you want me to be different?' she asked him, smiling.

'Course not, Auntie Paula, but yer new name does sound posh an' t'day you are going back to that big house to look after your twin boys. Don't suppose we'll see yer for a long time now.'

'Oh, Jack, I suppose sometimes it does seem as if I don't see enough of you and young Ronnie. I promise I will try harder to get over here, but you do know that I am always thinking of you both, don't you?'

'Suppose so, t'ain't the same thing though.'

Now Paula was experiencing an emotion never before known to her: jealousy. Jack had said she was going back to the big house to take care of *her* twin boys. Was that how he looked at it? It suddenly seemed wrong – no, not wrong, that wasn't the right word. But she couldn't think of one that fitted how she was feeling. She looked into the indignant young face frowning up at her and she felt at sixes and sevens. 'Jack, you are a big boy now, aren't you?'

'Yes,' he muttered, sounding almost rebellious.

'Well, my darling boy, I want you to try and understand what has really happened to me. After I have gone if you still have any questions please ask your mum and I am sure she will do her best to answer them truthfully. For now I am going to give you a quick summing up. Just over two years ago I left my home because I didn't have a good father like you have and I wasn't happy living there. I was lucky to get myself a job looking after twin baby boys whose mother had died only hours after they had been born. You just referred to them as "my boys", but really I am only their nanny. It isn't hard for me to love them and I hope they have learned to love me, but that doesn't alter the fact that I truly love both you and Ronnie – after all I have known you two from the day you were born and that is a lot longer than I have been caring for the twins.'

The minute Paula stopped speaking Jack was up on his feet and had thrown his arms around Paula's neck. 'Sorry, Auntie Paula, I am jealous when you go back to that big house but I didn't properly understand that the twins didn't 'ave no mother.'

Paula spent a couple of minutes rubbing Jack's back, unable to speak to him because his words had choked her.

Finally it was Laura who saved the situation. 'Come on, lad, yer brother is out in the scullery; he's all ready to leave an' yer don't want to be late for school now, do yer?'

'I'm ready, Mum,' he said solemnly before breaking away from Paula. Lifting his face up, he said, 'Will you come back soon?'

'As soon as I can, but you must remember I have just spent two weeks here on holiday. But how about if I write a letter now and again to you and to Ronnie?'

'Yeah, that would be smashing – will we be allowed to write back?'

Laura thought it was time she stepped in. 'Jack, you write to yer Auntie Paula whenever you like. I will give you paper and an envelope and I will also buy you the postage stamp. Now if all of that is settled will you please fetch your cap and get yerself off t'school?'

Both Laura and Paula breathed a heartfelt sigh of relief that the boys were long gone when Arthur Blackmore arrived in his car to pick up Paula, otherwise they would have asked for a ride in the car and never have got to school on time.

It was an emotional parting. Between Paula, Molly and Laura, each one had their own thoughts but the unanimous decision was that it had truly been an eventful two weeks.

*   *   *

Almost before Paula had a chance to get out of the car Peter and David came bursting out of the house and thundering down the steps, shouting, 'Paula! Paula! We've missed you!'

She laughed. 'I've only been away for two weeks,' she said, catching them both within her arms. 'Oh, you darlings, let me look at you,' she cried, tilting David's face up and patting Peter's head. 'Golly, you're both so handsome and I love you so much I just want to kiss those lovely rosy cheeks.'

It felt such a long time since she had seen them and she felt such emotion she could hardly contain herself.

'You will stay now, won't you, Paula?' David sounded uncertain while Peter was tugging at her hand and having a job to hold back his tears.

'Ssh, ssh, both of you,' Paula soothed, tears welling up in her own eyes too. 'I am not going anywhere – everything is going to be all right.'

'Get yourself away into the house; I'll bring your luggage,' Arthur urged her.

Paula thanked him and with the boys on either side of her, holding on to her hand, they mounted the steep flight of stone steps. 'David, how have you been? Has your head healed up nicely?'

'Yes, thanks.'

Joyce was waiting in the hallway and from her demonstrative welcome Paula gathered that she had been missed. 'Mrs Blackmore has insisted that she be allowed to prepare lunch today and the boys have made all kinds of things for your tea this afternoon – at least that's what I have been told. Practically banished from my own kitchen, that's what it's boiled down to.'

Paula wasn't mistaken at the resentment she heard in Joyce's voice. *Oh dear*, she muttered to herself, *I'd better tread very carefully for the next few days! And right now I had better find Jeffrey's mother and see how the land lies between her and me.*

In spite of its odd beginning the rest of the day went surprisingly smoothly. Mary appeared to be amenable while Joyce was still a little on the prickly side. Arthur as always kept the boys amused, although at regular intervals the twins came close to Paula, talking to her, touching her, almost as if making sure she had returned.

At one o'clock Mary told her grandsons to wash their hands

and come into the dining room for their lunch. That in itself was a surprise: meals were only taken in the dining room when their father was at home. However, Mary had prepared a delicious crown of lamb with a great assortment of fresh vegetables. It was Arthur who carried the dishes to and from the table and there was no sign of Joyce Pledger. Paula really did have to bite her tongue, she so badly wanted to comment on her absence, but with difficulty she refrained. The pastry on the fruit pie that Mary served for dessert was as light as a feather, indeed the whole meal was perfect, but the enjoyment was spoiled for Paula because every time the boys so much as uttered one word they were reprimanded by their grandma.

'Well brought-up children do not speak at meal times; it takes time and effort to produce a meal such as I have served today and you, Peter, and you, David, will do it justice by eating slowly and properly and not talking.'

Although it was painful for Paula to remain silent, she kept smiling at the boys and shaking her head should they attempt to converse with her. As soon as lunch was over she dressed the boys warmly, for summer had long since gone and the windy October days could be extremely cold, and together they set out for a walk. They hadn't been out long before she felt as if she had never been away. They sat on a bench at the side of a five-bar gate and watched two men riding their horses.

'Did you really miss us?' David asked, somewhat awkwardly.

Paula laughed at this. 'Of course I did. I really and truly missed you and every day I thought about both of you.'

He looked surprised but a great deal happier. 'And you did look forward to coming home?'

'Without out a doubt. I was longing to see you. Look, the horse riders are waving to you; stand up and wave back.' Paula was glad to have something to divert their attention.

Both lads did as she suggested, entering into the spirit, and when both horses sniffed and snorted, noisily forcing air out through their nostrils, both boys were so delighted, jumping up and down, laughing loudly as the men waved again.

Paula made sure that they walked the long way back home; she couldn't put into words how she felt, it had only been a matter of hours that she had been back in the house but it was strange, almost as if she were trespassing. As they approached the house Paula was lost in thought and when the boys let out a great whoop of delight the noise made her jump.

'Daddy's home!' they both yelled.

Ignoring Paula's plea for them to walk, they were off like a shot, eagerly covering the yards of the long driveway. Their father must have been watching from the house, for he came out, leaped down the steps and was running to meet them. There were yells and hoots of laughter as he gathered his two sons to him and Paula too was encircled within his arms.

This was so typical of Jeffrey that now Paula was laughing with them, partly from relief that she seemed to have reverted to being completely at ease with being back at Ridgeway and, even more so, at ease with Jeffrey.

'Welcome home, Paula. Was your holiday worthwhile?' he asked, smiling as he gazed into her bright green eyes.

'Yes, it was, and thank you for arranging it.'

'My pleasure.' Jeffrey grinned at her, still keeping her within the circle of his arms. He liked it when she and the boys were dressed for the outdoors, although it made her look still more like a young girl. God, he'd missed her, and so too had Peter and David; the very atmosphere in the whole house had changed. Even Esmé Wright hadn't been able to get on with his mother and she had stopped coming to the house daily, calling just to collect the washing, take it away and return it later all neatly washed and ironed.

Jeffrey freed his arms and broke up the group but no one seemed in a hurry to go into the house. 'Dad, you've come home really early today, why can't you do that every day?' Peter's voice and the look on his face showed that he considered this a serious question.

'Because I have an important job which in turn pays me a lot of money and allows us all to live in this lovely old house and enjoy a good life. Do you understand?'

Peter looked at his twin and quietly asked, 'Do we?'

It was as much as Paula and their father could do to keep straight faces. It was obvious that the twins had had a serious discussion on this matter.

'I think we do,' David answered. 'Anyhow, it won't matter so much now that Paula is back home.'

Jeffrey was shocked. Extremely pleased that the boys thought so much of Paula but having now been made aware just how lonely life had been for them this past two weeks. 'I will try to get home early on more days, I promise, but now aren't we supposed to be giving Paula a special welcome-home tea?'

'Yes!' they cried in unison, each grabbing hold of her hand and pulling her along as they raced towards the house.

Jeffrey stayed where he was for the moment, silently thanking the Lord for having sent Paula into their lives. If two weeks away from her had upset the boys he wondered what their lives might have turned out like had he continued to employ professional nannies. The boys weren't the only ones who had missed her. For him the evenings had seemed long and the weekends had dragged endlessly despite having his mother and Arthur staying in the house. Even while at work he had found himself picturing her beautiful young face in his mind's eye and remembering the time when he had held her in his arms and kissed her, the feel of her gorgeous hair when he had laid his cheek against her head. It was what he had allowed himself to dream of so often, but always he had cautioned himself that he was that much older than her and he had no right to take advantage of the fact that she was living under his roof.

They had both agreed that the time had not been right for making known their feelings. At that point in time it was as if an entirely new life was being offered to Paula – with a new surname, a large sum of money invested in her own name, she could be entirely independent. The world was her oyster, and he had no right to imagine that she would want him to be part of it.

'Daddy, come on!' Peter called loudly from the top of the steps.

Jeffrey shook his head. He had to stop all of this daydreaming. Anyway, Paula had her head screwed on all right; she was capable of making her own decisions.

'I'm coming,' he called, breaking into a run; to upset his mother was the last thing he needed to do.

A touch of excitement took hold: the next few months were going to be ones of change and he found himself praying they would be good for all of them.

Thirty-Nine

In some respects so much had happened since Paula's mother had died, but in others the legalities seemed to drag on for ever. The mountain of paperwork that had continued to arrive from the probate officer was almost beyond belief.

Very little had been heard of the O'Brien brothers but both Jonathan Griffith and Anthony Perkins had been quick to reassure Paula that every threat of legal action had been withdrawn by Michael O'Brien and since she and Laura had paid that visit to Milner Road she hadn't heard anything about any member of the family, a fact for which she was truly grateful.

Today Paula was waiting with the twins at the end of the drive for a car to arrive bringing Freddie and Raymond Burrows home from school; they had already been staying at Ridgeway for the past week and were likely to remain there for at least another two weeks. Their mother and father, Hilda and Andy Burrows, were in Malta because Hilda's mother had died and there had been no one else to see to her burial and to wind up her affairs. Her father had been born in Malta, had lived in England since he had married, but once he had retired both he and her mother had expressed a wish to return to Malta. They had been there just three years when her father had died and now just eight months later her mother had also died.

Jeffrey had consulted Paula before he had accepted the responsibility of caring for the two boys while their parents were away. Paula had felt she couldn't refuse because Hilda and Andy were godparents to the twins and they had been there to help Jeffrey through his loss of his wife. Andy was also a business colleague and they were both good friends.

Several times Jeffrey had pointed out that the bulk of the burden of having two more boys would mainly fall on Paula and that she was at liberty to refuse if she thought she was unable to cope. Of course she hadn't refused and Esmé Wright, as usual, had come to the rescue. 'My kids mainly look after themselves, so I can come in every day if you like,' she had said, grinning broadly and murmuring, 'Four boys! That should liven this old house up.'

Peter and David liked Freddie and Raymond; they liked having someone to play with although they were a few years older. Ridgeway was a nice place for children to be, with plenty of room to play hide-and-seek. Paula sometimes gave them lessons, which always turned out to be fun, and Joyce made all the things that they liked to eat. All the boys liked Mr Tompson, Joyce's friend, who came to the house every day, bringing his dog with him. It was a big friendly dog that did lots of tricks and never failed to retrieve a ball no matter how far the boys threw it. Freddie and Raymond missed their parents, of course they did, but Paula had put them both in one bedroom and they were sleeping together in a big soft double bed. Back home they each had their own room, but here the rooms were very big and they didn't feel lonely snuggled up together; in fact they thought it was good fun.

The car was now coming into view, and Peter and David couldn't wait to tell Raymond and Fred that Paula had this morning bought four painting sets, lots of big sheets of special paper and lots of colouring pens and pencils. Having given out that information as they all ran along the drive, Peter suddenly said, 'Before we start, Paula says on any picture we have to write our name in the left-hand corner of the page if it's in a book or on a big sheet of paper, so there won't be any mix-up.'

Eyebrows raised, Fred glanced across at Paula, and Raymond, younger by two years, also looked despondent. Paula had the feeling that the boys had misconstrued her meaning.

'Don't you want to put your name to your work?' she carefully asked.

Fred was quick to speak up. 'Oh, it's all right for Raymond and myself – our surname is Burrows, same as our parents – but I was thinking it must be confusing for David and Peter.'

Paula felt her cheeks flare up. The impudent little devil! She knew exactly what Fred was alluding to. There must have been a time when he had heard his parents discussing the fact that she was legally changing her surname.

'Oh, it's all right,' Peter said quickly. 'Our name is easy: Lawson.'

'Yeah, but Lawson is your father's name, not hers.' Fred stopped suddenly, frowning, probably realizing he had gone too far.

They had reached the flight of steps that led up to the front door and Paula had not been aware that Stanley Tompson had been walking behind them with his dog on a lead. 'I won't come in just now, Paula,' he murmured, 'but remember I'll be close by. I reckon you've got some explaining to do, not to that cheeky one, but to Peter and David.'

Paula raised her eyes to his and because he knew full well that she was a kind young lady and he had her best interests at heart, he answered her unspoken question without hesitation.

'Both you and Mr Lawson must know it's time you sat the twins down and told them *all* of it,' Stanley Tompson said softly, as he walked away.

All of it! Paula closed her eyes. Before either of them said a word to the twins a talk between herself and Jeffrey was long overdue. And the delay she knew was down to herself. Jeffrey had made so many attempts to put their relationship on a firmer footing but always she had been afraid to take that one step further. The boys were not the only ones who needed to know what was happening in their lives; Paula felt she was at a crossroad and the decision to take the right turning was of infinite importance. She had so much to lose. The twins had become her whole life but was that the only reason that Jeffrey was interested in her? She had to be decisive. Yet should her decision turn out to be wrong the result would have a momentous effect on four lives.

Feeling guilty as she settled the four boys, letting them each choose whether they wanted to paint or to draw, she went off to find Joyce and to help her prepare tea for all of them. She really didn't want to think about all the decisions she was going to have to make but even when a certain prospect did penetrate her thoughts, she knew in her heart that whatever the outcome might be, nothing, but nothing, could be worse than going off on her own, leaving Peter and David whom she regarded as her own children – and, yes, she had to admit she couldn't bear the thought of losing Jeffrey.

Paula's expression showed traces of unease and Joyce tactfully said, 'I've made a pot of tea; let's sit down and have a cup before we give the boys their tea, they won't starve if they have to wait half an hour or so. Come on,' she said, pulling Paula into her arms, 'it doesn't take a wise man to know that you've been eaten up with worry for some time now and by the look on your face it has suddenly come to a head. Do you want to talk about it? A trouble shared an' all that . . .'

'Oh, Joyce, in one way I thought the whole of my life had been sorted out for good after my mother died and the solicitors produced her letter.'

'And surely that's turned out to be true, hasn't it?'

'Financially yes, and to be able to shrug the O'Brien family out of my life has been great. But having some problems solved seems to have created a whole lot more.'

As Joyce tried to think how to answer that, Paula said, 'It was something that young Fred just said that upset me, and your Stanley overheard and offered me a piece of good advice, but I don't know if I've got the courage to take it.'

'I'm sorry if you think Stan was interfering,' Joyce said, stroking her hair. 'I'm sure he meant well, most likely he could tell that you were a bit stressed.'

'Oh no, Joyce, I didn't think that at all. It *was* good advice, I do need to sort out what I am going to do, because I can't just let things slide along as they are; it isn't fair on the twins.'

Joyce frowned. 'Do you mean you're thinking of leaving here?'

Paula nodded. 'I no longer know where I stand, and Peter and David no longer need a nanny.'

Joyce wanted to tell her that no, they really needed a mother. Instead she asked, 'Do you really want to leave here?'

Paula shook her head. 'I don't think I've got much choice.'

Joyce smiled sadly and reached out to hold her hand. 'What you're afraid of is that Jeffrey might be wanting you to stay on merely for the sake of the twins, is that about the size of it?'

Paula nodded.

'You want my opinion?'

'Yes please.'

'I think our Jeffrey is going through the same trauma as you are. Doesn't feel he can ask you to marry him because of the baggage that comes with him. Before your mother died, and you inherited so much, he had a lot to offer you. Now you don't need a roof over your head and you certainly do not need to work and get paid as a nanny. So you both need to put your heads together and make sure each one of you has got your priorities right.'

Paula managed a weak smile. 'Thank you.'

Inwardly Joyce gave a sigh of relief. 'You go and fetch the boys while I set some food out on the table cos if we leave it much longer we'll have a riot on our hands.'

The rest of October had disappeared in the blink of an eye, although with Hilda and Andy back from Malta, and Freddie and Raymond leaving Ridgeway to return to their own home the house did seem very quiet.

The relationship between herself and Jeffrey puzzled Paula a bit but she had decided not to be too critical, and to take each day as it came. On the face of it there seemed to be no pressure on either of them.

Joyce Pledger worried over Paula; these days she herself was so happy to have Stanley in her life that she longed to see Paula settled, happy and safe. She had anguished for hours over whether or not she should say that she and Stanley were more than willing to look after Peter and David any evening that Jeffrey wanted to take Paula out. She had at last plucked up enough courage and was more than pleased at the reaction she received from Jeffrey Lawson.

'I know that Stanley is a good man and that he has taken a lot of trouble to prove to my sons that he is their friend – and please, Joyce, be assured that I appreciate all his efforts. It is good for my boys to have a man to whom they can turn when I am at work. I will take up your offer and I'll personally thank Stanley.'

Joyce had smiled to herself. It worked both ways. On the evenings that Jeffrey took Paula out in the future Stanley would be in his element, playing cards or whatever with the boys and when they had gone to bed she and Stanley would have the comfort of the big lounge in which to sit.

And so the arrangement suited everyone.

Jeffrey took Paula out for meals, once to the theatre, and once to the Odeon at Leicester Square. They talked about anything and everything except what mattered most: their future.

It seemed to Paula as if day by day she was putting her life on hold. They both appeared to be happy in each other's company. No questions were asked, no answers offered, and nothing was promised. They just enjoyed spending time together.

Each night he went to his own bedroom and Paula went to hers.

It wasn't until the eleventh of November, Remembrance Day, that things had taken a notable change. Andy and Hilda had taken the twins together with their own two boys up to London on the Saturday, staying one night in a hotel in order to be out in the Mall early enough on the Sunday morning to get a good place from which they would be able to view the parades, listen to the bands, and take part in the Armistice Service to remember the dead of the Great War.

Stanley had taken Joyce to visit his brother and his wife and Paula was cooking dinner for Jeffrey that night when he suddenly reached out and pulled her to him and kissed her.

He had wanted to do that again for so long, but was now suddenly terrified he had upset Paula. So many complications had set in lately. Letting her free from his arms, Jeffrey was thrilled as she looked at him with a slow smile spreading across her face and he felt relief wash over him. Neither of them said anything and they both enjoyed a good dinner in an atmosphere that was pleasant and companionable.

Later they sat in the lounge, in the dark, he with his arm around her shoulders, and both of them staring into the glowing logs burning in the huge open grate.

It was turned midnight when he suggested a nightcap and as he handed Paula her drink he said, 'I feel like a young lad again, Paula.' To her he sounded irresistible.

Paula smiled and softly said, 'I want to thank you, Jeffrey, for having had so much patience with me. I am sorry I've given you such a hard time.'

'I'm not!' He laughed at the idea. 'It was well worth the wait. I know what hateful memories have been bothering you. It was a great step for you to take but I have to know you are quite sure you believe that what you're doing is going to be right for you.'

'Oh, Jeffrey,' was all she managed to murmur before his lips covered hers again. Only minutes passed as they sipped their drinks and then they were lying on the carpet in front of the fire and he was holding her, kissing her, and she was returning his kisses with equal passion. Slowly they removed each other's clothes and Jeffrey felt he had to ask whether she was sure she wanted him to make love to her.

'You mean the absolute world to me, Paula. Never did it occur to me that I would be able to really love a woman again, but to find you and day by day come to realize that you had made my life worth living again – there aren't enough words to describe how very much I do love you.'

Paula didn't say anything. She wrapped her arms more tightly around him and buried her face into his neck. They both wanted and needed each other and at that point in time neither of them were wondering whether or not they were doing the right thing.

What Paula felt filled her with wonder. Jeffrey treated her body as if it were a shrine. 'The most beautiful body in the whole world,' he had whispered to her.

Although in reality this was not Paula's first time, she had no memory of that awful incident all those years ago, and therefore she had no idea that intercourse between a man and a woman could be such a wonderful and loving experience. Jeffrey felt he had been granted so many wishes all at one time as they shared their passion and even afterwards as her young body lay quietly beneath him.

They slept in one bed that night and next morning she woke in his arms, as he caressed her breasts and looked into her eyes with such a sweet smile that was full of love. She lay still for some time, not really knowing what was expected of her now. So, she slipped out of bed and walked across the room, and then as she turned to look back at him, she felt and looked like a timid young girl.

'Are you all right, Paula?' He looked at her, wanting to make love to her again, but suddenly feeling worried. She seemed totally different.

'I'm not sure,' she answered quietly, then sat down on a chair, still naked, looking at him, she said, 'I can't believe we did that last night.'

My God! Fear raced through his veins. 'Are you saying you're already regretting it?'

'Oh no, no, no, quite the reverse! But Jeffrey, I have to somehow tell you what is going on in my mind. Because of what happened you have wiped a whole lot of demons out of my head. The one thing that has terrified me for years was the thought, the agony of having intercourse. Because of that I promised myself I would never form a relationship with a man. Not ever. If I did think about it, all I could recall was the morning after my thirteenth birthday when I woke up to find the bed covered in blood and my body a mass of bruises . . .'

'Please, Paula, stop there!' The colour had drained from his face and his limbs were trembling. 'Just don't tell me I forced you or it was the drink I gave you. I couldn't bear that, Paula.'

Paula sighed softly. 'Jeffrey, you are a darling man and what I am saying is nothing of the sort. It was beautiful from beginning to end, the lovely evening, the firelight, you kissing me, and the generous, gentle way you made love to me. I love you dearly, Jeffrey, and I loved every minute of last night.'

'Thank God for that!' He took a deep breath and let it out slowly before walking across the room to her, kneeling down beside her. He knew she was what he wanted for the rest of his life. Her early life had dealt her some very cruel blows and all he wanted now was to be given the chance to make it all up to her and to see that she was happy. He had never thought that he would have been able to experience such contentment again, not after his Sheila had died. Now he was being given a second chance and he meant to grab it with both hands.

Gently he lifted her to her feet, took her into his arms and held her against his own body; it was as if both their hearts were beating as one.

Paula was a wonderful person, his sons loved her, and together they were going to have a great life.

Forty

'Maybe we should tell Peter and David,' Paula said sleepily as she lay in bed snuggled up to Jeffrey.

'Hmm, great idea, but I think we should wait a while.'

'Why?'

'Because you haven't yet agreed to marry me.'

'Oh, Jeffrey, you're crazy, you really are.'

'Well, name the day and let me make an honest woman of you.'

'Anytime to suit you, my darling,' she said, turning on her side toward him as he kissed her.

'Are we to have a big wedding or a quiet do with just friends and relations?' Jeffrey wondered.

'You choose . . .' But she was already falling asleep in his arms as she said it, and as he looked at her a slow smile was forming over his face. She really was something, just looking at that mass of shining reddish hair spread out over the pillow made him want to wake her up and make love to her.

He wouldn't have given up his sons for anything or anyone in this world, but God had been good; it had taken time and there was much to sort out yet but from now on he was going to work on making his family complete for all of them. Mr and Mrs Lawson and their two sons. It sounded wonderful and he was going to make sure their new life as a family was as good as he could possibly make it.

Saturday morning, three weeks after Christmas, and they had the house back to themselves, apart from his mother and her husband, who were staying on until the end of the month. It had been a great holiday, the house alive with relatives and friends dropping in. Arthur Blackmore had taken his car to Blackshaw Road on the day after Boxing Day and picked up young Ronnie and Jack, bringing them to a children's party at Ridgeway. The party had been a great success and all the lads and lasses who had been invited had been thrilled with the gifts that Jeffrey had so generously provided for every guest to take home.

Now the beautiful grounds of Ridgeway looked beautiful; plants, shrubs and branches of the trees were covered with a layer of new snow, turning the whole area into a fairy wonderland. Paula, Jeffrey, Peter, David and Stanley were kicking a ball about, and Arthur was keeping up a pretence of being the goalkeeper. Their faces were glowing and the breath coming out of their mouths steamed as it hit the frosty air and hung there a moment or two.

Jeffrey thought Paula was incredible. No matter what the twins wanted to do, she was all for it. Even today, dressed in a cherry-red coat, white woolly hat, gloves and scarf, she was a picture, looking and acting as if she were no more than sixteen years old. She could rough and tumble out here with a ball and still manage to look beautiful and yet recently when he'd taken her to a business lunch she had done him proud. She had looked so elegant and with her natural, gentle grace she'd had all his colleagues in raptures. Everyone had loved her. At times it worried him that his life was suddenly turning out so well. Almost too good to be true.

Now he couldn't take his eyes off of her as she raced to reach the ball, then without warning she floundered, staggered and fell to the ground and he was startled to see she wasn't moving. He reached her side at the same time as Peter and David did. Her eyes were closed and her face was deathly pale. He tried to raise her head and felt her fingers tug at his sleeve.

'I'm . . . sorry,' she mumbled. Now not just pale, but a ghastly grey colour, she was blinking as though she was having trouble seeing. He got an arm under her shoulders and another one under her knees and lifted her to the height of his chest.

'Whatever happened? Is she all right?' Arthur puffed and his chest was heaving from running as he spoke.

'I'm not sure what has happened,' Jeffrey murmured, but even as he uttered the words, Paula's eyelids fluttered, her eyes rolled back and she passed out.

Both Peter and David were close to hysteria while Paula lay lifeless in his arms.

'Boys, Paula will be all right,' he told them with a faith he was far from feeling, 'but I want you both to run up to the house, find Joyce and make sure that Stanley has telephoned for an ambulance. Go on, go quickly, please,' he ordered, but he had hardly finished speaking before they were off, racing towards the house, yelling for Joyce at the tops of their voices.

Jeffrey somehow managed to walk, with Paula in his arms, to the foot of the front steps. There he sat down, cradling her close, her head resting against his chest. The wait seemed endless. Paula began to stir and glanced up at Jeffrey, with no idea of what was happening to her. Thankfully at that moment the sound of the ambulance arriving could be heard and within minutes the ambulance men were taking charge.

'Can you tell us your name?' one of the young men dressed in a green uniform was kneeling by her side and urging her to answer him.

'Paula,' she muttered. 'I am so sorry.'

'There's nothing for you to be sorry about, Paula. Can you tell me if you have any pain?'

'No, no pain, just my head is muzzy and I feel sick.'

'Well, we'll soon have you feeling better,' he told her as he let go of her wrist and made notes on a form that was attached to a clipboard. 'Just as a precaution we are going to lift you into the ambulance and take you off to hospital; my mate is fetching a stretcher.'

'No, I don't need to be taken anywhere . . . I'm fine,' Paula protested, struggling to sit up. But the ambulance men would have none of it. No matter what she tried to say, they wouldn't listen.

'I'm coming with you,' Jeffrey said firmly, relieved that she had recovered consciousness.

'I just don't know what came over me.'

'Don't worry about it, Paula, probably you ate too much over Christmas and shouldn't be rushing about out here in the cold.' Jeffrey knew full well he was talking a load of rubbish but he was so upset he said the first thing that came into his head.

At the hospital they had to wait a while and Jeffrey never moved from the side of the trolley on which she was lying. All the while he held her hand, his thumb moving slowly over the back of her hand, his thoughts flying in all directions. He had lost Sheila and for something as sudden as this to strike down Paula was terrifying. He must stop imagining the worst, he told himself as he gazed at Paula, who was sleeping peacefully, but it was no good; he had to swipe at his eyes because he realized they were brimming with tears.

It was a relief when two nurses came and said the doctor was ready to see Paula now and if he wanted to go to the cafe and get a drink for himself they would come and find him once the examination was over.

Jeffrey wasn't at all pleased when, two cups of coffee and almost an hour later he had heard no word from anyone. When finally they did come to fetch him, seeing Paula lying on a bed, all her clothes removed and wearing only a thin white hospital gown did nothing to reassure him.

A smartly dressed man aged about fifty with a thick head of dark hair but greying at the sides was washing his hands at a hand-basin as Jeffrey entered the consulting room. 'Roger Bradford, resident gynaecologist,' he said cheerily as he threw down the towel he'd used to dry his hands and held out one hand to Jeffrey. Jeffrey took it very gingerly, still dreading to be told what had caused Paula to have such a bad turn.

Dr Bradford had noticed that Paula wore no wedding ring; nevertheless he deemed it proper to address this couple as husband and wife. 'Good news, Mr Grantham.'

That surname alone rang alarm bells in Jeffrey's head, but of course Paula had had to give her details on arrival and she was so enjoying using her rightful surname.

'Although your wife seemed totally unaware of her condition, I can now, having examined her, confirm that she is pregnant. I'd say she is just about two months gone. My congratulations to you both. I do advise you, Mrs Grantham, to see your own doctor as soon as possible; this morning's little blip I think we can put down to overexertion but you will need to take more care during your pregnancy.'

It would have been hard to say which one of them was the most shocked. The colour had drained from Jeffrey's face and Paula was muttering, 'Oh no!'

'I take it this is a surprise for both of you.' Dr Bradford smiled sympathetically. 'I wish you both all the best – take care of her,' he added, looking at Jeffrey as the nurse helped Paula down off the bed and told him to wait outside until she was dressed.

'I don't believe it,' he muttered as soon as she appeared. He now looked worse than she did. She actually felt better since being told that there was nothing drastically wrong with her, but she glanced at Jeffrey in embarrassment as they slowly walked toward the entrance of the hospital.

'I'll get one of the receptionists to phone for a taxi for us,' he said, keeping his head lowered. Neither of them said a word until the cab arrived and they got into it.

'I didn't want this to happen to you,' Jeffrey blurted out, agitated. 'It feels like a repetition of what happened to Sheila and I couldn't face going through all that again.' Jeffrey's voice was still harsh and for a moment his reaction frightened her.

Paula was doing her best to understand how he was feeling but it was just as bad for her. The very thought of giving birth brought back all the horrors of what she had been made to endure whilst in that madhouse and she had never really stopped feeling guilty for letting them take that small baby away without telling her what was going to happen to it. Not that she had been given any choice in the matter, of course.

'Jeffrey, would you like to go somewhere and talk about this? Or just go home and let things take their course?'

'Best if I take you somewhere for lunch, somewhere quiet, where we can decide how best to deal with this. I'll phone from the restaurant, tell Joyce to feed everyone and that we'll be back later.'

'I don't know what to say,' Paula said softly, looking at him. To her this was amazing, but frightening at the same time. But this time shouldn't everything be different?

'It's my fault,' he said dolefully. 'I should have taken precautions; I just got carried away.'

'I never gave this situation a single thought either,' she said, still in shock.

'At least we won't let it interfere with our marriage plans; you're not far gone so it won't take much to fix it.'

'What do you mean by "fix it"?' she asked, her voice very low and taut.

'Well, I don't think we need any more children; we have the twins and I am just reaching the peak of my career. We're fine as we are, all set for a good life, I promise you, Paula.'

The taxi was cruising through Wimbledon High Street when Jeffrey leaned forward and tapped on the glass partition. 'Let us off here, please, driver, this will do us fine.'

hadn't really had time to come to terms with the fact that she was going to have a baby yet, but when she did give it serious thought she placed her hands across her stomach and she smiled gently.

Jeffrey had been quick to notice her action and he angrily said, 'I'm asking you to be reasonable, Paula. Sheila died giving birth to the twins and I don't want to lose you the same way. Please, don't even consider keeping this baby.'

'I will *not* get rid of it.' She hadn't even thought about it properly yet, but suddenly she knew it would be so wrong. They were going to be married, the baby would have a mother and a father and two dear brothers and a lovely home. Where was the wrong in all of that?

He realized that she wasn't far from tears, and he did his best to control himself before he started again to reason with her. 'Look, my darling, I know this has been a shock to you. This morning I was terrified there might be something seriously wrong with you, and now there is nothing to worry about. You just have to start thinking clearly. What we have is too good to spoil, don't you see that? In any case you have to let yourself be guided by me.' He sounded so determined, as if his decision had been made with a rod of iron.

Now Paula was crying. She hadn't seen this dominant side of Jeffrey before and she didn't like it. 'I'm sorry, I can't do it,' she said firmly.

'I'll give you time to think it over,' he said. 'I'm sure you'll see the sense in my reasoning.'

But still his voice sounded so harsh and certainly not as if he was going to listen to anything she had to say.

'No, Jeffrey, I don't need time. It's as big a surprise to me as it is to you but I am going to accept it and hope and pray that I will eventually be delivered safely of a healthy boy or girl that I will love with all my heart.'

'And what about Peter, David and me? I thought we meant the world to you?'

'You do, all three of you, and you always will, but I will not get rid of this baby you fathered just so that you can carry on with your safe and comfortable way of life.'

'That's your final word and nothing I can say will sway you?'

'Nothing you can say, Jeffrey, will convince me that we should not have this baby.'

'All right then, keep the baby, but I want no part of it. If you agree to do things my way, I'll be there for you, and we'll get married as soon as you like, but I am not going to be forced into having another baby that neither of us want.'

'That is where you're wrong, Jeffrey. I suddenly know without any doubt that I *do* want to have this baby and I shall do my best to care for it – and if you are so sure that you don't want to be part of its life then I will provide for it and care for it without asking for any help from you.'

He stared at her and his jaw dropped as she stood up, gathered her gloves, buttoned up her coat and pushed her chair back against the wall. And she never looked back as she walked through the restaurant and out into the street and disappeared among the throng of shoppers.

'All right, all right, I'm coming,' Molly Owen was shouting as she lumbered up her narrow hallway in answer to the thunderous knocking on her front door.

'God above, whatever's 'appened to you?' she practically screamed as she put her arms around Paula and gently eased her through the doorway at the same time calling, 'Laura come an' give us an 'and 'ere, will you?'

Laura put her head around the living-room door and was as shocked as her mother had been. Paula's coat was smeared with mud, her white gloves were filthy and as they were watching her now, stepping out of her shoes, they could see that they too were coated with mud.

'By the look of you anyone would think you'd been in a field playing football,' Molly declared as she handed Paula over to her daughter.

Paula did her best to smile, took a very deep breath and admitted, 'That is exactly what I was doing early this morning, but then I slid over, passed out, and was taken to hospital where they told me there was nothing wrong – except I am pregnant. Jeffrey is emphatic that if I keep the baby he wants nothing more to do with me, so I walked out on him, found I had nothing on me, not a penny, so I had to walk all the way here.'

Having said all this Paula almost slid from Laura's grasp.

'Come this side of her, Mum, an' let's get her sat down in a chair.'

That was accomplished with difficulty and when at last Molly was able to straighten herself up she looked down at the sorry sight of Paula and sighed heavily as she said, 'Well, love, I 'ave t'give it to you, you don't do things by 'alf, d'yer?'

Paula was out for the count. Her hat and coat had been removed, a pillow placed behind her head and a thick blanket tucked in around her legs. Laura and Molly were drinking the inevitable cup of tea and still staring at Paula with utter disbelief showing on their faces.

'Wonder how this lot will work out,' Laura said, not expecting any answer.

'God only knows; at least she knew where to come, bless her. There was me thinking she was set up for life cos when that Arthur Blackmore brought our boys home from that party and I asked him how our Paula was he tapped the side of his nose and told me to listen out for wedding bells.'

'Yeah well,' Laura sighed, 'yer never can tell with them city gents.'

'And you'd know all about that, would you?' her mother sneered.

'Not really, but I've got a funny feeling we're about to learn a lot more over the coming days.'

Forty-One

The past twelve days had been a nightmare for all of them. For the first time in years Fred Wilson was glad to get out of the house. Paula knew she was the cause of all the trouble but she couldn't help herself.

Paula couldn't bring herself to go outside the house and she wasn't eating enough to keep a bird alive. She played games with Ronnie and Jack but even the boys remarked that her heart wasn't in it.

'She's just letting us win,' Jack said, more wisely than he knew.

Paula herself felt she was struggling in what seemed a deep mire and the more she struggled the more entangled she became. She was absolutely lost without the twins; they had been her whole life, twenty-four hours a day for years and she had been totally committed to them. She had blocked from her mind all thoughts of a future without them, even as they grew away from her, which inevitably they would as they grew older, she had never envisaged such an abrupt parting. It had been a strange relationship that she'd enjoyed right from the beginning in the intimacy of their beautiful home, yet there had been a number of times when she had warned herself against the danger of becoming too strongly attached to them. Not that the warnings had counted for much. She loved those two boys as if they were her own flesh and blood. Thanks to her mother she would now be able to make an independent life of her own, though what that independent life would turn out to be, she had as yet no idea. All she had at this moment was this firm resolve to keep her baby, but that way forward seemed a very lonely path.

Meanwhile, her thoughts lingered on Ridgeway Manor. It was such a beautiful house and, more than that, it was a happy home and Paula told herself that at least she could take part of the credit for that. So many memories she had stored up, every day of the twins' lives: their birthdays, Easter and the joy and excitement of Christmas. How could she even contemplate a life without them?

But the only option Jeffrey had offered her was to marry him and become a real mother to Peter and David, something so wonderful it had seemed a dream beyond reality, but for that to happen she had to give up this baby of her own. It was so illogical.

How could he even bring himself to think about getting rid of their child? In truth he had done more than just think about it. How could he dismiss her just like that? He knew well enough how deeply she cared for the boys. They had been seven months old when she had first come to Ridgeway and she could honestly say from day one she had been devoted to them. They had been her responsibility and never had she shirked that fact; without a doubt she had given the twins her total commitment. Was it any wonder that she missed them so very much?

And what about the feelings she and Jeffrey had for each other?

She couldn't possibly have imagined what had passed between them. Surely it had been true love; nothing else could begin to describe what they had meant to each other. Perhaps it was a pity that she had become pregnant so early in their relationship, but to her, after the first wave of shock, it had become a matter to rejoice over.

But there had been no love in the look he had given her when he had declared, 'I am very clear about how I feel about this, I don't want to lose you but if you have this baby you are on your own.'

Had she been rash in walking out on him? No. Her feelings were still the same. It was horrid to think of how lonely her future might become, but on the other hand she would be a real mother. Jeffrey could bellow and shout but she would never come round to his way of thinking.

'Get yerself dressed an' come shopping down the market with me and Laura this morning; it'll do yer a world of good and you can 'ave a coffee in the cafe, you know I'm no good at making coffee.' Molly was trying everything she knew to coax Paula but there was no moving her.

'What's really wrong with yer, love?' Molly finally asked in desperation.

'Surely you've worked that out for yourself by now?' Paula said, more sharply than she had meant to. 'Jeffrey doesn't want me because I'm having a baby.'

'Oh, come on, love, you don't really know that; you 'aven't given him much of a chance,' Molly chided her, and Paula was startled by the harshness of the remark.

'What, are you agreeing with him?'

'No, I'm not, and you know better than to ask; that isn't fair.'

'Oh, Molly, I'm sorry. I do know your feelings on the matter but I am all at sixes and sevens in my head. I just cannot come to terms with the fact that he wouldn't want to know his own baby, and, Molly . . .'

'Yes, love? Finish what you were about to tell me.'

Paula's cheeks flushed red and she lowered her head. 'It wasn't as if he had forced himself on me. It all happened so . . . well, you know, nicely, lovingly. Jeffrey made me feel I was so special; it wasn't dirty, not at all.'

Paula hadn't really been able to come to terms with Jeffrey's attitude. She still didn't really believe it. What on earth had caused him to react like that? It wasn't her fault she'd fallen pregnant, she knew it takes two, but the fact that he had threatened to have nothing more to do with her if she persisted in having the baby disgusted her. He could go to hell!

And then, just as she was telling herself that was all right by her, she would remember how kind and considerate he had been when making love to her and in the morning when she'd woken up and he gently kissed her and told her how much he loved her. All of this, going over and over in her head, was driving her crazy!

Molly had been worried before; now she'd worked herself into a frightful temper.

'Come on, get yer arse up from that bloody couch and get yerself ready to go out.' She was shouting and Paula was shocked. Why would Molly suddenly turn on her?

'It's about time you looked on the bright side of this ruddy mess. It isn't as if you're penniless; thanks to your dear mother an' yer grandmother you're sitting pretty. You can afford to book into a decent nursing 'ome to have the baby and when you're good an' ready you can buy yerself a nice little 'ouse. The baby won't be lost for folk t'love it, you'll find that out soon enough, and me and my Laura, we'll be there for you every step of the way. Now I've got that off me chest you can stop being such a pain in the backside. Laura's just gone up the road to take the bag wash and you an' me are gonna 'ave our coats on ready to go down the market with 'er the minute she gets back.'

One look at Paula's face and Molly's annoyance melted away.

'Tell yer what, Paula, as you're going be eating for two now you can 'ave a Bath bun as well as a doughnut when we get to the cafe. Now, move yerself and stop being such a pain in the backside.' She had said the words strongly but there was now a hint of a smile to soften the blow.

Paula grinned at her and stood up. She looked better already.

Molly looked at her fondly. To herself she vowed, *I'm gonna get my Laura to give that Jeffrey Lawson a ring tonight; he at least deserves to know where Paula is. And then we'll see what happens!*

The pair of them cheerfully made their way through the market crowds to meet Laura. It was a cold but fine dry day and the market was particularly busy. The stall they were aiming for sold masses of knitting wool, paper patterns, needles and everything needed for sewing and embroidering. The adjoining stall, owned by the same family, sold a vast assortment of baby clothes and all the equipment that would be needed for a nursery.

Quietly, Laura stood to one side of her mother and Paula pushed her way through the many customers to stand on the other side of Molly.

'What d'you think you're doing, Mum?' Laura asked, having a job to keep a straight face as she eyed the various coloured balls of wool Molly was holding.

'Oh, reach over there to the back of the stall and get me a few patterns to look through, will yer, love?'

On the other side of Molly, Paula looked astounded but she was also feeling far happier than she had been since she had walked away and left Jeffrey in the restaurant.

'Thanks, Laura,' Molly grinned as she took hold of the patterns and began to leaf through them. 'What d'yer think, love?' she asked, turning to face Paula. 'Shall we start by using all white wool, maybe edge the matinee jackets with a bit of colour, or shall we risk a few items in pink?'

'Oh, Molly!' Paula exclaimed loudly, causing a load of women to turn and look at them.

'Proud Granny you're going to be, then?' a stout, jolly-looking woman asked of Molly.

Alice, who had stood behind this counter serving customers with her parents long before she'd even left school, looked up sharply and then grinned. 'Molly Owen is not unused to being a granny, but as far as I know she's never 'ad a granddaughter – two boys you've got, ain't it, Laura?'

Laura laughed loudly. 'You're on the wrong track, Alice, me old mate. You know I've got two boys an' I ain't aiming to 'ave any more. No, it's my friend 'ere. Say 'ello, Paula, this is Alice. What she don't know about babies' needs ain't worth knowing.'

Paula stretched her arm across the wide counter of the stall and Alice, who was standing on a box, reached forward and shook her hand. 'Your first, is it, love?'

Paula couldn't find her voice so she merely smiled and nodded.

'Well, you've picked a great one to 'ave as its gran; they don't come any better than our Molly.' Turning her gaze to Molly she remarked, 'I'd 'ave thought you'd 'ave had enough knitting patterns to last you a lifetime. Still, I ain't grumbling, it's all good for business.'

'Long time since I did any baby's clothes, our Jack's all grown-up now, but I don't mind starting again, not for our Paula, I don't.'

In the end Paula watched as Molly paid Alice for six ounces of white two-ply wool, one ounce of the palest blue and also one ounce of the very palest pink plus three paper patterns – and it was only then that her conscience struck her.

She hadn't any money! For almost two weeks she had lived off Molly, worn clothes that belonged to Laura while her own clothes, the ones she had been wearing when taken to the hospital, had been washed and ironed by Laura. From the grounds of Ridgeway she had been taken by ambulance, without so much as her handbag or even a purse. What a damn fool she'd been to walk off and leave Jeffrey just like that. And she hadn't been very good as a guest in Molly's house. True, she hadn't eaten very much, but Molly had done her best to tempt her and all the family, even Jack and Ronnie, had put up with her black moods. She would repay them, make it up to them one way or another, but how was she going to do that without going back to Ridgeway at least once to collect her belongings? Her thoughts turned to Peter and David. Whatever must they be thinking of her? Whatever would Jeffrey have told them?

Had she been utterly selfish? Perhaps she had, but here a little self-pity began to creep in. She had only just been told that she was carrying a baby, it was a total shock to her and given her past history she had every right to feel afraid. If only Jeffrey had been happy about the situation! He needn't have been on the top of the world about it but then neither should he have rejected her so completely. He made it seem like the very idea of their child was repulsive to him.

She still had a lot to think about, a lot to decide, she realized later when she was in the cafe drinking a lovely cup of coffee that Molly had ordered for her.

Laura had not yet come into the cafe; she was still out in the market filling two shopping bags with fresh vegetables. When she did make an appearance she heaved the heavy bags on to an empty chair and moaned, 'I'm absolutely knackered; go to the counter and order me a large tea an' two of toast, will yer, Mum?'

'I'll go,' Paula offered quickly as she slid from her chair and made her way to the counter.

Mother and daughter looked at each other and both grinned wickedly. 'Mission accomplished,' Laura told her, winking her eye at the same time. 'I got through to that Esmé. I've always liked the sound of her and straight off she fetched Mrs Pledger – you know, Joyce. Anyway, she said she didn't think she could telephone Mr Lawson because he was in court today but promised she'd let him know what I'd said the minute he got home. Said he got home as early as he could every day now.'

'Watch out, Paula's coming back. Here, quick, take this ten-bob note, shove it in yer pocket and when we're ready to go you pop up to the counter and pay the bill, that way the poor love won't be so embarrassed.'

It was nine o'clock that night when the knock at the door came. Fred had gone to the pub, the two boys were in bed and the three women were sitting in the front room where a nice fire was burning. This was unusual in itself; the fire in the front room wasn't usually lit on a weekday, only at weekends.

No one said a word as Laura went to answer the door.

Several minutes ticked by and a quiet conversation could be heard. Nothing had prepared Paula for the shock of seeing Jeffrey Lawson walk into Molly's front room with Laura standing behind him. Still not a word passed between either of them. Molly had already wound up her wool and she got to her feet, crossed the room, nodded her head as she passed Mr Lawson and, joining her daughter in the hallway, she put a hand out and firmly closed the front-room door behind them.

Paula's heart felt as if it had missed a beat. All she could think of was how terrible she looked; she hadn't bothered to wash her hair since she had been here, and she hadn't worn any make-up since she last saw him.

'May we sit down and talk?' he asked, smiling at her, but she only shook her head. She looked so sad, and he thought she had lost weight.

'You made your views very plain. I don't think we have anything to say to each other.' Her voice was little more than a whisper but as they looked at each other she couldn't believe how much she still loved him, and although she was going to kill Laura for arranging this meeting she was so pleased to see him.

'Come on, Paula, please,' he begged her, and she thought about it for half a minute before flopping down in the armchair and he took the chair facing hers. Tears were glistening in her eyes and he thought she looked so young and so vulnerable that it almost broke his heart to look at her, and he wondered for the umpteenth time how he could have been stupid enough to let her walk away like that.

'I suspect Laura must have telephoned you, but why have you bothered to come and see me?' she asked, with a wretched look that tore his heart out.

'Because I love you, and I wasn't thinking straight . . . and because I can't go on lying to the twins any longer.' He smiled sheepishly as he said the words. 'Joyce has threatened to leave me, Stanley has said I am one brick short of a load and I won't tell you what Esmé's comments have been.'

'What have you told Peter and David?' she asked forcefully, determined to distract him from all other matters.

'That the hospital has sent you somewhere nice, a convalescent home.'

'What? What am I supposed to be recovering from?'

'I told them you were overtired and in need of a rest.'

'And the twins didn't ask why I'd gone away without so much as a goodbye?'

'That was your own fault, Paula, not mine. Besides, I didn't think that you would have come here to your friends; I imagined you would have been holed up in a nice comfortable hotel.'

'And how did you think I was paying my way?'

'You have plenty of money in the bank; you could have written a cheque.'

'Yes, I could have, if I had my purse and my handbag with me. I was taken to the hospital straight from the grounds of Ridgeway; I hadn't a penny piece on me, not even a few coppers to make a phone call.'

The colour drained from his face and he looked absolutely sick. 'How did you get here? How have you managed?'

'Bit late in the day for you to start showing concern, isn't it, Jeffrey? I walked here and my clothes and food have been provided by Molly and Laura.'

To say Jeffrey looked shocked would have been an understatement.

'Honestly, I have been imagining you going off on some mad shopping sprees – most women I know would have.'

'Just goes to show you don't know me as well as you thought you did, Jeffrey.'

'My God, things have reached a bad pitch when you couldn't even phone and tell me you had no money with you. All this worry can't have been good for the baby.'

'What do you care?' She looked him straight in the eye as she asked that question. 'Showing concern now is nothing short of being hypocritical, since it was you who said I had to get rid of the baby.'

'Oh, come on, Paula . . .'

'You said I could keep the baby if that was what I wanted, but you would wash your hands of me. That's what you said, wasn't it?'

'Hang on a minute. I was just so afraid you might die . . . giving birth . . . just as Sheila had . . . I didn't want to lose you. I really do love you, Paula, with all my heart,' he finished sadly.

Silence hung heavy between them.

'I don't suppose you'd let me take you out for a meal, say tomorrow evening?'

'Why? I can't see any point in that.'

'I need to tell you how much I have missed you and just how

sorry I am. I have been a complete moron these past two weeks. It's a wonder the twins haven't run away from home, I'm sure if they were just a little bit older they would have come looking for you.'

'I haven't been all that great myself. I've slept for hours during the day and paced the floor at night. It's a wonder Molly has put up with me.'

'I wish you hadn't left me.'

'So do I,' she said softly, 'but I am still going to keep this baby.'

'Would you consider coming home if I promise I will go along with whatever it is you want to do – as long as you will promise to take care of yourself during the pregnancy? If you promise me that, I'll get you extra help in the house; I'll see the twins don't tire you out so much and we'll go together and buy all the things that a new baby will need.'

'I am not an invalid, I am only going to have a baby, a perfectly natural thing for two people who love each other to do.'

'Are you saying you do still love me?' he asked, rising to his feet and holding out his arms.

Paula didn't answer him but only seconds passed before she too stood up.

Jeffrey looked long and hard at her before gently taking her into his arms and holding her close.

'Oh, Paula, my darling, I have been such a fool,' he murmured. 'I just can't find the words to tell you how sorry I am.'

At that moment, she too felt more emotions than she could ever hope to express, and she quietly started to cry.

'Ssh, ssh,' Jeffrey soothed her, tears welling up in his own eyes. 'Everything's going to be all right.'

'I didn't want to live without you,' she whispered. 'It was only the thought that the baby inside of me was part of you that kept me going.'

'And I love you so much I thought I would die if you never came back home – and the twins have been giving me hell. They are not daft; they know something is really wrong. We've both of us acted far too hastily, wouldn't you agree?'

'Yes, I would, Jeffrey, but I think if this blip has taught us anything it is to appreciate what we have and to love and cherish each other.'

'Shall I leave you here for tonight?' he asked cautiously.

'I think you should give some time to the twins, maybe even tell them the truth, so I think it's best if I stay here until the end of the week. But please will you ask Esmé to pack a few things for me and to remember to bring my handbag? Esmé lives quite near to here so I'm sure she won't mind.'

Jeffrey reluctantly released his hold on her and reached inside his jacket pocket to withdraw his wallet. He laid some notes on the table and then added a handful of loose change. 'For Jack and Ronnie,' he grinned. 'Should I say goodnight to Mrs Owen and to Laura?' he whispered once they were out in the passageway. 'I don't know how I am ever going to be able to repay them for their kindness to you.'

'No, I'll say it for you, and I'm sure you will think of a way,' she assured him.

Paula opened the front door and when they were both in the porch she pulled the door to behind them and he took her into his arms again, holding her even closer. Before they parted this time they each knew with certainty that they still did truly love each other.

He walked a few steps down the pathway and then came back to say, 'I can hardly wait for you to come back home.' He laughed. 'And I will have your very first job lined up for you.'

'Oh yes, and what will that be?'

'You will have the job of arranging a hasty wedding!'

'First off, together we have to talk to Peter and to David, sound out how they feel about us getting married.' Paula still sounded a little uncertain.

'If you aren't absolutely certain that when they hear that you are going to be their mother for real they aren't going to feel over the moon then you don't know them as well as you've made out.'

'I pray to God that you're right, Jeffrey, because then *all* my prayers will have been answered.'

He laughed at her, and he kissed her again, and it was a while before either of them remembered that they were out in the street and that he was supposed to be on his way home, alone.

Epilogue

On the following Sunday morning Jeffrey Lawson appeared on Molly Owen's doorstep bright and early, bearing gifts for everyone. Half the street turned out to see Paula climb into his car and her departure was to the sound of good wishes from all quarters.

However, her arrival back at Ridgeway was an entirely different matter: it was gloomy and dismal in comparison. Both Peter and David had obviously been on the lookout for her arrival and came flying down the steps as their father's car turned in to the drive. They didn't run to fling their arms about her but instead held back, smiling and telling her how glad they were that she had come home.

'Don't I even get a hug?' she cried out in disbelief.

'You first, Peter,' David said, hanging back.

Paula was bewildered, and flinging her arms wide she said, 'Haven't I always been able to hug both of you at the same time? Surely you haven't grown that much in the short time that I have been away.'

The twins stood still, each looking undecided and it was Peter who spoke. 'Daddy said we have to be very careful and treat you gently because you haven't been very well.'

Paula felt if she were to dare look at Jeffrey she might lose her temper and say something that she would regret. So instead she told a white lie. 'I have had a good rest and I am really quite well now, so come here.'

Neither lad needed a second telling; they flew at her and she gathered them both in her arms and held them close. Her chest did feel tight and the lump in her throat was choking her but it was only because she felt so relieved. A great sigh of happiness escaped as they hugged her in return.

Mentally she made a resolution: Jeffrey and she needed to talk and then when they had things straight in their minds they needed to tell Peter and David about their plans for the future and when the changes were going to happen. And she wasn't going to let much time pass before her plan was put into action.

'Are you going to stay out there much longer? I have made coffee and some extra-special gingerbread men.' Joyce at least didn't hold back her joy at seeing Paula return home.

'Coming right now, Joyce,' Paula called out in answer, and taking hold of a hand of each twin she began to run. Peter and David, their fears alleviated, caught her mood and they were whooping with joy as they, three abreast, climbed the stone steps.

Sunday lunch had been a happy meal, and Jeffrey had insisted that both Joyce and Stanley sit down to eat with them in the dining room. Now Stanley had taken Joyce for a drive through the countryside. The curtains at the French windows were drawn back and the winter sunshine was doing its best to make the garden look as if spring might not be too far away, but still a great log fire was burning in the grate.

Jeffrey was reading the Sunday papers and the twins were attempting to do a jigsaw puzzle that Paula had laid out on a very large tray.

'Peter, David.' Paula's voice sounded strange. It caused them both to lift their heads at once. 'Your daddy and I have a lot of plans to make and I think you both should stop what you're doing and listen because we need your approval before we go ahead. Is that all right? Because it is important.'

They both put down the pieces of the jigsaw they were holding, sat up straight and nodded their heads. Paula's face was serious so it was to their father that they turned. Jeffrey knew he couldn't shirk this responsibility.

'You've always known that your mother died on the same day that you were born. What you've never known is that I had a very hard time doing my best to look after you and to keep my day job. My job is important because it pays well and provides us all with a good life. However, the nannies I employed to take care of you did not do a very good job and they didn't stay long. People suggested I wasn't coping well and that I should think about having you both put up for adoption. Do you know what adoption means?'

Each boy solemnly nodded his head but never uttered a word.

'I was at my wits' end but parting with you two never entered my head. Not for one moment. Then I found Paula, and from the very first day she came into our lives she has loved you and has taken care of you, do you both agree?'

'Yes, yes,' the answer came in unison. Then Peter looked at his brother and very quietly said, 'Why can't Paula be our mother since she lives here all the time?'

Tears were pricking hard behind Paula's eyes and she had to run her tongue over her lips because they had gone so dry. But finally it was she who broke the silence that had followed Peter's question.

'You *want* to have me for your mother? Both of you?'

What happened next absolutely overwhelmed Paula.

The twins scrambled to their feet, flung themselves on to Paula, almost knocking her off her chair. 'Oh, my darlings, my two dear darlings,' Paula was murmuring, and Jeffrey looked as if a load had been lifted from his shoulders and at the same time his ship of good fortune had come in. There were tears in his own eyes as he came across the room and spread his arms to enfold his two sons and his wife-to-be.

'Will you change your name again, Paula?' David asked.

'Of course she will,' Jeffrey told them firmly. 'Now that we know we have your approval I shall acquire a special marriage licence and Paula and I will get married and we'll be Mr and Mrs Lawson.'

'Will we be able to come to the wedding?' David thought that would only be fair since it was he and Peter that had given their approval.

'Most certainly, and you shall each have a proper suit to wear,' their father told them. All the while Paula was looking at them, loving them desperately and over the top of their heads she mouthed the word 'baby' to Jeffrey. He in turn shook his head hard and said aloud, 'Enough excitement for one day; let's go into the kitchen and see if Joyce has left us anything nice for our tea.' The twins ran on in front. 'The reason I didn't tell them wasn't because I didn't want them to know you're pregnant, my darling. I just think enough is enough for one day. We will tell them they're going to have a brother or a sister as soon as I've put that ring on your finger and I know for sure that you are my wife. I couldn't bear any more hiccups, but I must say, you leaving me, Paula, certainly made me realize just how much I do love you. I just couldn't begin to think of a life without you in it.'

Having said all that he reached out and, clutching at her sleeve, he pulled her back into his arms. 'About time some of your hugging came my way.' He grinned before lowering his head to kiss her.

It was a long, soft, lingering kiss that told Paula everything she needed to know. 'Oh, Jeffrey,' she said in a whisper as he released his hold on her.

He murmured, 'I know, my darling; what we almost lost doesn't bear thinking about.'

Paula and Jeffrey's wedding was a beautiful day, with forty guests and a reception at the Victoria Hotel.

In the days and weeks following, Paula was often amazed that Jeffrey chose to show his love for her in so many ways. He had increased the household staff, for one thing. Joyce Pledger no longer lived in, because she was now Mrs Tompson, but she still came to Ridgeway to cook for them five days a week. Esmé still came to do the washing and the ironing and a regular daily cleaner had been installed. He also now employed two permanent gardeners who diligently had begun to bring the grounds to a state of perfection and had them install a huge summer house. To Paula this was his greatest gift, the one in which they could all spend many happy hours together.

Jeffrey enjoyed making Paula happy; he felt it was her due, since she had been through so many years of pain and hurt growing up. Most of all he loved to watch her face each and every time the twins called, 'Mum, where are you?' And even more so each night before they went to bed when they kissed her and said, 'Goodnight, Mummy.'

Paula herself was truly happy, and never more so than on the last day in August when she was safely delivered of a seven-pound baby daughter whom Jeffrey immediately named Frances after Paula's mother, and on seeing the baby the twins instantly decided they would be calling her Frankie.

Later that night as she lay resting Paula recalled something that Molly Owen had said to her a long time ago.

Molly had urged her not to waste her life but to find herself a good man. She now knew, without any doubt, that Jeffrey Lawson fitted the bill.